CROWNING HOPE

CROWNING Hope

CROWNING HOPE

Half Moon Bay
Book 8

ERIN BROCKUS

Chapter One

THE AFTERNOON St. Croix sun warmed the wooden railing beneath Hope Monroe's hands. She stood on an elevated deck overlooking the aquamarine Caribbean Sea. The deck was attached to the second story of a long building halfway down a wooden pier, a large palapa at the end. A lock of reddish hair blew in front of her face, and Hope tucked it behind her ear. Her fingers paused on her neck, and a smile rose as a memory flashed into her mind.

A vivid, life-changing memory.

She had stood in this same position nearly four years ago, though the railing had been replaced since. This was where she and dive operations manager of Half Moon Bay Resort, Alex Monroe, had shared their first kiss. And just the previous month, they had celebrated their two-year wedding anniversary.

Her gaze drifted to the right, taking in the long crescent of white sand beach which gave the resort and bay its name. Hope shook her head. What she saw now hardly resembled the humble resort of her arrival. Since taking over—and especially since she and Alex had married—they had nearly doubled the number of guest bungalows, as well as building an art gallery and spa toward the northern half of the beach. She inspected a bare stretch of land at the far northern end, her next big project.

But not quite yet.

Hope's smile lingered as she turned around and opened the glass door at the other end of the covered deck, entering a wonderfully cool open room, now in its third incarnation. Originally, the area had been Alex's apartment. But after a hurricane, he had moved in with her and she had turned the space into a modest spa they had quickly outgrown. Once Aqua, their new destination spa on the beach, had opened the previous spring, Alex had been quick to reclaim his territory, moving the dive shop to take advantage of the newly freed area. She'd had a few ideas for the space herself.

Now Hope looked around the finished product, very pleased with the result. The long check-in counter was the only thing left from Hibiscus Spa. Two-thirds of the wide-open room was taken up by the dive shop, filled with wetsuits, regulators, buoyancy compensation devices, and other diving necessities. The other third was the resort gift shop, an idea she'd wanted to implement for years.

As usual, the first thing that caught Hope's eye was the group dive staff photo on the wall. Specifically, the picture of Alex smiling at the camera. His crystal blue eyes, sandy hair, and tall, muscular body only increased her desire for the real thing.

Alex, along with their dive boat *Surface Interval*, was out on the afternoon dive trip, so the shop was deserted except for two people working in it. An average-height young man with closely cropped black hair turned from arranging dive masks on a wall display. His dark face breaking into a smile, Zach Turner spoke with a lilting Caribbean accent. "Hey, Hope. What brings you by?"

Twenty years old, he'd worked for them for over two years and was addicted to diving. Alex was slowly bringing him along and had plans to make Zach a divemaster for the resort. Often, the young man worked on the boat, assisting the staff, but he was covering the dive shop that day.

And helping orient their new employee.

Hope smiled as a nineteen-year-old young woman approached from the gift-shop side of the room. Jasmine Olson lifted her lips in response, an irresistible expression of brilliant white teeth against her caramel-colored skin. She had a tiny, upturned nose that gave her pretty face a youthful cast.

"I just came by to see if Jasmine had any questions," Hope answered Zach, then turned to the young woman. "Is he treating you ok?" She'd hired Jasmine to work in the gift section, but Zach and Hope would cross-train her to work the dive shop as well.

"Oh, yes!" Jasmine said. Like Hope, she was dressed in the usual uniform of a staff polo and capris. Her shoulder-length straightened hair was pulled into a low ponytail. "I'm learnin' the ropes, and Zach's showin' me where everythin' is."

"Sorry you couldn't go out on the boat, Zach," Hope said. "But after Alex starts our divemaster class, you might be longing for an easy afternoon in air-conditioned comfort."

Zach widened his eyes, his expression aghast. "No way! I can't wait to start. Do you know how long I've wanted to be a divemaster?"

Hope laughed. "Pretty much as long as I've known you. Unlike me." She shook her head. "I'm still a little surprised Alex wants me to take the class too."

The young man shrugged. "Don't know why. You've been divin' a lot longer than me."

Hope had never thought of herself as an expert diver. She'd come a long way since her near-drowning shortly after becoming certified, but she still viewed diving more as recreation than profession.

Better change that line of thought.

"We'll figure it out together, just like we've been doing." Hope smiled at him. She and Zach had been partners in their last two classes. The previous summer, Alex had brought them through the rescue diver course, the prerequisite for divemaster, which had been a challenging and fulfilling class. Hope was proud to be one of the only non-dive staff members who could assist in water emergencies.

"Leadin' people on dives is a lot of responsibility," Jasmine said, giving Zach an admiring smile.

He visibly puffed up. "It's just a matter of gainin' confidence. Maybe I'll show you sometime." The two couldn't tear their eyes apart, their mutual interest obvious. Hope refrained from groaning.

Oh, boy. I should have foreseen this!

Though she couldn't exactly cast stones in this area, now could she? At thirty-nine, Hope was a long way from young, blushing love, and her experience with first love had been a disaster. An abusive relationship had wounded her spirit deeply, and it wasn't until she met Alex that she was able to trust completely. Old demons still rose to the surface now and again, for both her and former Navy SEAL Alex. But neither Zach nor Jasmine had experienced their traumas. Hope wished them every happiness, but she wasn't paying them to make moon eyes at each other.

Behind Jasmine stood a half-full display of resort-themed coffee mugs. An open cardboard box sat on the floor. "Did the mugs arrive undamaged?" Hope asked.

As desired, her question brought Jasmine back from

admiring Zach. She whipped her head toward Hope. "Oh—yeah. I'll just get back to unpacking them."

"Excellent," Hope said. "I need to head over to Aqua and check on things there. See you two later."

After stepping back into the afternoon heat, she headed down the staircase to the wooden planks of the pier, passing through a tunnel created from the gear room on one side and the compressor room on the opposite. The dive shop spanned overhead.

Hope continued, stepping down onto the white sand beach. An emergency station sat next to the stairs, a life ring and flotation device ready to assist rescues. An identical station was placed near the spa. Heading north along the beach, she passed a rectangular infinity pool with a restaurant behind and pool bar to one side. The resort faced due west, giving it a full view of the sun as it made its daily progress toward the western horizon.

Hope approached a seventy-year-old woman laying her towel on a chaise lounge. "Getting a little sun this afternoon, Peg?" Hope asked. The woman was vacationing alone, so Hope had made a point to talk to her and make sure she felt welcome.

"I'm lathered in sunscreen, but I just love the heat," Peg said, ruffling a hand through her short, wavy gray hair. "I'll head into the ocean if it gets too much."

"It's a beautiful afternoon, so enjoy."

Hope continued toward the white building in the distance. The left third of it was encased in smoked glass, streaks of red and orange running through it. The art gallery Ember had been a success from the very start, benefitting its exhibiting artists as well as the charities Hope donated profits to each month. A local pet shelter, veterans support center, and domestic abuse shelter were her primary beneficiaries.

Aqua took up the other two thirds of the building. The same smoked glass graced a large wall with a patio facing the ocean.

Tables were placed on the brick pavers, and several guests were enjoying an afternoon drink. The ocean-facing row of massage rooms also incorporated the one-way glass, allowing the guest to enjoy the scenery and stay cool.

Hope entered Aqua's lobby and was met with soothing spa music. A meandering four-feet-wide river ran through the lobby, leading off to the salon on one side and the massage wing on the other. She crossed a bamboo bridge, enjoying the trickling water as it flowed through the river-rock-lined channel below. On the far side of the room, a long aquamarine-colored glass counter stretched before a gigantic stacked-stone wall. A sheet of water flowed over it.

Aqua's receptionist, Violet, stood behind the counter. In her mid-forties, she was tall and willowy with a natural elegance Hope admired. Her black hair was arranged in a neat bun at the base of her neck. She smiled at Hope's approach. "Afternoon! You here for a little pamperin'?"

"No, I'm here to talk to Sara. Is she in the salon?"

Violet's smile faltered slightly. "Yes. They're just finishin' up. Sara doesn't seem to be feelin' real great today."

Hope kept a straight face as she clucked sympathetically. Her empathy was as much for the Aqua staff as her sister Sara. Due to give birth in a few weeks, Sara's crankiness increased with the size of the baby she carried.

As Hope crossed over a bamboo bridge and entered the salon, Sara stood in the far corner, sweeping her station. Hope strolled over two more bridges as the river ambled across the salon. "How's my favorite sister today?"

Sara looked up and drew her brows together. Dressed in a voluminous lavender maternity dress, her dark-brown hair fell in styled ringlets down her back. "Glad the day is over. My back hurts, and just look at my ankles!" She thrust a leg out, tapping one sandal-covered heel on the white tile floor. "Correction —cankles!"

They were rather swollen, and Hope winced in sympathy, genuine this time. Sara had never been known for a meek personality, and she became ever fiercer as her pregnancy progressed, causing the staff to treat her with wary respect. Even Sara's husband Jack, one of the most easy-going people on earth, treaded carefully around her now.

"Well, why don't we get some smoothies and sit on the patio? You can put your feet up."

Sara's irritated frown softened, and a smile peeked out as she set her broom aside. "Thanks, but I just want to go home."

"I don't blame you. I came in here to let you know I talked to Patti, and she agreed the two of us can manage Aqua just fine while you're on maternity leave." Patti Thomas was the general manager of the resort. She dealt more with the housekeeping and guest-relations side of the resort, but was a quick learner and wouldn't have any issues adapting to being a temporary spa manager.

Sara grunted, placing both hands on the small of her back. "At first, I was so scared of this baby coming. Now I can't wait for the birth so this damn pregnancy can be over."

Hope shifted from one foot to the other. With no children herself, she was at a bit of a loss around Sara these days. "Can I help with anything?"

Sara's shoulders fell, then she gave Hope a hug. "No, you're a sweetheart for putting up with my bitching. Not as much as Jack is, but then again, he's responsible for this. So I refuse to completely give him a free pass."

"I think it takes two."

Sara made another derisive noise, then lifted her eyes to the windows facing the ocean. "Go on and get out of here, sis. The dive boat's coming back, so both our husbands will be off soon.

And Alex doesn't have to tiptoe around you." She sighed and gave Hope a crooked smile. "I'm married to a saint."

Hope couldn't help but breathe a sigh of relief as she left the salon, but the soft breeze restored her good mood. The life ring from the spa emergency station hung askew. She was heading over to straighten it when she became distracted by a much more appealing sight, *Surface Interval* snugging up to the dock. She quickened her steps, eager to see Alex and discuss the other adventure they were planning, involving a submerged tunnel exploration.

Peg's empty lounger lay just past Aqua, and Hope shielded her hand as she walked, looking for the older woman in the water. Peg was further out than Hope expected, and she waved to her. The woman waved back and Hope smiled, continuing on her way. A few moments later, she looked again.

Peg was nowhere to be seen.

The ocean's surface rippled somewhat, but the waves weren't large enough to hide a person in the troughs. Hope raised both hands to her brow as she stopped at the water line. Peg surfaced and feebly raised one hand over her head, making no noise.

Instantly, Hope kicked off her shoes and sprinted into the water, heart racing. She swam toward the woman with fast, powerful strokes, grateful that swimming was a regular part of her fitness routine. In their rescue class, Alex had explained that drowning people rarely splashed and screamed.

They simply slipped beneath the waves, exhausted.

As Hope neared Peg, the woman surfaced again, gasping for air. Then she disappeared beneath the waves.

Hope dove after her.

Chapter Two

HOPE'S HEART nearly beat out of her chest as she took sweeping strokes with her arms, driving herself downward from the surface. Peg was about ten feet below with her eyes screwed shut and arms above her head. Her arms and legs were moving slowly, prompting Hope to kick harder.

I can save her—she's not unconscious yet. Come on!

Hope swam down until she was in front of the older woman, whose face was relaxing. She scooped her arms under Peg's armpits and kicked as hard as she could for the surface. Her lungs were screaming when they both broke into the sunshine, and she took a great gasping breath before shouting into the woman's face. "You're ok! Breathe, Peg."

But she already was—coughing and sputtering, taking enormous whooping breaths. Hope kicked toward shore with one arm wrapped around Peg's waist, amazed at how heavy she was.

The older woman's arms looped around Hope's shoulders. She opened her eyes, unfocused and half-lidded. "Help," she said weakly.

"Everything's fine, Peg. We're going back to shore. You're

"

doing great." Hope still breathed hard, kicking to keep them both afloat as they slowly moved toward the beach.

Peg's eyes cleared, growing larger as her head whipped around. "I can't breathe! Get me out of here." She tightened her arms around Hope's neck.

"Loosen up, Peg. You're gripping too tightly. Peg!"

At Hope's shout, the woman loosened her grip, still holding tightly but no longer choking her. Hope lowered one leg and her toes landed in soft sand. "We can stand here. Can you do that?"

Peg nodded and Hope kept her arms around her as the woman stopped struggling and stood in the waist-deep water, wobbling slightly.

"Good job," Hope said, rubbing Peg's back. "Just breathe, ok?"

Peg nodded, no longer gasping. "I'm doing better now."

"Can you walk back to shore? I'll support you every step of the way."

"I can. Let's just go slow, dear."

The two women slowly made their way in, Hope's arm held tightly around Peg's waist. As the water became more shallow, fierce pride rose inside Hope, bringing tears to her eyes. Taking that rescue class had paid off, and the sense of accomplishment she felt now was like nothing she'd ever experienced. She gripped Peg's shoulders, supporting her as they moved toward the shore.

ALEX LOOKED toward the beach as *Surface Interval* entered Half Moon Bay. He sat in the elevated wheelhouse on a padded bench behind captain Tommy Williams. Next to him sat his other instructor and brother-in-law, Jack Powell. As Alex looked at the white façade of Aqua, the door opened, and Hope walked out. Even from a distance, he had no trouble recognizing her gorgeous hourglass figure and reddish-brown hair tied in a ponytail. Sara had dyed Hope's hair several months ago, and Alex was still amazed at how the red color turned him on.

A figure climbing the ladder in the wheelhouse distracted him and he turned away from his wife. Will Powell, the third dive guide on the trip, and Jack's brother, flopped down on the bench next to Jack. "Ok, everything's broken down. Should be quick work to clean up after we get back." Will shared Jack's dark hair and average height, but his face was longer as he frowned at them. "I guess since I'm the lowly divemaster, I get to do the dirty work while you two bask in the breeze, huh? Maybe I'll take the next instructor course that comes along."

Jack laughed. "Bite me. You're barely a competent divemaster. At least you finally figured out your compass."

"More than competent at this point," Alex said with a smile. "I've gotten a lot of compliments from guests. Good job."

Will smacked Jack on the side of the head. "See? He appreciates me."

After a rocky start, Will had come a long way. Jack had asked Alex to mentor his brother, knowing he was a divemaster in name only. Alex had clashed with the twenty-eight-year-old man's easygoing—bordering on lackadaisical—attitude. At one point, Jack had asked him to lighten up on Will.

That had been a bit of a wake-up call for Alex. He'd spent years training and commanding Navy SEALs and enjoyed teaching. But Will was the first employee he hadn't personally chosen, and he'd been more than skeptical at first. But a diving mishap had badly shaken Will, and Alex made sure to take more of a positive, reinforcing position with him. The young divemaster had bloomed in response.

In some respects, the situation had shaken Alex as well. He'd always had absolute confidence in his ability to judge people quickly and how to best interact with them. But he'd been wrong about Will.

This isn't the military, is it?

Alex had lightened up over the years and learned to enjoy life more. But sometimes he needed a reminder.

As Tommy eased the boat next to the dock, Alex's eye was drawn back to the shore. Hope wasn't visible anywhere. Will descended the ladder and hopped off the boat to secure the lines. As Alex stood to follow, he froze, detecting movement in the water. His perception narrowed to a laser focus at two people struggling in the ocean in front of Aqua. "Someone's in trouble off the beach!"

He burst into action, sliding down the ladder without using the rungs. A quick mental calculation determined he'd reach the swimmers more quickly by running along the beach rather than swimming from the pier.

Alex pounded up the pier at top speed, and the wooden floorboards shook underfoot as someone followed just behind him. As he jumped over the steps into the sand, Jack joined his side. Alex automatically grabbed the nearby life ring, tossing the other rescue aid, a long red rectangle, to Jack. Both men raced up the beach.

Patti appeared from the lobby, her plump form hurrying down the brick path, worry lines creasing her dark brow. The two swimmers were now wading out of the ocean. Alex nearly stumbled when he recognized Hope. She had her arm around the shoulders of an older woman, who was breathing heavily and leaning against Hope.

What made Alex's blood freeze in his veins wasn't that Hope had been involved in a rescue. It was the fact that she didn't carry any type of flotation aid. As the two women stopped on the beach, his eye darted to Aqua where the other emergency station sat unused.

My God, Hope. You could have been killed!

She was dressed in khaki capris and a staff polo, both dripping wet. As he neared, his breath searing in his lungs, Hope made eye contact, and the pride in her eyes was unmistakable. Relief flooded through him that she was uninjured. As he slid to a stop, Jack joined his side. Both men breathed hard, and Patti appeared on Alex's other side.

Her gray hair dripping, the older woman looked at the trio. "Oh my. I've caused quite a stir, haven't I? I'm so sorry."

"Don't be," Hope said, her voice soft and warm.

The woman turned to her with giant, haunted eyes. "I just got so tired while I was swimming back to shore. If you hadn't seen me, I don't know what might have happened."

"Let's head to the lobby," Patti said, joining the woman and sliding an arm around her waist. "We'll call an ambulance and get you evaluated."

"Oh, I'm quite all right. There's no need for that!"

"We need to get you checked out," Hope said. "That was quite an ordeal."

Jack had trotted to the towel display near the pool and now returned, draping a towel over the woman's shoulders.

Alex cast an appraising eye over the woman. She was at least seventy, and thin. There was no question she needed to be checked out by a medical professional. "Better safe than sorry. Why don't you go with Patti?"

Peg nodded and gave the general manager a shaky smile. "Of course. Let's go, dear."

Hope started walking with them when Alex called her name. "Let's head back to the house. You could use a change of clothes, and Patti's got this handled."

Hope's face registered blank surprise as she glanced at her still-dripping body, then she stared at the two men with a broad grin. "I never even realized I was wet!" She was humming with energy as she looked up the beach at a pair of sandals tumbling in the waves. "I need to get my sandals too."

Alex turned to Jack and spoke quietly. "Can you, Tommy, and Will handle cleaning up without me?"

Jack nodded, then pointed to the life ring Alex still carried. "Want me to take that back to the pier?"

With his heart sinking, Alex shook his head. "No, I'll take it to the house."

Jack held his eyes for a long moment, then nodded. Jack knew as well as Alex that Hope had broken one of the fundamental rules of water rescue. And it was just as obvious she was completely unaware of it.

Hope chattered all the way back to their house, which sat on the beach south of the resort, giving Alex a blow-by-blow description of her experience with Peg. He had rescued enough people, not to mention performed enough military operations, to understand the rush of energy that followed. So he stayed quiet and let her talk. Carrying the life ring loosely in one hand, Alex swung it gently as he walked at Hope's side. Her pride and sense of achievement were palpable, making him feel even more awful about bringing up that she'd made a very serious error.

Their house was a white, one-story cottage. A covered porch which ran the length of the house faced the sea and provided a 180-degree ocean view. As they neared the three steps that led up to it, a medium-sized yellow dog appeared at the head of the stairs, wagging his tail.

"Hi, Cruz!" Hope hopped up the steps and scratched the dog behind his floppy ears as Alex unlocked the slider. They entered a great room with a kitchen to one side. Their master bedroom lay on the other.

Hope pulled away her wet polo shirt from her neck, laughing. "I'm going to take a shower. Too bad we don't have any champagne." Trailing a hand lightly across Alex's shoulders, she headed into their bathroom.

Cruz padded over to Alex after drinking from his water bowl, and he bent down to pet the dog. "She's not going to like what I'm about to tell her, boy. Wish me luck."

But the two of them had never shied away from difficult conversations. Alex set the life ring on the granite kitchen island before retrieving two beers. Hope was back shortly, freshly scrubbed and dressed in shorts and a T-shirt.

She raised an eyebrow as she accepted the beer. "You've been awfully quiet. Everything ok?"

Alex enfolded her in his arms. At 6'1", he could easily rest his chin on top of her head, but now he pressed his face into it, inhaling the coconut scent of her shampoo. "I love you so much."

She pulled back, lines forming in her forehead. "I love you too. What's wrong?"

He moved to the other side of the island, running a hand over the life ring. "You were just outside Aqua when you saw Peg struggling?"

"Yes."

He hesitated, taking in a long breath before finally meeting her gaze and speaking softly. "Why didn't you grab one of the flotation devices that were right there?"

Hope immediately dropped her eyes to the life ring. "I never even thought about it. I just wanted to get to Peg as quickly as possible." She met his gaze. "But I probably should have, huh?"

Alex's heart hammered but he kept his voice soft. "Yeah, Hope. You should have."

She stepped to the ring and trailed a finger over it. "You did mention that during the course. But everything turned out fine. I'll try to remember next time."

He moved to her and cupped her face in his hands, staring

at her. "You need to do better than that. You could have died out there today. Drowning people grab onto the first thing that's available, even the person trying to save them. Especially the person trying to save them."

Hope frowned. "Peg did get a pretty hard grip on my neck."

Alex briefly squeezed his eyes shut, trying not to picture that. "You can't save someone if you're dead."

Hope stared at him, her jaw firming. "She's a seventy-year-old woman, Alex. And she let go as soon as I asked her to."

"Would your response have been any different if the person had been a thirty-year-old linebacker?"

"Uh... probably not."

Alex nodded. "And he would have grabbed you and held on, drowning you in the process. There's a reason rescuers *always* carry something to hand to the victim. People can be incredibly strong when they're panicked."

Her shoulders slumped, making him feel even more terrible.

"Hope, you have to stop and evaluate the situation before you act. I need to understand you're hearing me right now."

She nodded, and his hands moved with her head. "I know I can be impulsive."

A small smile rose on Alex's face. "It's one of the things I love about you. But you can't be impulsive when you're rescuing someone."

She sighed, but her eyes weren't troubled any more. "Message received. I guess I was a little premature on wanting the champagne."

Laughing, Alex drew her into his arms again. "I'm so proud of you, baby. You've got every right to feel good about this." Then he placed his knuckle under her chin, tilting her face up. He whisked his lips over hers, then settled in for a longer kiss. "You're the most important thing in the world to me."

She reached up and brushed a finger along his jawline.

"And you are to me. I noticed you and Jack both had rescue aids. It won't happen again." Then a sparkle appeared in her eye. "But you have to cut me a little slack. Unlike you, I don't go around saving people five times a day."

Alex rolled his eyes. "God, not this again."

She burst into laughter. "I'm serious! This was my first rescue. Did you do everything perfectly when you were training to become a SEAL?"

Reluctantly, a smile crept across his face. "Not even close. I got wailed on pretty good."

"Well, there you go." Hope returned to her beer and took a drink. "What do you have planned for your day off tomorrow?"

"I'm going to walk the perimeter fence around the grotto and make sure there aren't any breaks."

"When were you thinking about diving that passage off the pool? You haven't said anything about it in a while."

A small thrill rippled through Alex's stomach. "It's been on my mind lately. I need a new challenge. But first I need to check the fence."

"You want some company? I'd like to explore that area a little more, and I haven't been hiking in ages. We could take Cruz with us—just like old times!"

The dog woofed at his name, making Alex laugh. "You've got yourself a date, Mrs. Monroe."

Chapter Three

THE THICK VEGETATION cut the morning heat as Hope walked along a well-marked path, Alex at her side. Ahead of them, Cruz loped along the trail, periodically darting into the jungle to chase something enticing. Hope swiped an arm over her sweaty brow—the temperature might be lower, but the humidity skyrocketed under the dense canopy.

"I'm still not used to this path leading to the grotto," Hope said. "You could probably drive a car down it."

Alex laughed. "What? The whole thing was your idea."

"I know. It's just such a change from the animal track we started with."

Soon they came to a chain-link gate within an eight-foot fence. But instead of unlocking the gate, Alex turned right and led as the pair continued parallel to the fence. Hope nearly tip-toed, trying to be quiet. Yet even she could hear her footfalls while Alex's steps were nearly silent. Quiet movement was so second nature to him, he wasn't even aware of it. Except for the delight he took in sneaking up on her.

The fence was placed in a loose circle surrounding Half Moon Grotto, a stunning cobalt-blue spring. A large cave anchored one end of the pool, and the scene was so picturesque and peaceful Hope made it a feature for their guests. But the pool wasn't their destination that day.

"Your grotto has been a big hit," Alex said as he kept an eye on the chain-link fence, which was in excellent shape. "Divers remark on it just about every day."

"They like the idea that it's a secret hideaway just for them," Hope said, then laughed. "But we've managed to keep the real reason for the fence under wraps."

"I thought someone would have mentioned the gate covering the passage in the grotto pool by now, but no one has," Alex said. "It's visible from the surface if you look, and anyone free diving could see it easily. But I doubt anyone would find the tunnel in the cave unless they knew it was there. Which is a good thing."

Their exploration of the submerged passage deep within the cave had resulted in finding a fantastical Spanish treasure box, placed there by a marooned sailor. After bringing out the loot, two highly discreet auctions at a Miami auction house had provided the funds for expanding the resort. The underwater tunnel, as well as the one in the rock pool, were sealed, and they built the fence to keep out unwary adventurers.

As they continued around the enclosure, Hope studied her left hand and smiled. Alex had commissioned her engagement and wedding rings using a diamond from the treasure. A jeweler had custom designed her set, dominated by a Princess-cut solitaire of nearly two carats.

The fence ended at a large rocky hillside, which rose into a nearly vertical cliff. From where they stood, the grotto to their left was invisible. Hope had insisted the fence be placed far into the jungle so people enjoying the pool would only see the undisturbed area around them.

Alex turned to her, wiping his forehead. "The fence looks good. You want to explore some?"

Nodding, she bit her bottom lip as a grin escaped. Alex's light-gray T-shirt was covered in sweat, and nearly sheer where the material stuck to him. His chiseled chest and shoulders were easily visible, as were the defined muscles of his abdomen. Unable to resist, Hope sidled up to him and slid her hands under his shirt and up his torso, standing on her toes to kiss him. His skin was hot and slick under her fingers. A bolt of hot electricity ran through her as she opened her mouth and swiped her tongue over his.

Alex gave a surprised hum, which quickly became a laugh as he broke the kiss. "I thought you had another kind of exploration in mind. I'm kind of gross here and I probably smell."

Hope grinned back and leaned into his chest, inhaling deeply. "Pure, one-hundred percent Alex Monroe. Yum."

"Unless you want me to throw you against this cliff and ravish you, you might need to hold on to that thought until we get back to the house."

"Wouldn't be the first time you've thrown me against a rock-hard wall, would it?"

He brushed his thumb over her lips. "No, it wouldn't."

She blinked and took a firm step back, breaking away from his mesmerizing blue eyes. "But you're right. I actually did want to explore a bit. Do you remember this part from when you explored the entire parcel?" Most of the property she and Alex owned was jungle-covered. Only twenty of their seventy acres were oceanfront.

Alex adjusted his shorts, making her grin. "Nice change of subject there," he said. "But I didn't comb over every foot of the area. I mostly stuck to the ridgelines, looking for clearings where drug runners might have been hiding out. We are in unknown territory here."

In the two years since discovering the cave, Alex had scouted the area periodically, making sure their hidden grotto remained hidden. He had never come across any signs of clandestine human activity.

Hope examined the dense vegetation. "How do we bushwhack our way in there? Did you bring a machete?"

Alex grinned. "No, but there's an animal track branching off not far from here. Let's go down that."

He continued along the fence perimeter and Hope fell in behind him. She hadn't noticed the path but wasn't at all surprised Alex had. Cruz appeared from out of the bush and padded behind Hope. As they walked, Hope studied the back of Alex's shirt, but couldn't detect any telltale bulge at his waistline from the pistol holstered there.

After an unexpected altercation left Alex with a souvenir gunshot wound in the shoulder, he never went into unknown situations unarmed if he could help it. And few people were better prepared to use a weapon. His need to protect what he cared for—especially Hope—ran to the core of him and was undoubtedly part of the reason he'd been upset the previous day over her misstep in the swim rescue. Fortunately, after a thorough checkup, Peg had been released back to the resort with instructions to take it easy for the remainder of her trip.

Alex veered off the flattened brush next to the fence, following a narrow, barely discernable track into the lush vegetation. Cruz picked up his pace, slingshotting around them both to lead the way.

"Wonder if he's been down this path too," Hope said.

Her formerly stray dog had helped her discover Half Moon Grotto, and she suspected he'd lived in the area prior to trying his luck with her.

"Wouldn't surprise me," Alex answered. "He's probably familiar with this whole area." He leaned under a large branch which overhung the path, and Hope followed. The steamy jungle was quiet around them except for birds singing and occasionally taking flight.

Hope hadn't been in the area since she and Alex had visited it several months ago with Sara and Jack. A small trembler had shaken the ground, adding a little spice to their outing but not causing any damage to the island. The shaking had never been repeated.

After a quarter mile, they caught up to Cruz, who stood on a broad shelf of black rock. The tree canopy arched overhead, providing dappled shade to the clearing. A narrow fissure, six feet long, ran through the middle of it. The dog stared into the tight opening, nostrils flaring as he sniffed. Alex hunkered down at his side, giving Cruz's side a solid pat. The dog turned and licked Alex's face before returning his attention to the hole.

Hope kneeled next to Alex and leaned over the crevice. It was only a few inches wide and continued downward through several feet of solid rock. But only blackness could be seen at the bottom.

"I wonder if there's an opening under there," Hope said.

Alex reached his arm down but could only extend his hand and wrist into the narrow hole. Hope was able to slide her hand through to the elbow, but the seam continued.

"I don't know," Alex said. "This rock shelf is thick though. We already know this area has caves and caverns in it. I wonder if there's a room down there?" He scrabbled in the dirt until he dug out two rocks the size of a golf ball, then looked up at her and grinned. "Only one way to find out. Bombs away!"

He dropped one rock into the seam, and they leaned down. Hope pressed one ear over the opening. After a long pause, a *plink* emanated from the crevice. Hope took the other rock and dropped it in. She got the same result—a long pause followed by the sound of the rock hitting solid ground.

"There's definitely a cave down there," she said, and examined the pathway they had just traveled. "The underwater passage in the grotto goes this direction. Could it lead right below us?"

Alex sat up on his knees and shrugged. "It's possible. I've never investigated that tunnel, so who knows where it goes?"

At the prospect, an excited shiver rippled through Hope. A similar expression showed in Alex's eyes. At the same time, both of them broke into wide smiles, and Hope laughed. "You wanted to investigate that passage. Now you've got a reason to! Maybe we'll find more treasure."

Smiling, Alex stood and helped her to her feet. "I wouldn't count on that. Barnaby didn't say anything about putting his loot anywhere else, and I'm sure that rock pool tunnel has always been flooded."

Barnaby Morgan, Henry Morgan's younger brother, had been marooned in the giant cave after absconding from a Spanish galleon with a box of treasure he'd purloined. After hiding it deep within, Barnaby had left a letter describing his travails. No trace of him had ever been found again.

Cruz hopped over the fissure and continued down the path, branching off the other side of the clearing. "Let's keep going," Hope said and stepped after the dog. "Maybe there's something else out here."

Alex fell in behind her and she could hear the smile in his voice. "By all means. The view is much better from back here."

Rotating around, she arched a brow at him. He dropped his eyes to her breasts, his smile getting bigger. Turning frontward again, Hope said, "Oh, no you don't. You're supposed to be on the lookout for monsters and creepers. Don't go getting all distracted on me."

"Mmmm. I'm pretty good at multi-tasking, you know.

Besides, the monsters rush up from behind. They'll get me, not you."

"Uh-huh. How reassuring."

Cruz had bounded ahead, so Hope continued down the track after him. A short distance later, the dog's yellow form could be seen to the left of the path, sniffing at some stones. Hope moved in his direction, finding an overgrown area that might have once been a clearing. As Cruz moved down a neatly laid out row of stacked rocks, Hope realized they were too regular to be natural. "What did you find, boy?"

Alex moved along the short wall until it turned ninety degrees to the left. He hunkered down and ran his hand over the formation. Flat rocks were stacked on top of each other, with crude flaking mortar in between. Long shoots of grass grew along the formation.

"This looks like an old foundation," he said. "I think this was a house once upon a time."

Hope continued around the corner. The wall crumbled into a jumble of stones before reforming on the opposite side and making another corner. "Who would want to live in the middle of the bush like this?"

"There's no sign of the structure, just the foundation stones, and it looks really old. It might have been someone who wanted their privacy. Maybe escaped or freed slaves."

That made Hope frown. "I guess the grotto is nearby for fresh water, and they probably had rain collection systems too."

Cruz curled up in one of the corners and closed his eyes with a long sigh. Hope and Alex poked around the area, but didn't find much of interest except some old, rusty tin cans. The area was beautiful and peaceful, with trees arching overhead and filtered sunlight bathing the area in welcoming warmth. Hope dropped a tin can back to the ground, wiping her hands on her shorts, then saw several more stones a short distance away. She crossed to the formation, Alex following just behind.

Three broad, thin stones stood upright in a neat row. Two were three feet tall and the third slightly shorter. Hope knelt before them, running a hand over their mossy surface. "I think these are grave markers, but I can't make anything out." Her fingers traced over indentations chiseled into the stone. "I might come back out here sometime with some blank sheets of paper. I could do a rubbing and maybe make out what's written on these."

Alex glanced back at the foundation. "They might belong to whoever lived here. Maybe that foundation was a family dwelling, and this was their cemetery."

Hope examined the three markers. Instead of making her sad, the idea filled her with sentimental tenderness. "What a lovely idea. They kept their loved ones near, and obviously cared for them. This area is so peaceful and serene. I think this was a happy home." She smiled at Alex. "I'm glad we discovered this."

He pulled her to him, kissing her temple. "Me too. It's a good reminder of how lucky we are."

She slid her arms around his waist, pulling him tight. "Absolutely. Let's head back. I'm sure you're excited to start planning the next cave diving adventure."

"I am, especially since the grotto passage might lead to that cavern below. Given what we discovered before, I can't wait to explore."

Chapter Four

THE NEXT AFTERNOON, Alex sat behind his desk, glaring at the screen of his computer. Said desk was inside what had been his old bedroom and was now his office off the new dive shop. But he was unable to appreciate the changes at the moment, instead trying to decipher why the scuba teaching supplies he'd ordered a month ago hadn't arrived yet.

After verifying that he had placed the order, Alex picked up the phone, scowling as he stabbed the numbers with his forefinger.

"Professional Dive Instructors International," the professional female voice answered. "How may I help you?"

"Hi. I need to know why I haven't received the order I placed." Alex gave her the order number, then listened to the woman type on her keyboard.

"Oh, you're in St. Croix. We've been having problems syncing our order systems there."

Alex ground his teeth but kept from snapping at her. The PDII regional representative had been fired several months earlier, which Alex considered a blessing. He'd thought corresponding with the main office in Miami would work just as well, but apparently not. After nearly twenty years in the Navy, the one thing he could not abide was disorganized, shoddy operations.

"Look, I need these orders yesterday." He tried to keep the irritation out of his voice. "I've got dive groups coming soon who need certifications, and we've been without a regional rep for months now. Can I talk to the head instructor there?"

"Oh, I'm so sorry. He just headed out on vacation."

"Of course he did."

"Tell you what. I'll go pull your orders myself and make sure they go out tonight."

At that, Alex put some politeness back in his tone. "Thank you. Please overnight everything."

After confirming the office had everything he needed in stock, he slammed the phone down. It made a satisfying clunk as it connected with its cradle. Alex leaned back in his chair, rubbing his eyes with both hands. Jasmine stopped by his office to wave goodnight, and he looked at his watch, startled it was 5 p.m.

"Lock the door on your way out, would you, Jasmine?"

"Sure thing. See you tomorrow."

Then Alex was alone in the silence. His cell phone vibrated on the desktop and a smile broke over his face at the caller's name on the screen, his agency troubles disappearing. "Baker. How's life in the Beltway?"

Alex had been Mike Baker's commanding officer within SEAL Team Four for nearly a decade. They'd lost touch after a combat debacle in Syria that had killed eight other members of their Team and been nearly fatal to Alex. The two men reconnected two years ago, and Mike had been Alex's best man when he'd married Hope. They'd kept in touch ever since.

"It's getting colder, and I've been working my ass off on this latest job." Mike worked for a private defense contractor and specialized in tactical weapons. Notably his specialty—demolitions. "Emma and I need to escape. Desperately. I tried to book through the Half Moon Bay website, but there wasn't anything. Can you work any magic for December first through the fourth?"

Alex cradled his phone between his ear and his shoulder as he brought up the resort scheduling program on the computer. "That's between Thanksgiving and Christmas, so you might be in luck." He frowned at the mysterious colored blocks on his screen. Alex had a superficial knowledge of the program, but guest bookings were firmly in Hope's wheelhouse, not his. Running a finger down the screen, he blinked at a row of purple dots by one room, which meant it was blocked but couldn't be booked online. "How about that? Waterfall looks like it's being held open manually."

"Waterfall?"

Alex grinned. "That's one of our new bungalows. They sit just behind the beach. Hope calls them Rainforest Bungalows, so they all have names like that."

"Better than cockroach and viper, I guess."

"I'll have Hope make a reservation for you. I don't have a clue how to do that. Your timing's great—I'm going to be teaching Hope and Zach in a divemaster class. You want to help?"

Mike laughed. "Sure you want me to?"

"Definitely. They need to be able to handle emergencies. And I don't need to worry about you freaking out for real."

"No promises on that. I haven't dived since Em and I came down for your wedding."

"Lazy ass."

"Not all of us live in a tropical paradise, you know. I actually work for a living."

"It's not all piña coladas every day. Just most days," Alex

said with a grin, then it faded. "You've been putting in the hours, huh?"

Mike hesitated. "Yeah, it's been rough the last few months."

The tone of his voice made Alex straighten. "Everything ok?"

"Emma and I just need to get away and reconnect a little. She's not real happy with me. I've been working too hard and have a lead on a new job that would mean more travel."

"Well, Half Moon Bay might be just what you need, then."

"That's what I'm counting on, Alex."

AFTER ENDING THE CALL, Alex sat back in his chair and laced his fingers behind his head. His mood was much improved after Mike's call, and he was looking forward to the visit.

Got plenty to keep me busy with the divemaster class, Mike's visit, and planning the Grotto dive.

Probably too busy. The cave dive might need to wait until after Mike's trip. Thoughts of Mike brought back memories of his and Hope's wedding, and a smile rose as he stroked a finger over his titanium wedding band. Alex swept his gaze around the room, remembering the times he'd spent here with Hope before the hurricane had demolished his apartment.

They had been long nights with very little sleep, two new lovers learning about each other. Hope had saved him, every bit as much as he'd saved her. After learning about Hope's abusive relationship, those initial months had been a delicate dance for Alex. It was nothing short of a miracle to him that she loved him so unreservedly—a man who had spent nearly two decades as a Special Forces operative. Their pasts still haunted them on occasion, but less and less over time.

A slow smile raised the corners of his lips as he closed his eyes, imagining her in his mind. Hope was of average height, with a spectacular athletic body, kept toned with regular swimming and running. Her full breasts fit perfectly in his hands and her mouth was beyond delicious. Inhaling deeply, a wave of desire rolled over his body, arousal steadily building.

"I *have* to know what you're thinking about."

Alex didn't need to open his eyes to recognize Hope's voice. He didn't startle, though she must have let herself in quietly through the locked door. Slowly, he opened his eyes. She leaned against his door frame, smiling and wearing a blue strappy sundress which showed plenty of tan skin. Her tattoo also peeked out on one shoulder, a chrysalis becoming a butterfly. He loved it.

Alex rose and strolled over to her, pinning her with his eyes. "You, actually."

"I'm glad to hear that, since you had quite the hungry expression on your face." Hope's voice was low and husky, and it doubled the blood flow to his groin. Her greenish-gold eyes met his and her lips parted slightly as he slid one hand behind her head.

Bending his neck, Alex pressed his lips to hers. He kissed her softly, keeping the pressure light until she pushed hard against him. She opened her mouth and circled his tongue with hers, a quiet moan escaping. The sound seared through him.

After softly nipping her lower lip, he pulled back. "Since you're here, I guess I'm not the only one having wicked thoughts."

Giving him a sultry smile, Hope slid her arms around his waist, grinding her hips back and forth against his shorts. He inhaled sharply, a hot molten core forming within.

"I passed Jasmine on the pier, and she told me you were still up here." She darted her eyes around the room. "And we are in your old bedroom, after all."

He bent his head to nibble on her earlobe. "Did you lock the door?"

She gave a throaty laugh that made his whole body shiver. "Oh yes," she whispered. "We learned that lesson already."

As she ran her hands under his shirt and up his back, his skin caught fire.

Alex ripped his shirt off and tossed it aside. Cupping her face in both hands, he kissed her again. This time harder, immediately pressing his tongue inside her mouth. He reached around and unzipped her dress, sliding the straps off her shoulders. Breaking the kiss, he took a step back so he could watch. The dress had a built-in bra, so when he let go and the fabric dropped to Hope's feet, she stood before him dressed only in pink panties.

His heart pounded at the sight. He stepped in again to stroke both breasts, her skin soft and warm beneath his fingers. With a whispered moan, Hope unzipped his shorts and reached beneath, grasping him firmly in her hand.

Growling, Alex slid his hands around to her back and pulled her tightly to him, crushing his mouth to hers. Their kiss was loud and wet in the silent room. Rushing now, Hope pushed his shorts off.

He kicked them and his boxers away, whispering against her mouth, "My God. I want you so much."

"I'm all yours, Alex." Hope quickly stepped out of her panties, then pressed her naked body against his, their hot skin meeting.

He walked her backward until her butt pressed against his desk. He reached around her and swept the desktop clean—pens, his desk calendar, and wire file holders clattering to the ground.

Spinning Hope around, he bent her forward and lifted one smooth leg aside. Entering her depths with one hard thrust, he leaned over her back as she gripped the opposite edge of his desk with both hands. He slid in and out, deeply each time, and pressed his mouth to her ear. "Oh, the things you do to me."

Hope didn't reply, just breathed in deep, ragged breaths.

Maybe it was because he'd just been thinking about their early days, but he felt the exact moment the experience changed for her. They had never broken in his new desk, but they'd made love in this exact position multiple times. He was exquisitely attuned to her, and something had just changed. Alex opened his eyes, and her fingers were white where they gripped the edge of the desk.

She froze beneath him. "Alex. Stop." Her voice was tight and small.

Instantly, he withdrew and straightened, holding her hips loosely with both hands. She stood up, slowly turning around. Her eyes were clouded, and shame flickered through them, which cut him to the bone. She couldn't meet his eyes, dropping hers to the ground. He wrapped her gently in his arms and whispered, "What do you need?"

She melted against him. "I'm sorry. I don't know why—"

He pressed a finger against her lips. "You never need to apologize. What do you *need*, baby?"

Hope breathed hard, her breasts moving with the force of her emotion. She slowly stroked her hands over both his shoulders and biceps. Closing her fingers around his arms, she finally met his eyes. "You. Only you, Alex."

With a small smile, he took her hand and led her around his desk. Still fully aroused, he sat down in his chair. She sat on his lap, straddling him.

He watched her, letting her take the lead.

Hope's breathing was quieter now and she skipped her fingers over his chest. Taking his shaft in one hand, she slowly stroked him. Then she leaned forward and drew her tongue slowly over his collarbone. He remained still, even as her wet touch sent a shooting bolt through him.

"I want you, Alex. Only you." Hope laid a row of soft kisses across his jaw, then pulled back to meet his gaze. The troubled, haunted look was gone, and a faint smile rose before she leaned against him, rubbing her breasts against his pecs.

She touched her mouth to his.

Alex kissed her back tenderly, keeping the pressure light. Hope moved her hands to his shoulders, sliding over them as she deepened the kiss, plunging her tongue into his mouth. Throbbing with every beat of his heart now, he held himself tightly in check. He moved both hands to her back, dancing his hands lightly over her damp skin.

Letting her stay in charge.

Holding him with her eyes, Hope lifted and guided herself onto him. He moaned, whisking his lips over her neck as he became surrounded by her warmth. "You feel so incredible, so warm." He whispered the words against her ear.

She established a slow, deep movement that drove him wild.

Clasping his face in both hands, Hope returned her mouth to his, kissing him deeply. He traced his fingers over her hips, slowly drawing them over her skin. She gasped, breaking the kiss to press her head against his neck, moving faster now. He slid his right hand across her flat stomach. He traced circles with his first two fingers around her navel. Teasing her as she moved, breathing hard now.

In one hasty movement, Hope grabbed his hand and moved it from her stomach to their joining between her legs. He needed no further instruction, continuing the circling movement.

Hope tipped her head back and closed her eyes, panting in short, moaning gasps. She gripped his shoulders with both hands, and he matched her breaths, his climax building just watching her. Her pants became cries and finally he couldn't keep his eyes open any longer, letting them fall closed as he was swept away with her.

He moved his hand, once again embracing her within both arms. She nestled her head into the hollow of his neck as he drew her to him, gathering her inside his love and protection.

THEY ATE at the outdoor table on their back porch. After their intimate encounter, Hope couldn't face the bustle of the restaurant, instead picking up two entrees to go. The sky was black as she refilled their glasses with white wine, her wind chime singing deep, soothing tones in the breeze. Still coming to terms with the emotional roller coaster she'd just gone through, Hope put her fork down to meet Alex's eyes. "I'm sorry about this afternoon."

He reached out and squeezed her hand. "Don't apologize. Neither of us can predict when old wounds will reopen."

"Maybe not, but I still hate it when they do. I got a call from Caleb's parole officer this morning. I'm sure that's what brought it up."

Alex's face became guarded, a sure sign he was feeling strong emotion. And fewer subjects brought out strong emotion in him more than her abusive ex-boyfriend. "Is he getting out of prison?"

"No, just the opposite."

The parole officer involved when Caleb had been convicted the first time—mainly due to Hope's testimony—had kept in touch over the years. Apparently, she had made an impression on him. The man would call her when something significant happened with Caleb, which wasn't often. Years went by without hearing from him. "The parole officer said Caleb got into a fight with another inmate and was transferred to a maximum-security prison. Now there are more charges pending against him."

"Doesn't sound like he's going anywhere soon."

A wave of relief ran through her. "No, which is a good thing." She reached forward and held Alex's strong, reassuring hand. "Thanks. You know exactly what to do." Alex had an uncanny ability to read her. Whenever these ghosts of the past came up, he let her be in charge, instinctively knowing that was what she needed.

The skin around his eyes crinkled. "Hardly. But when I'm hurting, you've always given me what I need. I just try to do the same for you."

After a long, intimate look that said more than words, they went back to their meals. The comforting sound of wind chimes filled the night as a half-moon broke free of the clouds, sending a broad, sparkling strip of light over the ocean.

Chapter Five

HOPE TOOK a seat at her usual corner table in the resort restaurant. It was just past 11 a.m., and she was there for an early business lunch with an important co-worker. Her table afforded a wide view of the ocean and pier. *Surface Interval* was still out on the morning dive trip, and Hope smiled, remembering her and Alex's encounter in his office.

A week had passed without further word from Caleb's law enforcement team. And more important, without further unpleasant memories. She and Alex were back to their usual passionate relationship, with no hesitations on her end. It was because of his sensitivity when she occasionally had dark moments that she could enjoy such a vigorous—even rough at times—physical relationship with him.

She was always safe with Alex.

Hope let her eyes wander over the open-air dining room. As the resort grew, they had placed additional tables in the large room. One row of tables fronted the beach, while another overlooked the pool. Divemaster turned professional photographer Robert Davis's photos hung prominently on the walls, all for sale.

The restaurant was beautiful, but Hope had higher ambitions. Which brought her back to her imminent meeting. As she turned her gaze toward the kitchen, a pair of double swinging doors opened, and executive chef Gerold Harrigan breezed through them carrying a plate in each hand.

A broad smile lit his face, his teeth brilliant against his dark skin. Effortlessly placing Hope's plate in front of her, he took a seat across after setting his own lunch down. Both entrees were the same, and Hope leaned over to inhale the wonderful scent. Gerold had prepared one of her favorite dishes on the menu. Blackened mahi-mahi with tropical salsa, mango rice, and whatever vegetable was fresh. That day it was broccolini.

Since Gerold hadn't started his shift yet, he was still in street clothes, wearing shorts and a St. Croix Triathlon finisher shirt. Hope smiled fondly at the sight of it. "That was a fun race, wasn't it?"

Gerold grinned at her. In his mid-thirties, the St. Croix native was a cycling fanatic. "I had a blast. We should do it again sometime."

Hope nodded. "I haven't run a half-marathon since, just shorter races. I've been looking to do some kind of team building activity, since we have so many more people on staff now, but I'm not sure what."

Gerold picked up his fork. "I'm sure you'll think of somethin'."

Hope took her first bite of the fiery, yet flaky, mahi and moaned, closing her eyes. "Oh, your blackening spice is *so* good! Did you have to hunt down the broccolini?"

"No. I cycled by a farmer's stand yesterday and bought his whole crop. He delivered it here this mornin'." He held her gaze. "I was talkin' to Percy. He asked if we plan on startin' our own garden here."

Percy was one of their longest-standing landscapers and a

gardening fanatic, so Gerold's statement didn't surprise Hope. "That's a great idea, but someone besides me needs to spearhead it. I'm going to have my hands full once Sara has the baby."

"I've always wanted to have a true farm-to-table restaurant concept and would love to serve ingredients we grew here at the resort. I'll talk to Percy some more and see what we can whip up."

"Go for it."

Conversation paused while they ate their lunches, giving Hope time to approach why she'd called this meeting. Setting her fork on her plate, Hope wiped her mouth with a napkin. "As much as I like having lunch with you, I have a reason today."

"Yeah? What's up?"

Hope swept her gaze around the dining room once again. "This restaurant is doing really well. Mostly because of you. We have to take dinner reservations now because we're so busy."

Gerold winked at her. "There are worse problems to have."

"Oh, I'm not complaining! Just the opposite." She tented her fingers, resting her elbows on the table. "I have another building project I'd like to discuss with you."

He stared at her but didn't interrupt. Gerold was an intelligent man and undoubtedly knew she wasn't bringing the subject up as idle chit-chat.

"When Alex and I purchased the land at the north end of Half Moon Bay, it gave us the space we needed to expand the resort. The building that houses Ember and Aqua is the first of those projects. But I've been saving the piece of land at the very northern end, which has a nearly 180-degree ocean view." She paused and his eyes were riveted to hers. "I want to build a formal restaurant, Gerold. Dinner only. We'll keep this one for casual dining, but I want the new one to draw people from all over the island, locals and tourists."

He blinked, as if shaking himself out of a trance. "That sounds incredible. How far along are you in the plannin'?"

A smile crept across Hope's face. "I haven't even started. The only ones who even know about this are Alex and Sara. And I only mentioned it to Sara once or twice—she's probably forgotten about it. This will be *your* restaurant, Gerold. I want you to take the reins and design it yourself. We might work out a co-ownership opportunity if you're interested."

Gerold pressed his fingers into the table, the pads of his fingers turning pale. "I don't know what to say, Hope. I've always dreamed of my own restaurant."

"This project won't start building for at least a year, but that's why I wanted to tell you about it early. So you'd have plenty of time to think about it. And you might give some thought about where to place that garden too."

Gerold barked out laughter and sat back in his chair, swiping a hand over his closely cropped black hair. "Thank you, Hope. What an incredible opportunity."

She smiled back at him. "You are one of the most talented chefs on the island. This is strictly self-preservation, you know. I don't want to lose you!"

He shook his head and they both laughed. Hope happened to be looking at her half-full glass of water when the liquid started dancing inside. Her smile faded as the silverware vibrated against their plates. The hanging flower baskets suspended from the edges of the restaurant swung in long arcs. Two glasses on the table next to them fell over and rolled off the table, shattering on the tile floor.

Hope and Gerold's smiles both fled as they froze, looking around themselves.

"We're havin' another trembler," Gerold said.

"Should we get under the table?" Hope asked, but the shaking was already decreasing.

He shook his head. "Nah. It's fadin' now. Stronger than the one we had a few months ago, but no major damage that I can see."

After another few seconds, the quaking stopped completely, and birds began singing again. Gerold turned his head, frowning toward the kitchen. "I need to make sure there's no damage in the kitchen."

Hope nodded as she stood. "I'll go to the lobby and check in with Patti. Fortunately, most guests are out on the dive trip, but there might be some damage in their bungalows when they get back. Hopefully it's minor."

Half Moon Bay Resort's lobby was a separate building near the restaurant. It was painted a soft yellow and a porch encircled the entire unit. As Hope entered through the rear, beach-facing door into the large room, Patti and front-desk clerk Martine were on their hands and knees, using rags to mop up water spilled when the large container of fruit-infused water fell onto the tile floor. Martine tied her black braids in a knot, getting them out of the way.

"Are you two all right?" Hope asked.

Patti looked up. "Yes, we're both fine. Just a little spill."

Hope crossed the room to the front desk. A large flat-screen television hung on the wall, cycling through pictures of St. Croix and the resort. Picking up the remote control, she changed to a local channel, where news anchors had already broken into regular programming.

A bleached-blonde anchorwoman smiled at the camera. "We have Professor Stuart on the phone, a geologist at St. Croix University, who was kind enough to give us some information. How strong was the earthquake, Professor?"

The screen cut to a static image of the island with *Earthquake* in bright red font running across it. A man's voice with an American accent said, "We just got the official reading from the

US Geological Survey, which registered it as a 4.1. We've had increasing tremors for several weeks, so this wasn't entirely unexpected."

The woman appeared on screen again, her eyes wide. "We've been having quakes for weeks?"

"Microquakes, so small they can't even be felt. But often they're a sign of a stronger quake building, and that's likely what we just had."

"So can we expect any stronger earthquakes in coming days?"

"That's unlikely. The Virgin Islands have tremors periodically, but they're usually not terribly strong. This one, coupled with the 3.6 magnitude quake we had several months ago, was likely the main event. I would expect a few more aftershocks, which might not even be noticeable, before they diminish altogether."

"Well, that's reassuring to hear." The anchorwoman flashed a big fake smile at the camera and repeated the information.

Hope turned the TV back to the scrolling images and turned to Patti and Martine, who now stood next to her. She exhaled in a long, cleansing breath as she glanced at the wall clock. It was noon. "That sounds like good news. I'll head down to the pier to meet the returning guests and let them know there might be a bit of a mess in their rooms. Can you two stand by here? I'll have guests call if they need anything cleaned up."

"Of course, child," Patti said. "Don't worry. We'll be back to normal before dinnertime."

After visiting the kitchen and being reassured by Gerold that no damage would prevent lunch from being served, Hope headed toward the pier. The dive boat was sidling up to the end of the pier as she hurried down it. She inspected the wooden planks but couldn't detect any damage. No windows were broken either downstairs or in the new dive/gift shop on the second floor.

She stepped aboard as soon as the boat was secure and raised her arms, asking for everyone's attention. Alex, Tommy, Jack, and part-time divemaster April all stood in the wheelhouse, wearing identical questioning expressions.

"Did you guys notice anything unusual during your second dive or the trip back?" Hope asked.

She was met with blank looks and shrugs all around. Alex climbed down onto the main deck. "Nothing out of the ordinary. What's up?"

Hope explained about the earthquake and the expressions changed to alarm. She quickly reassured them. "It was a minor trembler, but call the front office if you need anything cleaned up in your bungalows. Lunch will be served as usual."

The guests hurried off the boat to check their belongings, chattering about missing the excitement. The rest of the crew joined Alex on the main deck. "Is there any damage to the dive operation?" he asked.

Hope raised a hand to her brow, wiping away the sweat. "I haven't checked. The tremor wasn't long ago, but I didn't see any broken windows or signs of damage when I walked down here."

Alex nodded and turned to the crew. "Tommy and April, can you check out the dive shop? Jack, you go to the gear room. I'll make sure the compressor and NITROX membrane system are ok."

Half an hour later, they all met in the lobby, and Hope was grateful to work with such an incredible group of people. One bungalow had minor damage and Patti dispatched workers to repair it. But there was no lasting damage to any of the dive equipment.

Patti had been correct. By dinner time, all would be back to normal.

Chapter Six

AS ALEX STEPPED on the stern dive platform of *Surface Interval*, the sun burst from behind a bank of clouds, throwing a sparkling blanket over the ocean before him. That had to be a good omen following the trembler two days ago. His group of six bobbed on the surface, waiting to start their dive. He couldn't resist a smile as he made a giant stride into the water.

Wonder what I'm going to get today?

Everyone in this mixed group of guests was new to him. He joined the loose circle of divers and cast an eye around, pleased not to see any large, panicky eyes behind masks. "Everyone ready?"

He got six nods back and gave everyone the thumbs down, initiating their descent. As the group drifted downward, Alex kept a close eye on everyone, evaluating from their form and position in the water those who might need extra help. He noticed two middle-aged men descending like rocks. As they approached the reef, they added air to their BCDs, slowing themselves quickly to hover a few feet above it.

Ok, don't need to worry about those two.

As the dive progressed, Alex helped a new pair of divers

several times, gesturing to inflate or deflate their BCDs. The two experienced divers kept to themselves but stayed near the group. He checked on them but didn't ask for their remaining air supply. He had a firm policy that experienced divers should be left to manage their own dives, and most didn't appreciate being babied.

The two men were eager to inspect all the fish and creatures he found on the dive, though. Alex was particularly pleased when he found a large toadfish hiding in a shallow cave on the sand. The odd, flattened fish had a frilly fringe around its large mouth, camouflaging it to resemble the sand it rested on. Any unsuspecting fish which swam too close became a quick meal when the toadfish struck with lightning speed.

For their second dive, they went to Sea Fan Haven, one of Alex's favorite dives. The reef was a carpet of soft corals, fans, and sponges in a dizzying array of bright colors. Large schools of yellow-tailed snappers parted gently as he swam through them, followed by the rest of his group.

By the time they reboarded after the second dive, the clouds had completely burned off, leaving a vault of vivid blue sky above. Alex was removing regulators from tanks when the pair of experienced divers approached him.

"Thanks for the dives." The man, who introduced himself as Leonard, was around fifty, with short salt-and-pepper hair.

Alex smiled back. "You're welcome. On days like this, it's as much fun for me as it is for you."

The other diver, Ed, was heavier with dark brown hair. "We noticed you didn't watch us too closely."

Alex straightened, then shrugged. "I saw in about two seconds you guys knew what you were doing. I try not to coddle experienced divers, but if you want me to ask about your air consumption, I'd be happy to."

Leonard laughed. "God, no! It's a nice change. Besides, you had plenty to watch with that new pair."

Alex wasn't about to put down anyone in his group. "They were fine. Just needed a little help now and again. You guys diving tomorrow?"

"Yes, and then we head home on Monday," Ed said. "We had to get out of town. Our skin was drying out—saltwater's the only cure."

"I hear you," Alex said. "Where's home?"

Leonard watched him closely. "Miami."

"Do you two own a dive shop or teach?"

The two men exchanged a look, then Leonard shook his head. "Not exactly. I'm the east coast director of operations for PDII. Ed here works in course curriculum setup."

Alex flashed back to his irritating phone call with the Miami office, though he'd finally received his delayed materials once they'd been overnighted. He grinned. "I called the Miami office a few days ago and actually asked to speak to you. Your receptionist told me you had just left on vacation, but I had no idea it was going to be at Half Moon Bay."

Leonard returned his smile. "I wanted to check out St. Croix personally. I realize there's been some hiccups since our last regional rep left."

"A few," Alex said noncommittally.

"We'd like to pick your brain a little about how to improve things," Ed said. "You want to meet us for lunch?"

Alex covered his surprise. Talking about bureaucratic channels sounded about as much fun as a root canal, but he wouldn't get a better opportunity to express some of the frustrations he'd experienced recently, as well as those of other dive shops on the island. "Sure. Let me take a quick shower and I'll meet you at the restaurant."

. . .

ALEX ENTERED the dining room at the same time as the two men, and they gathered around a table lining the beach. Hope had promoted head server Charlotte to work at Ember, and her replacement came over to take their order. Lucinda wore her black hair in a halo around her head and gave them a warm smile as she approached the table. She glanced at Alex first. "Iced tea?"

He nodded and was surprised when Leonard and Ed ordered beers. Before leaving the boat, he'd looked at the afternoon roster, and both had been listed for the afternoon dive. "You guys change your mind about diving this afternoon?"

The two men glanced at each other, a look passing between them. Leonard shrugged. "A beer sounds terrific, but I guess we can have one tonight. Diving sounds better. Change our orders to iced teas too, please."

As Lucinda walked away, Alex stared at the two men, suspecting he'd just passed some sort of test. As employees of PDII, Leonard and Ed would certainly know that alcohol was strictly prohibited before diving.

"You run a good operation here," Leonard said, looking Alex in the eye.

"Thank you. I try to."

The older man sighed and folded his arms on the table. "I'm sorry things have been a wreck since Cody left. We got several complaints about him and quickly discovered he had to go."

Alex had had his own run-in with their former representative. But it was water under the bridge now, and he didn't feel like getting into it. "Not having a rep for the Virgin Islands has created more problems than I thought it would."

"Us too," Ed said. "We might have a solution, though. We'd like to run it by you."

"I'm all ears."

Leonard eyed him steadily. "We need another representative. One with solid credentials and serious credibility."

Alex shrugged. "No argument there. I imagine plenty of people in Miami would love the job."

A faint smile rose on Leonard's face. "That's true, but we already have someone else in mind. You."

This time, Alex didn't hide his surprise. "Me?"

Even more of a surprise, he didn't hate the idea.

"Yeah," Leonard continued. "You're the perfect guy for the job. It wouldn't be too much extra work, but we would like an annual meeting to start up here."

Alex was stunned at the excitement fluttering in his stomach.

I hate bureaucratic shit. Then again, what better way to change how things are done?

They spent the next half hour discussing the job and what exactly it would entail. With Half Moon Bay's extra dive staff, plus Hope and Zach becoming divemasters, Alex could easily handle the extra work. "All right. Let's give it a shot."

"Excellent!" Leonard said, raising his glass of iced tea. "We'll ease you into the position and start by having a meeting in Christiansted so you can introduce yourself."

"How come you've never become an instructor development course director?" Ed asked.

"Never needed to. Until recently, Half Moon Bay has always been a small operation. I was the only instructor until earlier this year."

"Having an IDC at Half Moon Bay is something else to think about long term," Ed said. "Alex, you've got a very unique set of qualifications. Leonard and I would love to see what you come up with."

Alex sat back and laughed. "Well, let's take it one step at a time, ok? This will affect resort operations, so I can't formally accept your offer before discussing it with my wife. But something tells me she's going to like the idea."

THAT EVENING, Hope sat on their porch couch, Alex next to her. Filled with excitement, she bolted upright at his news. "Alex, that's fantastic! Of course you need to accept."

She settled back into the hollow of his shoulder as he draped his arm over her shoulders. The sky was completely black, and the evening was warm and balmy, with hardly a ghost of a breeze.

"I'm kind of amazed how much I want to do it," Alex said. "I've spent the last six months grumbling about how I could do a better job managing all this agency crap. Now I'll get to put my money where my mouth is."

"I'm so proud of you."

He made a derisive noise, and she bit her lip to keep from smiling. Alex hated praise.

Instead, he asked, "You still have your get-together tomorrow? What do you call it?"

"GNO. Girls' Night Out. Not very original, maybe. But we're meeting at Marimba tomorrow evening. It will be the last one before Sara has her baby. That will sure change things." She looked at the distant pier, its palapa lit up with LED rope lights. "So many changes around here. And maybe someday you'll be training instructors too."

"I'm in no hurry for that. Plus, I'd have to go to Miami to take the course for the credential." He laughed and stroked Hope's hair. "I gave Jack a hard time about being separated from Sara when he took his IDC, but I don't like the idea of being away from you either."

She turned and looked into those blue eyes. "That's a problem for the future. Right now, nothing can keep us apart."

Inhaling deeply, she took a long breath of fresh, salty air. She pressed a soft kiss to his lips, then snuggled closer, savoring the warmth of his arm around her.

Chapter Seven

MARIMBA WAS a beach bar a few miles north of Half Moon Bay. An almost-hidden local hangout, it was a favorite setting for their semi-regular Girls' Night Out. Hope and Sara arrived early so they could talk for a few moments before the others arrived. They chose a picnic table on the beach, sitting across from each other as a palm tree cast its shade over them.

Ted, the middle-aged bartender and owner, came over. He tossed a dish towel over one shoulder as he smiled at the two women. "How you two doin'? You want the usual tonight?"

Hope nodded. "One bucket of Leatherbacks and whatever Sara's drinking."

"Just a large ice water, Ted."

After he brought their drinks, Sara adjusted her position on the wooden bench, wincing. "Only a few weeks left. Thank God."

Hope fished an ice-cold beer out of the steel bucket and opened it using the built-in device on the side of the bucket. "Next time we meet, you'll be able to have a beer."

Sara shot her a rueful glance. "Maybe. It's more complicated when you're breastfeeding."

"That's true. Guess you don't want baby Powell getting all drunk, huh?"

"Probably not very parental. You're ok with me keeping my maternity leave flexible?"

Hope smiled and clasped Sara's swollen hand. "Patti and I are working out a schedule, so don't worry about it. Concentrate on your family."

"I just can't decide how much time I want off. I can't imagine not working for three months. I'm afraid I'll be climbing the walls."

"You might feel differently after the baby is born."

Women's voices drifted toward them as the rest of their group crossed the sand to the table. Hope's friend Cindy sat next to her with roommate and Ember manager Heather on her other side. Massage therapist Selena settled next to Sara, with April taking the end on that side.

After everyone got their drinks, Hope caught them up. "We were just discussing the impending birth." She glanced at April. "We've got Aqua covered, but Jack's going to need some time off too. Has Alex talked to you about it?"

April nodded. Her long honey-blonde hair was still damp, and she had it wrapped in a messy bun. "I'll cover some while he's out, but Will and Alex have a lot of it worked out already."

"That's great. Thank you."

Sara leaned across Selena to look at the divemaster. "Jack said two weeks sounded about right to him."

Hope glanced at her sister in triumph. "See? All covered. Nothing for you to worry about."

Sara burst into laughter. "No. Nothing at all."

"You'll do great. I can't wait to meet my niece or nephew."

"I can't believe you've never wanted to find out the sex," Cindy said, twisting her long black braids over one shoulder.

She had a successful career working in a local physical therapy office.

Sara smiled and ran a hand over her round stomach. "BB will be here before we know it, so we'll find out soon enough."

"BB?" Heather asked. "I thought you were calling it Bump."

Sara's brows flew up as she pointed at her belly with both hands. "Does this look like a bump to you? No, Bump graduated to Basketball a couple of months ago. BB for short."

"Your other dive shop doesn't mind you filling in?" Hope asked April.

"They don't care, and hours are hours. I've been trying to save some money, so I'll take whatever I can get. Especially since I'm not working at the restaurant anymore."

Like many people on the island, April worked multiple jobs to make ends meet. She'd recently broken up with a co-worker at the restaurant where she'd worked for years. They'd taken a romantic trip to St. John, and he decided to stay. Without her. Hope felt bad for her. April was an excellent divemaster, and normally would have been a top choice when Half Moon Bay needed more dive guides.

Except for one complicating factor.

April had long harbored romantic feelings for Alex. Even when he was single, he'd never felt the same way toward her. Hope was completely secure in her marriage, and April had always been respectful of their relationship. She wasn't a threat, but having her work beside Alex full time was a complication Hope could do without.

April studied the label on her beer, picking at it. "I've been talking to my friend Maia at Calypso Key a lot lately. She just found out she's pregnant so she can't divemaster until after the baby's born." She looked up and met Hope's gaze. "She offered me a job. I'm thinking about moving."

A round of disappointed mews went around the table, but Hope's primary emotion was relief. She genuinely thought April would be happier somewhere else. Somewhere without Alex.

"Where's Calypso Key?" Selena asked April.

"In the Florida Keys. A bit up from Key West."

"Alex and I really enjoyed the resort when we visited on our honeymoon. It gets our seal of approval."

April gave Hope a smile, but it was forced. "I'm still mulling it over. If I take the job, I'll let you or Alex know ASAP." Then she brightened. "I don't think Calypso Key has had all the growth of Half Moon Bay, though. It will be sleepy by comparison."

Hope shook her head. "There have been so many changes. We've hired a lot of new staff—not just Aqua and Ember, but support staff due to the new bungalows. I've been trying to find a way to bring the team together. I don't want to lose the family-feel of the resort, even if we are larger now."

"Anything specific?" Selena asked.

"Not yet. I was thinking about something involving photos. If you guys have any of you working, send them my way. Maybe they'll inspire me."

Sara smiled. "Maybe I can find some of the two of us. But you are absolutely prohibited from using any pictures of me looking like the Good Year Blimp."

"Oh, stop it, Sara," Cindy said with a laugh. "You're even more gorgeous pregnant."

Sara just waved her off, but a small smile formed on her face.

"Did you guys have any damage from our little trembler?" Heather asked.

April shook her head. "Some stuff fell over is all."

"Jack had to repair a pipe that burst under our kitchen sink,"

Sara said with a laugh. "Fortunately, I went home shortly after the tremor and got the water shut off or we would have had a major flood in the kitchen."

"I'm just glad we only had two small tremors," Heather said with a shudder. "I'm from San Francisco—I hate earthquakes."

"It appears we've had our excitement on that front," Hope said. She lifted her glass and nodded at Sara. "Now it's time to look forward to the next excitement."

WHEN HOPE RETURNED to the house, Alex was in their great room watching a military history documentary. "Have a good time tonight?"

She flopped onto the couch next to him. "Yes. We had lots to talk about. Did you know April is thinking about moving to Florida?"

Alex's face went blank, and he muted the television. "No, not at all. That just makes it more important to get you and Zach certified as soon as possible. Starting next week—ok?"

Hope nodded. "I've cleared my schedule for the times you gave me." Then she frowned at him. "Do I need to be worried that Mike is going to help with our class?"

Alex grinned. "No. He's down here for vacation, so I'll only ask him to help with one session. We'll all go on a dive beforehand, so he'll at least get one day of regular diving in. Thanks for booking that bungalow for them."

"Of course. I try to keep one blocked for last-minute reservations. I have no doubt Emma will be thrilled with Aqua. She can get all the treatments and pampering she could ever want."

Alex's smile faded. "Hopefully not too much. Mike didn't say too much on the phone, but they're coming down here because things have been a little strained between them. We need to make sure they have plenty of alone time."

Hope ran her fingers over his short, sandy hair. "That shouldn't be too difficult. This is one of the most romantic places around. We'll give them a private key to Half Moon Grotto. If that place doesn't put them in the mood, nothing will."

Chapter Eight

DECEMBER...

ALEX STOOD in the arrivals hall of the St. Croix airport. Hope was in a business meeting, so he was alone as he craned his head, searching the group of passengers streaming out of the security zone. After a few minutes, he recognized Mike Baker's athletic form, his wife Emma at his side. Several inches shorter than Alex, Mike had stayed fit, his dark-brown hair short and neat. Emma wore a long white sundress with navy-blue streaks running through it, her long, blonde hair loosely curled.

Mike spotted him and broke into a wide grin, quickening his step. The two men shook hands, then pulled each other into a hug.

"Wow," Mike said. "Two years of marriage and you're not fat yet."

"Just following your lead. You've been married longer than me."

Alex turned and gave Emma a quick hug. "Decent flight?"

"Ask me after our luggage arrives," she replied with a laugh.

They moved to the carousel, and Emma breathed out a sigh as two gray bags appeared. "Ok. Now the vacation can begin."

Alex arched a brow at Mike, who laughed. "I know. It's only four days, but she packs like a movie star."

"Oh, stop complaining," Emma said, smiling. "You're the one who wanted to pack a wetsuit."

Mike grabbed a suitcase in each hand and joined Emma's side as they made their way toward Alex's Land Cruiser.

"You didn't really pack a wetsuit, did you?" Alex asked.

"No. I figured even a slacker like you would have rentals available."

"Uh-huh. Like the one I lent you last time you visited?"

"Exactly. See? I keep you in line."

They climbed into Alex's car, Mike in the back and Emma riding shotgun. As Alex pulled onto the highway, Emma's text tone went off. She lifted her phone. "Ooh, look at that! I just got the confirmation for my spa appointment tomorrow morning. I'll be relaxing while you all get salty and wet."

Alex grinned at her. "Hope is dying to know what you think of Aqua. I had to talk her into diving with us tomorrow morning. I think she'd rather go to the spa with you."

Mike leaned forward between the two seats and rubbed his hands together. "I'm glad she's coming. I need to evaluate both her and the kid's abilities before I plan my mission."

"Mike, you be nice," Emma said mildly.

Alex looked in the rearview mirror, meeting Mike's eyes. "You might be surprised when you see Zach again. He's shot up six inches since you last saw him."

"Oh cool. So now he can stand fully upright with his tank on instead of tipping over backward?" Mike laughed. "I talked to him for a while after your wedding. I like him."

"He's a good guy."

Zach had started off at Half Moon Bay with a strong case of

awe-struck hero worship toward Alex. Fortunately, over the past two years it had tempered to respect and admiration, much to Alex's relief.

"You guys have any big plans while you're down here?" Alex asked. "Sights you'd like to visit?"

Emma leaned her head against the headrest. "We both just want to relax. Our jobs have been way too busy lately, especially Mike's. Hanging out at the resort sounds like paradise."

"That can easily be accomplished," Alex said, turning onto the access road toward the resort. "I know Hope is putting together a private beachfront dinner for you guys, but you'll have to talk to her about the details."

Emma rolled her head toward him, breaking into a smile. "That's sweet of her. You guys don't have to go to all this trouble for us."

Alex laughed. "I'm getting free help with my divemaster class, and Hope lives for planning special touches for people. It's no problem, trust me."

As he pulled into the sand parking lot, the trail leading toward Half Moon Grotto appeared. Mike craned his head at it. "That's new. Where's the path go?"

Alex parked and they got out of the car. "That is the other special surprise we have for you two. Tomorrow afternoon, Half Moon Grotto is all yours. The path is a mile and a half to a really cool freshwater pool and cave. It's fenced so we can control access. We'll make sure you two have the only key, so you have your privacy."

As they entered the lobby, Mike beamed. "That sounds awesome! Spending the morning diving in the Caribbean, and the afternoon on a private retreat with my girl. What more could a man want?"

After an answering smile, Emma's attention was diverted as

she moved toward the center of the lobby. "Oh wow! This is gorgeous!"

Alex's smile became thoughtful as they approached the six-foot glass dolphin sculpture, captured as it leaped out of a wave. Hope had first spotted it at a gallery inside a private airport in Miami when they'd brought their first lot of treasure to be auctioned. She'd been entranced by it. So entranced, she hadn't noticed the clever thief who stole their loot. But they got it back, and when they returned the following year for the second auction, the statue was still there. Hope insisted it was a sign they were meant to have it and marched right in to buy the figure.

After handing Alex the bag which contained their incredibly valuable items.

For Alex, the dolphin sculpture was a vivid reminder of the woman he loved. And something deeper. A representation of a bond he shared with the animal brought to life by the artist. He'd experienced two personal encounters with dolphins, and both had occurred at pivotal turning points in his life. This statue would ensure he never forgot how taking a leap of faith can change an entire life.

After examining the dolphin, Emma spied a large glass photo hanging on the wall of staff photos. She approached, exhaling another, "Oooh."

The photo made Alex straighten, like it always did. The sight of himself in dress whites automatically put some starch in his spine. Robert had captured the moment beautifully, seconds after he and Hope had become husband and wife. Mike walked up to the picture and grinned. "Gotta admit. That's pretty good advertising for the resort." Then his eye dropped to the framed articles beneath. "You hung the article that guy wrote about you, huh?"

Alex shrugged, somewhat embarrassed. When Mike had

been at the resort for their wedding, Hope had shown him the article a nosy newspaper reporter had written about Alex's past as a SEAL. But it had taken more cajoling before Alex had let the article be displayed. "Hope and Patti finally wore me down."

Mike nodded sagely. "Even SEALs are no match for determined women."

They moved to the front desk, and as Martine gathered their keys, Alex turned toward the pair. "I'm sure you're both wiped out from the trip, so I'll leave you to get settled in. Enjoy the rest of your day." He pointed at Mike. "0900 hours at the pier. Don't be late."

Mike saluted crisply. "Yes, sir."

Smiling, Alex ambled out of the lobby, already looking forward to their dive.

BRIGHT SUNBEAMS SHINED through holes in the ceiling of the hollow underwater seamount. Alex hovered near the arching wall, waiting for Robert's group to exit the structure. He was with Hope, Mike, and Zach, diving separately from the other two groups on *Surface Interval*. Alex had personally arranged to go to this dive site, called Chapel, which was one of his favorites. He had very fond memories of diving it with Hope, and Mike would love it too. The water was less clear than normal since they were the last of the three groups to transit through the large domed structure.

But the silty, cloudy water was an advantage here. The sunbeams shining through the ceiling became even more vivid, reflecting off sediment in the water. Alex glanced at Mike, who nearly gave himself whiplash as he took the scene in, his eyes wide.

Alex nodded to Hope, who took the lead, demonstrating how to negotiate the dive's calling card. Two large holes in the dome, one on the ceiling and the other on the side wall, allowed a large volume of water to pass between them with the ocean's surge. A diver timing their exit just right would be propelled out of the Chapel, giving the feature its name of The Cannon.

Hope rushed over and got into position, gripping the edges of the hole in the side of the seamount. Alex frowned slightly, wishing she'd evaluated the feature more before jumping in. She swept her gaze over the group, ready to demonstrate The Cannon. Despite being a superb diver, Hope had other responsibilities and wasn't able to dive as often as Zach. Alex had been mentoring Zach for two years, slowly giving him more responsibility and challenges on dives, and had been impressed by the young man's progress. Both were ready to become divemasters.

Though Hope had the added complication of being Alex's wife. Zach easily took instruction from him and followed his direction. Hope could be more prickly about it, though her feisty independence was one of his favorite things about her.

The large surge of water moving into the Chapel became visible in Hope's vibrating regulator hose. Then there was a lull. She made eye contact with everyone, then she waggled her eyebrows, making Alex laugh out loud. The water flow reversed, surging back through The Cannon as she let go and was thrust on a horizontal column of water and out of the seamount.

Even underwater, Mike's muffled, "Oh, yeah!" could be heard clearly. Alex gestured for him to go next.

Since they were the last group to exit The Chapel, they had the advantage of being able to repeat the ride through The Cannon, doing it once more before needing to move to shallower water to conserve their air supply.

· · ·

ZACH TOOK the lead on the second dive, a tricky navigation through a narrow channel in the reef. He kept his face glued to his compass, not looking for any interesting creatures or fish to show the others. Alex held back and didn't correct him—that was what the divemaster course was for. As they exited the channel, Zach stared for a long moment at his compass, then at the wall rising next to him, fans and spiral corals teeming with a palette of fish. Finally, he looked up at Alex, his eyes wide and sheepish, then shrugged.

Alex laughed, unable to help himself, then nodded. *Ok, I'm not surprised you're lost.*

Beckoning the group, he took over guiding them back to the boat.

THEIR QUARTET WERE all in a good mood as the boat motored back to the resort. They huddled at the stern, letting the paying groups enjoy the covered main deck and sundeck on the bow.

"It was great to be in the water again," Mike said.

"You were flopping around like a landed fish. I might have to work with you some," Alex said with a big grin.

Zach stared between the two men. "How do you two stay so... quiet in the water? When you guys hover, you don't even *move*. I thought it was just Alex, but you do it too, Mike."

Mike grinned. "You don't want to know. Let's just say it was in our best interest to learn quickly."

Hope shot Zach a rueful grin. "Trust me. You don't want to get these two started. Let's break down the gear."

Alex beckoned to Mike, and they moved to the front of the covered deck. Alex went to his dry bag and retrieved a key on a large wooden keychain, handing it to Mike. "Here's the key to the grotto. You might want to pick up a bottle of wine and some glasses when you're at lunch. They can set you up at the restaurant."

"Thanks. Emma was super excited when I told her about this. And Hope got our private beach dinner all set up for tonight. We'll have a good time." He paused, then met Alex's eyes. "I'm looking into a new job, and that's what's led to some of the tension between us."

"Why's that?"

"The position is for another contractor. A lot more money, but a lot more travel too. We'd see each other even less."

Alex nodded, trying to be supportive, even though he couldn't imagine wanting a job that took him away from Hope. "More money is a good thing."

Mike shrugged, watching the ocean as the boat raced over it. "We don't really need the money. Both of us bring home good salaries. But I can't help wanting to reach for the next thing, the next challenge. I'm really torn."

"Maybe being here will give you some perspective. You guys could make sure you take regular vacations to stay connected."

"Perhaps. If I could get the time off on the new job." Mike shook himself and turned back to Alex, holding up the grotto key. "Anyway, we're here to have a good time. And with this, I'm sure we will. Maybe I'll pick up two bottles of wine."

"You'll like the grotto. It's a special place."

"I'll try not to be too hungover for tomorrow morning's class."

Alex crossed his arms and grinned. "You better not be, unless you want some extra tasks to perform."

Mike closed his eyes and shuddered. "God, don't even say that."

Alex clapped him on the back. "Have a good time, and don't get your ass too sunburned."

Chapter Nine

A LIGHT MORNING breeze blew a ripple across the placid ocean surface as Hope stood under the palapa with Alex, Mike, and Zach. She'd been tapping her hand against her hip and stopped, glancing at it and relieved her fingers weren't shaking.

Alex had explained they were splitting into two teams for their first divemaster class water session. He would work with Zach, while she and Mike teamed up. They would be performing an advanced skill—one she'd never attempted before.

Alex leaned down and patted the metal first stage of Zach's regulator, already attached to the tank. "Mike and I are going to toss your kits into the ocean and sink them, including masks, and we'll all jump in. Then you guys dive down, put everything on, and surface again."

Zach chewed his lip. "It's about twenty feet here, right?"

Alex shrugged. "Twenty-five. You guys will be fine. I don't expect you do to it perfectly the first time."

Mike leaned casually against the wooden support pier of the palapa, his arms folded. His face split into a wide grin. "Are you going to tie their hands?"

Alex burst into laughter. "No, I think that would be crossing into cruel and unusual punishment territory."

Hope alternated her gaze between the two laughing men. "You guys had to do this with your hands tied?"

Alex slid his eyes to her. "Uh, not exactly."

"You guys are getting off easy," Mike said, trying not to laugh. "This was one of Alex's favorite training drills. He used to drag us out to Chesapeake Bay in the dead of night. If the weather was awful, even better. One of our support guys would drive us out into the bay in a RIB."

Hope sighed, knowing Zach didn't know the acronym either. "RIB?"

"Rigid Inflatable Boat. Zodiac," Alex added helpfully, still grinning.

"So, we'd get out to about fifty feet of water and Alex would toss our kits overboard, one guy at a time," Mike said. "He'd tie our hands in front of us. Then we had to dive down in the pitch blackness, find our kit, untie our hands with our knife, put everything back on, and surface."

"Quit your bitching," Alex said. "I gave you a headlamp."

Mike's eyes became round. "Yeah! It only lit up the mud in the water around us! It usually made things worse, not better." He turned to Hope and Zach, equally exasperated and amused. "If you couldn't find your kit and had to surface to breathe, Alex would make you continue until you came up with your gear on, ready to go."

"Seems reasonable," Zach said.

Mike shot Alex an irritated glare and he burst out laughing again.

"I'm not done yet," Mike continued. "Then he made us swim back to shore and run back to the boat launch. In full gear! We called it the Shame March. It *sucked*."

Alex just shrugged. "You're still alive, aren't you?" He

turned to Hope and Zach. "I tried to keep the swim to around half a mile and the run to about one. He's a whiner."

Despite her nerves, Hope couldn't help smiling. "You never did the exercise yourself, Alex?"

His brows flew up. "Of course I did. I'd never ask my men for something I wasn't willing to do myself."

Mike rolled his eyes. "Oh yeah. Mr. Free Diver, who can hold his breath for four hours."

Zach grinned as he studied the two men, his admiration obvious. "Did you ever do the Shame March, Alex?"

At that, Alex and Mike looked at each other and roared laughter, bending forward at the waist.

"Only once," Alex said, wiping his eyes.

"Oh, God," Mike said, still laughing. "I'll never forget that as long as I live."

Getting hold of himself, Alex turned toward Hope and Zach. "It was a terrible night—wind, rain, just nasty. By the time we got out into the bay, conditions had deteriorated even more. The waves were huge. I knew I'd have to modify my plan, so we all threw our kits out at once. What I didn't realize was that a current was *ripping* that night."

Mike rubbed his face, still laughing. "You are such an asshole."

"None of us could find our gear," Alex said, and started laughing again. "The current carried them *way* farther than I thought it would. We swam around forever, but eventually we tracked the gear down and everyone got his kit on. Then we all swam back to shore and ran back to the boat launch as a team. The support guy got to drive the boat back alone."

Mike groaned. "Our kits were down over seventy feet, and we were over a *mile* offshore. Our run ended up being four miles."

Alex was still laughing. "I decided to pause that particular exercise after that. Figured I'd have a mutiny on my hands otherwise."

"No one would speak to him on the drive back to base."

"Did you recover all the gear?" Hope asked.

"Are you kidding?" Alex asked, his eyes growing wide. "Eight military-grade rebreathers with full night-vision comms? That gear was worth more than we were."

Zach stared at the two men, his face slack. "What if one of you had been killed?"

Mike scoffed, waving a hand. "Please. We were SEALs. It was an interesting diversion, nothing more."

Hope smiled sweetly at her husband. "If you try to tie my hands, I'll castrate you."

Laughing, Alex held up both arms. "I already said I wasn't going to do that, didn't I?" Still smiling, he checked his dive computer. "Let's split up and get started. We have several exercises to get through this morning."

Hope moved to where her and Mike's scuba kits were lined up some distance from Alex's and Zach's, butterflies fluttering wildly in her stomach. "You couldn't have told that story *after* we'd finished this?"

Mike smiled. "Sorry, but don't worry about it. You'll do fine."

He lifted Hope's inflator hose and pressed the exhaust button, expelling all the air out of her BCD. Then he slid his right arm through the shoulder straps, lifted the scuba kit, swung it back, and launched in into the ocean as far as he could.

Hope watched it sink and swallowed the lump in her throat while Mike got into his own kit. "Put your weight belt on and hop in."

Dressed in a wetsuit, she did so, buckling a canvas belt with several lead weights attached. She stepped off the dock and popped back to the surface. The additional weight tried to pull her beneath the gentle waves, an unsettling feeling. Her BCD had integrated weight pockets, so she normally didn't use a weight belt. But the exercise would be very difficult without additional weight to stay submerged while she donned her scuba kit.

She and Mike swam to where her tank rested twenty-five feet below. They treaded water above it, Hope working harder than usual to stay afloat.

"Ok," Mike said. "What are you going to do first when you get down there?" His casual, joking nature was gone. He was serious and intent, focused completely on her.

"I won't be able to see clearly, so I'll go for my mask first."

"What's more important—seeing or breathing?"

"Oh. Good point. I'll put my reg in first."

"Exactly. Secure your air supply first, then grab your mask and put that on. The water will sting your eyes, so be prepared for that—it's expected, not an emergency. Get your BCD on and drop your weight belt before you buckle it. Then surface. Easy peasy."

Hope stared down at her kit twenty-five feet below, her heart pounding. "Sure. Easy."

"I'll be there the whole time with air in case you need it. I won't let anything happen to you, Hope."

That made her glance back up, and she smiled at him. "I know. Thanks."

"Whenever you're ready."

Hope took several deep breaths, jackknifed her body, and swam down, taking long sweeping strokes with her arms. She kicked as hard as she could. After opening her eyes, they immediately stung as the saltwater contacted them, making her squint. She closed one eye.

Ouch, ouch! I don't need to breathe yet. I'm going for the mask.

Through the fuzzy water, she located where it lay on the bottom, still clipped to a buckle on her BCD. Hope fumbled with the clip, now growing more panicked as the urge to breathe increased. Finally getting the mask unclipped, her lungs were nearly bursting, so she switched tactics, locating her second stage mouthpiece. Reaching out, she fumbled with it, and the regulator slipped out of her grasp. She also dropped the mask.

Oh, no. I need to try this again. Breathe, Hope!

Pushing forcefully with both feet, she launched herself upward off the sand. Hope burst through the surface, taking a deep, gasping breath. She closed her eyes, legs pumping hard beneath her as she concentrated on getting her breath under control.

Mike surfaced next to her. "Take long breaths. In and out. You're doing fine."

She concentrated on lengthening each inhale, still pumping her legs to stay afloat. Opening her eyes, she stared at the horizon, focusing on it to calm herself.

"Hope, relax. Hold on to my shoulder. Stop fighting. The wetsuit will keep you afloat."

She grasped Mike's shoulder and relaxed her legs to a gentle scissoring. Her breath slowed slightly.

"Why did you go for the mask first?"

"The salt water stung my eyes. I didn't need to breathe, and I thought I'd be more comfortable if I could see. But before I got the mask unclipped, I had to breathe."

"Hope, look at me."

She turned her eyes from the horizon to Mike's bright green ones. He stared at her intently, completely serious. "You knew the water would sting, and you knew getting that second stage in your mouth was more important. Yet you still deviated from the plan."

"I know. It was stupid. I'll do it right this time."

Mike shook his head. "It wasn't stupid—don't put yourself down like that. But it was impulsive. You can't be impetuous and fly by the seat of your pants down there. Follow your plan unless it becomes impossible."

Hope narrowed her eyes at him. "Have you been talking to Alex about me?"

His face went blank. "No. He just told me you might prefer working with me instead of him for this exercise."

Hope broke into reluctant laughter. "He tells me all the time I'm too impulsive."

Mike smiled faintly. "There's a time for that, but only after you've learned the fundamentals. Like this exercise. You were impulsive yesterday too. You entered the flow of The Cannon without judging the strength of the water movement. Take a deep breath and slow down. We're not in a race here. You're not being timed."

She took a long inhale, forcibly calming herself. "Slow down. Think first. Got it. Let's do it again."

Mike nodded and she let go of his shoulder, no longer out of breath.

Hope closed her eyes and breathed deeply, centering herself and visualizing her task. This time, instead of taking several gasping breaths, she just took one deep inhale and sunk below the surface. Bending at the waist, she kicked steadily and let the weight belt draw her downward, keeping her eyes open from the start. She was ready for the sting. Reaching her tank, she followed the fuzzy-looking hose from the first stage to its second stage.

Hope pressed the purge button as she placed the mouthpiece between her lips, expelling the water. She took a breath of pure, clean air and blinked. Her mask was lying on the sand next to her BCD. Picking it up, she placed the frame against her face before breathing a long exhale through her nose into the nose pocket of the mask, clearing the water out of it. After she secured the strap over her head, the water around her was crystal clear.

Hope opened her BCD and lifted her tank upright on the sand. It was tricky maneuvering the heavy scuba tank, but eventually she got into the vest with the tank on her back. She was reaching to close the cummerbund of her BCD when she remembered her weight belt. Quickly opening the buckle, she let the belt slip onto the sand and closed her BCD. All the while, she breathed calmly through the second stage, intent on her task.

A smile rose on her face as her eyes met Mike's.

He grinned back and held up a hand for a high five. She slapped him back and they rose to the surface.

They repeated the exercise twice more, Hope gaining confidence and skill each time.

Then Mike and Alex changed places.

She and Alex bobbed on the surface, facing each other. Hope looked into his crystal blue eyes, a deep sense of calm safety enveloping her. "Want me to show you how this is done, sailor?"

A slow, sexy smile crept across his face. "I'm counting on it, Boss Lady."

Hope shrugged out of her kit, deflated it, and watched it sink before glancing back at Alex. "Let's go, then."

She performed the exercise flawlessly as Alex watched closely. Kneeling on the bottom in her gear, pride filled her as she met his eyes. He applauded her and gave her the thumbs up to ascend. They rose together almost in slow motion, eyes locked together. He stopped them at the ten-foot mark, pulling his regulator out of his mouth.

She'd dived with him enough to know what that meant.

Hope removed her own regulator and moved toward him,

closing her eyes. She tilted her head to the side and met his lips, warmer than the water. She traced a finger over his jaw, the hint of stubble catching under her digit. As their kiss became more heated, she could feel them ascending again. Hope pressed a hand against his face and opened her mouth to graze her tongue over his. They broke through the surface, still kissing. His lips were firm, yet yielding under hers, and she couldn't resist a breathy moan.

Hope reluctantly pulled away. "So did I pass, teacher?"

Alex's eyes were fixated on her mouth. At her words, he blinked several times and met her gaze. "If your intent was to distract the instructor, definitely."

"Hey, you're the one who wanted to kiss."

His gaze softened. "Because I was so proud of you. You more than passed that, baby. You were perfect."

Hope's eyes were wrenched away as Mike and Zach surfaced. She and Alex shared a smile before swimming to meet them. Though she'd much rather be alone with her husband, her instructor had a class to continue.

Chapter Ten

ALEX STOOD on the bungalow deck, watching the retreating forms of Hope and Emma as they headed toward the spa. Though Mike and Emma were staying in one of the northern-most bungalows, there was still plenty of room between it and Aqua, in keeping with the private vibe of the resort.

Both Hope and Zach had done well that morning, despite their nervousness at the start. Alex and Mike had traded off often to keep the session fresh and unpredictable. Both had simulated being divers in trouble, challenging both students to correct the issue. Working with Hope again had created a curious mixture of emotions in Alex. Intense pride at watching her overcome difficulty. She struggled with some exercises, sometimes showing flashes of insecurity. Then her eyes would fill with determination, and she would repeat the exercise until she mastered it.

Which had brought about his other strong emotion. Hope's feisty, passionate determination to succeed, coupled with her flirty banter while on the surface with him, had made him horny as hell.

Now Alex grinned as his eyes slipped down to Hope's ass.

Sexual arousal when working with students was *not* a typical response from him. Fortunately, this particular student could scratch his itch perfectly, which she had accomplished as soon as they were done with the session. Alex had practically dragged her back to the house.

Still smiling, he turned away from the two women and sat in an armchair. Mike sprawled on an ocean-facing couch. He sat up and pulled two bottles of beer out of an ice-filled bucket, handing Alex one.

"Sounds like Emma enjoyed her morning at the pool," Alex said, taking a drink.

Mike nodded. "She's never had any interest in diving, but she doesn't resent that I do. She said Clark doted on her."

"I suspect Hope had something to do with that."

Clark was the main bartender at the resort and was working at the pool bar that day. He had been a guest at Alex and Hope's wedding along with Emma, and Hope would undoubtedly have told him about her return.

Alex put his feet on the coffee table, crossing his ankles. "I'm sure the ladies will have a lovely afternoon at Aqua. They've got several hours booked."

Mike smirked. "I'd much rather sit on the deck with a beer and watch the ocean."

Alex raised his bottle. "That makes two of us. How was the grotto yesterday?" A pang twisted through his gut. He'd never told Mike about what he and Hope had found there, and it had been weighing on him since Mike's arrival.

A satisfied smile lifted Mike's lips. "Exactly how you described it. Private. It was just what we needed. Thanks."

"You're welcome. Hope and I have had some good times there ourselves."

"I swam around that pool and explored a bit. I came across a gate covering an underwater passage. And that fence surrounding the whole thing! I kept looking for velociraptors." Mike leveled a stare at Alex. "What's really going on out there?"

Alex twitched one side of his mouth as he turned to face the ocean. His troubled conscience wouldn't be a problem anymore. "Did you go in the cave?"

"A little, but I stayed in the water. It looks huge."

Alex nodded. "Along the back wall, about fifteen feet under-water, is a second gated-off passage. I've never explored the one in the rock pool, though I'm planning on checking it out soon. But Hope and I followed the one in the cave extensively." He returned Mike's even stare. "We found a box of Spanish treasure inside a large cavern. We've very quietly sold off two portions of it at auction—that's what has paid for all the expansion here."

Mike's eyes were round, and he barked laughter. "A *treasure?* Are you serious?"

"Very."

Mike sat up and faced him fully, grinning. "Were there booby traps, and arrows shooting out of walls?"

Alex couldn't help laughing. "No, but the final passage leading into the cavern is half silt. That caused enough problems. Hope kicked it up and almost got lost in there."

Mike's smile disappeared. "Shit. Did that turn her off cave diving?"

"You dove with her. What do you think?"

"I think your wife is a pretty determined person."

"I was the one who didn't want her going back in there. But we worked it out and she did great."

Mike swept his gaze from one side of the resort to the other. "I can't believe how much this place has changed since your wedding. I've wondered how you financed it, but figured the resort was doing really well."

"It is, but not *that* well. I wanted the grotto fenced off and the passages covered in case word ever got out about the treasure. Though we've been very tight lipped to keep any dumbass treasure hunters from getting killed in those tunnels. And our lawyer didn't want us to have the liability if they did. Hope came up with the idea of a private guest oasis to cover why the fence is there."

"What kind of treasure? Gold coins and stuff?"

"Gold and silver coins, plates, and crosses. There are chalices and jewelry, as well as emeralds the size of your fist, and other gemstones. It's pretty incredible. We keep it in safe deposit boxes at the bank."

"Not something you want to leave lying around the living room."

"Definitely not."

"Pretty amazing, man. Congratulations."

Alex relaxed, his conscience clear at last. "Thanks. So your job has been pretty hectic lately?"

Mike swiped a hand over his face, rubbing his scruff. "Yeah, to put it mildly. Emma and I haven't been spending much time together, and things have gotten strained between us. This trip has helped."

"I'm glad." Alex thought about bringing up Mike's new job prospect but remained silent. The resort spell seemed to be working so far. He didn't want to rock the boat. "Half Moon Bay has brought more than a few couples closer."

Mike took a swig of beer, then laughed. "You and Hope are obviously still happy. You damn near threw her over your shoulder and ran after we finished this morning."

Alex laughed, enjoying being with someone he could be completely open with. "What can I say? Watching my wife become a divemaster is a major turn-on."

Mike sighed and looked out at the pier. "Too bad Em and I have to leave tomorrow, but I'm glad we came down. You impressed me this morning—I only needed to give you a few pointers. You might learn to dive yet, Monroe."

Alex smiled fondly. "It was fun working together again. Thanks for your help. I should be able to finish up their class within the next couple weeks."

"Zach didn't know what to do when I put my mask on upside down. I had fun messing with him."

"He's come a long way."

"No shit! I hardly recognized him. I tried to keep a straight face when he was showing off for his girlfriend."

Alex groaned, rubbing his face with both hands. "Yeah. We hired Jasmine to work in the shop and sparks flew between them right away. But Hope and I can't exactly discourage them, can we?"

"Not unless you want to be total hypocrites, anyway."

"He's taking Jasmine diving on the house reef this week. She's open water certified, so it shouldn't be too much of a disaster. I hope."

Mike laughed. "Ah. Young love. Don't you miss those days?"

"Not even in the slightest."

Mike fished another beer out of the bucket. "You'll have to come visit Em and me sometime. I'll take you diving in Chesapeake Bay."

Alex stared at him. "Why the hell would I do that when I can dive here anytime I want to?"

"Hey, we could do the Shame March for old time's sake."

"You do it. I'll watch."

Mike grinned. "At least we can laugh about it now."

Alex had been about to make a smartass retort, then considered Mike's statement carefully. "You're right. A few years ago, I would have reacted completely differently to that story you told this morning. You have no idea how good it feels to laugh about those days now."

WHEN HOPE and Emma returned from the spa, Alex was sitting with Mike on their front porch. She felt wonderfully relaxed after a massage, body treatment and mani-pedi. Plus, Emma hadn't stopped raving about Aqua. Hope took Alex's hand and led him toward the bungalow stairs. "We'll leave you two alone, since you're leaving in the morning. Enjoy your dinner tonight." She smiled into Mike's eyes. "And thanks, Mike. You were a big help this morning."

As they walked down the beach, Hope caressed the back of Alex's hand. Her afternoon had given her plenty of time to rerun their brief, but very hot, encounter earlier. She was still flush from it.

"Have a good spa... session? Is that what you call it?"

"A treatment. And it was *wonderful*." She peaked a brow at him. "I even got my red hair color enhanced."

Alex grinned wolfishly. "I noticed that. You might not be safe from me just yet." She laughed and he draped his arm over her shoulders, pulling her in to kiss the top of her head. "I was really proud of you this morning. You'll be a great divemaster."

"I'm not sure how often I'll be able to lead dives. Especially with Sara going on maternity leave soon." She frowned at what Violet had passed on to her. "Sara went home this morning. Her blood pressure is up a little, and Dr. Grainger wanted her off her feet."

"That doesn't sound good."

Hope shrugged. She'd called her sister immediately and gotten reassurance. "Apparently, it's fairly normal, but Sara's cutting back to half days now, just to be safe."

"When's BB due?"

"December 10th. Another week."

"We need to get cracking on finishing this divemaster course. Maybe the baby will be late. That will help."

Hope laughed. "Don't say that to Sara! Did you have a good visit with Mike?"

"Yeah. He and Emma really enjoyed the grotto. By the way, I told him everything. He picked up right away that the fence was a bit much just to keep the grotto private for guests. Keeping it from him had been bothering me."

"I'm glad you told him."

They climbed onto the porch, letting Cruz in as they entered the slider.

"I need to answer a few emails," Hope said.

"I've got some things to work on while you do that."

Hope headed to her office, waking her computer and groaning at the list of unread emails.

Get started. It won't take long if you power through now.

An hour later, she sat back with a satisfied sigh. As usual, Cruz had curled up on a rug next to her desk. He raised his head. "All done. Now I can face tomorrow morning's class with a clean conscience. Let's see what Alex has been up to."

Cruz followed at her heel as she re-entered their great room. Alex sat at the kitchen table, a large yellow pad in front of him and a pencil tucked behind his ear. She brushed her hand over his broad shoulders and peered down at the pad, where he'd written a long list of items. Bullet-pointed, of course.

"What have you got there?" She moved to the fridge and took out two beers, handing him one before sitting in an adjacent chair.

"A list of things I need to bring to the small cave in the grotto. I want to stage everything and start exploring soon. First step will be getting my rebreather secure there, along with other supplies I'll need. Then I'll head in and do an exploratory—"

"Wait a minute," Hope interrupted. "What's all this *I* stuff? What about me?"

His face clouded. "I just thought I'd check it out first, like last time."

She made sure to keep her voice soft. "Last time, I had never dived in a cave. Now I've got a lot of experience—including how to handle an emergency—and I'll be a divemaster before too long. I think I've earned the right to go with you this time."

Alex's brow smoothed, blank surprise showing on his face. He glanced at his paper, then returned his eyes to hers. "You're right. I didn't mean to exclude you."

"I know. But I really want to be there and see whatever we discover by your side."

He grasped her hand. "I do too. But what if the passage is too narrow for us to swim next to each other?"

He was staring at her evenly, and she knew what he was getting at. "Then you can lead. I defer to your expertise. The first trip anyway."

Alex grinned. "Compromise! I like it. Does this mean you're going to help me schlep tanks and gear all the way out there?"

That had never occurred to her, and she swallowed, already picturing how exhausting it would be. "Fair's fair. I'll do whatever it takes."

Alex's smile softened and he raised a hand to smooth her hair. "I was just teasing. I'd never put you through that. We'll use the cart this time, especially since we've got a decent access path now. We can hide the extra keys when we're exploring so we don't get any looky-loos while we're there."

Excitement tickled her. "When do we start?"

Chapter Eleven

AFTER PUSHING the cart through the chain-link gate, Alex replaced the padlock but didn't close it, uncomfortable with the idea of being locked in if their key got misplaced. The cart was filled with several tanks, his rebreather, plus Hope's BCD and regulator, and everything else they'd need in the passage.

Nearly a week had passed since Mike and Emma left, and this was his and Hope's first day off together. Today was just for staging equipment and Hope's little project at the old homestead. The weather was perfect—a light cloud cover and soft breeze would keep things comfortable. Alex glanced at her, trying to tamp down the uneasiness rising in him. She walked confidently at his side, smiling at a tropical bird which streaked overhead.

He agreed with her logic that she was qualified to accompany him on his initial exploration this time. But over the past week, his mind had enjoyed tormenting him with memories of her getting lost during her silt-out in the cave tunnel.

Syria might have been the most traumatic event of his life, but he had no memory of the actual ambush. But he vividly remembered every excruciating second when he hadn't known where Hope was, or if she was ok.

We're not going in today, so I can relax for now.

They arrived at the small sandy beach, and he pushed the cart toward a nearby ten-foot-tall rock covered with vines. Pushing aside the foliage, Alex revealed another metal grate covering a small cave.

"I'm sure you feel better leaving all this here locked up."

Alex nodded. "A necessity now that people visit here regularly."

It only took a few minutes to unload the cart. Their two wetsuits were the last to be placed inside the small cave. Both were 5mm suits, thicker than those they wore in the ocean. The water in the rock pool was significantly cooler. Alex looked everything over, making sure he hadn't forgotten anything before turning to Hope. "Ready for part two of today's adventure?"

She patted a backpack she wore. "Absolutely. Let's go."

They headed back to the gate and relocked it, then followed the perimeter of the fence as they had last time. They had left Cruz at the house, so it was only the two of them heading down the faint animal track to the old ramshackle foundation.

Hope took the lead and headed toward the three gravestones. Kneeling, she opened her backpack and removed three large sheets of butcher paper and a charcoal pencil. She smiled up at Alex. "I got the paper from the restaurant kitchen and Jack lent me the pencil." Sara wasn't the only artist in the family— Jack was a talented sketch artist.

Alex studied the worn surface of the three grave markers. "Do you think you can get anything legible off those?"

"Who knows? They're really eroded. Let's start with the one on the right. It looks the most overgrown."

The worn granite slab was a foot wide by two feet tall. The

other two monuments were larger. Alex held the sheet of paper against it while Hope used the charcoal pencil to draw broad, sweeping strokes on the paper. When she had covered half the surface, faint traces of white could be seen on the paper, negatives of the words etched into the stone.

"I think it's working," Alex said.

Hope nodded. "Doesn't mean we'll be able to read it. Or that it will be in English, for that matter."

She continued scratching across the paper until she reached the ground, then stood again. She held the sheet of butcher paper spread between both hands, and both she and Alex studied it. It took several minutes, but between the two of them, they were able to decipher the faint letters. The marker read: *Sebastian Percival Morgan, Beloved Son, November 21, 1675-January 14, 1679.*

"He only lived four years!" Hope said. Letting the rubbing roll up, she placed it gently on her backpack. Then she turned her attention to the other two graves. "Come on. Let's do these other two and see what we get."

Thirty minutes later, they each held a similar rubbing, and both were stunned to speechlessness. The sweat lining Alex's back became chilled. He looked from one sheet of paper to the other, finally finding his voice. "We're reading them correctly. I'm sure of it."

"What does it mean, though?"

Alex read the rubbing in Hope's hands: *Mercy Morgan, Beloved Wife, 1641- September 16, 1708.* There was a small, chiseled character before the first date they finally decided was a *c.*

The rubbing he held in his own hands was what had caused their stunned reaction: *Barnaby William Morgan, Devoted Husband, June 4, 1636- September 16, 1708.*

Hope and Alex had brushed their fingers over the gravestone several times but couldn't detect the small letter c on Barnaby's headstone.

Hope gave an incredulous laugh. "Looks like we were wrong. Barnaby didn't get killed escaping the cave after all."

Alex shook his head, a strange sense of dislocation running in a numb wave through him. "According to this, he died at the ripe old age of 72."

"But he never went back to the cave to retrieve the treasure!"

Alex looked at Hope's rubbing and the phrase *Beloved Wife,* his dislocation turning to certainty. "I think he found something more valuable than treasure. Home."

"Barnaby got his happy ending after all!"

Alex rolled up his rubbing. "Let's head back to the house. We can figure this out on the way."

They were silent until they reached the fence and started following it around the grotto. "Why did they live all the way out here in the middle of nowhere?" Hope asked, sweeping her gaze around the dense jungle surrounding them.

"That's what I've been thinking about. They had a source of fresh water and plenty of game to hunt. I think the key is who Mercy was."

"You're thinking the same thing as me, then. That she was a runaway slave?"

"Yeah, or maybe a freed one who didn't want anything to do with the colonists and plantation owners. I keep thinking about that c on her gravestone."

"Circa," Hope said. "As if her exact birthdate wasn't known."

Alex nodded. "Which would make sense if she was a slave. Also, Barnaby is listed with three names, while Mercy only has two. And one of them was his."

Hope took his hand, and he gripped hers tightly.

"I wonder who carved the stones," Hope said.

"They had one son who didn't survive. It's reasonable to assume other children did. Maybe one of their adult children buried them."

"Barnaby gave up everything to be with her," Hope said. "He probably had an estate of some sort in England. I think they loved each other very much."

Devoted wife. Beloved husband. "I think they did too."

"They died on the same day," she said quietly.

"That way, neither had to live without the other." Alex ran his thumb over her smaller hand, tight within his. "That's how I'd like to go."

She smiled at him, but her eyes were clouded. "Me too. But not for a really long time, ok?

He pulled her in and kissed her. "I don't plan on going anywhere."

"Neither do I."

They walked quietly for a while, dropping hands to cross the highway. When they reached the end of the path, they turned left toward their house.

"They died in September," Hope said. "I wonder if a hurricane killed them."

Alex studied the gentle sea, his mind's eye seeing the times when it had been anything but serene. "That's a good guess. A hurricane would certainly do it."

"I feel happy and sad at the same time." She laughed and took his hand again. "How can I be sad that we know he's dead? He lived over three hundred years ago!"

Alex nodded. "It is kind of weird. But look at it this way. Where would we be if he hadn't found the love of his life? He would have gone back to the cave for his treasure and sailed back to England."

Hope stopped and slid her arms around his neck. He lost himself in her green-gold eyes.

"But he didn't," she whispered. "Instead, I found the love of *my* life. With or without the treasure, I don't ever need more."

Alex pressed his forehead against hers. "Me either. There's a lot to be said for true love, you know. It saved me. And maybe it saved Barnaby too."

As the pair resumed their stroll toward home, Alex ran this thumb over the soft skin on the back of his wife's hand. How strange it was that an event over three hundred years ago had completely changed his and Hope's lives!

Chapter Twelve

HOPE EASED into the cool blue waters of the grotto pool, grateful when she was deep enough for the water to support her tank. Beside her, Alex wore his rebreather. Two black corrugated hoses arched over his shoulders from the rectangular canister on his back, meeting on either side of the large regulator in his mouth. Wearing the rebreather, along with the black wetsuit and a black mask, she could easily envision the SEAL he'd once been.

"Been a while since you've worn that rebreather, hasn't it?"

Alex grinned and removed the regulator, letting it rest against his upper chest. "Yeah. Feels good to wear it again. A reminder of what I used to do."

She pressed her lips into a thin line before saying, "Don't go getting any ideas about tying my hands."

His smile became a laugh. "I like my balls right where they are."

"I'm glad we're on the same page."

His smile faded. "You ready?"

Hope nodded, a shiver tickling down her spine. Even

though she was confident in her skills, entering a pitch-dark underwater passage was a daunting prospect.

"I'll go in first," Alex said. "It's narrow at the entrance. If it widens out, feel free to come up next to me." His jaw tightened and she nodded gently back, understanding this was difficult for him. Underwater caves were highly dangerous. Alex's need to face any unexpected danger first conflicted with her desire to be recognized for how far she'd come.

They descended and swam across the rock pool, hovering in front of the gate. After unlocking the padlock, Alex pocketed the lock. Hope was relieved. The thought of being trapped if someone closed the padlock was enough to make her want to turn around. She smiled at Alex's quiet, assured form, confident in his ability to make decisions to keep them safe.

He unclipped a spool of bright orange line, wrapping one end around a protruding rock near the entrance. After confirming Hope was ok, he finned into the black passage. Holding the spool in one hand, Alex let it loosely spill out as he continued. Hope followed, watching the orange line—literally their lifeline to get back to the entrance. After ten feet, the passage turned left, and the ambient light disappeared. The tunnel was pitch black except for the light emitted from their headlamps.

The passage consisted of the same black rock as the pool, unlike the tunnel inside the big cave, which had been tan to reddish-brown in color. The dark walls appeared to suck the light into them, making it disappear. Hope tilted her head down, illuminating the stone floor, which was also different from the cave passage. Instead of a smooth rock surface or muddy silt, the ground here had many small rocks scattered over it. The walls around them soon became uneven and jagged.

After twenty-five yards, the tunnel widened, and Hope swam up to Alex's hip. He turned his head slightly, keeping track of her position. She rose to travel just above him, ensuring their fins wouldn't interfere with each other. Cave divers used a different finning technique, called a frog kick. Instead of moving their legs up and down from the hip, they moved them sideways, holding their fins horizontally like a frog starting its leap. This fin style prevented silt from being kicked up, which could destroy visibility in an instant.

Something Hope had learned the hard way.

The tunnel widened further, forming a large oval. It couldn't be called a room or a chamber, just a widening big enough for several people to cluster together. Alex looked up, studying the surface above, which looked like a flat mirror in Hope's light rather than the black rock of before. Several brown discs were scattered through the water above, but Hope didn't know what they were. Alex signaled for her to wait and ascended. She studied the irregular walls around her, noting stacked layers of black, gray, and dark brown. After a long moment, Alex descended again with an ok signal, then led again.

The spring-fed, fresh water was crystal clear, their lights making the tunnel appear to be in air. Alex tilted his head up, slowing, and Hope followed his lead. After thirty feet, the ceiling had changed from bare black rock. Multiple parallel ridges now ran in the same direction they were traveling. It was a curious feature—one she hadn't seen before. More loose rocks were scattered over the floor, some pebbles and some the size of her fist.

Alex continued, studying the ceiling as he swam. The ridges ended after twenty feet and the passage narrowed again. Hope dropped behind him. The tunnel was four feet across, plenty wide enough to travel without constriction, but narrow enough to *feel* like the walls were pressing invisible fingers against her shoulders and hips.

An opening appeared on the right, taller than their tunnel. Alex stopped and tied off his orange line to a rock in the passage they were in, clearly marking their direction. He verified once again that Hope was doing ok. Her nerves had settled, and as they slowly swam down the same narrow tunnel, a surge of confidence filled her.

I've earned my place here.

The passage meandered in a loose S-pattern for another ten yards. A rock protruded into the side of one turn, making the opening narrow enough to scrape Alex's shoulders as he passed through.

After another fifteen feet, the walls on either side dropped away, leaving a void around them. But it wasn't black. They were surrounded by a gray half-light. Hope looked straight down and spotted the black rock floor twenty feet below. It gently sloped up in the direction they swam.

Alex had tilted his head up again. His rebreather emitted almost no bubbles, but her exhalations rose toward the surface in a steady stream. He watched the progress of her bubbles, studying the surface. Then he met her gaze and gave her the thumbs-up.

He thinks there's an air pocket up there!

Excitement quickened Hope's heartbeat as she eagerly nodded back. The pair rose to the surface and gently broke through, holding one hand high to prevent their heads from colliding with a low ceiling.

But that wasn't a problem.

They emerged into a large cavern. Sunlight beamed into the cave through several holes of varying sizes in the dome. A few were the size of a baseball, but most were smaller. The ceiling was the same black stone, but with large swaths of dark red and tan streaking across.

Alex pulled his regulator out of his mouth and inhaled a

deep breath. "The air's nice and fresh. Warmer too, than the other caverns we were in. There's a good exchange with the surface here."

Nodding, Hope removed her regulator and tilted her head down, following the gently sloping floor. "You want to keep going the same direction? Maybe there's dry land here."

He nodded. "Let's stay on the surface to conserve your air."

"Good idea. I'm almost down to 2000 psi." Two thousand psi left in her scuba cylinder marked the turnaround point, when they needed to head back to the grotto. Alex had a much larger supply of air, since his exhalations were being continuously recirculated into fresh air. Rebreathers were highly technical pieces of diving equipment and very dangerous in inexperienced hands. Hope had no desire to use one.

They kicked in the direction of the rising floor and several murky shapes took form in the distance. Their lamps illuminated large columns meeting a black stone floor, and other stalactites and stalagmites created an otherworldly landscape. The pair's movement created a gentle wave which splashed upon a rocky shore.

Alex stopped and took his fins off, the water waist deep. Tucking her fins under one arm, Hope nodded toward the rocky shelf in front of them. "Shall we?"

He nodded and placed a supportive hand on her tank valve, helping her ease into gravity once again. Alex tied off the orange line and sliced it with his dive knife, leaving the spool on a rock. A cut in the stony shore created a three-step staircase of sorts and they climbed it, Hope breathing harder at the effort involved with hauling an extra sixty-plus pounds uphill. The slope diminished, but continued ahead. "I want to get this tank off before we look around."

"Me too." Alex removed his rebreather as Hope unbuckled her BCD and slid off her tank, placing it next to Alex's kit.

"Why did you ascend at the beginning of the passage?" Hope asked.

"There was a small air pocket. Not a room or anywhere we could exit the water though. But an air supply makes this a cavern dive instead of a cave dive."

Hope turned off her headlamp, not really needing the extra light. Plus, Alex had drilled into her head on their previous explorations never to shine her light into his eyes.

"Where do you want to go?" Hope asked.

Alex swept his head around, his beam lighting up the far reaches of the cavern. Ahead was a much lighter area, suggesting an opening to the outside. "Let's go over there."

Before moving, they pulled their wetsuits down to their waists. The air temperature was high enough that the wet neoprene would make them cooler, not warmer in the air.

Hope fell into line behind him as they walked up the slope, watching the muscles of his bare back at play as he walked. Concentrating on the cavern wasn't easy with the tall, male form right in front of her. The air got warmer by the second as she examined his broad shoulders and torso, which tapered to slim hips. Though she was the one heating up, not the cave. She hardly noticed as they wound around rocky formations, some several different colors.

Then Alex stopped as they emerged onto a broad plateau. Hope halted just behind him. Her nose was inches from his back, and she was riveted by the play of his shoulders as he raised his hands to rest on his hips. She closed her eyes, inhaling his masculine scent, then couldn't resist pressing her lips to his warm skin. She opened her mouth to taste him. His skin had nearly no flavor after being submerged in the fresh water.

"What are you doing back there?" Alex laughed and turned around, wrapping his arms around her as she smiled up at him.

"Getting very distracted. And maybe a little flustered."

He whisked his lips over hers playfully. "I can see that."

"I'll try to focus." Laughing, Hope stepped around him and continued toward the area with more light. A ribbon of sunbeam lit the ground. She tipped her head up, revealing a long gash in the cavern's ceiling thirty feet above. "Well, would you look at that!"

"More enticing than my back, I hope."

She grinned at him. "Not even close."

Stopping under the long cut, Hope studied it, shading her brow with her hand at the bright light. "This is that long seam we saw from up top. Before we found Barnaby's house."

Alex stopped close behind her, his mouth next to her ear. His breath tickled her as he murmured. "I guess this answers the question of an accessible cavern being below."

"How exciting!"

"Extremely." Alex's voice was deep and throaty as he brushed his hands over her shoulders. Then he pulled her back hard against his chest, nuzzling her neck.

With a hot wave of desire rolling through her, Hope turned around in his arms and laced her fingers around his neck. "I thought you wanted to explore."

"I do. You can't imagine how much."

Her eyes flitted around the cavern. "No need to investigate the area further?"

Alex shook his head. "Later. I've reconned the grotto parcel enough, and I can tell by the lack of scent in here it's empty." He slowly traced his finger along the string of her swimsuit top to where it tied around her neck. Her skin caught fire with every inch. "Anytime you wear a bikini top, all I can think about is what's underneath."

"I wear bikini tops a lot, Alex."

"Exactly."

With a quick pull, he untied the knot, separating the two

pieces. Her breasts tumbled free, and he cupped them with both hands.

Hope leaned into his touch, tilting her head to give him a flirty smile. "We're in the middle of a cave. Do you intend to toss me on the rocky ground and have your way with me?"

Alex shrugged one shoulder, but desire radiated off him, his eyes molten. Hope took a deep breath, inhaling him again.

"That might be uncomfortable," he said. "I was thinking more of holding you against that wall over there." He glanced over Hope's shoulder, and she turned to follow his gaze. A sheer black wall rose on the far side of the lighted area they stood in.

She slid her eyes back to his and fanned her hands over his pecs. Even with her fingers spread, his chest was bigger than she could touch. "I'm not sure that would be more comfortable."

"With what I'm planning on doing, you won't even notice." His mouth was parted, his lips full and begging to be kissed.

Hope slid her hands to his shoulders, tracing their contours before sliding them down to grip his large forearms. "Still, why should I suffer? You're the big, strong SEAL. What if I want to throw you against that wall?"

Her hair was in a ponytail. Alex grabbed it, yanking her head back to tilt her face to his. She gasped as he closed in, and an electric current sizzled through her body. He stopped with his mouth an inch from hers. "Then I'd say we've got a battle of wills on our hands."

Chapter Thirteen

HOPE CLOSED the distance between them, slowly sucking Alex's lower lip between hers. She ran her tongue over it, back and forth, making him groan. Sucking harder, she drew his lip between her teeth. She bit down gently, her threat implicit, and Alex froze. Letting go, she laughed softly and pulled away to meet his eyes. "Such a smart man."

He let go of her hair and rushed both arms around her, locking his hands together as he pinned her arms at her sides. She moved her right arm, testing him, and he tightened his hold. His arms were like steel, his biceps rippling.

A smile started at the corners of his mouth.

Slowly, it grew. "Do you really think you're in charge here?"

Iron encircled her ribcage—she could hardly breathe. Desire rocketed through her, and she ran her tongue slowly over her lip. Alex dropped his eyes to follow the movement, his nostrils flaring.

"Think, Alex? No. I *know* I'm in charge."

She let her eyes blaze at him, matching his sensuous smile. Without warning, she put every ounce of strength she had into her arms, forcing them upward. Instantly, Alex let go. Hope cupped his face in both hands, his chin rough under her fingers, and yanked his head down.

Their mouths smashed together, teeth raking each other. Alex made a deep, throaty growl as she lowered one hand, fanning it out over his chest and down his abdomen. Slipping it under the thick neoprene of his wetsuit, she slid her hand beneath the board shorts he wore underneath and grasped his impressive length firmly.

She broke the kiss to laugh softly in his ear. "You *do* like it when I'm in charge, don't you?"

Alex shook his head, rushing his mouth back to hers and answering against her lips. "No. I love it, baby."

Hope moved her hand up and down, and he moaned again, resting his forehead against hers, nearly panting now. Hope whisked her tongue in his ear, and his entire body jerked. "Is there any hot, sexy way to get out of wetsuits?"

That made him laugh. "None. It's impossible to accomplish without flopping around like a fish."

"I won't laugh at you if you don't laugh at me."

"I'll try, but no promises."

Hope sat on the rocky ground, unzipping her neoprene booties.

Despite his statement, Alex whisked off his boots and pulled his wetsuit off in one smooth, practiced motion along with his board shorts, standing before her naked.

And very ready for action.

Hope awkwardly pulled one bootie off, then frowned at Alex. "Oh, sure. Make me feel inadequate."

He dropped to his knees in front of her, leaning forward to tip her chin up. He softly kissed her, brushing his tongue over her lips. "Inadequate is the very last thing you should be feeling. Let me help."

With a smile, she leaned back on her hands, watching as he

pulled her other boot off. Alex lifted his eyes, settling them on her breasts. He crawled up her legs and drew one breast into his mouth, pressing her onto her back. The rock floor cooled her bare, blazing skin. With one hand, he stroked her other breast, and she arched her back, leaning toward him. "I thought you were taking my wetsuit off."

Alex broke off to stare at her, his eyes intense. "I am."

Hope lifted both arms over her head, knowing it made her breasts rounder and more shapely. Alex inhaled sharply, then returned his mouth to her breast, rolling his tongue around the peak. She gasped and started to bring her hands down.

Alex whipped his head up. "No. Don't move."

She returned her arms to their prior position, raising an eyebrow at him. "Oh, we're back to the battle of wills, are we?"

A ghost of a smile crossed his face. "We never stopped. Stay still."

"Or what?"

He smiled fully this time, and the look in his eyes went straight to the center of her. "You don't want to find out."

He crawled back down her legs and hooked his fingers over her wetsuit, folded over her waist. With one firm motion, he pulled both it and her bikini bottoms down. Grasping the wetsuit by the arms, he tugged it to her ankles, inside out. Darting his eyes to hers, he said, "Don't move now."

She nodded but didn't speak, dying for him to touch her.

With two hard tugs, he pulled the legs of the suit over her ankles and feet, tossing it on top of his. Meeting her eyes again, he lifted one foot and drew her big toe between his lips. It disappeared into his warm, wet mouth and Hope cried out, the sensation rocketing through her whole body. He ran his tongue over the arch of her foot and up the inside of her ankle.

Hope closed her eyes. "Oh my God. You're killing me here."

He laughed softly but didn't reply.

He slowed when he reached her inner thigh, moving his tongue in soft circles as he moved slowly upward.

Agonizingly slowly.

Hope wanted to move her arms, to grab his head and pull it where she desperately needed him to be. But he'd stop immediately. That was part of the game. He pressed her legs apart, dancing his fingers up her other thigh as his mouth made her insane.

He reached the top of her thigh and kissed his way to the front of it, running his tongue over the crease at the apex of her leg. Hope groaned in frustration. She started to throw her leg over his back, but he pressed his hand against it, preventing her.

She was breathing so hard his soft laugh was barely audible.

"Have I convinced you yet?" he asked.

"Alex, so help me God, I'm going to make you pay for this."

He nipped her inner thigh and her shout echoed through the cavern. She joined her hands together above her head, trying not to squirm.

At last, Alex moved in, swiping his tongue in one long stroke. Hope arched her back, gasping, and he moved with her. He circled his tongue relentlessly, swirling and sucking. She couldn't hold still anymore.

Grabbing his head with both hands, she pressed her hips hard against his mouth as the wave rolled through her, screaming his name. Her climax was both endless and over too soon, leaving her spent and yet yearning.

Hope rubbed her hands over his broad back as he kissed his way up her body. Brushing his lips over hers, he spoke softly. "You moved your hands. I told you not to do that."

She dug her fingernails in, making him inhale.

"It doesn't matter what you tell me."

He settled on one elbow above her. "Oh? And why is that exactly?"

In one fierce motion, Hope moved both hands to his chest and pushed him off her as hard as she could, rolling with him so she was on top. She grabbed both his hands and pulled them over his head, holding both wrists. "You're a smart man. I'm sure I don't need to draw you a picture." She rolled her hips from side to side. He felt huge between them. She relaxed her hands and brushed them up the inside of his arms. Goosebumps rose along his skin. "Hold still. You're not allowed to move."

Hope ground harder against him and he closed his eyes. "Oh God."

She bent down and kissed his neck, opening her mouth when she reached the hollow between his collarbones. Tracing a wet stripe, she moved down the center of his chest, his hard pecs on either side of her mouth. When she reached his navel, she nipped him, making him tense all over as he gasped.

Hope looked up. His eyes were closed, and his arms were still above his head. Both hands were clenched into fists, his knuckles white.

Smiling, she resumed her downward march over his abdomen, the length of him hot against her cheek.

Alex moaned, not the soft sounds of before. This echoed around them. "Please, Hope."

She laughed gently. "You've hardly suffered yet. Be patient and don't move."

Shifting her head to the other side, she continued her soft, wet kisses over his abdomen, tracing the ridges of each defined muscle with her tongue. She kissed each of the small scars scattered across his lower abdomen, the result of shrapnel, then drew a long, wet stripe down his V. She pressed her hand flat against his right hip and caressed the many ridges of scar tissue covering it. At the same time, she grasped him with her other hand, holding on as she enveloped him with her mouth.

Alex clenched both his legs, pressing them together to keep

from moving as he cried her name. Hope moved her head, drawing the same movement with her fingers over his scars, loving all of him.

It didn't take long before Alex took a deep breath and spoke in a rush. "Baby, if you want to have sex, you'd better stop that. Now."

Smiling, Hope lifted her head. "Maybe I don't want to. Maybe I'll finish you right here."

With his arms still over his head and his eyes closed, Alex broke into a wide grin. "Suit yourself. I'm not going to complain either way."

That made her laugh out loud, and she climbed up his body, stopping briefly to bite his right pectoral muscle. His whole body twitched. "Just in case you need a reminder," Hope purred.

Alex opened his eyes and they stared at each other. With one hand, she grasped him and lowered herself, easing him inside. He let out a long, deep moan, and she bent down to him, moving her mouth to his ear. "Mmm. Do you like that?"

"I'm way beyond like at this point." His voice was thick and strained, making her smile again. A deep drawing sensation built within her. Again.

Alex's arms were still above his head and Hope stretched her own out, lacing her fingers through his as they moved together. He gripped back tightly, cradling her hands within his. She raised her head, and he stared back at her. His lips were parted, and he breathed in gasps but held still otherwise. Hope bent to him, softly brushing her lips over his, then encircling his tongue with hers.

She broke the kiss to close her eyes, another climax building quickly. Alex still held still below her, letting her take the lead. But she knew what he wanted.

The same thing she did.

She moved her lips to his ear once more. "Now, Alex."

Instantly, he exploded into motion, rolling her onto her back. He pressed her against the hard rock, but she hardly noticed, wrapping her legs around his waist. He crushed his mouth to hers as her arms swept around his back. She raked her nails down it, and he gave a deep, gasping moan against her mouth. Their tongues plunged, each welcoming the other.

Together, they crashed into each other, the skin where their bodies touched becoming slick with sweat.

Together, they gave every last portion of themselves.

Together, they rode the same all-encompassing wave as the cavern around them reverberated with their cries.

Chapter Fourteen

HOPE LOCKED the door to the dive shop and headed down the stairs, shading her eyes against the sun as it neared the horizon. A smile rose on her face at the sight of Zach and Jasmine under the palapa, nuzzling as they took their tanks off.

Where does he get the energy for another dive?

A week had passed since she and Alex discovered the new cavern, and they had been working overtime. Alex was learning the responsibilities involved with being the new scuba agency regional representative and working to finish her and Zach's divemaster course. They only had one class left, plus the final exam. One of their exercises had been drawing a detailed topographic map of a site and giving Alex a dive briefing about it. She had thoroughly enjoyed the challenge.

Hope and Zach had also assisted in several of his and Jack's classes, helping students master skills. It was a good thing they were nearly done, because Sara was now several days overdue and crankier than a wet cat. Two days prior, she had called Hope, announcing, "That's it! I'm officially starting my maternity leave. Between the swelling, my sore back, and the damn tropical heat, I'm not leaving my house until Jack and I go to the hospital."

"That's fine, Sara. Patti's enjoying working in the spa and the resort employees don't need to be micromanaged. Concentrate on BB."

"Like I have any choice." Then she laughed. "I'll keep you updated."

When Hope entered through the slider, Alex sat at the kitchen table, which usually meant he was engrossed in a project. "Working on the regional meeting you're setting up in Christiansted?"

Alex pinched the bridge of his nose. "Not at the moment, but I was putting that together earlier. I'm going to open the meeting up to anyone who works as a dive professional—instructor, divemaster, or shop owner. I want to set a new course and make people feel welcome and a part of the team."

She slipped off her sandals, leaving them by the door. "Creating good teams is a subject you're an expert at. If that stuff isn't about your new rep duties, are you pondering when we'll have the next cavern session?"

An amused glint entered his eyes. "I was hoping we wouldn't have to wait that long."

Hope laughed as she crossed the room. Following their tryst, they had redressed, then performed a quick survey of the cavern, but found no obvious offshoots. But making love in the cool, damp cavern had made them both eager to return to the sunny grotto, so they left quickly with plans to return in the future.

But not until after they finished the divemaster class.

"And our bed is much more comfortable too." Hope stopped next to him, drawing her brows together as she studied what was spread before him. "That doesn't look like cave drawings."

"No. When Mike was here, he told me he'd found a bunch

of old photos of us and the Team. He sent them and I printed some out."

Smiling, Hope picked one up. The picture showed a group of eight heavily armed, yet smiling, men in desert tactical gear, lines of sand dunes behind them and a cloudless blue sky above. All wore helmets and sunglasses. Hope peered at the picture, unable to pick Alex out. "All I see is a bunch of guys I wouldn't want to mess with. Which one is you?"

"Here." Alex pointed to the middle of the back row, and like a switch being flipped, he was instantly recognizable. A smile rose on her face at his happy expression.

"Where was this taken?"

Alex shrugged. "Hard to tell. Probably Afghanistan or Iraq."

Hope set the picture down and picked up a second, raising both brows. It was the same environment, and the same men, but now all were shirtless. None wore helmets or sunglasses, and she gave a low whistle. She had no problem picking Alex out in this photo. The Alex she was married to was a muscled, fit man in superb physical shape. The man in the photo was on a completely different level. His chest, arms, and abs were much bigger and more sharply defined. He had an arm thrown loosely over Mike Baker's shoulders and grinned at the camera with a brash, self-assured glint in his eyes.

"You look like the Incredible Hulk!"

Alex laughed and shook his head. "Not quite, but I carried ten to fifteen more pounds in those days. And it wasn't fat."

"I can see that."

Her Alex was still confident, but more compassionate and understanding. He was a different man than the one in the picture. She glanced at the others in the print, knowing some of them weren't alive anymore. But she would never force Alex to relive terrible memories by asking which.

Hope set the picture back on the table and stood on her

tiptoes to kiss him. "You may have been a specimen of the perfect soldier in those days, but I prefer you now."

"So do I. I was a cocky bastard back then. You probably would have hated me."

She burst into laughter. "I don't know about that. But it does make you think about how the life phase where you meet someone can make all the difference." She sifted through more of the photos. "I've been asking staff to give me pictures. Sara texted me one earlier I haven't looked at. Can I use some of these in a project I'm putting together?"

Alex stiffened, growing still beside her. "Pictures of me are fine, or me with Mike. But please don't use any of the whole Team."

She turned to look at him. His jaw was set hard, and his face was carefully guarded. Hope pressed a hand against his cheek. "Of course not. I understand."

The tension visibly drained from him, and a smile appeared. "I know you do. I'd like to see what Sara sent you."

Hope opened her phone and brought up the picture. It was of her and Sara as children. She looked about ten, meaning Sara was six. Hope's hair was nearly blonde, but Sara's was the same dark brown as it was today. Both girls smiled big, toothy grins at the camera.

Alex laughed and put an arm around Hope's shoulders. "You were both pretty cute kids."

Hope's smile was a bit more reserved. "This was taken before Dad left and everything fell apart. It's a good photo, though I'm not sure it would be appropriate for resort promo."

"Have you decided what you're going to do with them?"

"No. I'm still waiting for inspiration to strike. Maybe a collage on a big piece of poster board? I'm not sure, but—"

Her phone chimed with a notification of a Facebook memory.

"Maybe that's some inspiration," Alex said.

She opened Facebook and a photo appeared on her screen, Alex looking over her shoulder. Hope's breath froze in her lungs. It was of her and two friends, taken during college. The younger Hope smiled at the camera, but her face was thin. All of her was thin, and deep black smudges lay under both eyes. Eyes that held a haunted look.

Alex's hand tightened on her shoulder. "Or maybe not."

Hope's heart twisted at the sight of herself. *How might my life be different if I'd never met him?* She glanced at the date. "This was taken about a year after... Caleb. I took an entire semester off school and disappeared inside my apartment to heal. Or to try. You can see I wasn't very successful. When I came back to school, I got all new friends. None of them knew about Caleb."

She was careful not to say more. Alex had never asked the details of what had happened that final night. He only knew she'd ended up in the emergency room and filed charges against Caleb, who had been convicted. With her own eyes, Hope had seen Alex level a man who had threatened her, and easily knock him unconscious. She was relieved Caleb was in prison for many reasons. Not the least of which was fear of what Alex was capable of doing to him.

Not because she worried about Caleb. Because she worried about Alex.

He tightened his hold and kissed the top of her head. "I'm so sorry you had to go through that."

She put her phone down and smiled at him. "Just as I'm sorry for what you went through. But both events led us here. To each other. Good can come from even the most horrible experiences."

Slipping her arms around his waist, Hope pressed against his chest. Alex's arms enveloped her, and he moved one hand to hold her head against his beating heart. Leaning his cheek against her head, he rocked her gently in his arms. She closed her eyes and breathed out a relaxed sigh, safe in her favorite place in the world.

When her phone rang, she was tempted to let it go to voice mail. But a quick glance revealed Sara was the caller, so she broke away from Alex. "Hey, what's up?"

"Well, there's a big puddle of nasty fluid all over our kitchen floor that Jack's mom insisted on cleaning up. So, unless my bladder went on strike, my water just broke."

Every muscle in Hope's body contracted. "Oh my God! Is Jack there? Do I need to drive you to the hospital? Should I call 911?"

Sara's laugh came through the phone. "Settle down there, Auntie. Jack's right here and putting my bag in the car. I just wanted to call and let you know the show is starting."

"Do you want me at the hospital? Or Alex?"

Alex wrinkled his nose. Hope frowned and waved him off.

Sara burst into laughter. "No! Jeez, relax, Hope. This is probably going to take a while. We'll call or text you when BB gets here, ok?"

"That sounds great. We'll keep a phone handy."

Alex visibly relaxed, and Hope stuck her tongue out at him.

Sara inhaled sharply.

"Was that a contraction?" Hope asked. "Are you ready to scream?"

"I will be if you don't shut up. Oh, look at that! Jack's back, so I need to go."

Hope laughed. "You'll do great. I love you."

"Love you too. I might keep you updated myself, but if we actually get to the screaming part, it'll probably be Jack."

Chapter Fifteen

HOPE AND ALEX were getting ready for bed when her text tone went off with a message from Sara. Hope glanced at him. "She's progressing steadily and about to have an epidural put in. Jack will let us know when the baby is born."

"That sounds like good news," Alex said.

Hope sent an encouraging message back and climbed into bed after making sure Jack could ring straight through. She rolled onto her side and closed her eyes. "I wonder if I'll be able to sleep tonight."

Alex curled his body behind her like a giant comma, stroking his hand down her arm. "Are you ok not having kids?"

Hope's eyes opened. She was surprised he'd asked, having thought this issue was settled. "I'm looking forward to being an aunt, but you and I are pretty much through that life phase. Besides, adoption is a long, difficult process." She'd had an emergency hysterectomy two years prior. "Has something changed for you?"

He snuggled closer. "No. I can't see myself with a baby in my forties. I just wanted to make sure we were on the same page."

She lifted his hand to her mouth. "I love you, and I love what we have together."

"So do I." After a gentle sigh, Alex was asleep in seconds.

HOPE'S PHONE rang just after 3 a.m. Instantly awake, she fumbled for the phone, confirming the caller was Jack.

Who else would it be?

"Jack! Is everything ok?"

"Everything's perfect." His voice was thick with emotion. "We have a baby girl. Magen Elizabeth was born at 2:24."

"Magen! What a lovely name, and I'm sure she's beautiful. Sara's ok?"

"She's doing fine. She didn't even scream. Much."

Hope laughed, tears filling her eyes. "I'm so happy for you two. Can Alex and I come by in the morning?"

"Of course. The nurse said if things continue to go well, we'll probably go home in the afternoon. So there's plenty of time. My mama will be here in a little while."

"Thanks for calling, Jack. We'll see you a little later." Hope tossed the phone on her nightstand and rolled over.

Alex pulled her into his arms. "Mother and daughter are both fine?"

"That's what Jack said. We'll head to the hospital before you go to work. I can't wait to meet my niece!"

HOPE HELD Magen in her arms, enjoying the soothing motions of the rocking chair she sat in. Sara lay in the hospital bed while her nurse evaluated her. Jack's mother, a plump woman named Trish, sat on a couch. Jack stretched out in a recliner, snoring softly.

The baby was tightly swaddled and wore a soft pink cap

which covered a prodigious amount of dark-brown hair. She slowly blinked a pair of dark-blue eyes at Hope, then yawned. Hope grinned and brushed a finger down Magen's tiny button nose.

Trish frowned at her son. "Maybe I should wake him up. You're the one who did all the work."

Sara smiled at Jack. "Let him sleep. He was a wreck last night and almost passed out."

Trish laughed. "That doesn't surprise me at all. His father did the same thing when our first, Mary, was born."

Jack's mother had arrived two days previously to help with the baby's first week. But since Magen made a late arrival, she'd been able to enjoy a little vacation before the big event. She would no doubt be a big help to Sara and Jack, having raised six children of her own.

Hope and Alex had arrived at the hospital just after seven o'clock. Both got a chance to hold the baby and visit a bit with Sara and Jack. The new father was still awake then, though he'd looked more disheveled than Sara had. In fact, there was a calm serenity about her Hope had never seen before.

After a half hour, Magen began fussing, ready to nurse. Alex took that as his cue to leave and practically bolted out the door. Hope enjoyed watching him with Magen. He had more experience with babies than she did, having been around both his nephew and niece when they were young. But he drew the line at watching Sara nurse, stating he needed to work out the dive schedule while Jack was off for two weeks.

Sara brought Hope back to the present. "Do you have everything worked out to cover Aqua?"

Hope nodded. "Patti hired a temporary stylist to fill in for you. Some of your clients rescheduled with her and others just made appointments for a couple months out. You're irreplaceable, sis."

Sara gave her a tired smile. "I'll take two months off, then reevaluate."

"Whatever you need to do, we'll work it out."

"Are you working today?"

Hope nodded. "I need to head out. Zach is helping Alex and Will today, so I'll work in the dive shop. Speaking of Will, does he know?"

Sara nodded. "Jack called him, and he's planning on stopping by the house later."

Hope looked down. Magen was sound asleep in her arms. She stood and placed her in the bassinet, where the baby cooed before settling down again. Hope approached the bed and embraced Sara. "Congratulations again. You did an amazing thing."

"Thanks. I'm glad to have that over with, though I think the work is just beginning."

Hope turned to Jack, whose head was tipped back, his mouth open. "If he ever wakes up, tell him congrats too."

ALEX SAT IN HIS OFFICE, chewing on a pencil. Several days had passed since Magen's birth, and he'd been able to get the dive schedule covered. Jack had called him the previous day, confirming he'd be back after two weeks' leave.

"You sure?" Alex had asked. "Hope and Zach are both officially divemasters now. I gave them their exam yesterday. Hope has her hands full with the resort, but I put Zach in the water right away to lead dives."

"Yeah, I'll be ready to come back after another week. I've caught up on a bunch of projects, and helped with the nighttime feedings, but I miss diving."

"We miss you too. I'll put you on the schedule for that Monday."

After hanging up, Alex breathed a relieved sigh as he stared out the window at the beach. Despite what he's said, finding dive guides had been a challenge. Robert was only able to help two days, but April had worked several, including today. They had three groups most mornings now, and Alex needed to drive twice a week to give Tommy days off.

He glanced at his watch and confirmed he had an hour before his scuba meeting in Christiansted. Turning to the schedule again, he studied it, drumming his fingers on the desk. He wanted to go back to the cavern—and explore it properly this time. A smile tugged at the corners of his mouth as he remembered *why* he and Hope hadn't explored it thoroughly. He wanted to celebrate Hope and Zach becoming divemasters, and a grotto dive would kill two birds with one stone. There weren't any tight squeezes in that passage, which made it safe for Zach to join them.

Someone rapped on his open doorway and Alex looked up.

April stood there, dressed in a resort rash guard and swim skirt, her golden-blonde hair in a neat bun. She held a sheet of paper in one hand. "Got a second?"

"Sure. Come on in." Alex gestured to the simple folding chair in front of his desk.

She sat and placed the typewritten paper on her lap, smoothing her skirt and tucking an errant lock of hair behind one ear. One foot bounced rapidly.

What's she nervous about? "Everything ok?"

She met his eyes and her foot stopped bouncing. "Yes. Really good, though this is hard." She handed him the paper. "I'm giving my notice."

Alex took the piece of paper. "Hope told me you'd been

talking to the resort at Calypso Key, but I didn't know you were ready to leave quite yet."

"I feel like it's time for a change."

He set her resignation on the desk and sat back in his chair. "I'm sorry to hear that. We'll miss you." He silently thanked God that he had two new divemasters ready to go.

"I'm not moving quite yet, so I should be able to help out while Jack is off work."

"He's taking another week, then starting back the following Monday."

She smiled, but it was strained. "That works perfectly. I leave that Wednesday."

Alex couldn't deny he was relieved. April was a great divemaster, but there was always a slight edge of strain between them. Hope wasn't the jealous type, but he never wanted her to feel insecure about their marriage. April was an attractive woman, and he didn't know why he had never been romantically interested in her, but he wasn't. He never even noticed other women after meeting Hope. He admired April's integrity in honoring their boundaries, even though she felt differently.

They had never talked about it out loud, but both knew he would never return her feelings. Alex wished her the very best, but her moving on was best for everyone, including her.

LESS THAN AN HOUR LATER, Alex stood in an adult education classroom in the Christiansted community center, the traditional venue for scuba agency meetings. It was 3:58 p.m., and he glanced around the room filled with rows of desks with attached chairs. They were about three-quarters full, which pleased him.

At precisely 4:02 p.m., he walked over and locked the door before returning to stand in front of the room behind a lectern.

A guy in the front row laughed. "You're locking out the stragglers?"

One of Alex's brows edged up. "You all made the effort to be here on time. Why should we wait for people who didn't?"

Several people laughed, and he let a smile rise. "I'm Alex Monroe and I'm the new PDII regional rep. I have a military background—" a titter of laughter rose again, but now it sounded slightly nervous. A knock sounded on the door. "—and that's made me a stickler for punctuality. But this isn't the military. Should I let them in?"

The guy who spoke shook his head, grinning. "No way. I hate it when meetings go on because they didn't start on time. Let them eat cake. They'll know for the next one."

Several others nodded, though there were some frowns as well. Unease slithered through Alex's gut. *This isn't the Navy, Monroe. These people aren't SEALs.* Alex saw his friend Mark Lowry from Ocean Surf Resort and held his eye for a moment. Mark gave him a nod, and Alex placed a finger on his agenda. "Ok. Let's get started then..."

AFTER THE MEETING, Alex sat with Mark at a nearby bar. He looked around and smiled. The last time he'd been there was when he and Hope had met up with Mike and Emma Baker unexpectedly at a festival.

Mark raised his Leatherback in a toast. "To new opportunities."

Alex clinked his bottle to Mark's and took a drink. "Not sure if it's more of an opportunity or a pain in the ass."

"We need a rep here, and I'm glad it's you." Mark laughed, lifting his ball cap to run a hand over his curly brown hair. "You shook things up right from the start. That let people know not to screw with you."

Alex didn't smile back, disquiet once again creeping through him. "I hope that wasn't a mistake. I didn't mean to come across as a hard-ass. I just hate wasting my time."

Mark shrugged. "I think it was a good move. Sets the tone you want. Jack mentioned you're very clear about your expectations." Jack had worked for Mark before coming to Half Moon Bay.

Alex gave him a reluctant smile. "Pretty sure that's just a fancy way of saying I'm an asshole."

Mark laughed again. "No, it's not. How is Jack, by the way? I miss him."

"He just became a father. And I'm sorry I poached your best divemaster."

"Tell him congratulations for me. I think he'll make a great dad—he's got the patience for it. And I'll forgive you if you buy me another beer."

"You've got a deal."

"Besides, he married your wife's sister, right? Might as well keep everything in the family."

"I hired his brother as a divemaster too."

They shared a laugh, and Alex tried to ignore the qualm that rose yet again in his gut. Will was another example where he'd maybe come across too hard. He'd mentored the divemaster, but it hadn't been an easy road.

Alex took another pull, enjoying the moment with a friend as a warm breeze blew across his face. He pushed the negative feelings away, and Magen's sweet face appeared in his mind with her mop of brown hair.

There were too many good things he'd rather think about.

Chapter Sixteen

BIRDS TWITTERED in the trees as Alex stood with Hope and Zach at Half Moon Grotto. Magen was now ten days old and doing well. Jack's mother had extended her stay to help the new parents. Alex had plenty of work for his two new divemasters, but he wanted to celebrate their accomplishment with something special.

"I can't believe we're diving in a cave!" Zach said, eyes open wide as he swept them around the blue waters of the grotto.

Alex held up an index finger. "Cavern. Not cave. There's a big difference, and you're not qualified to dive a cave."

The young man turned a big smile to him. "What do you mean? I'm a divemaster now—so is Hope. What's the difference between them?"

"Air." Alex didn't smile back. He liked Zach's confidence, but the kid still had plenty to learn. "Caverns have an accessible air source. Caves don't."

Hope smiled indulgently at him as she set up her tank. "I suppose air is a good thing when you're diving."

They hadn't said anything about the cave passage where they'd found the treasure or the fact that Hope was already an experienced cave diver, only that they had explored the passage in the rock pool together. Alex crossed his arms. "You can both call me overprotective if that makes you feel better. But Zach, you need to follow my lead here."

Zach's smile faded. "I will."

Hope straightened from her tank, a frown turning down the corners of her mouth. "What about me? I have been in the cavern before. Can I lead?"

Alex suppressed a sigh. "Maybe next time, ok? Zach, I want you to follow me and watch how I move." When he'd brought up the plan to perform a celebratory dive here, Hope thought it was a great idea. Zach thought it was beyond great. But Alex was nervous enough taking Zach in there without the experience Hope had.

The young man nodded enthusiastically, but all Alex saw was the irritated flash in Hope's eyes. "Why don't you get your kit together, Zach?" While he moved a short distance away, Alex crossed to Hope and spoke quietly. "I'm not discounting your skills, ok? But Zach has a tendency to get cocky. I want him between us."

"Can't you keep a better eye on him if you're in the rear instead of me?"

"I'm his instructor. I want him watching me."

She gave him a nod and picked up her wetsuit. "That makes sense. But I'm not letting you off the hook about this, ok?"

They shared a smile, the faint tension between them fading. "Noted. Let's dive."

Thirty minutes later, they entered the pool tunnel. Alex had recently worked with Zach on his frog kick, satisfied he understood how to perform it, and more importantly, why.

With all these rocks on the floor, at least I don't need to worry him kicking any silt up.

They reached the area with the air pocket Alex had noted

on the first dive. That time, he'd ignored the flat circular disks dipping into the water from above, each with a carpet of short, thread-like strands hanging from them. But now, he was excited to show them to Hope and Zach. Halting, he spun around and removed his slate. The nearest, eight-inches-in-diameter disc was above him, and Alex pointed at it before writing:

Do you know what that is?

The passage widened here, and Hope moved to Zach's side as they peered at the strange object. Both shook their heads, making Alex smile. He gave them the thumbs up, and the trio ascended into the shallow air pocket he'd discovered on the first dive. The ceiling was less than three feet above them. Above water, the strange disc became a long, brown gnarly growth reaching from a hole in the ceiling of the tunnel into the water.

Hope studied it, then several others that were scattered around. "It looks like a giant root."

"The lady gets a gold star," Alex said softly, and she slid her eyes to him, a seductive smile forming. He returned it, memories of their last encounter in the cavern flashing in his mind.

"They're roots?" Zach said, pulling him back to his task.

"Tree roots. That's how a lot of the vegetation around here gets water. The big trees send roots through holes in the rock, and they soak up the ground water like straws."

Hope's smile turned to sheer delight. "That's so cool! I've never seen a tree root from underneath before."

"Not many people have," Alex said. "That's why I brought you guys up here. And this is what makes this passage a cavern, not a cave, in terms of diving."

Alex took the lead again and next they passed under the ridged ceiling section. As he studied the strange formation, a small rock broke off and skittered down the wall of the tunnel, settling with the others on the ground. After emerging back under a normal ceiling, they came to the offshoot. When he and

Hope had left on the previous dive, Alex tied off a section of orange line in a diagonal slash across the side tunnel, clearly marking it as a No Entry zone.

They entered the serpentine and Alex kept a close watch on the headlamps shining on the walls around him, easily able to tell Hope's from Zach's, even without looking back. Zach's beam bounced everywhere as he tried to take in every possible feature of the tunnel.

Before long, they followed the orange line up the slope and surfaced where it was tied off to the rocky shore. Zach stood, spit out his regulator, and pulled his mask down around his neck. He was slack-jawed as he stared at the dim cavern around them. "This is *awesome!*"

Alex and Hope shared another smile, this one tinged with regret. This cavern was nothing compared to the one where they'd found Barnaby's treasure. But of course, they couldn't say anything about that to Zach. Even without the treasure, Alex would have kept the cave passage, with its far more dangerous diving, to himself.

"It's like being in a different world, isn't it?" Hope asked Zach, smiling.

He just nodded his head in long sweeps.

Alex grinned, glad they'd brought him. "Let's move to shore and get our gear off. We can explore and see what's here."

They turned off their headlamps and climbed up to the rocky shelf. "Why was the ceiling different in that stretch of the tunnel?" Zach asked Alex.

"I can't help you with that one. Geology isn't my strong suit."

"Maybe it's just a different type of rock," Hope added with a shrug

As Zach deposited his tank on the stony ground, he gaped at

a nearby multi-colored stalactite. "You guys didn't check this place out when you were here the first time?"

"Sure, some of it," Hope said, her voice betraying no hint of what they'd actually been up to. "But mostly where that big seam is in the ceiling that's letting in all the light. We can check out the other side this time."

"Don't just stand there, guys," Zach said. "Let's go!" He turned on his head lamp, striding forward to the dim reaches.

Alex couldn't help laughing. "Don't get too far ahead. We're doing this as a team, remember?"

Zach turned around and shined his light directly in Alex's face. He clenched his eyes shut, flinching as he raised an arm in front of his face, but he bit back a sharp retort.

"Oh, sorry! You told me not to do that."

Alex opened his eyes again, blinking to dispel the blinding flashes. "That's ok. Try not to do it again, though, ok?"

Hope moved to his side and slid an arm around his waist, her laugh echoing around them. "You're getting off easy, Zach. Apparently, Alex was a terror in his old days about that."

"Yeah, I can see why that wouldn't be good." Zach adjusted his light, so it sat higher on his head. "That should help. Let's go, we're burning daylight here!"

Alex expelled a long breath as Hope grinned and squeezed his hand. "Aye aye, captain."

The trio walked side by side. Stalagmites rose from the floor, periodically reaching toward the ceiling as they came to a point. Matching stalactites grasped downward to meet them, and some had joined, forming columns stretching the full height of the cavern.

The area wasn't overly large, and they soon came to a solid wall that met the curving ceiling. Hope looked at Alex and shrugged. Zach followed it to their right and shouted after ten feet. "There's a passage here!"

They quickly joined him, and Alex stepped in front. He inhaled deeply, all his senses on full alert. But there was no other scent except the chalky, damp smell of the cave around them. "Let's follow for a little while."

The passage was narrow, and his shoulders scraped the sides, prompting him to move sideways. He had to hunch over, though the tunnel was tall enough for Hope and Zach to move unimpeded. After ten feet, the tunnel veered sharply left, narrowing tightly. Alex stared at the stricture, moving his headlamp up and down. "This looks like the end of the line. I don't feel like contorting myself through that thing."

"You're just too big," Zach said with a bark of laughter. "I bet Hope and I could fit."

Alex smiled but shook his head. "Not this time. Let's go back and look around a little more." They returned to the cavern, but there wasn't much more to discover. They ended back at the flat area where he and Hope had spent most of their time previously, near the narrow rend in the ceiling.

She ran a hand over the smooth black wall. "I don't see any other offshoots here."

"That's all right," Zach said, standing with his hands on his hips as he looked around the area. "This is an incredible find."

Alex nodded. "I agree. And since it's a cavern, not a cave, we might be able to open it up to divers. Though I'd be pretty careful who I brought in here."

Zach whipped his head toward him. "That's a great idea!"

Alex laughed. "You say that now, but you might be singing a different tune when you're the one hauling all the gear out here. That's the main problem—how isolated the grotto is."

"I don't know," Hope said as they moved toward the shore once more. "Maybe we can have a staff dive day and see what some of them think about it."

"I'm glad you two are the first to be in here," Alex said.

"Congratulations to both of you. Half Moon Bay now has two more divemasters."

Zach broke into a blinding smile. "Thanks, man. I really enjoy leading dives."

"You've done a terrific job," Alex said, pride filling him at how far Zach had come. "With Jack at home, I'm doing a lot of teaching, so it will be you, Will, and April leading most of the dives. Robert's even helping out a couple days." A smile crossed his face as he looked at Hope. "Maybe I can get Boss Lady into the mix too."

A frown tugged at the corners of Hope's mouth. "I'd like to, but I've got my hands full right now. With Sara out and people on vacation, I'm not sure I can jump in quite yet."

Alex sighed theatrically and picked up his rebreather, tossing Hope a smile. "That makes sense. But I'm not letting you off the hook about this, ok?"

She laughed, acknowledging her exact words from earlier. "All right. You made your point, sailor. Let's head back to the grotto."

A tiny bird flew through the seam and circled the cavern before exiting the same way, reminding Alex of how different this cavern was than the others he and Hope had explored. A smile rose as he placed the regulator in his mouth and helped Hope wade into the black water.

And if we weren't divers, we would never have discovered any of this.

Chapter Seventeen

HOPE PLACED several handmade bead necklaces inside the glass display case, then stood. She looked around the dive/gift shop as bright light streamed through the windows. The dive shop took up about two-thirds of the room, and the other third was devoted to resort T-shirts and sweatshirts, coffee mugs, hats, and other St. Croix souvenirs. On the wall behind her, a large flat-screen television cycled through Robert's images of the island and resort. She leaned backward against the counter, watching the colorful images scroll past.

I need to get more photos from Robert.

It was just past noon, and *Surface Interval* should be returning from the morning trip at any moment. Alex was driving, with Zach, April, and Robert leading dives. As Hope watched an image of yellow Fort Christiansvaern transition into a sunset beach, the idea for her project came in a flash. She smiled, excitement running through her.

The front door opened, and Jasmine entered. The initial sparks between her and Zach had blossomed into a romantic relationship that never failed to bring a smile to Hope's lips when she saw them together.

"You're right on time," Hope said. "I'm going to go wait for the boat. Can you hang up those new T-shirts we got?"

"Sure. Did you see the Frederiksted display I made?"

Hope turned to the corner, where several coffee-table books about the town were displayed along with jigsaw puzzles and handcrafted pottery. "That looks fantastic! I sold one of the pottery pieces this morning. You've got a great eye."

"Thanks," Jasmine said with a shy smile. "I like workin' here a lot."

"Been diving with Zach lately?"

"Not since last week, but we're talkin' about goin' again in a few days. Thanks for lettin' me dive for free and use the resort's equipment."

"Of course! As long as it's not needed by guests, there's no point in just letting it hang in the gear room."

The dive boat was already tied up to the pier when Hope reached the bottom of the stairs. She crossed under the palapa and stepped aboard. Alex was still in the wheelhouse, while Robert, Zach, and April scurried around the deck, removing the empty tanks.

"Robert, can I talk to you for a second?" Hope moved under the covered canopy, where Robert joined her. "I'm working on a project to showcase our staff. Could you go through your Half Moon Bay photos and pick out some that show people working? Or just take new ones if that's easier?"

He grinned, sweat beading on the dark crown of his shaved head. "I can get you plenty. All my photos are organized on my hard drive. I separated the resort pictures into landscapes and people. Anythin' specific you want?"

"I'm still putting the project together. But I'd like pictures of the staff at work. Clark mixing drinks, Gerold cooking, Jasmine in the gift shop. And the dive staff too—in and out of the water. Things like that."

"No problem. Heather and I are goin' out tonight, but I should be able to get you somethin' tomorrow."

"That would be great. Date night tonight?"

"Yeah," Robert replied. "I've been workin' a lot. Had a bunch of sunset photo shoots, so we haven't seen much of each other lately. Today was cool too. I forgot how fun divin' is!"

"You still remember how, huh?"

He laughed. "Yeah, gotta show up here once in a while now that you're gunnin' for my job."

Alex's tall form climbed down from the wheelhouse to the deck. "If we get fully staffed around the resort so she can free up some time, you're in trouble, Robert." He wore a light-blue staff polo shirt, making his eyes even more vivid.

Hope swept up to him for a quick kiss. "Things have been a little hectic. Now that Jasmine's here, I'm headed to Aqua to fill in for Patti, who has an appointment this afternoon. And Corrine at the front desk is taking a week off, so I'll be in the lobby starting tomorrow."

Robert gave her his dazzling smile. "Speakin' of bein' too busy. You've been slackin' in the bakin' department."

"I know!" Hope said. "Pauline has been making treats for the divers and you guys. I'll get back to it as soon as I can." Hope had gained something of a cult reputation for her baking skills and loved providing goodies for the divers and staff. She always threw in something special for Alex.

He patted his flat stomach. "Glad to hear that. I'm wasting away over here."

As Hope strolled up the pier, her mind was taken up with ideas for baking. *Tomorrow afternoon! Right after I get off work. If I make it a priority, it will get done.*

. . .

HOPE OPENED the slider and Cruz slipped in with her. After tossing the mail on the kitchen island, she grabbed a beer from the fridge. The afternoon had passed quickly, mostly in Sara's office. On the whole, she preferred working in the lobby or the dive shop, and didn't mind relinquishing Aqua back to Patti the following day.

She took a long drink of cold beer. "I need to carve out a morning next week to lead a dive." She had led several during her course, with Alex bringing up the rear of the group and available if she needed help. But she hadn't.

The prospect of leading a dive by herself filled her with a mixture of anticipation and nervousness.

Probably how most new divemasters feel.

She was lifting the bottle to her mouth when her phone rang on the counter. Her hand froze as she looked at the name on the screen. John Salisbury.

Caleb's parole officer.

Her heart skipped a beat, then marched in double time. John didn't call just to chit chat. Hope answered the phone. "Hello, John."

"Afternoon, Hope. How are you doing?"

After assuring him she was fine, she asked, "I take it you have some information about Caleb?" A momentary fear that he'd been released ran through her brain. She pushed it away, irritated at her reaction.

"I do. Caleb was involved with a fight with another inmate."

"You already told me that. And that he'd been transferred to a different prison."

"Not that fight. This incident was just a few hours ago. He was fighting with another inmate in the prison laundry room when Caleb produced a homemade knife. Prison officials aren't sure how he got it."

Hope stared out the window at the beach in front of her, not really interested in hearing about yet another fight Caleb had been involved in. "And he hurt the other inmate? Or did he finally kill someone?"

John paused on the other end. "Neither. The inmate wrestled the knife away and stabbed him. In the chest. Caleb is dead, Hope."

An involuntary gust of breath exploded from Hope's lungs. Her ears rang. The ghost who had haunted her for almost twenty years was... gone? "You're sure?"

"Yes. He didn't have any family in the area, so I identified the body. It was him, Hope. I thought you'd want to know."

"Yes. Thank you for calling." Even to her own ears, Hope's voice sounded formal and shocked.

After John hung up, she stared at the phone in her hand, now full of empty silence. Tossing the phone on the counter, she turned fully toward the back wall of windows, wrapping her arms around herself. Trying to decipher what she felt.

Mostly empty. And relieved.

There was no grief, no sadness, but no anger either.

Hope looked at her left upper arm. The arm Caleb had broken in multiple places. Without thinking about it, she had been rubbing up and down it with the other hand. Opening her fingers, she placed her palm flat on the cool granite countertop. "He won't ever hurt anyone again."

Cruz lay in his bed in the corner and lifted his head at her words. She smiled at the dog. "Looks like we're both free of our pasts now."

The sliding glass door opened, and Hope jumped. Alex was brought up short as he closed it. His eyes scanned her face. "Are you ok?"

A tiny smile rose. "Yes, I am. I'm still trying to process a phone call I just received from Caleb's parole officer. Caleb was killed in a fight this morning."

Alex strode across the tile floor and clasped her hands. "And how do you feel about that?"

"Relieved, mostly. Now that chapter of my life can truly be closed. I won't have John Salisbury calling periodically with updates. It's finally over."

Alex wrapped her tightly in his arms and she closed her eyes, leaning against his solid warmth. He held her for several minutes, stroking his fingers through her hair. "I've never asked what he did to you. It wasn't because I didn't care." He pulled away, staring at her. His forehead was deeply lined. "It was because I wasn't sure what I'd do. If you need to tell me, I'm here to listen. That son of a bitch is safe now... from me."

Hope glanced at the floor. Even when Caleb had been out of prison, he'd never shown any interest in coming after her. It was like he refused to acknowledge her existence. But after she fell in love with Alex, she had spent a few sleepless nights worrying about what might happen if the two men ever met face to face.

She suspected only one would walk away. And not Caleb.

Alex just confirmed that.

A flashback ran through her head. Of her wired-shut jaw, the cast on her arm, the liver laceration. Of the times Caleb wouldn't take no for an answer.

Then Hope returned her gaze to the man before her. An honorable, deeply committed man. A man who would stop at nothing to protect her. How could he possibly benefit from knowing the sordid details? He already knew everything that mattered.

"I mean it, Hope. You don't need to keep this inside if—"

Hope stopped him with a finger placed against his lips. "I

don't need to. Caleb hurt me, and that's all there is to it. He means nothing... and you're everything."

Smiling, Hope pulled Alex toward her, resting her head against his chest. Closing her eyes, she felt his heart beat steadily beneath her ear. She was home.

Chapter Eighteen

WATER TRICKLED GENTLY down the massive stacked-stone wall behind Hope, filling the air with its relaxing song. The sound of women's voices emanated from the salon on her right as she stood behind the lengthy, turquoise-colored glass counter of Aqua. She held the soft, solid warmth of Magen in her arms. The infant scrunched up her face, crying and waving one balled fist. Hope bounced her and Magen quieted, staring at her aunt. "Are her eyes turning brown?"

"Yes," Sara said as she leaned backward against the desk. "We didn't figure those blue eyes would last for long since Jack's and mine are both brown."

Violet, Aqua's receptionist, chucked Magen under the chin, tickling with her finger. Magen kicked her feet and cooed. "Oh, what a sweet child! Thank you for comin' by." She arched a black manicured brow at Sara. "And I'm guessin' I don't need to ask why she's named Magen? I know you got married in St. Thomas."

Sara laughed. "You're right. We picked the name out early for a girl. She was likely conceived on our wedding night, which we spent on a secluded spot of Magens Bay." The baby resumed her fussing and Hope handed her off to Sara. As soon as Magen was in her mother's arms, she quieted again.

Hope smiled. "You've got this motherhood thing down pat."

"I wouldn't go that far, but we're getting there. Jack and I have a system worked out where we trade off feeding her during the night so we both get some sleep." She turned to Hope. "What do you have going on this afternoon?"

"Covering the front desk, then I am absolutely baking afterward. I grabbed a bunch of ripe bananas from the restaurant. They're sitting on my counter, ready to become banana bread. Which just happens to be Alex's favorite."

"Who knew you'd turn into Betty Crocker, and I'd become a mother?" Sara grinned and glanced at her watch. "I'd better head back. I just wanted to come by and show Magen off a little."

"I'm so glad you did!" Violet said.

After Sara left, a woman appeared from the massage wing to pay her bill, readjusting her dark hair into a bun on top of her head. "My massage was fantastic. I have an afternoon planned at the pool, and I managed to snag a dinner reservation for me and my husband. I plan to make the most of it."

Hope gave her the slip to sign. "We resisted reservations for dinner, but it was a losing battle. We've got big plans on the restaurant front. You'll have to visit in the future and see what we've got up our sleeve."

"That sounds exciting!"

Hope and Gerold had met again to discuss ideas for the new restaurant—without any earth tremors. The plans were still in the early stages, but his vision for their new showcase was stunning.

After the guest left, Patti rushed through the front door. "I'm here! My meetin' with the laundry service ran long."

"No problem," Hope said. "It's been a great morning. You missed Magen, though."

Patti's round, dark face fell. "Oh no! I was hopin' I'd make it in time."

"I'm sure Sara will bring her around again. I need to head down to the pier, then I'll be covering for Corrine this afternoon if you need me."

Hope entered the dive shop. She had hired a second woman to work with Jasmine, and Maribel finished checking in a diver for the next day's tour. "Everything going ok?" Hope asked.

"So far, so good." Maribel was in her mid-twenties and an advanced level diver. She'd recently moved to the island from Michigan and her sunburned skin was now a tropical tan. "Jasmine has been showing me the ropes. Today's the first day I've worked alone, but it's going fine. She was excited to spend the day with Zach."

Hope smiled in agreement, biting back a laugh. Zach had pestered Alex relentlessly to give him a matching day off with Jasmine. Alex had brought the dive schedule home to make it happen, griping at Hope about it.

She descended the stairs, enjoying the sunny day before she headed to the lobby for the afternoon. *Surface Interval* was tied up, but all was quiet at the moment as the staff ate lunch. The door to the gear room was ajar, and Hope entered, peeking around the neatly organized room. Their former dive shop had completed its transformation, and Jack had constructed several racks and pegs to hold scuba equipment.

"Is anyone here?" she called.

"I'm back here." Alex's voice drifted out of the classroom and Hope crossed to the room with its three long tables and whiteboards on the walls.

"What are you up to?" she asked.

"Two divers asked to do a Nitrox class late this afternoon, so I'm getting set up."

She nodded. "How many people are on the afternoon dive today?"

Alex picked up a green and yellow enriched-air analyzer. "Eight. Will and I are both scheduled to work, but I'm thinking of giving him the whole group and teaching the class early."

Hope glanced around the room where she'd spent so much time lately. "I'm looking forward to leading my first group tomorrow!"

Alex slid his eyes to her, a mask coming over his face as he tightened his jaw. It was an expression Hope was very familiar with. Her heart plummeted.

He kept his voice even. "I want to delay your debut a few more days."

"Alex! You wanted me to become a divemaster. Here I am!"

"This isn't a great group for you to start with. I only want to wait a few days, ok?

He met her glare evenly, refusing to back down. She'd have an easier time trying to negotiate with a mule. "Why don't I take the other group, then?"

Alex crossed to her, tucking a lock of hair behind her ear. She tried to stand strong and resist his nearness. "Because Will is getting along famously with his group. I don't want to break them up, and I want your first day as a divemaster to be a success. Hang in there, baby. You'll get your chance soon." He cupped her face and brushed his lips over hers.

She tried not to smile as she narrowed her eyes at him. "I'd better. I'll nag until you give in."

He caressed his index finger over her collarbone and her insides rearranged themselves. A smile slowly crept over his face. "Nagging's never been your style. Maybe I can talk you into something else."

Taking a deep breath, Hope stiffened her spine and took a big step back. "Simmer down there, sailor." She glanced around the room and let her smile rise. "Despite the memories being in this room brings back."

He laughed. "Very good memories. Let's head back to the gear room. I need a Nitrox tank."

Hope studied the repurposed room as she entered. Rental gear and guests' private equipment, staff gear, and her and Alex's own supplies were all in neat, separate areas. Her eye stopped at the staff equipment section, where two sets of equipment were missing. "Are Jasmine and Zach diving the house reef? They didn't go out with you this morning."

Alex wrinkled his brow. "I'm not sure. Today was the day he harangued me into giving him off."

Hope grinned at the image of Zach pestering the much taller and more imposing Alex. "Jasmine mentioned having a special date today. Maybe they went for a shore dive somewhere else on the island."

"That could be. Though he didn't say anything about taking gear, which is weird. He usually gives me a head's up, so I don't wonder why it's missing—" Alex stopped mid-sentence and whipped his head to the right.

To the corner where the scuba cart was kept.

The corner that was now empty.

"Oh *shit*!" he yelled. "Goddammit, Zach."

"Alex, what are you swearing about?"

"The cart is gone!"

"So? Maybe they used it to haul their stuff to the parking lot and left it there."

He hissed a breath through his teeth. "No. Zach is meticulous about putting things back. They've still got the cart."

Hope breathed a long sigh. "I don't understand why you're so upset."

Alex shifted his eyes to her. "Hope, there's only one place we take that cart to. And Zach knows about it."

"You think he took her to the grotto?"

"Not just to the grotto. I think he took her to *dive* the grotto. You saw how excited he was in that cavern. And everyone goes on about how romantic and private the whole thing is."

She couldn't help smiling at that statement. Alex returned it briefly, then laced his fingers on top of his head and started pacing. "I need to go after them. Make sure they're ok."

Hope frowned. "Why? Let them have their private dive."

Alex froze, gaping at her. "Jasmine is a new diver and has absolutely no experience in overhead environments. And Zach isn't qualified to lead anyone in there yet! I can't believe he did this."

An uneasy squirming slithered through Hope's gut. "You don't know for sure that's where they are."

He resumed pacing. "I'm willing to bet money on it."

She thought for a moment, her heart beating double time now. "I wouldn't take that bet. You're probably right."

"We don't know when they left. Maybe I can stop them before they head into the tunnel."

Hope checked her watch and frowned. "I have to work the front desk this afternoon, and I need to head up there. Keep me updated, ok?"

"Sure. I'll text Will and tell him he needs to take the afternoon group, then I'll reschedule the NITROX class." He crossed the room and pulled his rebreather off its hanger, opening the canister. "This is ready to go. I'll take it just in case I need to go in after them."

"Let me know what you find out."

He nodded as he screwed in his full air bottle on the opposite side of the oxygen cylinder. Then he closed the unit, his face drawn.

"Alex, how much danger are they in?"

His hands stilled and he glanced up without moving his head. "Impossible to say. That passage is long enough that if they weren't paying close attention to their air, they could run out on the way back."

"There was that air pocket with the tree roots."

"If Zach remembers. He's had plenty of drills about emergencies, but the real thing is rather different."

"You don't need to convince me of that." The vision of her rushing into the ocean to rescue Peg flashed into her mind. Hope crossed the room and placed a hand on his chest. "You be safe, too."

"I always try."

As soon as Hope took over front desk duties, she scanned the arriving guest roster, running her index finger down the page. They had a busy afternoon of arrivals. She paused when she saw the names Derek and Megan Riley. They sounded familiar, but she couldn't place their faces.

If they've been here, I'll remember when I see them.

Several flights landed in the afternoon, so she was busy with check-ins right away, which helped distract her from the situation at the grotto. One bungalow wasn't ready yet, and the arriving guests weren't happy about it. Hope sent them to the pool bar for a free drink, her stress level rising.

When Derek and Megan walked into the lobby, Hope recognized them immediately, and also realized why she hadn't quite put the pieces together when she'd seen their last name. Megan still had blonde hair, though it was shorter, just past her shoulders. Derek was still handsome, with neat brown hair. Their eyes were immediately drawn to the glass dolphin sculpture. Then Megan gasped at Hope and Alex's wedding picture hanging on the wall. Many guests were drawn to it.

Hope gave them a moment to enjoy the photo and the two articles below. Soon Megan turned around, a smile gracing her face. Her eyes bulged at seeing Hope and she screeched. "You and Alex got *married?*"

Hope burst into laughter, some of her tension dissipating. "Yes, two years ago. We're not the only ones, though, are we? Last time, I distinctly remember you two arrived alone and left together."

Derek slipped an arm over Megan's shoulders. "We were married about a year and a half ago."

"Congratulations."

"Same to you!" Megan still had a gigantic smile pasted to her face. "You have no idea how much we wondered about you and Alex! And why you weren't together."

Hope shrugged. "It took us a while to admit our feelings."

"Alex was a Navy SEAL?" Derek asked, tipping his head to Alex's article. "He didn't say anything about that last time. I'm sure I would have remembered."

"He was, but it's not something he brings up in day-to-day conversation. I take it you're checking in?"

"Yes," Megan said, then smoothed her hands over her protruding abdomen. "We're here on our babymoon. Baby Boy Riley will be arriving in four months."

Hope burst into a smile as she turned to her monitor. "Congratulations again! Let's see what we can do here."

"Since I'm pregnant, Derek will be diving without me," Megan said. "But I spent hours drooling over Aqua on the website, so I'll have plenty to keep me occupied."

"I can't believe how this place has changed," Derek said.

"We've been busy," Hope replied, tapping on her keyboard. "Hmmm, you booked one of our new Rainforest Bungalows, but we have one Beach Bungalow open for the days you're here. I'd be happy to upgrade you."

"That would be perfect! Thank you so much." Megan said. "There weren't any available when we booked."

"It helps to know the owner," Hope said with a wink, and handed them their key cards. "You're in Orchid Bungalow, which is also nearest to the spa. It sounds like the perfect room for you. The beach bungalows all have outdoor, Bali-style showers now, and they turned out pretty fantastic, if I do say so myself! Enjoy your stay."

Hope watched them exit the lobby, a smile remaining on her face. Catching up with returning guests was one of the best parts of her job. Then the next couple entered to check in, with a family just behind them.

Ok, back to work. Soon enough I'll be able to breathe a little...

Chapter Nineteen

ALEX FROWNED as he stepped onto the sandy beach at the grotto. A pile of discarded clothes and shoes lay inside the empty cart. The area was deserted. "I hate it when I'm right."

After pulling on his wetsuit which was still in the small cave with his other gear, he donned his rebreather and headed straight for the passage. The padlock hung on the closed gate but was unlocked. Alex added it to the pocket of his rebreather, then left the gate wide open behind him. He switched on his headlamp and moved down the tunnel, finning in long, sweeping strokes, wanting to get to the cavern as quickly as possible.

He spent the journey deciding how to confront Zach. He was mad as hell at his new divemaster. But laying into the kid would be counterproductive when they still had to get out of the cavern safely. A quiet, firm approach would be best.

As Alex left the tunnel, he turned off his headlamp and ascended to the surface near the shore. Soft voices drifted over to him, and a light female laugh. Unbuckling his rebreather, Alex softly deposited it on the rocky ground next to two fully assembled kits and discarded wetsuits. Gritting his teeth, Alex climbed up the slope.

Zach and Jasmine stood under the seam in the ceiling, both wearing swimsuits. They were locked in an embrace and trying to suck each other's faces off.

"Oh, you've got to be kidding me," Alex whispered.

A voice in his head gave a snarky laugh. Alex thought of the voice as his alter ego. It liked to tell him things he'd rather not hear, though it had saved his life while he'd been in the military. *"You shouldn't throw stones here, pal."*

Alex scowled. *Hope and I were completely different.*

The voice roared with laughter.

Shut up. I've got a job to do.

Apparently, the voice agreed. Though if Alex hadn't been in such a pissy mood, he would have appreciated the irony—and the humor—in the situation.

He stopped twenty feet away. The pair had no idea he was there. Zach's hand was on the front of Jasmine's stomach and edging upward. The last thing Alex wanted was for this situation to get any more embarrassing than it already was. He cleared this throat loudly.

The couple flew apart, Jasmine barking a short scream.

"Alex!" Zach called out, his eyes bugging. "What are you doing here?"

Alex let a cool smile rise. "Funny, I was about to ask you the same thing."

Jasmine wore a tiny floral bikini and scooted behind Zach, apparently shy now that Alex was there. Zach's face hardened, his shock fading. Was that a spark of anger in his eye? "I wanted to show Jasmine the cavern."

"Didn't look like the cavern was what you were exploring."

"So what?"

Alex walked across the plateau. "Look guys. I couldn't care

less if you want to screw like jackrabbits. As long as it's not deep within a cavern you've got no business being in."

"What do you mean we've got no business here?" Zach asked. "You said you were thinkin' about openin' the tunnel up for people to dive."

"Thinking about it! And I also said it would only be to highly qualified divers."

"I've been here, *and* I'm a divemaster."

"Jasmine, how many cavern dives have you done?" Alex asked in a quiet, even voice so he wouldn't alarm her.

She stepped out from behind Zach. "This is my first. It was kind of scary, but I did just fine."

Zach wrapped an arm around her shoulders. "She did. We're not hurtin' anyone or anythin' here. Why are you so mad?"

Alex breathed out a long exhale, grabbing his temper with both imaginary hands. "Because you have only been in this cavern one time, Zach. And Jasmine has exactly *zero* experience and shouldn't be in here without a qualified guide. And that means me. Sexy times are over, guys. We're heading back." Alex pointed at the dive computer on Jasmine's wrist. "How much air do you have?"

She peered at it. "It's too dim to see."

Alex shot an angry glare at Zach, who dropped his eyes.

Great, she doesn't even know how to operate the backlight.

But rather than correct Jasmine over something that wasn't her fault, Alex moved to her side and turned on his headlamp, revealing the number to all three of them. "1300 psi. Does that ring any alarm bells for you, Zach?" He whipped his head to the young man, deliberately shining his beam in his eyes.

Zach squinted and took a step back, but the alarm was clear on his face. "Oh, shit. I was going to check before we headed back."

Alex remained motionless and just stared at him.

"I've got over a third of a tank," Jasmine said. "That should be plenty, right?"

Zach flinched as he turned to her. "No, it's not. In a cave or cavern, you're supposed to turn around at 2000 psi, so you leave the overhead environment with 1000 psi in reserve."

Alex sighed, turning back to Jasmine, but softened his stance and his voice. "You don't have anywhere near enough air. You said you were nervous coming in here. Nerves make you breathe faster, using more air than if you were relaxed. I'll go back to the resort and get another tank. You two stay here. Congrats—you're getting your alone time after all."

Both stared at the ground, wearing matching guilty expressions. He was being a little hard on them but was too ticked off to care. "How much air do you have, Zach?"

He swallowed as he read his computer, but met Alex's eyes evenly. "1900 psi."

"And you really thought you were qualified to bring her in here?"

Zach sighed and squeezed his eyes shut. "Guess not. I'm sorry."

"I'll come back with two tanks."

"Thanks," Jasmine said. "My dive light was getting dim. Can you bring me a fresh one?"

Alex counted to five before replying, fighting to keep his voice calm. "You didn't bring backup lights, Zach? Into a *cavern?*"

"I forgot them."

After giving Zach a long, hard stare, Alex slid his eyes back to Jasmine, softening them. "I'll bring you a fresh light."

She stood with her arms crossed in front of her, then turned to frown at Zach. "Thanks, Alex."

"I'll be back within the hour. You two stay here. I mean it.

We only found one passage leading off this cave, and it petered out. If you do explore and find one, for God's sake, don't follow it!"

They both nodded.

As Alex turned away, Zach called out. "I'm sorry."

Alex stopped and looked over his shoulder. He nodded. "You might say the same thing to Jasmine."

As Alex buckled his rebreather and entered the water, Zach's imploring voice washed over the large room. He was glad he couldn't make out the words.

Once back on the shore, he deposited his kit and wetsuit in the cart and took it with him. Thoughts of the predicament kept him busy on the trek back to the resort. He was shocked at how many mistakes Zach had made.

I thought I trained him better than that.

During their course, both Zach and Hope had poked fun at how Alex harped on safety procedures and planning. He couldn't help it. That had been drilled into him for nearly twenty years—experiences where poor planning could be the difference between life and death. Even when things were planned to perfection, disaster could still happen.

Like Syria.

His thoughts of the class and Hope brought back her disappointment at his delaying her first dive as a divemaster. His group was a band of six college-age guys on a dive vacation. They were full of piss and vinegar, know-it-alls to a man. Alex knew exactly how to handle men like that—he'd done it for years. And he was getting along great with them. But he did *not* want some cocky, college age pissant hitting on his wife and making her uncomfortable. Hope could handle herself just fine, but leading a group for the first time was nerve-wracking enough without dealing with guys like that.

The present situation with Zach and Jasmine presented a

great opportunity to get her some experience, though. A smile rose on Alex's lips as he picked up his pace.

———

Hope smiled warmly at the florid, balding man in front of the check-in counter. "Don't worry. I'm sure the airline will drop off your bag shortly. I'll be here, and will call you the second it comes in."

He was sweating profusely and had been none too polite. But Hope had calmed him down. "Thanks. We had all kinds of delays and problems getting here. Losing our luggage was just the icing on the cake."

"But you made it, and that's what counts. Go have a beer by the pool and dig your toes in the sand. Your troubles will melt away."

"That is a fantastic idea. Consider it done." The man nodded and walked out the back entrance of the lobby.

Hope's smile plummeted off her face. Before the lost-luggage incident, she'd had to reassure a horrified guest that a gecko on the wall of their outdoor shower was normal, and the tiny lizard wasn't going to launch itself off the wall and attack.

In short, it had been a long afternoon.

Plus, Alex had been gone a while and she'd had no word from him.

Oh, stop worrying. Alex is Mr. Indestructible. He'll probably step into the lobby any minute now. Zach and Jasmine will be right behind him, suitably chastened.

Patti texted her that a massage therapist had gone home with a stomach bug.

Is it a full moon or something?

She was trying to hold on to a good mood, but it was slipping ever faster away.

The last of the guests had checked-in, and if not for the errant suitcase, she'd consider going home and leaving a phone number for guests to call if they needed her. Baking would help relax her. But she couldn't leave with missing luggage in limbo.

The sound of feet climbing the steps came to her and Hope snapped her head up as Alex walked into the lobby alone.

"You didn't find them?"

He stopped in front of the desk, wiping his face with both hands. "Oh, I found them all right. Exactly where I thought they'd be."

He recounted discovering them in a rather compromising position, and they shared a quick laugh. But Hope felt her eyes becoming bigger and bigger as he recounted Jasmine's nervousness, then her lack of air and lack of light for the return journey.

"I left them in the cavern with strict instructions to stay put. I'm on my way to the pier to get fresh tanks and lights." Then he gave her a crooked smile. "I've got an offer for you though. You said you wanted more responsibility. Why don't you come with me? Get someone else to cover the lobby."

"There isn't anyone else, Alex. Patti's at the spa. Corrine and Martine are both off."

His smile faded. "Can't you just leave Patti's phone number here?"

Frustration mounted, a hot whirling ball in her stomach. "I'm expecting a piece of lost luggage to show up at any time. I can't go. It's been chaos all afternoon."

"Is everyone checked in?"

"Yes."

"Then call the guest with the lost luggage to check the lobby in an hour."

"Dammit, Alex. I can't go!"

He braced his hands on his hips. "Hope, you wanted me to give you credit for the skills you've learned. That's what I'm trying to do here. You're telling me there's *no one* in the whole resort who can cover the front desk?"

"No, there isn't! I appreciate the offer, but I've got problems to deal with here too. We're stretched really thin. You do your job and let me do mine. All right?"

He didn't reply, just stared at her steadily.

Hope held on to her temper. "Just get Zach and Jasmine back!"

He shrugged and waved a hand as he turned away. "Ok, I'll go. Alone. Hopefully, we won't be too long."

She was opening her mouth to tell him she loved him when the phone rang, distracting her. Frowning, she looked at the display. The call was from a bungalow that'd had a plumbing issue earlier. Groaning, she picked up the receiver.

Hope flicked her eyes to the lobby doorway one last time. Alex was already gone.

THE MID-AFTERNOON SUN cast golden sparkles on the cobalt water of Half Moon Grotto, but Alex was beyond enjoying the peaceful scene. After he'd left Hope in the lobby, he'd taken the cart to the gear room and loaded up with everything he thought he might need. Then he'd quickly pushed it back to the rock pool.

He shifted his stance, getting used to the extra weight. In addition to the rebreather attached to his back, a full-sized scuba tank was attached to each of his sides. The combined rig was heavy and cumbersome, adding an additional hundred-plus pounds to his body weight. He couldn't wait to get into the water. The extra tanks would still be bulky, but at least the water would support their weight.

He clipped two additional dive lights to his rebreather, in

case Zach needed one too. Alex's own spare was zipped inside a pocket. His irritation and anger at Zach had faded, and now he just wanted the young couple safely out of the cavern and tunnel.

Gathering his fins and clipping his dive slate on the right side of his vest, Alex did a final check. A long sigh escaped, guilt over how snappish he'd been with Hope. The strain from the afternoon had been obvious on her face, and he hadn't helped.

"I'll apologize to her when I get back with Zach and Jasmine."

Focusing on the current mission, Alex trudged into the water, immediately feeling the difference of carrying two additional tanks. He traveled slowly as he swam into the tunnel, making sure he was properly buoyant in the narrow confines. The channel was wide enough that the tanks at his sides didn't scrape. But the story might be different after passing the ridged ceiling. The S-curve section at the end was narrower, particularly in one place.

Alex passed under the tree roots with hardly a glance, intent on reaching the cavern. He'd have to watch Jasmine closely on the return trip. If she had been nervous on the inward journey, the knowledge that she shouldn't be there would only increase her anxiety. She needed to be in the middle, with him leading and Zach in the back. A panicky diver in a cave environment nearly always went for the diver in front of them for help, so Alex would reassure her as often as possible.

His ears popped, which was strange.

The tunnel was flat here, without any depth fluctuations to change the pressure.

Must be residual from my descent.

The strange, ridged ceiling was ahead. It was an unusual formation, which had made Alex cautious from the start. He didn't like things he didn't understand.

After a few more kicks, a grinding, groaning roar sounded all around him.

The water around him shivered, and his body shook in the water, moving with it.

Confused, Alex stopped and looked around him.

The roaring amplified a hundred-fold and the floor of the tunnel jolted beneath him, throwing him violently upward. His rebreather slammed into the ceiling, and he rebounded off.

Oh shit! I'm in a goddamn earthquake!

Alex exploded into motion, finning as fast as he could. He was closer to the cavern than the grotto pool at this point. Rocks rained down around him, the water becoming cloudy as it roiled. He studied the ridged ceiling as he swam beneath.

It was *moving.*

The ridges shifted and slid against each other, rocks breaking apart. One tumbled down and banged off the tank on his right side, joining multitudes of others on the ground now.

Go, go, go!

The falling rocks became a steady rain. Most were small, but several large sections of ridge broke off and fell. Wrapping his arms around his head, Alex surged forward. The last place on earth he wanted to be during an earthquake was underneath a moving ceiling.

Underwater.

The tunnel heaved again. Alex was thrown sideways, and a scuba tank collided hard with the wall of the tunnel. The clang could hardly be heard over the all-encompassing roar, getting louder every second. The rock around him shrieked and bellowed as it ground against itself.

A few yards later, Alex was thrown against the left wall. Now he was grateful for the two tanks absorbing the impact instead of his body.

He moved his arms away from his face and glanced up. He

was nearly at the end of the ridged section, but it shifted and moved violently. A large section of rock fell on his right, barely missing him. He covered his head again and finned as hard as he could, bouncing off the walls like a pinball.

The bellowing thunder increased to that of a great beast, chasing him from behind.

Come on, come on—I'm almost past this part. Hurry!

The beast grew even louder, roaring and shrieking behind him.

Just ahead, the ridges ended, and the ceiling was intact. His heart hammering, Alex kicked even harder.

The deafening monster overtook him.

A great weight pinned his legs behind him. Then it buried his hips, trapping him at the bottom of the tunnel.

A bolt of white-hot agony exploded in his right lower leg.

Chapter Twenty

HOPE SMILED WARMLY at the man as she pushed his suitcase from behind the desk. Cruz snoozed behind her, and she had to make sure not to roll over any toes.

"I am so glad to see this!" the man said. "Thank you so much."

"The airline got it here pretty fast. Is your bungalow ok?"

He stopped to grin at her. "Ok? It's incredible!"

"That's what I like to hear. Enjoy your evening."

As the man left, her gaze returned to the lobby front entrance, and her shoulders fell.

Alex goes out of his way to include me, and I bite his head off. Nice, Hope.

"I'll apologize to him when he gets back with Zach and Jasmine."

With all the arrivals and departures done for the day, the rest of her afternoon should be a breeze. She brought up her email, finally having time to face her inbox. After that, it was home and baking.

Behind her, Cruz leaped to his feet and barked loudly, nonstop.

Hope whirled to him, frowning. He was a quiet dog, rarely making any noise.

"Cruz, hush!"

She was alone in the lobby, so at least no one could hear him.

His yellow rough was raised, and he stared straight at her as he barked.

Concerned now, Hope was bending down to console him when the earth jolted beneath her. With a startled cry, she fell to the ground behind the desk, curling into a ball as a great roaring enveloped her.

Cruz's barks turned to yelps as he dove next to her. Hope placed one arm around him and the other over her head as she scurried back against the check-in desk.

The floor shuddered and moved violently sideways. The keyboard fell off the counter and hit her on the side. Loud crashes sounded all throughout the lobby as items fell over, the sound of shattering glass competing with the earth's groaning.

Hope clenched her eyes shut, her heart nearly pounding out of her chest. Cruz whimpered and buried his head in her neck. She held him tighter, glad to have something to focus on as the formerly solid earth shuddered under her. The ground shook, it juddered, and once in a while, it moved in a long, terrifying roll.

After what felt like hours, but was likely less than a minute, the shaking abated. Crashing still sounded in the lobby as the quake stopped. Hope shivered on the tile floor, her hands shaking as she petted the trembling dog, trying to console him.

Something fell over with one final crash, which made both her and Cruz yelp. Then the grinding noise faded completely. The only sound was distant car alarms coming from the parking lot.

The scent of fresh soil filled Hope's nose, and she opened her eyes. A large potted plant lay tipped over in front of her, black potting soil spilled over the floor. Rolling onto her hands and knees, her right knee landed in something wet. She glanced down at the yellow puddle next to Cruz, who still shook on the ground.

Hope patted him on the head, and he licked her face. "That's ok, sweetie. I'm surprised I didn't pee myself too."

Slowly, she raised herself to her feet. The lobby was in a shambles and the lights were out. The television behind her still hung on the wall but had no power. Couches were knocked over and the five-gallon glass jug of infused water had fallen off the table and shattered on the floor.

Again.

An errant thought about replacing it with a plastic one next time ran through her head and she barked out a shaky laugh. But as she inspected the lobby more closely, she was surprised to see most of the floor tiles intact. The only visible damage to the walls was cracked drywall.

The front-desk phone rang, the double tone indicating an inside line. With shaking hands, Hope picked it up. "H-h-hello?"

"Hope!" Patti shouted. "Are you all right, child?"

"Yes. The lobby doesn't look real great, but it's standing. What about you? Is everyone ok at Aqua?"

"Yes. Maybe it's because the buildin' is so new, but other than stuff gettin' knocked over, there's very little damage. Just water splashed everywhere. We shut the water off."

Cruz climbed onto her feet, his tail tucked between his legs. "That quake was much worse than the others!"

"Jesus, Mary, and Joseph! Oh, here's Heather now. She looks fine."

"Thank God." Hope swept her gaze around the room again. Many of the framed staff photos had fallen off the wall and broken.

Including the large glass photo of her and Alex on their wedding day.

A large crack had broken the picture in half, separating her and Alex. Her blood turned to ice in her veins. She raised a hand to her mouth, retching.

"Hope!" Patti cried. "Are you all right?"

Hope stared at the broken picture, horrified shock sweeping over her body. "Alex!"

"What about him? The boat is back already. I just looked out there and the pier is ok."

"Alex isn't at the pier." She couldn't go on.

"Hope, where is he?"

When she tried to speak, her voice cracked. She cleared her throat and tried again. "Zach and Jasmine dove a submerged passage in the grotto, and they don't have enough air to get out. Alex found out and went to rescue them. Patti, he's in a big cavern! So are Zach and Jasmine!"

The thought of them being trapped in that narrow passage during the earthquake was too terrible to contemplate. She refused to consider it.

"Oh, Lord have mercy."

"Patti, I have to go check on them! Can you come up to the lobby?" Several guests shuffled into the room, including Derek and Megan. All wore scared, stunned expressions. Hope turned toward the wall and lowered her voice. "Please hurry. We need to reassure guests and check for damage. Patti, I have to make sure Alex is all right!"

"I'm on my way, child. I'm sure Alex is fine. Just wait until I get there."

Hope hung up, drawing solace from Patti's words. Pulling herself together, she turned to the guests. "Is everyone all right? How damaged are your bungalows?"

Several windows were broken and a wall surrounding an

outdoor shower had crumbled. She took a deep breath, forcibly quieting her panic.

This is Alex I'm talking about. Few people are better able to handle emergencies. Or have the skills to deal with them. They're all right.

By the time Patti arrived with Selena alongside, Hope had determined no one had been seriously injured. The guest with the delayed luggage had fallen and received a livid bruise on his arm, but other injuries were minor.

Another guest had a broken water pipe in the bathroom. "That's why we headed here," the woman said, holding tight to the man beside her. "We didn't know how to shut off the water."

Patti turned to Selena. "Can you go with her and shut the water off?"

Selena nodded. "I know where the valve is." Beckoning to the couple, she exited the lobby. The couple followed, staring at the ceiling as if it might fall at any moment.

"All right," Patti called to the remaining crowd. "We need to make sure everyone is ok, and we'd sure appreciate anyone who can lend a hand. We need to check out all the rooms, the kitchen and bar, as well as the dive shop."

Derek stepped forward. "Megan and I would like to help."

"Thank you," Hope said, panic slithering through her gut.

Patti squeezed Hope's shoulder, speaking quietly. "I've got this under control. You head to the grotto. They're probably on their way back here now. I bet you'll meet them on the way."

God, I hope so.

Hope swallowed the huge lump in her throat, embracing Patti. "Thank you. I'll be back as soon as I can."

Hope rushed out of the lobby, avoiding looking at the wall of shattered photos. Especially the big one. Cruz ran at her side. She leaped over the stairs in a single bound, tearing across the sand parking lot and desperate to get to the rock pool as soon as possible.

Then Alex's steady words reverberated in her head, cautioning her, and she skidded to a stop.

Squeezing her eyes shut, she took a deep breath.

I can't make the same mistake as the swimming rescue. I know better.

Hope reopened her eyes, Alex's face in her mind clear as he explained what she should have done in the water rescue. She knew what to do. "Stop. Think. Don't rush off to the grotto half-cocked. What if I need to dive? There are extra tanks there, but I brought my BCD and reg back here."

Calmer, and with new resolve, she turned around and headed toward the pier.

The wooden structure was mostly undamaged, except for boards which had been shaken loose. Some hung askew and others were missing altogether, presumably in the turgid water below. Hope unlocked the door to the gear room and gaped. The neatly organized room was in chaos. Wetsuits, BCDs, regulators, and fins were strewn everywhere.

She took a deep breath. "That doesn't matter. Focus." She tiptoed through the mounds of equipment until she located her BCD and regulator. A pony bottle lay nearby, and she grabbed that too. *If I'll be diving alone, I'll need a separate spare air source.* She slipped her arms into the BCD—it would be easier to just wear it.

Hope set off down the path at a steady trot, Cruz at her heels. When she reached the highway, she stopped in the middle of the asphalt, turning in a slow circle. Two large trees lay across the road, and several more lay in the distance, both north and south. "Looks like everyone's staying at the resort until they can get the road cleared." The trees weren't massive, but she couldn't imagine road crews being able to clear them before the following day.

Crossing the rest of the highway, she continued on the path. It was littered with branches and leaves, and she and Cruz had to vault over several fallen trees. They had just cleared one when Cruz pressed close to her leg, whining. As the leaves began shivering, Hope staggered. "Another one!" She dropped and covered her head, Cruz burrowing into her side.

But the aftershock was barely strong enough to rattle the trees, lasting only seconds. "Ok, that's reassuring. Hopefully the worst is over. Let's go, boy."

The chain-link gate hung wide open, and Hope hurried through it, her heart twisting that she hadn't met up with Alex coming back. She picked up her pace, breaking into a run.

Within minutes, she skidded to a stop on the beach of the grotto. In front of her, the cart lay tipped over, a jumble of clothing spilling over the sand. Alex's T-shirt lay on top. Breathing hard from her exertion, Hope moved her gaze over the area.

It was empty.

The only sounds were a chorus of singing birds, much louder than normal. As if they were reassuring each other of having survived the earthquake. Hope studied the blue water, the same color, but now hazy. She swallowed thickly, staring at the far end of the pool.

They're still in there. Something's wrong—I need to go after them.

Chapter Twenty-One

HOPE SET up her scuba kit, moving quickly and efficiently. Then she retrieved her thicker, 5mm wetsuit from the small cave, noting that Alex's equipment was gone, further confirming her worries that he, Zach, and Jasmine were still inside the cavern. Or worse—the tunnel. She pulled on the wetsuit and donned all her other gear, including the pony bottle. When she was ready, she took a moment to sit on a flat boulder, closing her eyes and breathing deeply.

Alex's voice continued speaking inside her head, advising her.

Hope opened her eyes, staring across the grotto and running through her plan. *I'll dive through the passage and into the cavern to make sure they're ok. Then we'll plan from there.*

She stood and waded into the cool water. Upon descending, the pool was noticeably murkier. The gate to the passage hung ajar, one hinge broken. Hope swallowed hard, breathing out a long line of bubbles and willing her anxiety to leave with them.

Turning on her headlamp, she entered the dark tunnel.

Though she itched to race through the claustrophobic passage, she moved in a slow, deliberate manner, using broad frog kicks. The water was thick with sediment, though she could still see. The floor of the tunnel was littered with rocks, both small and large.

Her mind presented her with a detailed image of what might happen if another earthquake occurred, but she pushed back hard, refusing to consider the idea. *If it happens, it happens. I'm moving forward no matter what.*

When she reached the area with the tree roots, it took her a moment to figure out why it looked different. Instead of barely reaching beneath the surface, now the roots hung a foot into the water.

The earthquake had lowered the ceiling above them.

An oily wave of nausea slithered through Hope's gut, nerves clawing their way up again, but she continued.

Past the tree root section, the visibility noticeably worsened. Now large shards of rock joined the pebbles lining the ground. Hope's heart pounded harder, and she couldn't deny the heavy, thick fear enveloping her.

Not just fear for herself, but fear of what might lie ahead.

Her answer came ten yards after the passage made a turn to the left. The shards and small boulders rose in a slope toward the ceiling of the cave. This was the section that had contained the ridged ceiling.

But no more.

The ridges had collapsed, leaving an impenetrable rock mountain.

Forcing herself to take long, slow breaths to quell her racing heart, Hope rose to the ceiling. Trying to find a way through. The cave-in had resulted in a variety of rock sizes and shapes. She tugged on several experimentally. Several came free, rolling down the hill to the base. But larger rocks lay behind. Stacked drunkenly together, there were no large openings.

There was no way through.

Tears filled her eyes and she tried to blink them back, to no avail.

They're trapped in that cavern! Are they ok? Has the cavern collapsed?

Then a thought just as terrifying...

I've got no way to contact them!

With a grunt, Hope set her face in determination and returned to the top margin of the cave-in. She inspected every inch, from the right side of the tunnel, over the top, and down the left side. But every time she dislodged a rock, more lay behind it.

She slammed her fist into the cool surface, relishing the pain.

"No!" Her voice was muffled through the regulator, the mouthpiece slurring the word.

Hope closed her eyes, once more centering herself.

Think. Assess. Solve the problem.

In the calm center of her mind, the answer came. She *could* communicate with them. She knew the way.

Spinning around, Hope swam for the exit, now moving quickly since she had assessed the condition of the passage. She turned her headlamp off as soon as she exited the tunnel, rising to the surface as she swam hard for the shore.

She slipped off her tank, dumping it on the sand and pulled off her wetsuit. Redressing in her shorts and staff shirt, she slipped back into her sneakers and sprinted for the chain-link gate. Cruz ran at her side, now back to his usual quiet, yet alert, self. Careening around the open gate, she took off at top speed around the perimeter of the fence.

The animal track on the other side looked the same as last time. She bolted down it, then skidded to a stop when she reached the rocky plateau near Barnaby's house. She darted her eyes around the darkening, stony clearing—the sun was nearing the horizon.

"Where is it?"

Breathing hard, Hope scanned the black rock as she stepped onto the hard surface, now strewn with tree branches and leaves. Cruz stayed at her heels, sniffing the rock and weeds instead of investigating on his own. A narrow, darker section of black steadied in her vision and she hurried toward the long tear in the rock.

She kneeled next to the seam. It was only a few inches wide, but it had to be the same one she and Alex had discovered on their first exploration. Cupping her hands around her mouth, she leaned over the hole. "Alex! Hello! Zach? Jasmine? Can anyone hear me?"

A scurrying noise drifted to her, followed by murmuring voices. "Is someone up there?" Hope almost wept at Zach's voice.

"Yes! I'm by the big seam in the ceiling."

Zach appeared in the slash of natural light illuminating the cavern floor. Jasmine stopped next to him, dressed in a wetsuit, and rubbing one arm with the other. Enough light shined through the seam to see her frightened face.

"Hope?" Zach asked. "Is that you?"

"Yes!" she answered, part sob. "You're unhurt?"

"Yeah. That earthquake scared the hell out of us though. We're ready to get out of here."

"I'm ready for you to get out of there too." Smiling, a happy tear slipped from her eye. "Let me talk to Alex and see what his plan is."

Even from thirty feet above, the confusion across Zach's face was clear. "What do you mean?"

Hope's smile turned into a frozen rictus. "Where's Alex, Zach?"

"He's not here. He went back to the resort to get more tanks."

"I know—I already talked to him. He came back!" The mountain of rock blocking the tunnel appeared in her mind.

Oh God! Please no!

"Zach, the tunnel caved in! It's completely blocked off from the grotto side. I tried to dive it just now but couldn't get through." She paused to calm her breath, stopping the panicky escalation of her voice. "Alex could be trapped in that cave-in. You've got to find him!"

Zach's mouth had dropped open at her explanation. Now it slammed shut, his jaw becoming firm. "I'll go right now. Wait there, Hope."

Jasmine turned, propping both hands on her hips as she stared at her boyfriend. "I'm comin' too."

Zach shook his head before Hope could say anything. "No. I'm doin' this alone. I've already put you in too much danger, Jas." He reached out and grasped her hand. "Please."

She stared at him for a long moment before nodding. "All right. But be careful."

"I will." He tilted his head up to Hope, the last of the day's light illuminating it. "I'll find him, Hope."

She nodded, her head thick and heavy. "Please..."

The word was little more than a whisper. Hope rolled up to sit on her knees, tears pouring down her face. Tears of dread, along with the deepest fear she'd ever known. Wrapping both arms around her torso, she couldn't stop the thought from running through her mind. Over and over like a loop.

What if Alex is buried under that mountain of rock?
What then?

Chapter Twenty-Two

AFTER THE GROUND finally stopped shaking, Alex blocked everything out, solely focused on decreasing his raging heart rate and slowing his frantic breathing. His right lower leg throbbed like a red-hot branding iron, but he ignored that too.

Control the situation. Nothing else matters right now. Slow breathing... in and out.

The tunnel around him still groaned occasionally, and pebbles rolled down the walls. Alex's training kicked in—his ability to compartmentalize and prioritize tasks to determine what needed his attention first.

What are my assets?

Not his legs—at the moment, they were a liability. Asset number one was his rebreather. His lifeline. He had fallen with his arms stretched out in front and could move both freely. He hadn't tried to move anything else yet.

Air first.

Alex opened his eyes, forcing himself to inhale deeply and slowly. His headlamp still worked—the water was cloudy and turgid. He brought his left wrist in front of his mask. The rebreather display was attached like a large watch to his wrist.

He quickly scrolled through different systems, immensely relieved all were working as designed. He had hours of air remaining.

Ok. Air supply confirmed. Move on to the second priority.

He slipped his elbows under his shoulders and pressed upward in a push-up. His shoulders moved unencumbered. Next, he tried to lift his butt, and immediately encountered resistance. He felt and heard the rocks shifting as he pressed against them. The slightest movement caused his right lower leg to scream—making him clench his eyes shut and focus on his breathing.

Ok, just need to peel these rocks off one by one. Slow and steady.

Alex rolled onto his right elbow, freezing immediately due to the pain. He held the same position until his injured leg adjusted to the new angle, the throbbing diminishing slightly. Craning his head around, he checked out how bad the situation was.

A large pile of rocks sloped up behind him, becoming a solid mass at the top. There was no indication of where the cave-in started and where the tunnel ceiling stopped. They had become one. His eyes followed the slope back down. The rocks thinned out at his upper legs and hips, leaving his torso completely free.

He had barely escaped being wholly buried alive.

Alex smiled grimly. *That's the good news? Oh great. I'm only partially buried alive.*

The voice in his head spoke up again. The same one that had found the situation with Zach and Jasmine so hilarious. There was no trace of levity now. "*Stop feeling sorry for yourself. That won't help. Find a way out—you've got plenty of air. So think. Do your damn job.*"

Alex lifted his left hand and pushed a large rock off his hip. It tumbled to the side of the tunnel, raising a small cloud of sediment. Encouraged, he pushed more off, bracing his jaw as every movement jarred his injured limb. After a rest to get his heart rate and pain under control again, he studied the rocks covering his legs.

He'd landed with his legs splayed, and by bending around—and with more accompanying shrieks from his damaged right limb—he was able to remove the rocks trapping his left leg. One by one.

At last, he pulled his undamaged leg free of the pile. Removing his fin, his left foot was now free to maneuver. He flopped down on his side, panting, and took a moment to rest. Sweat dripped down his face inside his mask.

Small rocks tumbled down the slope and he whipped his head up. The earth groaned around him once more. A subtle wave rippled over the floor. Alex covered his head with both arms, bracing for impact, screaming as the trembling shifted rocks and wrenched his leg. But the aftershock was minimal, and the ground quieted quickly.

He wiggled his two free hands and one foot. The voice spoke up again. *"All right. You've got three out of four limbs free. Progress. But the job's not done yet. Quit sightseeing, dammit."*

Alex uncovered his head. Clenching his teeth together, he shimmied up into a half-sitting position, bracing himself by bending his left knee. He blinked away the stinging sweat in his eyes. Any movement of his right leg was agony.

Yeah, that's broken for sure.

He studied his trapped appendage. His neoprene-encased leg disappeared into the rockpile just above the knee. He hissed as he moved the knee experimentally, ignoring the pain. His knee moved within the pile—his leg was pinned lower down.

Breathing like a freight train again, Alex closed his eyes, concentrating on a deep in and out, feeling his wetsuit expand and contract with each breath.

The pain faded once more.

Opening his eyes again, Alex continued carefully pushing rocks off his injured leg, taking care to move them sideways so none rolled straight toward him. An eternity later, he stared at a large, irregularly shaped black rock lying on his right lower leg. It was flat on top, and he could get his fist next to his trapped knee, so the underside must be pinning him in place where he couldn't see it.

Placing both palms under the rock, he lifted. It didn't budge, so he rested and tried again, his arms and shoulders trembling with the effort. His position didn't give him enough leverage. Taking a deep breath, he gripped the rock with both hands and lifted. Alex heaved until his shoulders screamed. The rock shifted, but it wouldn't move enough for him to pull his leg out. He relaxed, decreasing his breath and fighting for control. Then he tried yet again, lifting with everything he was worth, feeling like his shoulders were tearing. No movement.

Goddammit!

Alex let go and flopped onto his right hip, a frustrated scream escaping as his leg turned into a red-hot poker again.

The voice spoke again. *"Ok, that's not going to work. What's Plan B?"*

Alex ran over the problem in his head, searching for solutions. He only came up with one. And it was the absolute last resort. His right lower leg was a solid mass of pain. He couldn't move his toes without agony.

At least I think my toes are still there.

Alex raised his hand, running his fingers down the folded dive knife attached to the shoulder strap of his rebreather. Plan B...

Is this even a solution?

The six-inch blade was razor-sharp. He had no doubt it would do the job.

Could I really go through with it, though? And even if I could, what would I use as a tourniquet?

Alex closed his eyes and crossed both arms over his forehead. He wasn't ready to contemplate cutting his own leg off just yet.

Time grew malleable. He had no idea how long he'd been trapped. Not days, but surely hours. He returned to the rock—trying to lift it to no avail. He used his knife as additional leverage, placing it under the edge of the rock to wedge it upward and off his leg. But he stopped, afraid of snapping the blade.

What if I need it later?

Alex lay back down, setting the knife at his right side. The stone floor was cool, leaching his body heat through the neoprene. The water was still full of rock dust and particles, but clearer than before.

He wasn't giving up. That wasn't an option.

But his fingers kept returning to the knife. Stroking it.

The voice spoke more quietly this time. "*Not yet—you don't have a tourniquet. Don't think about that until there's no other option.*"

Angry frustration welled up within him and he pounded his fist on the rock ground. Then Hope's beautiful face flashed in his mind, and he stilled his hand. Calm strength rolled over him and he took a deep breath, exhaling the negative, useless energy as he stared at the rock.

A light bounced across the ceiling above his head.

Great. Now I'm seeing things.

The beam reappeared, holding steady this time. Alex's pulse raced and he twisted onto his right elbow to look down the open tunnel. A diver finned toward him, the headlamp a shining beacon of hope.

It was Zach.

His eyes were huge behind his mask as he darted them over

the mass of rock blocking the tunnel and pinning Alex. Fumbling with his hand, Alex unclipped the magnetic slate attached to the shoulder strap of his kit. It still worked, and he wrote on it and flipped it around to Zach.

My right leg is trapped under that flat rock. Between the two of us, we can lift it so I can get loose.

Zach nodded and swam above Alex toward the rock pile. Alex squeezed Zach's leg and wrote:

Take your fins off. You can maneuver better.

The young man removed both fins and placed them at the side of the tunnel. Then he approached the rock pile and positioned himself above it. He wedged his back against the side of the tunnel, spreading his legs and placing his feet carefully. The rockpile held steady.

Alex sat up and, with one hand, counted down from three to one, nodding excessively with each numeral. Zach nodded again, understanding. Alex threw out a silent prayer of gratitude that they had spent so much time together, and Zach understood Alex's nonverbal instructions so well.

Zach took his time forming his grip on the slab, then looked at Alex. The former SEAL gripped the leading edge of the rock and locked eyes with the young man. He repeated the exaggerated nods.

Three... Two... ONE!

Simultaneously, they lifted together. Alex shouted as he lifted with every muscle in his upper body. As the great pressure pinning his leg suddenly released, the limb howled with even greater ferocity. As his leg came free, Alex launched himself backward. The movement caused his limb to bounce against the rock, making him scream louder.

The pain was unrelenting.

He scrambled three feet backward and flopped onto his back. As he inhaled, water entered his mouth around the regulator. He coughed and sputtered, trying not to choke. Throwing both arms across his face, he breathed in wailing gasps, repeating a mantra in his head as he pictured a white sphere gently spinning in a void.

Don't hyperventilate. Don't choke. Master the pain.

That wasn't the voice. It was all him—he was under control.

Alex's breathing slowed, and the pain in his leg diminished to a steady, white-hot throbbing. Removing his arms from his face, he pressed both hands against the cool scuba tanks on both sides, grounding himself. His closed eyes stung from the sweat running down his face. He ripped his mask down, letting the cool water of the cave bathe his face and wash the sweat away. It relaxed him. Finally, replacing the mask and clearing it, he opened his eyes.

Zach kneeled at Alex's side, bursts of bubbles flying from his regulator and fists bunched on his thighs. His eyes had been large before, but now they were enormous. Alex smiled tiredly and gave him an ok signal. Relief transformed the young man's face, and the surge of bubbles decreased.

Alex shuffled onto his elbows to check the damage and was surprised to see his right leg and foot fully intact, though half his fin was missing. Freeing himself had hurt so badly, he'd wondered if his leg had been severed after all. But both legs lay fully attached to him, covered by his wetsuit and neoprene booties.

Thank God.

Both legs looked remarkably normal, and Alex was greatly relieved not to see any jagged white bone sticking out of the right one.

Or any blood clouding the water.

He glanced around the area until he found where his slate had ended up, then wrote:

Let's head to the cavern. I need your help. I don't think I can put weight on my right leg.

Zach's Adam's apple moved as he swallowed hard, but he nodded and replaced his fins. Alex found his knife and smiled grimly as he reattached it. He slipped his left foot into his fin, leaving the right alone. Adding air to his flotation system, he rose off the ground. He rolled onto his stomach and linked arms with Zach on his left. Alex gave one slow, careful sweep with his left fin, pleasantly surprised when the movement didn't hurt his right leg any further.

With a nod at Zach, Alex pointed ahead. The two men swam down the tunnel, carefully negotiating the S-curves. Alex maneuvered himself around the protruding rock that caused a narrowing, then they linked back up.

The two divers exited the tunnel, emerging into the cavern. Alex surfaced, pulled his mask down, and removed his regulator. He took a deep breath of fresh air. The chalky air entering his nose was one of the most incredible sensations he'd ever experienced. Even though they weren't out of the woods by a long shot, at least he wasn't trapped underwater anymore.

Alex wrapped Zach in a hug, making sure not to move his right leg. "Thank you. I've been trapped under that rock since the quake. I couldn't get free."

Zach pulled back and tugged his mask down. "You're welcome. Is your leg broken?" He rushed through the words, his voice cracking on the last one.

"I'm not sure, but probably. Were you checking to see if the tunnel was clear?"

Zach's face slackened. "No. Hope is up top. She told us about the cave-in and wanted me to see if you were trapped in the tunnel."

Oh my God, baby. You just saved my life.

A desperate yearning rose within Alex. He had to see her. Immediately. "Where is she?"

"Up top. There's a big open seam and she communicated through that."

A tiny smile moved one side of Alex's mouth. "Let's go. I'll need to use you as a crutch."

After they exited the water, Zach removed the extra tanks Alex carried, leaving them near the shore. Then he helped Alex to the ground. The former SEAL removed the broken fin from his right foot as carefully as possible, but the maneuver still left him heaving and sweating. Removing the rest of his gear was a much easier process. Both men kept their wetsuits on. Zach helped him up, and Alex threw his arm over the young man's shoulders. Together, they hobbled over to the seam, where Jasmine stood in a fading strip of light.

Her eyes lit up at the sight of Alex and she tipped her head back. "Zach found him! Alex is here!"

Alex made sure to put no weight on his right foot, and Jasmine moved out of the way, her face falling into a frown as she watched Alex more closely.

Heart pounding with anticipation this time, Alex looked up. His dark-adjusted eyes squinted at the light, dim as it was. All he could see was the silhouette of a head. But he'd know that voice anywhere.

"Alex! Are you ok?" Hope's voice was tinged with panic, and he tried to make his answering smile reassuring.

"A lot better than I was a little while ago."

"What's wrong? Why can't you walk?"

"I've got a twisted ankle, but it's not too serious." He squeezed Zach's shoulder hard, warning him to keep quiet.

Now there was a sob in her voice. "I'm so glad to see you standing there! What happened?"

"Me too, baby." He swallowed, not wanting to worry her or

cause any additional stress for her. "I got knocked around a little. How bad is the damage from the quake?"

"Some damage to the resort, but nothing catastrophic that we've seen so far. There are a lot of trees down. Several are covering the highway."

That caused a ripple of unease to run through Alex's belly, but he ignored it. "Are the phones working?"

"Patti was able to get through to me on an inside line. I'm not sure about cell signals. My phone is back at the front desk— I'll run and try to call the police." The silhouette of her head moved as she glanced around. "It's getting dark now. This fissure is narrow, but I should be able to toss some clothing and blankets down, maybe some protein bars or something."

"Sounds good," Alex said.

"I'll be back as soon as I can. Hang tight—all three of you!"

The shadowy head withdrew, and Hope was gone, leaving a hollowness inside him. With a sigh, Alex looked around the flat shelf of rock they stood on. "Well, this has been a hell of a day, hasn't it?"

Chapter Twenty-Three

HOPE STOOD from the seam and hurried down the path toward the resort. Cruz trotted at her heels. Relief rolled off her in waves that Alex was out of the tunnel. His twisted ankle was a concern, but she consoled herself that he wasn't injured any worse.

Except they were still trapped.

As she and Cruz hurried down the path next to the resort access road, the sound of chainsaws roared in the early evening calm. Tommy and Will were visible through the screen of trees, clearing the road from the highway to the resort.

Hope didn't stop to talk, instead picking up her pace into a steady jog. When she climbed the steps into the lobby, she found a room being transformed. Lanterns and candles illuminated the large space. A quiet hum filled the room, staff and guests working together and talking encouragingly. Two housekeepers carried a mattress in and set it next to another already lying on the floor. Derek and Megan pushed couches and armchairs against the wall, creating a large, open area.

Patti stood behind the front desk, giving instructions to a husband and wife to inspect the windows of the bungalows closely and note which needed to be boarded up. As they left, Patti saw Hope. Her eyes grew wide, immediately darting behind Hope to search for Alex, Zach, and Jasmine.

Hope shook her head as she approached the desk. The TV on the wall was plugged into a red emergency outlet. A colorful graphic was displayed by the local news station, indicating the earthquake had been confirmed as a 6.7 on the Richter Scale. A cooler filled with ice sat in front of the check-in counter, filled with sodas and water bottles. Hope grabbed a water, suddenly aware how parched she was. Taking a long drink of water, she joined Patti behind the front desk.

"You didn't find them?" Patti's face was stricken.

Hope spoke quietly. "I did, but they're trapped in a large cavern. The flooded tunnel leading from the grotto pool caved in. Alex has an injured leg, but I don't think it's too bad." Her stomach twisted at her words, and she hoped that was true. He tended to downplay injuries out of concern about worrying her.

Patti's mouth was hanging open. She blinked rapidly before saying, "Jesus, Mary, and Joseph! How are they gonna get out?"

"That is the question of the day, Patti. I need to call the police for a rescue team." The landscapers came back, carrying another mattress. "What's with the mattresses? Are the bungalows out of commission?"

"Only two. The access road is impassable. Tommy and Will are tryin' to clear a path, but I doubt anyone is leavin' here tonight. We're settin' up a ward for staff to sleep in the lobby."

Hope gave Patti a grateful smile and squeezed her arm. "Thank you so much. I don't know what I'd do without you."

Patti eyed her back evenly. "We'll survive this. And so will those three."

Hope refused to consider otherwise. "I saw trees down on the highway too. It's going to be some work getting roads clear around the island."

Hope picked up her phone from the desk, bringing up her keypad. The first time she dialed 911, all she heard was a rapid busy signal. The second time, she got an *all circuits are busy* recorded message. She took another swig of water, then kept hitting redial.

Over and over.

Hope almost dropped the phone when a woman's voice answered. "911. What's your emergency?"

"Hello!" Hope called out. "I'm Hope Monroe from Half Moon Bay Resort. We have three people trapped in a cavern. Please send police and search and rescue here as soon as you can!"

"Ma'am, I'm very sorry, but there's emergencies all over the island. Most roads are impassible and we're only able to respond to places we can reach on foot. Crews are already out clearin' the roads—we'll get to outlyin' areas as soon as possible."

Goosebumps broke out over Hope's arms. "What are you saying? You can't help?"

"I'm not sayin' that at all," the woman said, her Caribbean lilt calm and reassuring. "But your people are gonna have to hold tight tonight. I'll make sure the right people get this message, but don't count on anyone showin' up before tomorrow."

Hope raised a hand to her forehead. "They're trapped in a cave that just went through an earthquake. What if an aftershock brings down the whole cavern?"

The dispatcher paused, then answered, her real voice shining through her cool professionalism. "Then I suggest you pray tonight. I think maybe we all should."

Hope gripped the phone, unable to speak.

"Ma'am, are you still there?"

Hope's hand trembled, the phone vibrating against her ear. "Yes. I'm just in shock."

"I know the feelin'. Half Moon Bay isn't too far north of Frederiksted, so they should be able to get to you by mornin'. You just hang tight and have faith, ok?"

"We'll do our best. Thank you." Hope's voice was weak as she ended the call. The phone slipped out of her hand and landed on the wooden surface of the check-in counter. As she stared at it, she became aware the room was absolutely silent around her.

She lifted her eyes.

The lobby was filled with people. All were completely still as they stared at her.

"Hope, what's goin' on?" asked Percy, their head landscaper.

Hope slid her eyes to Patti, who shook her head slightly. "I didn't say anythin'," she said quietly.

Hope straightened, addressing the room. "We have a situation. Three of our own are trapped inside a cavern at Half Moon Grotto." An alarmed murmur rippled around the room. "The police know, but they can't come to help until the roads are cleared, which won't be until tomorrow."

Percy's eyes bulged, his dark face becoming even more lined. "Who's trapped?"

"Zach, Jasmine..." Hope choked back a sob, determined to stay strong. "And Alex."

AFTER HER ANNOUNCEMENT, Hope gathered supplies which might fit through the narrow seam. Tommy and Will returned to the lobby, and she got them caught up on events.

"*Surface Interval* came through the quake fine," Tommy said. "You want me to drive around to Frederiksted? Maybe I can go to the police and bring them by boat."

Hope thought for a moment. "That's a good idea. But the 911 dispatcher said the police and search teams are already maxed out tonight. We haven't had any more aftershocks, so let's wait until tomorrow morning."

"That works," Tommy said. "I'm sure people will be wantin' to get home tomorrow. Myself included."

"I'm sure glad you two were here," Patti said to Tommy and Will. "We'll do everythin' possible to get people home tomorrow to check on family."

Hope turned to Patti. "Can you try to call Zach's and Jasmine's parents? They need to know what's going on."

"Of course. I'll get right on it." Patti hurried back to the front desk.

"Speakin' of phone calls," Tommy said, rubbing a hand over his stubble. "I'm gonna try to get hold of Priscilla. She was at home with the kids."

"Of course," Hope said, her heart twisting. "I'm sure your family's fine, Tommy."

After he pulled out his phone and left the room, Hope turned to Will. "Have you been able to reach Jack or Sara?"

Will smiled. His long, slightly homely face only made him more endearing. "Jack and I were able to exchange a few texts. They're all doing fine. Him, Sara, and Magen."

Hope briefly closed her eyes. "Thank God. That's one less thing I have to worry about." She smiled and touched his hand. "Patti told me there's a sandwich buffet set up in the restaurant. Get something to eat. And thank you for all your help."

"If there's anything I can do to help at the grotto, let me know. I care about all three of those guys."

"I know. We all do."

Hope left the lobby and hurried to the pier, walking carefully in the twilight to avoid the damaged and missing boards. She climbed the stairs and entered the dive shop, sighing as she surveyed the devastation. The floor was strewn with merchandise.

Quickly locating a large backpack among the scuba wreckage, Hope picked it up before heading for the gift-shop side of the large room. Lowering to her knees, she sifted through the fallen display of snacks, placing all the thin candy bars, protein bars, and bags of chips she could find into the backpack.

"They've got plenty of fresh water to drink. I just hope it's safe." That gave her an idea, and she returned to the dive shop section and sifted through the debris until she found their selection of dry bags. She placed three in the backpack and straightened.

That should at least get them through the night.

As Hope passed by the restaurant, a voice called her name. She turned as Derek trotted toward her. "Are you headed to the grotto?" he asked.

She nodded. "Yes, as soon as I get some blankets."

He withdrew a small cardboard box from his pocket. "I thought you might want to give them this."

Hope took the box, turning it over in her hand. "What is it?"

"Water purification tablets. Megan and I were thinking of going on an all-day hike. She gives me a hard time about being such a boy scout, but I thought we might need to drink from some streams. I didn't want to take any chances with the baby. But I think those guys in the cave need them more."

Tears sprang to Hope's eyes, and she hugged him tightly. "Thank you! This is perfect." Pulling back, her eye drifted to the restaurant where several people sat around tables. "Are you and Megan getting enough to eat?"

"Plenty. I don't know how your chef did it, but there's a whole spread available."

A smile came to Hope's face. "Gerold is a genius. That's how he did it. Enjoy your dinner."

A large cinderblock shed sat next to the lobby and Hope opened the wooden double doors. The shed contained most of the housekeeping supplies for the resort, and she studied them carefully, realizing immediately most blankets would be too thick to fit through the narrow seam. She grabbed several sheets and located three thin, waffle-weave blankets.

With her backpack nearly full, she headed back to the lobby, where Patti frowned at her. "Why don't you take Tommy or Will with you? I hate the idea of you goin' all the way out there in the dark by yourself."

Hope shook her head. "I'd rather have them here, in case anyone needs some heavy lifting. I'll be back as soon as I can. Cruz will be with me." Turning on her headlamp, she descended the steps and headed across the sand parking lot. Cruz fell in at her side.

She looked down at him. "I'm sorry. You're probably getting hungry. I'll feed you as soon as we get back."

Without Alex.

Hope inhaled a giant breath, pushing down the threat of tears. The real reason she hadn't wanted anyone to accompany her was because of how close she was to breaking down. And she didn't want to put poor Tommy or Will through that. The constant motion and needing to manage the resort's response had kept her frightened thoughts at bay, but it was only a matter of time before they rose up in force.

Hope crossed through the open gate and went to the grotto. When she reached the cart, still by the sandy beach, she carefully folded Alex's shirt, then picked it up and took a long, deep breath of him. She teared up and slammed the shirt in her backpack.

No! I'm not doing that. I've got to stay strong.

She added Zach's and Jasmine's clothing, then placed her headlamp on her forehead and turned it on. Grabbing the handle of the cart, she pushed it down the path. She turned left at the gate and continued around the perimeter of the fence.

It was completely dark when she kneeled next to the seam and slipped the backpack off. "Hello? Alex?"

The sound of scurrying came from below, followed by Zach's face in the glow of her headlamp. He had stripped off his wetsuit and wore only board shorts. His arms were wrapped around his torso. "Hope?"

"Yes. Is Alex all right?"

"I'm here."

The tension Hope didn't realize she'd been holding in her shoulders drained out at Alex's voice.

"My ankle is swelling a bit, so I'm trying to stay off it."

Her stomach clenched. "How bad are you hurt, Alex?"

"My ankle's twisted. But you won't be able to collect that life insurance on me just yet. Sorry."

Hope dropped her head and gave a reluctant laugh. "Smartass." Then she unzipped the backpack. "I got hold of the police, but they can't come until tomorrow. The roads are impassible. So I brought some things to get you through the night. I grabbed the clothes you all left at the grotto."

She slid Alex's shirt through the narrow crevice, but she could only push it a short way. The rock seam within the cavern ceiling was over two feet deep. Frowning, she looked around the area until she located a good stick, then used it to push the shirt all the way through. Then she repeated the maneuver with Zach's and Jasmine's clothes.

"Thank you!" Jasmine called, smiling up at Hope. "I'm gettin' pretty cold. Alex told us to take off our wetsuits to stay warmer, but it's still gettin' chilly."

"I've got some sheets and blankets that should help too," Hope said. The sheets slid through easily, sliding against the smooth rock. The first blanket got hung up halfway, and Hope was afraid she'd just blocked half the seam permanently. But persistent shoving with her stick eventually pushed it through.

It plopped to the ground below, and the second two slid through easier.

Zach retrieved a blanket and tossed it over Jasmine's shoulders. When Hope slid the second one through, he grabbed it, then disappeared from her view. He quickly returned without it. That made her stomach clench harder. She could only hope Alex received some comfort from its soft warmth. She turned back to the backpack and grabbed a handful of snacks while Zach tossed the last blanket around his shoulders.

"Ok, guys," Hope said. "You officially have permission to eat as much junk food as you want." The candy and protein bars dropped through easily and she was able to push through the chips after slightly opening them to expel the air inside. Zach and Jasmine scurried around below, picking up snacks as if Hope were the great piñata above.

"Now for the *pièce de résistance*," Hope said, and tossed down the three dry bags. Then she held the box of water purification tablets in one hand and shined her headlamp on it. "See this box in my hand, Zach?"

"Yeah. What is it?"

She turned back to the seam. "The most important thing I'm giving you. Water purification tablets. They belonged to a guest, and he wanted you guys to have them. You can fill the dry bags with water and add the tablets so you each have your own safe drinking water."

Alex's laugh echoed up to her. "Hope, I love you."

"I love you too." Her voice wavered and she cleared her throat. "That's all I have. Can I get you anything else?"

Zach and Jasmine looked at each other and shrugged. "No," Jasmine said. "This is great. Thanks a lot."

"Patti's working on getting hold of your parents. We'll keep them updated. I promise."

Jasmine's face crumpled, and Zach pulled her toward his chest. He met Hope's gaze squarely. "Thank you."

Alex murmured something, but it was too faint for Hope to hear. Zach disappeared from view again. Moments later, he reappeared, Alex at his side with his right arm over Zach's shoulder. He held his right foot off the ground, and he was pale, his face drawn. But at that moment, he was the most uplifting sight Hope had ever known.

Alex gave her a smile, but it was tired. "Hey, you."

"Hi, love."

"How are things at the resort?" His voice was dry and scratchy.

"Most of the bungalows are habitable. Staff are bedding down for the night in the lobby. We're handling it."

"I never thought anything else. You'd better get back— you've had a hell of a day too. Get some sleep."

She smiled, and tears welled again. "I'll miss you tonight."

"Me too. It'll have to get damn cold before I consider snuggling up to Zach's scrawny ass, though."

Hope gave a laugh that was part sob, tears falling to splash onto the gray rock. "I'll be back first thing tomorrow, ok?"

"We'll be here."

Alex pressed his fingers to his mouth and blew her a kiss. Hope reached out and caught it.

She kept her fist closed the entire way back to the resort, holding tight.

Chapter Twenty-Four

ALEX SWALLOWED hard as Hope's headlamp disappeared from above. Jasmine hopped around the floor, picking up the snacks Hope had dropped. Alex pointed to the nearby area they'd set up as their home base. It was level without too many rocks to get in the way. It was also where he and Hope had made love. He needed that connection. "Let's get something to eat."

Taking care with his leg, Alex bent to pick up one of the dry bags. Zach helped him ease to the ground, and he handed Zach the dry bag. "Could you fill these up? Add one purification tablet and shake the bag up to dissolve it."

Zach nodded and picked up the other two bags before heading toward the shore. Alex cleared his dry, hoarse throat. Water had been his primary concern for a while, and he was beyond parched after his exertions in the tunnel. If he had any excess fluid left, saliva would be flooding his mouth at the prospect of the water Zach was gathering.

When the young man returned, Alex accepted the bag gratefully. The one-gallon container had a waterproof zipper at the top. He unzipped it and tilted it sideways, pinching the edge of the zipper. The cool fluid ran into his mouth. It tasted slightly metallic from the purification, but it was still heavenly. Some spilled over his chin, but he drank more than half the bag in one shot. When he was done, Zach refilled it.

Jasmine had separated the snacks into three equal piles and handed them out. Alex's first instinct was to conserve and ration the food. Then he laughed at himself. If there was one thing St. Croix had no shortage of, it was processed junk food. Even after an earthquake.

Jasmine, with her blanket wrapped around her shoulders, moaned in ecstasy as she bit off the end of a Snickers. "So hungry!"

Zach was quieter, darting his eyes around the cavern as he ate. His blanket was folded over his legs. The cavern was cool and damp—the perfect conditions to seep heat out of a body. "We should have had Hope bring us matches. A fire would be good right about now."

Alex had already disregarded the idea. "Good thought, but I haven't seen any wood. Hope brought everything we need to get through the night."

Zach barked a laugh. "I guess a fire wouldn't work too well if there's nothing to burn." He glanced at Alex. "Have you ever been trapped like this before?"

"No, but I've had a lot of training in survival situations." Alex pointed up at the seam. "That crevice is a game changer."

Jasmine stared at him. "I'm sorry you're here, but I'm also grateful. I feel better knowing you're with us."

Don't feel too good about it. I'm not of much use at the moment. But he'd never say that out loud. "We'll be fine, Jasmine. Think of it as an adventure."

Zach dropped his eyes to the ground and stuffed another Oreo in his mouth.

While trying to ignore the pain, Alex methodically worked

through his junk food, saving the chocolate chip cookies for last. They paled in comparison to Hope's, but he ate them anyway, grateful for every bite. His blanket lay nearby. Zach had brought it to him as soon as Hope tossed it down, but he had no need for it. Despite the cool air, a bead of sweat trickled down his face. He wiped it away surreptitiously, glancing at his right leg.

Zach's headlamp lay in the middle of them, pointing upward. Alex picked it up and pointed it at the far reaches of the cavern, where the water met the stone walls. It was too dim to make anything out.

He turned to Zach. "You up for a swim? I'd like to know if there are any tunnels on the far side of the cavern. We've never explored over there."

"Good idea." Zach nodded eagerly. "I can put my tank back on and check it out underwater."

Alex shook his head. "No. We need to conserve the air in those tanks. Only explore what you can see from the surface. Wear your wetsuit—it will provide flotation."

"I'll go with you," Jasmine said. "I'm tired of just sittin' around."

I know the feeling.

Alex nodded. "Stay together. I've got two fresh flashlights clipped to my rebreather, so take those."

Another line of sweat dripped down his face and Jasmine stared at him, a line forming between her brows. "Are you ok, Alex?"

The red-hot poker was back inside his right leg, but he just smiled as he wiped the sweat away. "I'm fine."

She looked dubious but didn't argue. She and Zach moved across the stony plateau and down the slope to where their kits lay at the water's edge. As soon as they disappeared from sight, Alex tipped the light toward his right lower leg and the real reason he had wanted the pair out of sight.

He still wore his neoprene booties and wetsuit, wanting the compression both provided to decrease the swelling. But the throbbing was increasing by the minute, and the garments were now doing more damage than good.

The boot had to come off. Then the wetsuit.

Taking a deep breath and holding it, Alex grasped his right leg with both hands, just below the knee. As gently as possible, he bent his knee, swinging his foot over his left thigh. A loud groan escaped as his leg screamed anew. He kept moving, eventually able to rest his knee over his left thigh.

He grabbed his nearby blanket, panting heavily as he wiped the sheen of sweat dripping off his face. After several more deep breaths, he unzipped the neoprene boot.

Ok, how am I going to do this?

He stretched the two wings of the open zipper experimentally. The slightest tugging on the fabric caused a lancing jolt of pain through his foot and ankle. Tilting the boot from his heel and pulling off like normal wasn't an option. The pain would make him pass out.

"Shit. I need my knife."

After a deep sigh, Alex shimmied over to the banked slope and his rebreather, scrabbling on his back with both hands and one leg, holding his right straight out. It wasn't fun, but he made it and unclipped his knife.

Scrabbling back to the light wasn't any more enjoyable, either.

This time, he needed to wipe his whole sopping head with the blanket. He stripped off the shirt Hope had tossed down, not wanting to get it soaked. Again folding his right leg over the left thigh, he adjusted the light closer and unfolded his knife. He smiled crookedly at it. *See? I did need it.*

Very carefully, Alex slipped the knife in between two of the zipper's teeth and started sawing the neoprene. Each pass of the knife jostled his lower leg. He clenched his jaw, refusing to stop when the shooting fireball exploded. Sweat dripped from his face, spattering on the rocky ground as he reached the sole. He continued sawing the fabric between the sole and the bottom of his foot, moving toward his big toe.

Better not slip...

When he reached his big toe, he had to stop for a rest and mop his head again. Taking deep, gasping breaths, he closed his eyes and waited for the pain and nausea to stabilize. He started sawing again.

Almost there... just a little more.

When he had freed the neoprene over his toes from the rubber sole, he set the knife down and gently lifted the boot off. The pain flared, then lessened immediately as he lifted the boot from his foot and ankle. He tossed his boot to the side.

Alex leaned back on both hands, closing his eyes and tipping his head backward. The difference after removing the boot was paradise. After a long moment, he sat up again and grasped the light to inspect the damage. Carefully, he unfolded his right leg, stuffing the blanket underneath so his heel wasn't lying against the cold stone ground. His entire foot was purple and swelling. He had unzipped the ankles of his wetsuit shortly after arriving in the cavern. But even so, the exposed flesh was an angry red bulge below where his wetsuit—and the compression it provided—ended.

He ran the fingers of his right hand slowly down the right leg of his wetsuit but couldn't lean far enough forward without jostling his leg. He wiped his forehead. "I can't do this myself. Guess I'll have to wait for them to get back after all."

Laying back down, Alex blinked at the ceiling of the cavern, grateful he'd been alone for the boot removal. He didn't want to show weakness in front of Zach or Jasmine. Only Hope got to see that side of him. *God, I wish she was here...*

But cutting the wetsuit off should be a less painful process. It wasn't long before Zach's and Jasmine's voices drifted up to him, shortly followed by the pair themselves. They peeled off their wetsuits, and Alex couldn't help but smile slightly at how easily they accomplished the maneuver. Both used a sheet to dry off.

Zach shook his head at Alex. "We searched thoroughly but didn't see anything. I even dove underwater, feeling against the rock with my hand."

Alex nodded, not surprised. "At least we know now."

Jasmine dropped the sheet to the ground. "The only way out is blocked. How are they goin' to rescue us?"

Alex thought of several responses to that question, but didn't feel like saying them out loud just yet. "We'll find out tomorrow when the authorities get here."

That was Alex's primary concern. He had the feeling he *was* the authority here.

"Prioritize!" the voice shouted in his head.

Oh, hey. You're still here.

It responded, *"I never leave. Just show up when you need a little kick in the ass. The wetsuit, remember?"*

Yeah, yeah. You can be quiet now.

As Zach wiped the sheet down his legs, he saw Alex's bootie on the ground. He froze, only his eyes moving as they traveled to Alex's leg on top of the wadded-up blanket. "How did you cut that off?"

"I used my dive knife."

Zach turned to look at the shoreline and Alex's rebreather. "But how did you get down there?"

Painfully. "Not very gracefully, I admit. But I got the job done. Well, half the job. Can you give me a hand getting my wetsuit off?"

Zach pressed his lips into a grim line, then nodded. Alex handed him the knife.

As Alex had predicted, cutting his wetsuit off was easier than the boot. Zach slipped the blade under the neoprene at the top of Alex's ankle zipper and slowly sawed his way up. The worst part was the beginning. Zach tried to be gentle, but it was impossible to slice through the thick material without jostling and tugging on the injured leg. When Zach reached his knee, Alex had to take a break to mop his face and head again, trying not to vomit. But from that point on, Zach gained confidence, quickly parting the neoprene. Then he performed the same operation on Alex's left leg, pulling apart the free pieces and leaving Alex in the board shorts he wore underneath.

By this time, the red-hot poker in his leg had subsisted to a steady, angry throbbing.

Alex drank the rest of his water, swallowing in huge, greedy gulps. Zach hunkered down next to Alex's leg, lighting it up with his headlamp. The two men inspected it. The foot was still purple and swollen. The leg was a mixture of red, yellow, and purple splotches. There was a noticeable purple and black bulge on the front of his lower leg. Zach tilted his headlamp up and looked at Alex. "I'd say that's broken."

"I'm pretty sure you're right."

While Zach freed Alex from his wetsuit, Jasmine had sat a distance away. Now she crept over. At the sight of Alex's leg, she opened her eyes wide. Then they unfocused and grew glassy.

"Grab her, Zach!" Alex yelled.

But his sharp voice was enough to snap Jasmine out of it. She whipped her head back and forth, avoiding looking at Alex's leg. "I'm ok."

Zach grabbed her hand and squeezed. "You sure?"

She nodded and sat cross-legged on the ground.

"It looks worse than it feels," Alex said, trying to sound optimistic.

Jasmine grinned, the difference to her previous expression startling. "I guess that's a positive. Your leg looks like shit, Alex."

He returned her smile. "I've been through worse than this. Tomorrow will bring answers, you'll see. Anybody have the time?" His rebreather used a wrist-mounted wireless monitoring system, but he'd left it next to the unit.

Zach nodded and looked at his wrist. "It's past eight."

Alex breathed a heavy sigh. "I don't know about you guys, but I think I'm ready to get some sleep."

Jasmine nodded. "Me too."

There wasn't much they could do about the stone floor. Alex's blanket was too damp with sweat to trap heat, so Jasmine spread it out to dry. Hope had given them plenty of sheets, so Alex wadded one under his leg and tossed a second over himself. Zach and Jasmine did similarly, settling under their blankets.

Soon, the cavern was silent except for quiet breathing.

After several minutes, Jasmine's soft voice came through the night. "Alex, are we going to get out of here?"

His heart clenched tight. "Absolutely."

Because the alternative wasn't something he was willing to acknowledge.

Getting back to Hope wasn't optional. She was his lifeline.

Without the headlamp, the cavern was very dark. Alex blinked at the ceiling. Eventually his eyes adjusted, and he could see the fainter black of the seam far above. The seam that separated him from Hope. It was hard to believe he'd held her in his arms just last night. Caressed her soft skin, tanned where the sun caught it and white as cream where it didn't. He closed his eyes, picturing her in his mind as he tried not to move. At last, his exhausted body relaxed.

Sleep tight, baby. We'll be together again soon.

Chapter Twenty-Five

HOPE BLINKED OPEN HER SCRATCHY, gummy eyes. Dim morning light filtered through the windows of their great room. Her face was tight. She raised a hand, wiping off the flaky, dried streaks of tears. She lay on the couch, facing their covered porch. Just beyond, the ocean softly lapped against the shore. Just like any other day.

How can it look so normal?

She held an 8 x 10 photo clutched against her chest and lifted it. The photo was of her and Alex. Not one of Robert's from their wedding. This was a simple selfie Alex had taken of them on their honeymoon in the Florida Keys. They sat on a chaise lounge, Hope laying back against Alex's chest. Her arms were folded around her bent knees, and he had one hand on the phone and the other wrapped around the front of her shoulders. Both of them wore radiant smiles, a reflection of the time they were spending together.

The photo was one of her favorites.

Hope brushed her finger over the image of his face, then scanned the ravaged great room with dull, disinterested eyes. Last night, she'd tried to sleep in their bed. Wrapping her arms around Alex's pillow, Hope had drawn it tightly against her. As she inhaled a deep breath of his scent, she had hoped it would make him feel closer.

She was wrong.

His scent had only opened a yawning chasm of terror and grief.

So she'd moved to the great room, clearing off the couch but leaving the rest of the wreckage strewn across the floor, unable to deal with it. The photo laid undamaged on top of a throw pillow. Remembering happier times, Hope gathered the frame in her arms, then flopped onto the couch. She recalled Alex had also slept there after her emergency hysterectomy, when she had spent the night in the hospital. Cruz curled up next to the couch below her. His usual bed was buried under a knocked-over bookcase.

With tears rolling down her face, and clutching the photo-graph against her breast, Hope at last fell into a troubled, rest-less sleep.

Now, it was just past 6 a.m., and the beach was slightly more visible as the sun continued to rise. She swung into a sitting position and placed the photo gently on a couch cushion. Cruz sat up, whining.

She gave him a scratch behind both ears. "You miss him too, don't you?"

Dragging a hand through her tangled hair, Hope padded to the kitchen and flipped a switch. Nothing—still no power. Lighting the stove with a match, she boiled water for instant coffee and let Cruz out. She spread peanut butter on a piece of bread, determined to face the new day.

Minutes later, after a fast, lukewarm shower, she walked down the pier wearing hiking shorts and a T-shirt. And running shoes—Hope had a feeling she'd be making several trips to the seam. Cruz stayed behind this time, lying on the porch.

Surprised by movement on *Surface Interval*, she crossed to the boat and stepped aboard. Tommy and Will clustered under the canopy, talking softly.

"Good morning, guys. You're both up early."

"I want to take the boat to Frederiksted and see what the town's like," Tommy said, his face sober. "Priscilla said she and the kids are ok, but I need to see it with my own eyes. Assumin' it's safe, Will can drive the boat back here and take anyone who needs to go to town."

"Of course," she said. "That sounds like a good plan. You need to be with your family."

"I'll go to the police station too," he continued. "Make sure gettin' to that cavern is a priority for them this mornin'."

Tears threatened again as Hope embraced Tommy, but she blinked them back. "Thank you." She turned to Will. "Why don't you stop by Sara and Jack's cove before you come back here? Make sure they don't need anything. I imagine their access road is blocked too."

Will nodded, his normally happy face tired and drawn. "I'll do that, thanks."

"Are you headed out to the grotto?" Tommy asked Hope.

"Yes. I was just heading up to the dive shop to get more snacks when I saw you two on the boat. I'd better get going."

"I'll be back here as soon as I can," Tommy told her, his voice grave. "Tell those guys we're thinkin' about them, ok?"

"Of course. Stay safe."

As Hope climbed the stairs, the boat started behind her and drove out of Half Moon Bay. She ignored the mess inside the shop and stuffed an assortment of snacks into her backpack, wincing at the unappetizing selection. Then she sat up on her knees. "I wonder if I can come up with something better?"

With purpose renewing her step, Hope marched toward the restaurant kitchen. As she pushed through the doors, the large room was fully lit. Kitchen staff and guests had worked tirelessly to clean up the mess. Backup generators were working as designed, powering the kitchen fully, including refrigerators and freezers. Gerold stood behind a counter, slicing a pineapple.

"Was I the last person to get up this morning?" Hope asked with a smile. "I just said goodbye to Tommy and Will. They're headed to Frederiksted."

Gerold twitched one side of his mouth. "I already talked to them. I couldn't sleep any more, and figured I'd get busy in here. What brings you by?"

"I was going to make some sort of a breakfast for Alex, Zach, and Jasmine. But I'm sure you can come up with something better. It needs to be something that's easy to eat."

Gerold paused his slicing, chewing the inside of his cheek. "What about a breakfast burrito?"

"They would love that."

The chef moved to one of the racks, tossing a package of large tortillas on the steel island, then retrieved sausage, eggs, cheese, and bell peppers from the walk-in refrigerator.

Hope studied the ingredients. "The fissure is narrow. Don't make them too thick or I won't be able to push them through."

Gerold grabbed a chef's knife and began chopping the bell pepper, his hand moving lightning-fast. "Well, how about a breakfast quesadilla, then? They're pretty flat."

"Perfect!" She slid the package of tortillas toward her and opened it, already feeling better now that she had a firm course of action.

"How many do you want?"

"How about six? That way they can have two each." Then she paused, reconsidering. "No, make it eight. I'm sure Alex is extra hungry."

She cut up the sausages while Gerold cracked a dozen eggs into a large mixing bowl and added the peppers.

As he cooked it all in a large frying pan, Gerold shot her a smile. "Good thing we hadn't gotten too far on the plans for the new restaurant, huh?"

Hope laughed and shook her head, enjoying the escape of simple laughter with a friend. "I'm afraid that project might be on the back burner for a while. But we'll get there. I promise."

Fifteen minutes later, eight quesadillas were each neatly wrapped in foil and stacked on the counter next to a large plastic bag of sliced pineapple. Hope carefully added the food to her backpack on top of the other snacks.

She crossed to the lobby and poked her head in. Patti was setting out packaged donuts next to a large brewing coffee pot. The delicious, rich scent filled the room. Mattresses still lay on the floor, some with sleeping people still on them, but most were empty. Patti finished with the donuts and came to the door, seeing the backpack Hope wore. "You're headed out to the cavern?"

"Yes. Gerold and I made them something for breakfast. Everything go ok here last night?"

"Yes." Patti wore the same clothes as yesterday, and lines creased her face. "Staff would like to go home today to check on their homes and families. Hopefully crews get the roads clear soon. I reached Zach's and Jasmine's parents last night. They're goin' to get here as soon as the roads open."

"Good. I'll make sure they get to the seam."

Patti nodded. "I'll call the police for an update soon. Cell service seems more consistent now."

Hope patted the back pocket of her shorts, verifying her phone was there. "Let me know if the police show up."

"You know I will." Patti drew her into an embrace, and Hope leaned into her broad frame, soaking up the softness. "Stay safe, child."

The eastern sky above the mountains was pink, fading to

blue and there was enough light to see unaided. The forest was alive with birds, but that wasn't the only sound. As Hope neared the highway, the roar of chainsaws drifted through the bush. She looked to her right as she stepped on the asphalt. The fallen trees had been cleared.

As she continued walking on the soft trail, steam rose from the surface. Some trees leaned against their neighbors and a carpet of leaves lay on the ground, but the jungle was little changed after the earthquake. Tommy and Will had chain-sawed away the fallen trees, their only trace the pale shavings lying on the broad path. Once again, the strange sense of the surreal washed over her. Everything seemed so normal, yet this morning couldn't be more different from yesterday.

Hope kneeled over the seam, tucking her hair behind both ears. "Anyone awake yet down there?"

Excited murmuring met her ears, making her smile.

Jasmine appeared below and waved before adjusting a blanket over her shoulders. "Good mornin'!"

"Is everyone all right down there?"

The young woman shot a troubled look to the side before peering at Hope again. "Yes. Do you have any news about a rescue?"

"Not yet. I'm sorry. But I brought you breakfast!"

Jasmine smiled as Zach and Alex appeared next to her. The light only lit their faces, so Hope couldn't see the extent of Alex's injury. That Zach was still helping him walk told her the problem hadn't improved overnight. But she was encouraged that Alex no longer wore his wetsuit. Getting off a wetsuit with a badly twisted ankle would be a painful process, so seeing him in his shirt and shorts was reassuring.

Thank God! It's not too serious!

She drank in the sight of him, even though he was obviously drained and tired. A scruff of stubble covered his jaw.

"Hey, you," Hope said.

"Good morning." His voice was stronger, and not as scratchy as it had been yesterday.

"You sound better. Did you get some water?"

Alex nodded. "Lots. That was a great idea with the dry bags."

"Thanks, honey. Is your ankle better?"

Both Jasmine's and Zach's smiles faltered slightly, but Alex's didn't. He held up a hand and waggled it in a so-so gesture. "Zach's helping me hobble around. You'll be happy to know I've had your voice in my head harping on me to let him, and not be stubborn. Though it's probably overkill."

A small laugh escaped her. "Good for you, Zach. Alex's stubborn side can be hard to deal with, so stay strong. I'm counting on you to keep him safe."

Zach's smile fell off his face. He stared at her, serious as a heart attack. "I'll do my best, Hope. I swear."

Something about his expression caused unease to wash through her belly, but she tried to focus on the positive. "All three of you look really good. I'm sure that ground wasn't comfortable."

Zach put on a brave smile. "We just pretended it was a campin' trip. A *rough* campin' trip."

Hope slid the quesadillas through the seam. "Here's breakfast. Gerold and I made them just for you. And there's fresh pineapple too."

Cheers greeted her, returning the smile to her face as she pushed through the chips, candy bars, and protein bars. "Do you need anything else?"

Alex shook his head. "Just the police with search and rescue."

"They're working on clearing the road now. I could hear

chainsaws all the way here. I'm going to head back and get an update. You guys stay safe, ok?"

"You too, Hope," Alex said.

They shared a long look, then she rose from the ground.

Hope could feel her heart breaking as she headed home. But today she refused the tears, determined to stay focused on the rescue. When she reached the highway, the chainsaw's roars were more distant and to the north now.

Just after she entered the thick jungle on the other side, car engines purred as they turned onto the resort access road. Hope froze and whipped her head to the right, where the flashing lights of a police car passed by, an SUV just behind.

Her heart leapt into her mouth as she broke into a run.

By the time Hope came out of the jungle, two uniformed police officers were entering the lobby, with two other people wearing brown vests just behind. She sprinted up the stairs, entering the lobby shortly behind them.

Patti was talking to one of the police officers. "Oh, here she is now."

The man turned and a smile broke over Hope's face. The two policemen were Officers Perkins and Watson, the pair who had helped her and Alex after the Charles Reed fight and shooting. "Hello again."

Officer Perkins tipped his cap and shook her hand. A fine sheen of sweat peppered his dark cheeks. "Nice to see you again, ma'am. We got here as soon as we could. I'm sorry we couldn't meet again under more pleasant circumstances."

"Me too, but it's nice to see two friendly faces." She shook Watson's hand, eager for news. Half Moon Bay and its family weren't the only people suffering. "How are things around the island?"

"There have been a few deaths so far." Watson's southern accent was as thick as Hope remembered, but his round face was redder. "The hospital has triage tents set up, and crews are getting debris cleaned up. The roads are getting cleared quickly and the airport is hoping to open again by tonight."

"That's good news!" Patti said.

Officer Perkins indicated the pair standing next to him. "Let me introduce you to Luke and Cassie of Search and Rescue."

Hope shook hands with them. Both looked around thirty. Luke's blond hair was cut in a flat top. Cassie was shorter, her light-brown hair pulled into a low ponytail.

"Let's head out to the site, shall we?" Hope asked, already moving to the doorway.

They followed, but Cassie placed a restraining hand on her arm. "Ma'am—"

Hope turned to her with a smile. "Please call me Hope."

The woman inclined her head. "Sure. I know you're eager to get going on this, Hope. But mostly we're here to get an idea of what the situation entails. Hopefully, we can put together a plan fast to get those people out. But for now, we just want to assess the site. We'll go back to base to formulate our rescue."

"Of course. I understand." Her heart sank.

I want answers now, dammit!

As they walked down the path, Hope gave them a summary of the sites, both Half Moon Grotto and the cavern where the group was trapped. She led them through the gate, describing the tunnel and the cave-in. Finally, they stood on the sandy beach. From here, the grotto looked none the worse for wear due to the earthquake.

Luke sketched the site on a pad he carried, while Perkins and Watson milled around, peering into the water.

Cassie stared across the pool, both hands on her hips. "The access tunnel is submerged?"

"Yes. Maybe you can get some machinery in there to scoop out the rock?"

Cassie's face didn't give anything away. "Did you say there's an overland access to the cavern?"

Hope pointed across the pool. "That way. There's a long seam in the roof of the cavern, but it's very narrow. We've been using it to communicate and get them food and blankets."

Cassie nodded her head slowly, casting her eyes over the blue water. "Let's head there. Maybe there's an easier access."

Luke snapped his pad shut and nodded. "I agree. Let's go."

Perkins and Watson returned to the group, and they walked to the fence, continuing along the outside perimeter. The two police officers huffed along, periodically raising their caps to mop their heads with a handkerchief. As the group moved away from the fence down the animal track, Cassie spoke up again. "Is this the only access to the site? There's no road nearby?"

"No. We only recently had the path to the grotto made."

Cassie and Luke shared a long look but didn't respond.

Hope turned around and led again. She kept catching herself speeding up, beyond eager to get the rescue started. Though she hadn't seen any usable surface access, she wasn't an expert in search and rescue either.

When they reached the seam, a smile swept across Hope's face.

Help is here, Alex! Let's get you out of there.

Chapter Twenty-Six

JASMINE SORTED through the foil packets, separating them into three piles of two. She held up the two extras, her brow wrinkling. "Either we're short one, or we have two extras."

Zach smirked. "I'm pretty sure those are for Alex."

Alex couldn't resist a smug grin as she handed him the two packets. The smile felt almost foreign on his face after the stress of the past day and helped dim the pain. "Hope likes to make sure I'm properly fed."

They unwrapped the foil packets and a spicy, heavenly scent filled the air around them. Zach took two huge bites and closed his eyes, giving a long, drawn-out groan. Alex dispensed with the theatrics but ate his first quesadilla in nothing flat. Two more followed in short order, and he stared at the fourth.

Should I save this?

His training and natural inclinations were hard to overrule, but there was no logical reason to withhold food, and he needed all the calories and protein he could get. The relief from removing his boot and wetsuit had been short-lived, and the pain had come roaring back. Within an hour, he'd retrieved his blanket and further elevated the leg, trying to decrease the swelling.

Zach had gotten up during the night, and Alex asked him to find a rock he could prop his leg on. After the quake, there was no shortage of those. The young man had quickly returned, carrying a bulky rock with a flat top in both arms. They had piled sheets on it to create cushioning, and eventually, Alex had found a tolerable position.

Though he used the word tolerable loosely.

Now he was sitting up, a fair distance from the seam but very near where he and Hope had lain. The thought brought him comfort. His leg was still elevated on the rock as he ate breakfast. Jasmine glanced at his injury, then swallowed hard, setting her quesadilla on the ground. Alex's lower leg, from knee to toes, was various shades of red, purple, and yellow. Originally, he had thought it was a simple break. But now he had to admit there were probably several fractures, maybe of both lower leg bones. His shoulders and upper back had stiffened overnight, adding to his chorus of pain.

He was just opening the foil on his final quesadilla when the seam above them darkened with several heads, all peering in.

"Alex! The police and search and rescue are here!" Hope called.

Alex beckoned to Zach. "Help me up and let's see what they have to say."

He nearly laughed after discovering the two policemen were the same ones who responded after Charles Reed shot him. But they didn't exactly fill him with confidence now.

Officer Watson listed their accomplishments in getting the infrastructure of the island going again, including the airport, but was vague about what the police could do to get them out of the cavern.

Luke and Cassie were more confident and assertive, but no less vague. Alex determined right away that Cassie was in charge. She made it clear they were just evaluating the site and would go back to headquarters to come up with a specific plan.

"Is there another way in?" Cassie called down.

Alex shook his head. He adjusted his arm around Zach's shoulders, ignoring the flash from his sore muscles. "We've looked around but haven't found anything. We'll keep exploring." *At least Zach and Jasmine will.*

"I don't see anything up here wide enough to be useful."

No kidding. "Do either of you have dive experience?"

"No," Cassie replied. "We've only conducted aboveground rescues. Mostly hikers who get caught in storms and flash floods."

"Super." Alex's breakfast congealed in his stomach.

"Luke and I are an experienced team. We also have teams working right now freeing others trapped because of the earthquake. Though none of those are underground."

Alex sighed, realizing the pain was making him crankier than normal. He forced a smile—it felt weary. But Cassie was trying. "We all appreciate the help, believe me."

"Listen," Alex recognized Officer Perkin's Caribbean lilt. "We have a dive rescue team on the island. We'll get you three out of there. Don't you worry."

Oh, now I feel much better.

The voice in Alex's head started laughing again.

The local dive rescue team were strictly amateurs, though one guy on the team thought otherwise. They had asked Alex to join, wanting someone experienced. The hotshot had acted like they were doing him a favor, but it was all a moot point. Alex just didn't have the time to spare.

Murmuring voices drifted down, then Cassie called out

again. "We're going to head back and get to work. Keep the faith, guys."

"Need anything else?" Hope asked.

Alex shook his head and Jasmine answered. "No, but a plan would be a real plus."

Laughter filtered down to them.

"We'll get to working on that," Luke said. "Be back soon, ok?"

Then the group was gone, and they were alone again.

Zach returned Alex to the floor and his rock. Then he wrapped his arms around Jasmine, boosting her up as he swung her in a circle. "Did you hear that? We're gettin' out of here!"

She laughed, placing her hands on his shoulders. "I sure hope so."

A smile crept across Alex's face. He was slightly envious of their naïve willingness to believe.

Zach set Jasmine down, and his smile could have cracked his face as he turned to Alex. "It's just a matter of time now. We've got search and rescue, police, and dive rescue working to get us out."

The two sat on the hard ground by Alex.

"How long do you think it will take?" Jasmine asked.

Alex hesitated, meeting her gaze. He didn't have it in him to crush her hopes, though he was concerned that a cave rescue might be a little more than the locals could deal with. "I'm not sure. But it's nice to have someone working on the problem, isn't it?"

Zach and Jasmine put their heads together, talking quietly. Alex mopped his forehead and lay down on his back, closing his eyes and trying to slow his heartbeat. That lessened the throbbing. He hadn't felt this helpless since Syria. It wasn't a pleasant sensation, and he hated not being able to influence and control the situation. But he was in no condition to control anything.

And there was no denying that his lack of influence was exactly why they were in this cavern.

This was the end result of a long list of his recent failures. *What the hell happened?*

Zach's and Jasmine's euphoria wore off and they returned to the rest of their breakfasts, sitting close together. Zach tried to tell her a story about a dive he'd led, but he faltered, breaking off. He stared at Alex for a long moment. "Do you miss Hope, Alex?"

A knife lanced through his heart at her name. He answered without opening his eyes. "Yeah, Zach. I do."

"How come you didn't tell Hope how bad your leg is?" Jasmine asked quietly.

Sighing, Alex opened his eyes and sat up. *I've still got a job to do, so it's time to stop moping and lead.* He met her gaze. "Because that knowledge wouldn't have helped her any. Hope is managing a natural disaster response for a whole resort. I don't want her worrying any more than she already is."

Jasmine took another bite of her quesadilla, then frowned. "If I were her, I'd want to know."

"I'm parsing that knowledge out on a need-to-know basis."

Zach grinned. "That's a real thing? Not just in the movies?"

Alex laughed softly, brought out of his funk. "Yeah, it's a real thing." He folded up the foil from his breakfast in case they needed it later. "Look guys. Hope and I both have a job to do. I'm managing a disaster situation too. I spent almost twenty years determining who needed what information to perform at their best."

"Does that mean if I ask you how you're doing, you'll lie?" Jasmine asked.

Anger flared, but Alex covered it quickly. She didn't mean to insult him. "Of course not. But admitting weakness isn't something that comes naturally to me. If my condition starts affecting our chances for survival, I'll let you know. I don't make a habit of lying to anyone."

Especially not Hope.

But lying and withholding information were two very different things. And his leg wasn't that bad. Yet.

Jasmine dropped her eyes. "I know. Sorry—I hoped we'd be out of here by now."

"The police and search and rescue are coming up with a plan as we speak. That's a big improvement over where we were a few hours ago. Why don't you pass around that pineapple?"

It didn't take long after finishing their breakfast for Zach to start fidgeting. "What are we going to do until they come back?"

"Why don't you two explore the dry part of the cave again?" Alex asked. "See if there are any passages we missed."

They nodded and rose, gathering two flashlights. As they disappeared into the gloom, Alex lay down again, tossing an arm over his eyes. The movement made his shoulder muscles protest, and his lower leg flared with every pulse of his heart. A quiet moan escaped from his mouth. In his mind, Hope's face appeared, and he focused on it. Her high cheekbones and full lips. Eyes that became golden in the sun. His pain faded to a tolerable level.

He couldn't measure time, but when the pair returned, he didn't think he'd fallen asleep. They were only away a short time, and their steps were quiet and halting.

"That didn't take long," Alex said.

Zach shook his head as he lay down and flopped onto his side. "There was nothing to find. I tried to squeeze through that narrow tunnel we found, but it's too small. The only way out of here is through that flooded, blocked passage. I'm goin' to take a nap."

Jasmine curled up nearby, closing her eyes too.

A bone-deep weariness filled Alex, along with trepidation

about what the rescue team would come up with. The worry that local rescuers weren't up to this challenge.

Whatever they figure out, they'd better hurry. I've got another few days before this leg is past the point of repair. Before then, I'll have to let Zach and Jasmine know how bad it is. Whether I want to or not.

The voice spoke softly. *"And Hope? When do you let her know?"*

When there's no alternative. And I'm not even close to that point yet—I've been in worse pain than this. So shut up.

Chapter Twenty-Seven

HOPE WATCHED the police car and unmarked SUV retreat up the access road. Officer Perkins promised to come back within a few hours, after they had formulated a plan. When she entered the lobby, Patti was talking to two middle-aged couples. All four wore wrinkled clothing and matching tense, exhausted expressions. Without being told, Hope knew they were Zach's and Jasmine's parents.

Patti made introductions. "Could you take them to the cavern right away?"

"Of course," Hope said. "It's close to two miles from here and the last half doesn't have much of a trail. Just so you know."

Zach's father was named Herb. He was a heavyset man, and his dark skin already glowed from exertion. "That's all right. We need to see our kids."

"Let me grab some waters. You might like a drink when you get there." Hope placed six bottles inside a backpack stashed in the office and set out for the seam once again.

Lucy, Jasmine's mother, wore her black hair tied up with a colorful scarf. "I still don't understand what they were doin' deep inside a cave."

Hope had been preparing for this question. "Alex took Zach and me on a dive to the cavern to celebrate our becoming divemasters. Zach thought the site was incredible and wanted Jasmine to see it."

"That doesn't surprise me. Sounds pretty private," Herb said with a smirk. "But why is Alex with them?"

Hope hesitated, answering carefully. "He was concerned whether they had the experience to be in there alone. He was on his way to get them out when the earthquake struck."

Lucy stumbled slightly. "Jasmine hasn't been divin' that long. Why would she dive inside a *cave*?"

Now was not the time to educate them on the difference between caves and caverns, so Hope said, "I'm sure they weren't planning on an earthquake. They just wanted a fun adventure."

Lucy sent Zach's parents a dark look. "Sounds like Zach should have known better."

Hope agreed, and she certainly knew Alex did, but didn't want them to get drawn into petty arguments. "All we're concentrating on now is getting the three of them out of there as quickly and safely as possible."

Lucy nodded curtly. "Of course. I'm sure he didn't need to twist Jasmine's arm."

"They're not the first young couple to do somethin' foolish," Herb muttered as he stared at the ground.

When they reached the seam, all four people gratefully accepted the water Hope had brought. She hung back while they kneeled over the seam, talking to their children. Alex must have been staying out of it, because she didn't hear his voice.

After half an hour of tears and worry, both sets of parents promised to stay at the resort until the group was rescued. They stood wearily.

Hope approached the seam. "We'd better get back in case the

rescue team calls. I'll be back as soon as I know anything." Jasmine and Zach both nodded, but Alex wasn't in sight. Hope hadn't intended to talk to him, not wanting to take the focus off the kids. But she couldn't help herself, a knot of worry growing in her gut. "Alex?"

"I'm here," came his voice. "Just staying off my foot."

"Ok." She wanted to ask how he was, but stayed quiet. "I'll be back soon."

They filed into a line as they headed back. "They look good," Lucy said. "Thank you for makin' sure they've got food and water."

"Of course," Hope said. "At least we can communicate with them."

"Why was Alex stayin' off his feet?" Herb asked.

"He twisted his ankle during the quake."

I hope that's all it is.

Herb breathed out a long, heavy sigh. "And he was goin' in there to make sure the kids were doin' all right. I'm right sorry about that, Hope."

She threw a smile over her shoulder. "Don't apologize. We're all in this together. And there's no one better qualified to help Zach and Jasmine right now than Alex. He'll keep them safe."

The group was quiet the rest of the way back to the resort. Hope concentrated on the rescue plan being formulated, her beacon of hope.

Soon!

When she entered the lobby, Patti was on the resort phone. But Hope's eyes were immediately drawn to Sara and Jack, who stood in front of the check-in counter, and her chest filled with warmth. Sara bounced Magen in her arms. The room was nearly empty of anyone else.

Hope turned to Zach's and Jasmine's parents. "Why don't

you get something to eat in the restaurant? We're keeping a buffet available all day."

"That sounds wonderful. We haven't eaten much," Lucy said, and the two couples filed out the back door.

Hope crossed the lobby and hugged Sara, pressing a kiss to Magen's forehead. "I'm so glad you guys are safe!" Then she and Jack exchanged embraces. "You didn't have to come here."

"Will gave us a ride in the boat," Sara said. "We couldn't stay at the house after we heard about the grotto. Are you doing ok?"

Hope took a deep breath. "I'm hanging in there. Handling it. The police are working on a rescue plan, so that's what I'm focusing on." She swept her gaze around the empty lobby. "Where is everyone?"

Jack smiled. "Will is leading a dive on the house reef and invited anyone who wants to go. That gives the guests something to do. Several of the staff went too."

"What a fantastic idea! I'll have to thank him."

Patti hung up the phone, frowning at the receiver.

"Who were you talking to?" Hope asked.

Patti lifted her eyes, which were troubled as they met Hope's. "It was that reporter. Strickland."

Hope groaned. John Strickland was a reporter for the *St. Croix Chronicle*. During the Charles Reed trial, he had become curious about the couple's reluctance to discuss Alex's past. Eventually, the reporter had uncovered the entire Syria story and printed a front-page article about the former SEAL.

To say Alex wasn't fond of Strickland was an understatement.

"What did he want?" Hope asked.

"He said the scanners are goin' wild with requests for help about the cavern rescue, and he wanted an official statement."

Patti shrugged. "I gave him the bare minimum, but it sounds like word is gettin' around."

"It was bound to, I guess." Hope studied the large room, now clean and neat. The glass shards left from the fallen pictures had been swept up. She swallowed hard at the memory of their broken wedding picture, now nowhere to be seen. "It's starting to look more like normal around here."

Patti nodded. "We're pretty much cleaned up now, and hopefully the power will be back on soon. A couple people are in the dive shop settin' that to rights. But the gear room needs someone from the dive team to work on it. No one else knows what goes where."

"I can work on that," Jack said.

"Tommy is drivin' in now," Patti said. "When he gets here, I thought I might go home for a spell."

Hope embraced her. "You've been working nonstop. We'll call you with any updates on the rescue. Get some rest."

Just then, Tommy walked in. Patti said her farewells and left, while Tommy informed them his family was uninjured and he'd gotten his house mostly put back together. "If any staff live on the coast and can't get to their home, I'll give them a lift in *Surface Interval*. But for now, I'll hang out here."

"Thank you. I'm sure Sara and Jack aren't the only ones with an impassable road." Hope closed her eyes and exhaled. "I should start working on our house. Last night I just cleared a path so I could get through. But it's a real mess."

"I'll bring Magen and help you," Sara said.

Hope turned to Tommy. "Can you and Jack give me a hand? The refrigerator tipped over."

AFTER GETTING the fridge upright again, Tommy and Jack left. Hope picked up the food that had fallen onto the floor and cleaned the interior before shutting the dented door. Magen went down for a nap in her carrier, giving Sara free rein to clean up the great room.

Hope moved to the master bedroom, righting both nightstands, which had fallen over. She kept her mind on her job, forcibly preventing herself from dwelling on the fact that she was cleaning up their house while Alex was trapped in a cavern with possibly no way out. Which was difficult when his presence was everywhere she looked.

She marched out of the bedroom. "I'm going to work in my office for a while." Her computer monitor lay on the floor but was unbroken. She placed it back on the desk and sighed at the tipped-over file cabinets, their contents strewn across the floor. *I wanted a distraction. Well, here it is.* Picking up a pile of papers, Hope went to work.

Several hours later, her phone buzzed with a text from Tommy.

> Tommy: The rescue crew is back. Come to the office asap.

> Hope: On my way!

Trying to keep her voice down, Hope ran out of the office and gave Sara the news. Sara scooped up Magen in her carrier and they hurried down the sand road toward the lobby. Hope's heart was in her mouth. The same police car was parked in the lot, but the SUV was missing.

She sprinted up the stairs two at a time and burst into the lobby. Perkins and Watson were both there, but the pair from search and rescue were missing. "Where are Cassie and Luke?"

Officer Perkins met her with a smile, but held both hands up. "It's just the two of us. We've got a plan, but we want to discuss it with the people who are trapped. So, we'd rather wait to talk about it until we're at the site. Ok?"

Hope nodded, so thrilled they were back she hardly minded the delay. "That's fine. Let's go!" She gave Sara a quick hug and led the way out of the lobby.

By the time they reached the seam, a fine tremor ran through Hope's body, a live current rippling back and forth.

Expectation. Anticipation. Excitement.

Several times she wanted to ask why Cassie and Luke weren't with the two policemen. But hearing Strickland report that the scanner was alive with requests for aid filled her with real hope for the first time. There must have been plenty of input.

Just a few more minutes until we all know the next step!

The trio kneeled over the seam, and Hope cupped her hands around her mouth. "Alex! I'm back with the police!"

Zach and Jasmine's expectant faces appeared below. Hope's stomach flopped at Alex's absence, her exhilaration dimming.

"Alex is restin' for a minute, but he's listenin'," Zach said.

What? Alex is resting?

That concept was so foreign Hope had a hard time picturing it. Her flopping stomach stilled and began filling with hot, burning acid.

"What did you come up with?" Jasmine called, pressing her hands together under her chin.

Perkins nodded at Hope, then shouted through the seam. "The police department has taken over the rescue. Everyone decided this was too specialized for search and rescue to oversee, so they've stepped back. But they're still on call."

"Ok," Zach said. "So, what's the plan?"

Perkins broke into a smile, his teeth blinding against his dark face. "Our dive rescue and bomb squad are teamin' up. A diver will enter the underwater passage wearin' a head-mounted video camera. Someone from the bomb squad will be watchin' remotely and will tell him where to place charges—very specific charges, positioned exactly. We'll remote-detonate them to clear the cave-in. Then the dive team will come get you guys!"

Next to him, Watson was nodding enthusiastically.

Zach and Jasmine both clapped. Happiness and sheer relief soared within Hope.

"Oh, *hell* no!" roared Alex.

The smile plummeted off Officer Perkins's face as Watson leaned closer. "No, it's a great plan! The bomb guy will tell the diver exactly where to place the explosives."

"Zach, get over here and help me up." Alex wasn't yelling now, but his voice came through loud and clear.

The young man disappeared, then returned with Alex leaning heavily against him, his arm around Zach's shoulders. His face was ashen and lined, his hair damp.

Hope gasped.

Good God. Alex, what's wrong with you?

"A great plan?" he yelled, his entire body tense and his eyes aflame. "Are you serious?"

Perkins and Watson were both slack jawed, while a deep uneasiness filled Hope.

"I am not entrusting our lives to the local version of the Keystone Cops!" Alex roared, back up to full volume. "You're going to have a *recreational* diver place shaped charges? In an overhead environment? Are you kidding me?"

Perkins and Watson exchanged a wide-eyed glance. Then Perkins returned his attention to the crevice, and he ran a hand over its surface. "Well, we could try to place the charges up here instead. Looks pretty thick, though."

Alex barked laughter. "Oh, even better! Place explosive

devices in a cavern ceiling that has *just been through an earthquake*! You're expecting me to trust a guy who doesn't know the difference between C4 and Silly Putty? You'll bring the whole goddamn thing down on top of us. My God, does anyone up there know what the hell they're doing?"

"Alex!" Hope called, shocked at his ferocity.

"We realize it's a risky plan," Watson said. "But explosives are the only way to clear the passage. Both the diver and bomb squad said they're up to the challenge."

"That's a lot easier for them to say, isn't it?" Alex called. "They'll be outside when that tunnel gets blown to hell. No way. I won't even consider it. I'm not putting Zach and Jasmine at risk like that."

Zach stared at Alex, his young brow deeply lined. Alex closed his mouth, breathing hard with his jaw set tight. He stared at Hope, though she wasn't sure he could see her face.

She spoke quietly, placatingly, even as her heart thundered in her chest. "If you won't agree with their plan, how are we supposed to get you out?"

Alex's frustrated sigh reached them. He shifted position, rearranging his arm over Zach's shoulder, but wasn't putting any weight on his right leg. Zach looked at the ground, like he wanted to disappear into it. There still wasn't enough light for her to make out Alex's injury, but Hope was getting more suspicious about the twisted ankle story.

"Hope!" Alex shouted.

She startled, refocusing on him. "Yes! I'm here."

"My phone is in the drawer of my workbench. Call Baker and tell him to get his ass down to St. Croix. Pronto! I don't trust anyone else to do this."

An involuntary gasp rushed out of her, accompanied by a blinding flash of hope. "That's a great idea!"

"Who is he talking about?" Watson asked her quietly, his brows lowered.

"You know Alex was a Navy SEAL, right?"

Both officers nodded.

"Mike Baker was on his Team for years. He's a demolitions expert. An *underwater* demolitions expert."

The two men exchanged another look, this one more calculating. "That might work," Perkins said.

"Hope! Did you hear me?" Alex called.

"Yes! We're discussing it. Just a sec."

There was loud murmuring and a lot of swearing.

"Normally, we'd never allow outside assistance," Perkins said quietly to Hope. "But we're a little out of our league here, not to mention stretched about as tight as we can get. I'm sure we can allow his friend to consult on the case."

Hope nodded and looked at Alex, who stared up at them, silent again. "I'll go and call Mike now. With the airport opening, he should be able to land." Her voice cracked on the last word and her next sentence was much quieter, fear creeping back in. "But what if he can't come down here, Alex?"

A smile rose on Alex's face, this one genuine and confident. Hope's terrified heart unclenched a bit at the sight of it.

"Don't worry, baby. He will. That's what we do."

Chapter Twenty-Eight

AFTER HASTILY MENTIONING she'd keep the two officers updated, Hope took off down the faint track at a dead run. When she reached the highway, an SUV drove by, further proof the island was recovering. She sprinted down the path and bypassed the lobby completely. During the journey, her elation regressed back into desperation. Alex was the expert, and he obviously thought the official plan was ludicrous. So ludicrous, he wasn't willing to take a chance on it. Even to save his and the kids' lives.

Not when he knew someone who was better qualified.

Hope jumped onto the pier and slowed, picking her way over the boards. Some had been replaced, but many were still damaged. She opened the door to the gear room, which had obviously been cleaned up, though Jack wasn't there. Dive equipment still lay on the floor, but now it was organized into separate piles. Alex's chair was tucked neatly into the well under his workbench. She pulled it out and sat in it, raising a shaking hand to the upper drawer.

Blowing out a long breath through her nose, Hope opened

the drawer. Alex's phone lay tucked into the front corner. Hope didn't think her pulse could race any faster, but now it did.

What if Mike isn't there? What if he doesn't pick up? What if he's on assignment in Timbuktu?

She entered Alex's password and his home screen lit up with dozens of missed calls, messages, and notifications. She opened his contacts, bringing up Mike. Hesitating, her trembling index finger hovered over the green circle. With a loud groan, she tapped the button and raised the phone to her ear.

Please, please, please.

Mike answered on the first ring. "Monroe! About time you called me back, though I know the phones have been shit. How was your little shaky-shaky?"

His warm, teasing tone almost brought a sob from Hope. She swallowed firmly, trying to hold it together. "Mike, it's Hope."

"What's wrong? Where's Alex?" Mike's joking tone was instantly gone, his voice urgent.

Hope opened her mouth, but no words came out.

"Hope! What's wrong?"

"Alex... Alex is in a cavern. With two others. He's trapped, Mike. He asked me to call you."

"Just me? Or the whole Team?"

"He didn't say anything about the Team. Just you."

"Ok, that makes it easier."

"The earthquake caused—"

"You can explain after I get there," Mike interrupted. "We're wasting time, and I need to book my flight. The news said the airport's opening soon. I'll text Alex's phone with my arrival info so you can pick me up."

He hung up and the line went dead.

Hope stared at the phone, hardly able to believe how quickly the conversation had happened. Then she gently set

Alex's phone on his workbench, leaned back in his chair, and closed her eyes.

What now?

She didn't really have any information to give anyone. Who knew when Mike could get a flight? Eyes still closed, she considered her next steps. Multiple choices and conflicting needs collided in her head.

Stop.

Think.

Plan.

Execute what Alex taught me.

Hope glanced at her watch. It was closing in on 6 p.m. The trio would need dinner. And the kids' parents were due—overdue—for an update. As Hope was prioritizing, Alex's text tone sounded.

Already?

She picked up his phone.

Mike: I got a flight out tonight. I connect in Atlanta and land in St. Croix at 9:15 tomorrow morning.

Hope's relief was so overpowering she dropped the phone. It clattered to the floor as a giant sob escaped. Tears streaked down her face. Taking a deep, shuddering breath, she wiped her eyes and picked up Alex's phone to answer Mike's text.

Alex: I'll be at the airport to pick you up.

He answered immediately.

Mike: Roger that. We'll get him out of there, Hope.

Alex: I believe that now. Thank you.

Mike: Gotta run. Over and out.

A teary smile rose on Hope's face at how Mike had slipped back into military parlance. She'd seen Alex do the same thing several times.

A quick scroll through Alex's missed calls and texts revealed that several were from his sister, Kate. "Of course she's been worried! I completely forgot."

Hope took several minutes and called Kate back, giving her the bad news of Alex being trapped, but following up with the good news that Mike was coming to lead the rescue attempt. Hope took solace in Kate's obvious relief at having Mike involved. Kate had known him for years, all the way back to when he and Alex had been SEALs, and she obviously had a high opinion of Mike's skills. Hope hung up after promising to keep Kate updated.

The sun had just dipped below the horizon when Hope entered the lobby. She stopped short, staring at the throng around her, which included many strangers. Most of the employees who had gone home were now back, including Patti. Sara, Jack, and Will stood in a huddle in the back. Jack held Magen against his shoulder, rubbing her back.

Patti had been bent over the kids' parents, a reassuring look on her face. That was replaced by palpable relief at spotting Hope. "Oh, thank goodness you're back! The two policemen didn't say much before they left. Just that the plan was bein' modified and you'd give an update."

No, I can't imagine they were real pleased with Alex's reception of their grand plan.

A tiny flame of pride rose at how Alex, despite being exhausted and in pain, had refused to submit to a plan he didn't believe in. And his natural authority was such that Perkins and Watson had agreed with him.

Hope hadn't made any type of official statement about the situation at the cavern, and who knew what rumors were flying around the resort grapevine. She held up both hands and the murmuring voices quieted. "The rescue plan has been in flux all day. Both the Police and search and rescue have been working tirelessly to help us, and I can't thank them enough. Alex, Zach, and Jasmine are trapped in a cavern near Half Moon Grotto. The only way in or out is a submerged tunnel, and the earthquake caused a cave-in, completely blocking it."

Several people scribbled on notepads, and an alarmed buzz rippled through the crowd. Hope raised one hand higher. "That's why we've been so careful. But we have a solid plan in place. I just contacted an expert who is arriving tomorrow morning. He's going to evaluate the site in order to place explosives and break apart the blockage so the group can be rescued."

Tommy's face registered blank shock. "Explosives? In a water-filled tunnel? Who do you know that's an expert on *that*?"

At last, the tight, hot ball of dread Hope had been carrying since yesterday relaxed. She smiled back at the captain. "A Navy SEAL. Who else?"

"Mrs. Monroe," said a man in the back she didn't recognize. "Is it true your husband is injured?"

"I'm sorry. Have we met?"

"No. I'm Travis McCloud from the *St. Thomas Dispatch*."

Hope tried to cover her surprise that the story had already spread to other islands.

The woman next to him spoke up. "And I'm with the *St. Thomas Herald*. There's a crew from Miami en route right now."

Hope swallowed hard and gave a vague update that Alex was slightly hobbled by a sore ankle.

Great. Now we're a media sensation.

After placating the reporters, she crossed the room and answered questions from Zach's and Jasmine's parents. "They're going to have to spend one last night in the cavern, but I'm hopeful we'll get them out of there tomorrow."

She mentally crossed her fingers, praying that was true.

Gerold prepared more quesadillas for Alex, Zach, and Jasmine's dinner. Pizza this time, which Hope delivered. With Zach's help, Alex hobbled over, still refusing to admit to more than a badly sprained ankle. The relief on his face was palpable when she told him Mike would arrive the following morning.

The power came back on, improving everyone's mood, and most of the staff departed again with plans to return the following day. Will gave Sara and her family a ride home in *Surface Interval* before returning to stay the night himself. Hope was beyond grateful.

He had been a stalwart pillar of support all throughout the emergency. But he brushed off her thanks with his customary casual joking. "My room in the house is probably completely trashed. I'm much more comfortable here."

Hope didn't believe him, which only made her more grateful as she thanked him.

The smile dropped from his long face, distress transforming his features. "I'm not leaving until Alex is out of that cavern. I wouldn't be here if it weren't for him. And it's the least I can do after what a shit I was."

Alex had mentored Will, though they had gotten off to a rocky start. That was behind them now, and Will was a treasured member of Alex's team. Tears pricked Hope's eyes and she blinked them away. "You were never a shit, but thank you, Will. Your support means everything right now."

On her way to the house for another night without Alex, Hope stopped by the restaurant kitchen. She couldn't help bursting into laughter when she saw Derek and Megan, both wearing aprons as they rinsed dishes. "Ok, I'm giving you guys a full refund. I probably need to put you on the payroll too."

Megan gave her a lovely smile as she placed a dish in the dishwasher. "This has been a babymoon to remember." Then she became serious. "We're staying right here until those three are out of the cave."

Hope raised her arms for a three-way hug. "Thanks. At least you can stay in your own bungalow again. With power!"

It was nearly 9 p.m. when Hope finally entered the house. Cruz met her at the slider, jumping up and down. She fed him quickly, feeling terribly guilty. She stared at the much cleaner great room, amazed she and Sara had been cleaning only hours ago. Time had lost all meaning. Hours lasted minutes. Then, a short while later, the next hour would stretch for days.

Too wired to sleep, Hope returned to the master bedroom to resume the clean-up. She flipped on the light in the master closet, surprised it wasn't in worse shape. The dresser was nailed to the wall, so while several drawers had shaken out and one was smashed completely, the damage was less than she'd expected.

She pushed the drawers back in, shoving clothing inside for now.

Progress, not perfection...

She tossed the smashed drawer in the garbage can outside. Returning to the closet, the floor was now clear enough to see that Alex's Navy box had opened and spilled its contents. With a sharp intake of breath, Hope dropped to her knees and crawled over to inspect the damage.

His medals were fine, secure within their hinged boxes. She smiled at his Purple Heart, then shook her head. Alex's medals had survived a hurricane and now an earthquake. They were as tough as he was. She picked up an 8 x 10 photo whose frame was undamaged, but quickly returned it to the box without looking too closely. It was a photo of Alex at the pinnacle of his career, shortly before starting a night mission. He glared at the camera, radiating lethal intent. Even years after she'd first seen it, the photo still unsettled her.

She much preferred the next one, though its frame was broken. Taken of Alex just after he became a SEAL, he was young and brash, facing the camera in dress blues and ready to take on the world. Drawing her finger slowly down his face, she set it aside so the frame could be replaced.

Hope continued picking up his things, smoothing photos which had bent during the jostling, and tipping pieces of glass off others. When she got to the prints Alex had shown her earlier, of him and the Team shirtless, tears streaked down her face. She returned them to the box and closed it gently. After wiping her face, she put the box back in the corner of the closet on top of the locked box containing his sniper rifle.

Her eye fell once again on the Young Alex picture, still on the carpet. She lifted it. "Do something productive. Something to give everyone as a thank you after this is over. Safely over."

Hope rose and moved to her home office, waking her computer. Cruz circled several times before lying down on the rug next to her desk. She'd been mulling her project over for weeks. It was time to start it.

Carefully removing Young Alex from the broken frame, Hope went to work.

Chapter Twenty-Nine

ABOVE THE SEAM, the sky gradually turned from black to gray. Alex watched the progression of his second dawn in the cave, both arms folded behind his head and his leg back to its elevated position on the rock. His sore shoulders and back had loosened up overnight, despite the hard ground. The pain in his leg, not so much. He hadn't slept much and was close to running on fumes—the rocky ground seeped the strength from his body. Zach and Jasmine lay a short distance away, Zach snoring softly.

I wonder if they'll be willing to speak with me this morning.

Things had been tense between him and the young couple after Alex shot down the police's amateur-hour plan, and Hope and the two officers had left.

Zach had been furious. "You hardly even let them talk! Maybe their plan would have worked great. We could have been out of here tonight! Who knows if your Navy buddy can even get here?"

Alex ignored the sneer in Zach's voice when he'd said, *Navy buddy,* though his own temper was on a very short fuse. "I'll deal with that when the situation becomes a reality."

"Oh, that sounds like a great plan."

"Zach, just shut up," Jasmine said, her face thunderous. "The only reason any of us are in here is because of you. You're hardly in a position to complain about anythin'."

Face stricken, Zach drew in a deep breath, wheeled around, and stalked off into the gloom.

The last thing Alex wanted was the two of them fighting. "This isn't his fault. And we need to work together if we're going to make it out of here."

Jasmine sighed, a tear slipping down her face. She swiped it away angrily. "I shouldn't have said that. It just slipped out." She stepped away, following in the direction Zach left.

They were gone a long time. Their quiet voices carried through the cavern, though Alex couldn't hear what they were saying. But they were holding hands when they returned. Alex wanted to give an uplifting talk about how he was positive they'd get out, but he just didn't have the energy.

The group was quiet until Hope returned with pizza quesadillas and confirmation that Mike would arrive the following morning.

This morning now. Even though Alex wasn't directly under the seam, he could see the sky just fine. It was edging from gray to pale blue.

With a jaw-cracking yawn, Jasmine lifted onto an elbow, and she exchanged a good-morning nod with Alex. Her gaze moved to his leg. "If you'd tell Hope about your leg, she could slip some first aid supplies through the seam."

"My leg's beyond the first-aid stage. And the skin's hardly broken, so nothing in the kit would help." *Except maybe ibuprofen or Tylenol.*

Jasmine snapped her eyes to his, acknowledging his admission that the injury was serious. "Even if they get that tunnel cleared, are you going to be able to swim out?"

"I'll swim out."

"If they get the passage open, they can probably bring in a stretcher," Zach said, his eyes still closed.

"No stretcher. I'll make it out under my own power."

Zach smirked. "Anyone ever told you you're stubborn?"

Alex laughed softly. "Only a few thousand times. Hope has called me a mule on multiple occasions."

That made them both smile, and the residual tension slid away.

"Mike will be here in a few hours," Alex continued. "He's forgotten more about explosives than I ever knew. Hang in there, guys."

His eyes drifted back to the seam, now with clear blue sky above. He was glad the negative energy had faded—he'd meant what he said about this not being Zach's fault. Alex slid his left foot up to bend his knee. As careful as he was, the movement still sent a stabbing bolt of agony through his right leg. Alex pressed his lips tight, refusing to give in to the pain.

There was no use blaming Zach. He wasn't responsible.

Alex was.

Hope walked into the kitchen, ideas for yet more quesadillas running through her head. The heavenly scent of bacon cooking interrupted those ideas. Pauline, wearing a fresh white chef's coat and her straightened black hair tied back, looked up from the grill. "Mornin'."

"Good morning. Did Gerold finally go home?"

"Yeah, but he's comin' back later to help with lunch and dinner."

"I came to get something for Alex, Zach, and Jasmine's breakfast."

Pauline's brows reached skyward. "The kids' parents just left with it."

"Oh," Hope said, strangely bereft. It was after 7 a.m., so that wasn't surprising. Hope hadn't set an alarm and had finally fallen into a restless sleep around three. And she really should check on resort operations before heading to the airport. Except she felt guilty not supplying Alex's breakfast. "What did you make them?"

"Johnny cakes and a bunch of bacon. With some maple-flavored pancakes to go with it."

Hope broke into laughter. "That sounds heavenly!"

"You want some?"

"No, I already ate. I need to head to the pier and see what's going on there. Thanks, Pauline."

The sound of hammering echoed from the pier, and Hope was curious to see the cause. She climbed the wooden stairs, where several fresh boards were now nailed down to the supports. Further down, Will and Tommy kneeled, each hammering away.

The dock was once again solid and secure under her feet. She stopped in front of the men. "You two started early."

Will looked up and grinned. "I had so many takers on my house reef trip yesterday, Tommy and I decided to take the boat out for a morning dive."

"We decided it wouldn't be good to have someone trip on the loose boards, so here we are," Tommy added.

"I'm sure the guests will love a little normalcy. Did you sleep here again?" she asked Tommy.

"Nah, just left the house early. Priscilla wants hourly updates on the situation at the grotto."

Will eyed her evenly. "We figured things wouldn't get going out there until this afternoon. If it's sooner than that, you'll let us know, right?"

"I'm sure that's true. This rescue is going to be planned *very* carefully. As much as we want them out, this is not the time to rush in, guns blazing. You should have plenty of time." She could almost *feel* Alex smiling at her and sent a warm thought back.

I've learned, honey—I won't make that mistake again. You taught me well.

When Hope reached the lobby, people had already begun to congregate. Patti stood behind the desk with Martine. They were speaking with a small cluster of people. Guests from three bungalows were checking out and the arrivals had cancelled. The departing guests standing before the desk had confirmed seats on the day's departing flights and were eager to get to the airport.

Zach's and Jasmine's parents were already back from the seam. Hope crossed the lobby to them. "Thank you for bringing breakfast out there."

"Of course," Lucy replied. "We needed to see our kids."

"I'm mighty relieved a SEAL is comin' to help with this," Herb said. "We have a lot more faith in Alex than what the locals came up with."

"Mike Baker should be landing soon, then we can get started. At some point, you might want to move out to the grotto, since that's where the rescue will be staged. I'll be busy with Mike, but I'll make sure Patti keeps you all updated."

Next, Hope moved to the other side of the lobby and set some ground rules with the reporters, whose numbers had swelled even more. They would be allowed at the grotto, including cameras. But none could venture to the seam. The last thing Alex, Jasmine, or Zach needed were nosy reporters asking them questions. The press tried to talk her into escorted visits, but Hope refused to be swayed. "Take it or leave it, guys. No one speaks to the three of them except family and rescuers.

And *no one* will interfere with the rescue attempt. If you get in the way, I'll pull all of you out."

The reporters grumbled, but eventually agreed, packing up their vans to stage their equipment at the rock pool. John Strickland strolled over, and she met him with a steel gaze.

"I was hoping I might be allowed special access to talk to Alex," he said. "For old times' sake?"

Hope stepped close to him. "If you step as much as one toe *anywhere* you're not authorized, I'll personally see to it you're run off this island and never find work again."

Laughing, Strickland took a big step back and held up both arms. "Take it easy! I had to try, didn't I? Believe it or not, I admire your husband a lot. If I was stuck in a cave only accessible by a flooded tunnel, he'd be the one I'd want with me."

Slightly mollified, Hope nodded. "I guess that makes two of us. But you get the same access as everyone else, no more or less."

"Fair enough."

She turned and strode to the exit.

"Hope?" When she looked over her shoulder, Strickland nodded. "Good luck out there today. I mean that."

Finally, she thawed. "Thank you."

Hope trotted down the stairs. It was time to pick up Mike.

Chapter Thirty

HOPE STARED OPENMOUTHED as she drove her Jeep Wrangler through Frederiksted and toward the southern part of the island containing the airport. The road was clear, and she didn't need to shift into 4WD once. But signs of damage were everywhere, including a large brown gash on the side of a steep hillside in the central portion of the island.

Several buildings had collapsed in Frederiksted, but the huge central pier was still intact. People wearing fluorescent vests and hardhats were everywhere, as were ordinary citizens, trying to help wherever possible. She pulled into the airport parking lot. A large section was cordoned off with yellow caution tape—a crack ran through the asphalt, the two sides several inches apart.

The check-in area was crammed with people. Overhead announcements boomed constantly—telling people to call the central reservations number, and that all flights out for the next two days were completely full.

Hope weaved around people, mothers holding the hands of crying children and sunburned tourists who had gotten more of an adventure than they bargained for. Now all just wanted to return home. Mike's flight was announced over the overhead speakers just as she reached the arrivals area. His plane had landed and was heading toward the terminal.

Hope looked around herself, just now realizing she was one of only four people waiting for an arrival.

Maybe it wasn't so hard for Mike to get a flight. Everyone wants out, not in.

Less than ten minutes later, Mike strode toward her. He moved with a serious intent she'd never seen before, dressed in olive green cargo pants and a fitted black T-shirt that contrasted with his green eyes. But after spotting her, he broke into his usual warm smile. They embraced and Hope nearly collapsed with relief that he had made it.

"Thank you for coming. I feel so much better about this now. You got here really fast."

Mike barked a laugh. "I barely made it to the airport in time. Let's head to the baggage carousel. I have a checked bag."

Hope couldn't hide her surprise as they left the hall. "You brought a suitcase?"

"I packed everything I thought I might possibly need. Except the ordinance."

"I wondered how you'd decide what to pack. You never asked me what Alex's situation was."

Mike shot her a side-eye. "I served with him a long time. I knew what to pack. Everything."

A large green canvas duffel appeared on the belt, TSA stickers covering it that indicated it had been opened and searched.

"Wow," Hope said. "Looks like they used a fine-tooth comb."

"Yeah, I told them at check-in they'd probably want to look

it over closely. I've got lots of goodies in there, including my pistol."

Hope reared back. "You brought your *gun?*"

Mike shrugged. "At first, I wasn't going to. But inside my head, I could hear Alex yelling. 'You came all the way down here and forgot your most important piece of equipment?'"

She laughed. "I can see him saying that."

He winced, squinting one eye. "I *have* seen him say that."

They were soon driving back, and Hope gave him a summary of the earthquake, as well as the tunnel and cavern. Mike asked several pertinent questions but didn't interrupt otherwise.

"I have a guest bungalow for you, which became available this morning," Hope said. "The key is in my purse. Do you want to go there now?"

Mike shook his head. "Take me straight to the cavern. I want to talk to Alex first, then recon the area and the tunnel before any *authorities*"—he used air quotes around the word—"show up."

"I'm sorry to take you away from Emma on such short notice. I'm sure she'd rather have you home."

"She understands. She's worried about Alex too."

"One more thing," Hope said. "Alex is injured. He says he twisted his ankle, but I think it's more serious. He hasn't put any weight on his right leg. Zach helps him move whenever we've spoken. But he refuses to admit it's anything more than an ankle sprain."

Mike breathed a long sigh. "Ok. Thanks for letting me know. We'll see if he's any more enlightening about it when I talk to him, but I doubt it."

Instead of turning onto the access road toward the resort, Hope pulled onto the grassy shoulder of the highway near the

Half Moon Grotto trail, relieved to find no other cars or news vans parked. She told Mike about the reporters.

Mike grunted. "Looks like word of your party is getting around."

"Unfortunately, yes. I gave the media strict orders to stay out of the way, or they'll be evicted. And none of them know where the cavern is located."

Hope set a hard pace, knowing Mike was fit enough to handle it. She followed the fence, then headed down the animal track, now more noticeable after all the traffic that had been over it the past two days.

Hopefully not for much longer...

They continued until they reached the bare, rocky shelf, with the ruins of Barnaby's house to one side. Hope knelt next to the seam. "Guys! I've got Mike here. Bring Alex over!"

It took longer than Hope expected. Jasmine appeared first, followed by Zach and Alex hobbling together. She inspected Alex closely, not liking what she saw. There were dark smudges under his eyes and his hair was damp, but he smiled gamely at her. "I've been waiting to hear your voice."

"Sorry I missed you this morning. Zach's and Jasmine's parents had already taken care of your breakfast when I got there."

"You can bring me breakfast tomorrow. At home."

She wasn't sure how realistic that was. Even if they got out of the cave soon, Alex looked like he needed to be in a hospital, not at home. But she wasn't about to say that out loud. "Count on it, sailor. Here's Mike."

Since arriving, Mike had been serious and completely focused. But as he hunkered down over the seam, his typical humorous, smartass countenance reappeared. He leaned over. "Well, look at that. Little Timmy fell in the well."

"Yeah?" Alex called. "I guess that makes you Lassie, then."

"Oh, shit! You're right. I guess that's my fate in life. To be the ever-faithful companion to Commander Monroe. Always sacrificing so you can receive the glory."

"Yeah, yeah. At least you're here."

"Are you and Zach an official thing now? Or are you two practicing three-legged races down there?"

Alex's face turned stony, but his voice remained even. "I've got a banged-up leg. I'm trying to be smart about not using it too much."

"Smart? Wow! I guess there's a first time for everything."

"Oh, shut up."

Mike affected a hurt look, holding one hand against his chest. "So cranky! Would you prefer I make a joke about *Silence of the Lambs* instead? I could get some lotion."

Face thunderous, Alex took a deep breath and shouted, "No, Baker. I would prefer you get off your good-for-nothing, wisecracking, lazy ass and get the hell down here!"

Hope gasped, whispering, "Alex!" Horrified, she darted her eyes to Mike, and was even more shocked at the wide grin splitting his face.

"Don't worry." Mike looked up and murmured to her. "This is the best sign possible. A grumpy Alex is an Alex in full command. It's when he gets quiet and withdrawn that you need to worry about him."

Hope snapped her open mouth shut and nodded, acknowledging that Mike had seen Alex in situations she couldn't even comprehend. And she'd heard enough conversations between the two men to know this was rather normal banter between them.

Mike returned his attention to the crevice. "Well, when you put your request so politely, how can I refuse? I'll go check out the tunnel and find the best areas to place charges. After that we'll meet up with the local yokels and see what they have for me to play with. I'll come back here and warn you before anything goes boom, don't worry."

Alex closed his eyes and breathed a sigh. "Thanks, Mike. I can't tell you how relieved I am to have you here."

"Ah, don't mention it. I wasn't going to do anything fun today. This beats the hell out of sitting in my giant corner office managing huge defense contracts all day long. You wouldn't believe the toys they give me! You want to hear the latest?"

"If you want to get started sometime this century, that would be peachy, Baker."

Mike grinned again. "Aye-aye, Commander." He hopped to his feet as Hope leaned close to the seam.

"Alex?"

He was pale and sweating, his sandy hair darker where it was matted to his head. He answered in a softer tone than he'd used with Mike. "Yeah, baby?"

"I love you."

A crack appeared in Alex's carefully constructed mask. Bare need shone through, then he covered it again. That told Hope all she needed to know about how much he was struggling.

"I love you too," he said, and finally a genuine smile rose on his face, as if she had just filled his empty tank.

"We'll be back as soon as we can. I promise." Biting her lip, Hope rose.

As soon as they began marching toward the perimeter fence, Mike became serious again. "How much dive equipment do you have staged at the grotto?"

"Just my kit plus a couple of extra tanks."

"Let's head to the resort and grab equipment for me. Do you have a rebreather I could use?"

She glanced at him over her shoulder. "We only have one. Alex has it."

Her concern must have shown on her face because Mike

shot her a smile. "Don't worry, we'll get them out of there. But I think you're right about his injury being more than a twisted ankle. He was sweating, and I imagine that cave is probably cool. Jasmine had a blanket wrapped around her."

Hope nodded as she faced forward again. "I hate the idea of him being in so much pain."

Mike barked laughter behind her. "Hope, that guy is the toughest son of a bitch I've ever met. People tried to kill him for *years*. I think he's pretty much indestructible. Stop worrying."

Relief washed over Hope, then she had to smile as she led the way down the path, realizing Mike was working his magic on her now. Her mind vividly flashed back to when Alex and Mike had met again at a festival in Christiansted. More specifically, to when she and Alex were driving home after having drinks with Mike and Emma. Alex had said, *"Every platoon has one guy. The guy who holds it all together. Who can joke when it's needed, or open up a can of whoop-ass when that's more appropriate. Mike was that guy."*

The smile lingered on her face. "I'm really glad you're here."

He laughed behind her. "Alex is one of those guys you'd cross deserts for. Any of us would. You remember my story about that awful night we all did the Shame March as one unit?"

Hope tried not to shudder, laughing instead. "Yes. That was hard to forget."

"We gave Alex hell about it afterward. But that exercise bonded us as a Team like you wouldn't believe. He kept all of us together, supporting anyone who faltered. When we were running on the sand, no one was allowed to pull ahead and get the damn thing over with. When one guy needed to walk, we all did. And Alex was right there with us. That night became a badge of honor for us. New guys were jealous they hadn't been there. Hope, *any* of us would come if he needed help. And Alex would do the same for us."

Soft warmth spread through Hope's chest. "Yes, he would. That's why he's in that cavern right now. He had to make sure Zach and Jasmine were safe."

AN HOUR LATER, they returned to the sandy beach of the grotto. Mike pushed the cart, now filled with dive equipment and several extra tanks. His duffel bag from the Jeep was tossed on top. Hope was relieved to find they were still alone. "I was afraid the press would already be setting up their turf, but they must be hanging out in the lobby. I guess they're waiting for the show to actually start."

"We were pretty stealthy when we picked up all this stuff. Hopefully no one saw us. I want to get the lay of the land before the circus starts."

Mike quickly put his dive kit together, including a pony bottle for an extra air source. Hope couldn't help smiling when he clipped a back-up light to his BCD, making sure he had redundancies in place. He glanced across the pool. "I remember where the tunnel is. I saw the gate when Emma and I came out here."

"You can't miss it. The earthquake broke one of the gate's hinges, so it's hanging askew. They're saying the tremors have nearly stopped, so hopefully we're done with the earthquakes."

Mike grinned as he buckled his BCD shut. "That would be greatly appreciated." Tucking a pair of black fins under one arm, he moved to the shore.

"Sure you don't want me to come with you?"

"Yes," he said quickly. "This is just a recon. I won't be gone too long. You can keep watch in case anyone shows up. Tell them the pool was so pretty I just had to dive it."

Hope laughed, though she wasn't entirely happy to be left behind. *He better not try to keep me out of there once the passage is open.* "Be careful in there."

He pulled the mask onto his face. "Don't worry. Careful's my middle name."

Chapter Thirty-One

AFTER HOPE and Mike left to plan the rescue mission, Zach helped Alex back to his rock. He was impressed by how well the divemaster was holding up to being his pack mule. Zach had grown several inches and put on quite a few pounds but was still much smaller than Alex. And he was leaning on Zach completely, unable to bear any weight on his right leg. He refused to even try moving his toes now.

Easing himself to the ground, he endured more agony propping his leg on top of the wadded-up blanket. Alex tried to hang on to the emotion that flooded through him at hearing Hope say those three words. She was his strength, what was getting him through this ordeal. And his last words to her before the quake had been irritated and childish.

I just hope I get the chance to make up for that.

He closed his eyes as a soul-deep gratitude rose in him. That Hope had stayed behind to work the front desk.

Otherwise, she might be dead right now.

One of them would be, certainly. Whoever had been trailing as they swam down the tunnel during the earthquake.

Then he thought of his conversation with Mike, and heat

rose up his neck. *Always the smartass. We've got a job to do, and he wants to joke about it.*

Then again, Alex had pretty much bitten Mike's head off when the man had dropped everything to come help.

Great, Monroe. What a super friend I am.

Alex's positive mood disappeared as quietly as Hope and Mike's shadows had. Lifting his arm, he sniffed his armpit.

Yeah, that's lovely.

He was sweating continuously now, and his shirt was soaked. He pulled it over his head and held it out to Zach. "Can you rinse this off?"

"Sure." Zach took the wet shirt and headed toward the water. He returned quickly, and Alex put it back on. At least it smelled better now. He didn't have chills or feel feverish, and figured the sweating was just a pain response.

Jasmine tightened the blanket around her shoulders and sat cross-legged nearby. "How long do you think it will take Mike to set the charges?"

"A long time," Alex replied quietly. "Hours. He's very methodical and won't rush this."

She nodded and picked at a loose thread on her blanket. "Alex, I'm scared to swim out."

He reached over and squeezed her knee, ignoring the bolt of pain. This was worth it. "You wouldn't be human if you weren't."

Jasmine shook her head, avoiding Zach's concerned gaze. "It's not that. I was really scared comin' in here. Even before the earthquake, I dreaded the return trip." She turned a pair of frightened eyes to him. "What if I can't do this?"

Alex dug deep. He wasn't sure he was even capable of a pep talk right now. But he had to try. "You've already proven you can. You're here, right? And you won't be alone. Plenty of people will be here to help."

Zach took her hand. "Jas, it's my fault you're here in the first place. Please let me try to make up for it. I promise. I won't let anythin' happen to you."

Jasmine stared at him, her forehead still lined.

She's not buying it.

Alex stared intently at her. "Mike might be a smartass, but he's the best at what he does. He'll find a way." *I hope.* "And I don't give up easily, either. Let's see what he comes up with. Maybe he'll find an exterior wall he can blow a hole in, and the return trip will be a piece of cake."

When Jasmine's face relaxed and she nodded, Alex hated himself even more. But she couldn't give up. Not now.

"I'm going to close my eyes for a while, guys." Alex lay down and clasped his hands over his stomach.

"I'm gonna check over our dive equipment," Zach said.

Jasmine rose to join him. "I'll go with you."

Alex closed his eyes as they left, trying to keep his mind a blank slate. It was impossible. He couldn't get Hope out of his head. But these weren't warm thoughts of the times they had spent together. All he could focus on was how his deficiencies had nearly gotten her injured—or worse—*twice* in the last few months. He was the teacher, the leader. *The example.* Or he used to be.

His recent track record screamed otherwise.

Alex opened his eyes to stare at the ceiling, imagining Barnaby's nearby home. Though there was no proof, he had a strong feeling his and Hope's idea of Barnaby falling in love with a freed or escaped slave was true. Why else would he give up everything to live alone in the bush with that treasure nearby? Only true love was worthy of that kind of sacrifice. Alex sent out a silent wish.

Barnaby, if you're still haunting this place, I could use a hand right now. I'd sure appreciate it.

Whenever Hope appeared above, Alex couldn't see her clearly. Her face was always in shadow. But every curve and plane of her face was etched upon his soul. He didn't need his eyes to see her.

Oh, Hope. Just a bit longer.

AFTER A LONG TIME, Zach and Jasmine came back. They sat huddled together, but away from Alex, and murmured quietly. Trying to let him sleep.

Zach's words ran through his head. That it was Zach's fault that Jasmine was there. She was there because of his decision, but the fault lay with Alex.

What kind of teacher—no, leader—could I possibly be that he thought this was a good idea?

Alex might have dozed off. It was hard to tell. He hadn't slept soundly since the night before the earthquake. But his mind insisted on treating him to a continuous loop of everything he'd done wrong in recent months.

He was used to being in charge, being in control. Now he was anything but. Alex was nothing but a feather in the breeze, dependent upon others. Just like after Syria.

When did I become such a failure? How the hell did this happen?

Eventually, Zach's and Jasmine's worried voices drifted over to him. "Do you think he's asleep?" Jasmine asked.

"He hasn't said anythin' in hours. And he doesn't look real great. I'm worried about him."

"So am I. Should we wake him up?"

"No," Zach replied. "Let him sleep. I'm not sure he can swim out on his own. He needs all the rest he can get. God, that leg—I can't imagine how much pain he must be in."

"I'm so scared, Zach. What if the explosions make things worse?"

"I know, Jas. I'm scared too. We'll figure this out. I promise."

Shame slithered through Alex, a creeping serpent bending its way through his abdomen. *I should be consoling them. But I just don't have the energy.*

The voice roared inside his head. *"Goddammit Monroe! Stop feeling sorry for yourself. You're pathetic! These two need you. They're kids, for God's sake. Are you going to lay there and mope about being a shitty leader, or are you going to do something about it?"*

Alex snapped his eyes open, pressing his lips into a thin line. The voice was right. Self-pity was a bottomless pit that would get him nowhere—he had personal experience with that. Taking a deep breath to prepare, Alex shook his right leg. Hard. A thousand knives exploded in his lower leg, blazing hot and eternal.

The voice became excited. *"That's it. Pain! What got you through, after Syria? What, Monroe?"*

Pain is a reminder I'm still alive. That I can influence the outcome.

"Exactly!"

I might be a lousy leader, but I can still get this job done.

"So do it, dumbass."

Strength flooded into Alex's muscles, determination setting in to rival the pain. *And I'm done talking to myself like this. Piss off.*

"Oh—so you figured out I'm not real?"

I've always known that. Go to hell, asshole. I've got this.

A soft laugh sounded in Alex's head. Then it faded away.

The agonized throbbing diminished slightly, and he was proud he hadn't screamed out loud. But his face was sopping again. He grabbed the nearby sheet and wiped it dry.

Just get through this. Prioritize. I've got a job to do here, goddammit. I might be a failure, but I can make up for it.

He turned his head toward Zach and Jasmine.

Both stared at him, fear apparent in their round eyes.

Alex managed a smile that weighed a thousand pounds. But he did it. "Don't count me out just yet, guys. I've been in some pretty awful situations in my life. A busted-up leg isn't enough to break me. We'll get out of here. All three of us."

Zach's face relaxed. He gave Alex a tiny smile. "Look at it this way. You'll have a hell of a story to tell at the next scuba agency meeting."

That lanced straight to Alex's heart. He shook his head. "Doesn't matter. I'm resigning."

"What?" The shock was clear in Jasmine's voice.

"Why would you resign?" Zach asked. "You just started."

Alex heaved a sigh, reality crashing down again. "Because I'm the last person who should be doing that job."

Zach stared at him. "What are you talking about?"

"Zach, a team is only as good as its leader. Look at what's happened the past few months. A divemaster I was personally mentoring fell off a ladder and injured a guest. My own wife rescued a swimmer in distress, completely forgetting basic procedures. And now we're here. You're wrong, Zach. Being in this cavern isn't your fault. It's mine. I didn't do my goddamn job."

"How is me being a complete dumbshit *your* fault?" Zach said.

"You brought Jasmine in here, didn't you? It doesn't sound like I did a real great job of discussing the risks of cavern diving."

Zach burst into laughter. It echoed around them. "I knew there was danger. I just didn't care. I thought this place was awesome and wanted to show my girl. Maybe get lucky too."

Jasmine rolled her eyes. "Great. You can shut up now, Zach."

Alex arched a brow at him. "Yeah. I got that part when I came in here the first time."

Zach sobered and leaned forward, looping his arms around his bent knees. "The point is, I knew *exactly* what I was risking. You made that extremely clear when I dove here with Hope. I used to think you went overboard with the safety shit. Then this happened." Zach rubbed a hand over his close-cropped hair, clearly frustrated. "Alex, this situation is exactly why you're a great teacher. And leader. You make your expectations clear—" He barked another laugh. "Extremely clear. Then you back off to let people make their own decisions. And mistakes.

"When things go to shit, you do everything possible to help. Will beat himself up all to hell after he fell off that ladder. You want to know why? Because he disappointed you. People screw up, Alex! Then they either learn or they don't. You give them the room to work that out for themselves."

Zach alternated his gaze between Jasmine and Alex. "I'm sorry. I want to say that to both of you." His voice hitched and he wiped a hand over his eyes, clearing the tears. "Jas, I put you in danger. And Alex, you're hurt and in a lot of pain. All because of me. The decisions I made—not you, Alex. You were just tryin' to help because you realized I was bein' stupid."

He stared at Alex for a long moment. "I screwed up. And we're payin' for it big time. You better believe I'm learnin' from this mistake."

Alex twitched the corner of his mouth, wanting to draw Zach out of his depressed, futile mood. That wouldn't help. "For a punk-ass kid, you're pretty smart, you know that?"

Zach's expression softened. "Yeah, boss. I am. So lighten up on yourself, ok?"

"Message received. I'll try."

"By the way, do I still have a job?"

Alex's smile steadied. "Yeah. You're not the first guy who did something stupid to impress a woman."

The young man gave a drawn-out sigh. "And I didn't even get laid."

Alex finally broke into laughter. "Guess I kind of ruined that, huh?"

"Hell yes, you did!"

Jasmine was laughing now too. "I've never been so embarrassed in my life."

"Sorry," Alex said. "But I really didn't want to see where that was going."

"I can't believe we were about to have sex in a cave," Jasmine said, gazing around. "It seemed like such a great idea at the time. But who *does* that?"

Alex's laughter increased to the point where he had to tone it down because his leg was getting jostled. "I have no idea."

He turned his gaze back to the ceiling. He'd memorized every bump and crease in it now. But his smile remained, reflecting the vision of him and Hope making love right here. The vivid reminder of her in his arms and being as close as two people can be.

His soul and mind were now lighter. Soon it would be time to go to work, and he would face the challenge head on. All three of them were getting out of this cavern.

Alex had found hope again.

Chapter Thirty-Two

BY NOON, the sandy beach and small meadow of Half Moon Grotto were transformed. The first news crews had arrived while Mike was still inside the tunnel. Hope directed them to the grass and tactfully told them to keep the hell out of the way. Mike explored longer than she expected, not surfacing until an hour after he entered the rock pool.

He walked across the beach and joined her. "You can call the police and dive rescue now. I've got the info I need to proceed."

Hope nodded and called Officer Perkins. Within half an hour, both he and Officer Watson arrived in their police cruiser, carefully exiting the narrow trail to park near the meadow. Behind them, two men climbed out of a black armored truck. The first man, wearing shorts and a T-shirt, introduced himself as Trevor. He was around thirty, of average height and with light-brown hair. The other was a towering man with ebony skin, dressed in an all-black tactical police uniform. Perkins introduced him as Josiah from the bomb squad.

Mike shook Josiah's hand, and a long, evaluating look passed between them. They gave each other a respectful nod. "Pleased to meet you," Mike said. "What's your background?"

"Army," Josiah replied in a deep, booming voice. "Demolitions."

"Glad to have you aboard." When Mike turned to shake Trevor's hand, an amused gleam entered his eye. "And you must be with dive rescue."

"I am." Trevor frowned, looking Mike up and down. "I take it you're the consultant they brought down to help."

"Mike Baker."

"No offense, man," Trevor said. "I don't know your background, but I have a lot of experience here in St. Croix. I don't mind you tagging along, but I want to make it clear I intend to lead this rescue."

"Is that right?" Mike smiled, glee openly sparkling in his eyes now. "Well, I certainly don't want to step on the toes of an expert."

"Thank you. I'm glad that's settled. Josiah is going to help me place charges. I'm happy to listen to you, but I think he and I can handle this."

Josiah's brow creased. "Uh, Trevor. I don't think you—"

"How many dives have you done, Trevor?" Mike interrupted.

The diver parked both hands on his hips. "Over a thousand."

Mike inhaled, his mouth forming an O. "Gee! A *thousand*?"

Hope had watched Alex in action often enough to guess where Mike was going with this conversation. She kept quiet and watched.

"Yeah. So do what I tell you, and we'll get along fine."

"How many times have you placed explosives, or worked with them?"

Trevor raked a hand over his head. "Never. But Josiah can

walk me through it. Are you just here to ask questions or are you actually going to help at some point? And who are you? What's *your* background?"

The polite expression plummeted off Mike's face. His eyes became steel, his jaw set firm as he took two rapid steps forward, stopping right in front of Trevor's face. The diver took a large step backward, his eyes growing large, and Mike advanced again. "I'll tell you who I am. I'm a former United States Navy SEAL with over ten years of combat experience. I'm a demolitions and ordnance expert in underwater and aboveground environments. I currently work as a defense contractor advising on tactical weapons. That means explosives. Because I'm an expert, Trevor."

He flung an arm in the direction of the tunnel, his eyes blazing. "I intend to do everything humanly possible to conduct this rescue successfully and safely. So I *strongly* suggest you modify your tone when you speak to me."

His nose was inches from Trevor's, whose face was bright red.

Hope could hardly keep from smiling. Next to her, Josiah straightened and crossed his huge arms, leveling a hard stare at the diver.

Trevor held up both hands, placating. "Ok, ok. I'm sorry. I thought you were just some guy they sent to complicate everything."

Mike stood still as a statue, both hands on his hips. "No. That job belongs to you."

"I won't interfere, ok? I want them out of that cave too."

Mike relaxed, moving back a step, though his face was still hard. "Good. And there's one other thing. One of the people trapped in that cave is Hope's husband and my former commanding officer. So you damn well better believe I won't let anything stop me from completing this rescue. Including you."

The diver darted a glance at Hope before returning his gaze to Mike. "What do you want me to do?"

"For now, Trevor, I'd like you to stand with Perkins and Watson and keep the hell out of my way. Later, I'd like your support when we ask for it." Finally, his expression softened. "You'll get the chance to help, don't worry. But right now, I need to concentrate on my job."

"Deal. I'll see if the cops need anything." Trevor exchanged a nod with Mike before crossing to join the two police officers in the shade. Mike turned to Josiah, speaking respectfully, peer-to-peer. "Do you have any C4?"

"Some," Josiah replied. "We don't have reason to use it here much."

"I don't need a lot. I'm going to set several small charges and try to blow that rock pile toward the grotto end of the tunnel. Without caving in the whole damn shooting match." He turned to Hope. "Any idea how long the cave-in extends?"

"I think it's pretty short," she said. "Fifteen to twenty feet of the tunnel had a ridged, unstable ceiling. From what Zach described after he got Alex, I think that's the only portion that collapsed."

"I'll set the charges in several places near the top of the tunnel. After the detonation, I'll go back in there and see if one series was enough to clear a path. If not, I'll do it again."

Josiah nodded across the beach to the black truck. "My gear is over there. I'll get the C4 and detonators."

After he left, Hope stepped next to Mike. "I want to go with you."

The former SEAL had been watching Josiah walk away. Now he slowly rolled his head toward her, his eyes going round. "When I set charges? Are you *kidding*?"

"No, I'm not kidding. Alex is in there, Mike! And he's hurt.

I want to help." She stopped for a moment, swallowing back her emotion. "I need to help."

"I understand. I know the last few days have been rough. But there's no way I'm letting you in there, Hope. I need to concentrate on what I'm doing, not worry about where you are or how much air you have."

When she opened her mouth to protest, he held up a finger. "No. You're not coming. You mentioned Alex. Do you seriously think he would want you with me when I'm setting explosives? He would have my head—parboiled—on a giant platter!"

Hope couldn't help but laugh, though it was equal parts humor and frustration. Mike was one hundred percent right about Alex. "All right. Only one thing matters right now. And that's getting the three of them out of there as fast as possible."

"Agreed."

"But if you think I'm staying behind when you go in there to reach the cavern, think again."

He stared at her, but Hope met his gaze head-on, unblinking. A staring contest ensued. Eventually, Mike broke eye contact with a laugh. "God, you're as stubborn as he is. Ok. As long as you stay behind for the detonation, I'll let you come with me to see if the tunnel is open."

"Thank you. Be careful in there."

It took an hour for Josiah and Mike to prepare the C4 and for Mike to get kitted up. He unzipped his large duffel, attaching pliers, snips, and other things Hope couldn't guess the purpose of to his BCD. He adjusted his pony bottle and put his mask on. A large spool of wire was attached near his hip. "Ok, I'm ready. I should be able to set the charges on one tank of air. Be back soon."

Hope had spent the morning keeping her worry and fear at bay, concentrating on getting Mike what he needed. But now there was nothing to distract her. The thought that she'd been pushing away all morning came roaring forward—of the last time she'd seen Alex close-up. When she snapped at him to go to the grotto without her. He hadn't been happy when he'd left.

He was only doing what I'd asked him to. To show support. And I bit his head off and sent him away.

Gerold and Clark arrived with lunch boxes and a cooler of soft drinks. Hope forced herself to eat, chewing woodenly. Nerves made her slightly queasy, but she forced down the meal. She had just tossed her trash in the garbage bag hanging from a tree limb when Sara arrived.

She crossed to Hope and embraced her. "How are you holding up?"

"Mike is setting the charges right now, so my mind is working overdrive on possible disasters."

Sara pulled back, gripping both Hope's upper arms. "Make it stop, then. He knows what he's doing."

"Where's Magen?" Hope asked.

"Jack's got her back at the resort. I came to get an update, and we'll all return when the rescue happens."

They crossed to the edge of the trees, sitting in the shade so they could have some privacy. Hope gave Sara a summary of what was going to happen.

"The rescue should be today?"

"Hopefully. Mike said he might need two tries to get the tunnel blasted open. I'm not sure my heart can take more than one."

Sara clasped her hand. "He'll be fine, Hope. Alex will be fine."

That was all it took for Hope to lose control. She buried her face in her hands, leaning over her crossed legs and sobbing. Sara rubbed her back, moving her hand in slow circles.

When she'd cried herself out, Hope sat upright again and

wiped her face. "I feel like half of me has been ripped out. I can't live without him, Sara."

"You won't have to."

"The last time we were together, I was a bitch to him. He wanted me to go with him to the tunnel, and I was too busy. Too busy!"

Sara cocked her head. "And if you had? You'd be stuck in there too."

"At least we'd be together."

"You'll be together soon. Hope, you moved mountains to make this happen. Literally! Plus, you've been dealing with getting the resort back together. If you were in there, things would be an absolute mess out here. Patti can only do so much."

"I should have never spoken to him like that." The image of their shattered wedding picture flashed before Hope's eyes, adding insult to injury. She shuddered.

"You'll get your chance to apologize. In person. When you rescue him."

Hope laughed weakly. "That's a change, huh? Alex is the one being rescued."

Sara grinned as she wrapped an arm around Hope and pulled her close. "And you're the one rising to the challenge and making everything happen. Queen of your realm. I'm going to start calling you Crowning Hope."

Hope leaned her head against Sara's and wiped her eyes again. "That's a bit much. If ever there was a team effort, it's this rescue." She laughed as something occurred to her. "I wanted a team-building exercise, didn't I? I guess I got it."

Across the clearing, Mike surfaced and finned toward the shore. Hope vaulted to her feet, trotting toward the beach with Sara at her side. Mike climbed onto the sand, letting out a long line of wire from the spool as he went. Everyone clustered around, including the police, as well as Josiah and Trevor. The reporters stayed where they were supposed to.

Mike nodded at Hope. "I set four charges. I think that will be enough to blast through the rocks without bringing down the larger structure above."

Hope straightened, swallowing her fear. "I'm sure it will be. You know what you're doing."

Officer Perkins spoke up. "We need you to give us a thorough briefing."

"Sure," Mike said. "Let's get out of the way so we don't bore everyone with the details. Then Hope and I will go to the seam above the cavern and let Alex, Jasmine, and Zach know when to expect the explosion. And hopefully us."

Hope insisted Mike eat lunch while he was talking to the authorities. After fifteen minutes, he returned. "Ok. We're ready to get this show on the road."

Hope said goodbye to Sara and headed down the path with Mike. Birds sang in the trees and dapples of sunlight moved over the ground. A soft breeze blew through the leaves.

Just your typical, lovely St. Croix afternoon.

<hr>

His heart lighter after the conversation with Zach, Alex dozed off for a while. But he was wide awake when two shadows appeared at the seam overhead.

"Yo!" Mike shouted. "Anybody still down there?"

Jasmine jumped to her feet and ran to the seam, letting the blanket drop from her shoulders. Zach helped Alex to his feet, and they hobbled over. Two shadowy heads were bent over the crevice.

"You have that lotion with you?" Alex asked, finally able to smile at the joke.

"It will not make rude requests," Mike replied, and Zach and Jasmine broke into nervous laughter.

"Oh, stop it, you two!" Hope snapped. "You can crack jokes later."

Alex nodded, but refrained from answering 'Yes, dear.' *The pain is making me giddy. Time to straighten up.* "How are things on the grotto end?"

"I got some C4 from a cool guy with the bomb squad. But I had to take the local dive rescue dude down a few pegs."

Alex laughed. "Is his name Trevor?"

"Yeah. You know him?"

Zach shifted under Alex's arm.

"I met him once when they asked me to join," Alex said. "He seemed to think his experience was on the same level as a SEAL's."

"Don't worry. He thinks differently now."

"What about the goddamn rescue?" Zach shouted.

"Oh yeah!" Mike said. "I forgot all about that."

Alex's smile widened as Hope's angry muttering drifted down.

"Fine," Mike called. "Your wife is getting cranky up here, Alex. So here's the deal. I've set four shaped charges and attached the detonators and fuses. After I blow them, we'll see if there's a big enough hole to swim through."

"And if there's not?" Jasmine asked.

"Then I'll blow out some more rock until there is."

"All right," Alex said. "What time should we expect the explosion?"

"At four o'clock."

"What time is it now?" Alex asked Zach quietly.

He glanced at his dive computer. "Three-thirty."

"Ok!" Alex shouted. "We'll be ready. And we'll see you soon."

"Stay safe, guys," Hope called.

"You too," Alex said. His eyes didn't move from the seam after Hope's head disappeared, imagining her face.

Soon, baby...

Finally, he snapped himself out of it and removed his arm from Zach's shoulder. "I'll sit down here. You two go down and grab all our equipment and bring it up here."

"Sure, but why?" Jasmine asked.

"The explosion might create a wave. I'm not real eager for our scuba gear to get washed away."

In a short time, three piles of gear were stacked near them. Then there was nothing to do but wait. And worry. The thirty minutes went by like a sloth moving through tree branches.

Finally, Zach counted down. "Four... three... two... one!" He snapped his head up, alternating his gaze between Jasmine and Alex.

A muffled boom shook the ground beneath them, an unsettling reminder of the earthquake. But this was much milder.

Then... nothing.

"What now?" Jasmine asked.

Alex sighed. "Now comes the hardest part. We wait."

Zach stood and aimed Alex's powerful flashlight at the water near the tunnel. The surface was agitated, rippling and whirling. Then a circle of bubbling water appeared and expanded rapidly. More frothing water appeared behind it, rolling out of the tunnel.

Finally, a silent wave rose, growing ever larger as it headed straight for them.

Chapter Thirty-Three

AFTER LEAVING THE SEAM, Hope and Mike returned to the grotto. More news reporters and onlookers had arrived, and Tommy was stringing a line of yellow caution tape for them to remain behind. Hope gave him a grateful nod.

Heather was also there. She approached Hope, a deep line between her brows. "I've been helping out Patti and Martine at the front desk, and they sent me to ask for an update on the rescue."

"We're about to start." Hope cocked her head as something occurred to her. "Why are you helping at the front desk?"

Heather widened her eyes. "Oh wow. The phones are ringing off the hook. Since Ember hasn't reopened, Patti asked me to lend a hand. We're fielding calls from all over the world! News outlets asking for details, and ordinary people calling to offer their thoughts and prayers. A florist just delivered a bunch of bouquets. I really need to take back an update. The news people are getting pushy."

Hope rubbed her temples. "Great. Alex is going to love this." Taking a deep breath, she met Heather's eyes. "Tell them the rescue has been a multi-agency operation utilizing resort staff, police, volunteers, dive rescue, as well as search and rescue. We're about to detonate explosives to clear the blocked tunnel. After that, Mike and I will go in and bring the group out. But I do *not* want anyone else coming out here except staff. We've got enough of a circus as it is. I'll have the two policemen start crowd-control measures at the highway. If people want to wait at the resort, welcome them with open arms. But no one comes to the grotto except staff and family."

"Got it. How's Alex? We keep getting asked if there are injuries, and word has gotten out that Alex is hurt."

Hope hesitated. "You can level with the staff—Alex hurt his leg, and I think it's worse than he's letting on. But tell anyone else who asks that you don't know the extent of his injury and can't speculate about it."

"Ok, thanks. I'd better get back." Heather embraced her before turning to walk toward the path.

"Heather?" Hope called out. "One more thing."

The redhead turned and Hope cleared her throat over a sudden, thick constriction. She took a moment to collect herself. "Could you call the hospital and see if they have an extra ambulance they could send to be on standby? Just in case?"

Tears filled Heather's eyes, but she blinked them back. "Of course. I'll call as soon as I get back. Please keep us updated, especially when they're out. All of us would rather be here."

Hope gave Heather a smile as she hugged her again. "I know. Instead, you're all doing what has to be done back at the resort. Thank you. Alex, Jasmine, and Zach thank you too."

After Heather left, Hope directed officers Perkins and Watson to the highway to monitor traffic and keep out anyone who wasn't authorized. She approached Trevor and pointed to the nearby equipment cart. "Could you help me with something?"

"Of course. I feel terrible just standing around."

"We appreciate you being here." Hope pointed to Tommy, who had finished tying off the cordon of yellow tape. "Tommy is our boat captain. Depending on what we find, Mike and I might need more tanks. Could you and Tommy go back to the resort and load up several extras?"

After nodding his agreement, Trevor jogged off to talk to the captain and Hope moved to the small cave. She picked up her wetsuit and set out a fresh tank and BCD with regulator outside the cave. Mike stood nearby, studying a handheld detonator.

He glanced up at her movements and straightened. "Hope, what are you doing?"

"Getting ready. We've only got a few minutes now."

"You're not coming with me right after the detonation!"

Frustration welling, Hope threw her wetsuit on the ground and stormed up to Mike. "Yes, I am. You said I could come with you."

"I was thinking more of when I had everything cleared and it was safe."

"What if you need help moving the rocks? Or you run into trouble and need help? It's never going to be safe, Mike. And every minute counts."

Jaw set tight, he stared at her. She glared right back.

I'm not backing down this time. Not with Alex in there. Not when I'm so close to finally seeing him—to being able to apologize.

"Dammit, Hope! There could be zero visibility in there."

"I've been in zero-viz conditions in a cave before. I've been in *that* passage before. I'm the only one on this side of the cave-in who has. I'll follow your directions, Mike. I'll do what you tell me. But I'm coming."

He breathed a long sigh. "Ok, then. Get ready."

Hope pulled on her wetsuit. "How long will you wait after the explosion?"

"A few minutes. Enough time to let things settle, but it shouldn't take long."

She checked her watch. It was 3:56.

The next four minutes were one of those strange passages of time she had experienced since the earthquake. Those particular four minutes took days, weeks, months to pass. The press and onlookers grew silent.

At 4:00 sharp, Mike depressed a large red button on the black device in his hand. The ground trembled faintly beneath Hope's feet, and birds took to the sky. A froth of bubbles surfaced on the far side of the grotto, followed by a long, low wave across the pool. It washed onto the sandy beach, several feet over the normal water line. But most of its energy was spent. Neither Mike nor Hope moved as the wave splashed over their neoprene-encased feet, reaching to mid-shin before retreating back into the pool.

Trevor returned with the cart, sweating and breathing hard. Six silver scuba tanks and several sets of full gear were stacked in it.

Mike nodded at him. "Good idea. Can you stage two tanks just inside the tunnel?"

"Sure. Just tanks, or whole kits?"

"Tanks for now. We don't know what their air supply is like on the far side. We might need full kits later."

"You got it."

Mike clapped him on the shoulder, all signs of his former hostility gone. "Thanks, Trevor." Then he turned to Hope. "Let's gear up and see what we've got in there."

Both got ready quickly and entered the water. Hope descended and swam across the blue pool with Mike at her side. The metal gate had been blown completely off its hinges and lay on the bottom of the pool, forty feet below the surface. The water in front of the tunnel entrance was murky and full of particulate. But there was minimal current, just a light surge as the water moved back and forth, working to regain equilibrium.

Mike hovered in front of the entrance. Alex's orange guideline lay side by side with the cord Mike had used to detonate the explosives. He unclipped a powerful handheld flashlight and shined it in a circular arc, studying the integrity of the passage walls. Hope waited behind him, trying to remain patient. He moved halfway into the entrance and repeated the motion with the light, illuminating the tunnel further down. Hope peered around him. The visibility was much worse than before, even when she'd been there just after the earthquake.

But it was a long way from zero visibility.

And that meant the main structure of the passage was likely intact. An excited flutter ran through her belly. Mike craned his head around and nodded, gesturing with two fingers for them to proceed.

The initial portion of the tunnel was nearly unchanged, except for a scattering of rock on the floor, which grew deeper the further they penetrated. They passed under the tree roots, and Mike paused to study them. When Hope shined her headlamp on them, the roots appeared the same from her previous trip just after the earthquake.

Oh please, oh please. This has to work!

The tunnel widened enough to swim side by side, but Hope stayed where she was. Mike had made it clear he wanted to be in the lead, and she gratefully acknowledged his expertise. As they grew closer to the rockslide, her heart pounded in her ears.

She slowed her breathing, forcing herself to relax. The rock scree they traveled over sloped up at a steeper angle than before. Then a boulder appeared in Mike's headlamp, with another just behind. Those were new.

The tunnel turned slightly to the left. After Hope negotiated the bend, they were at the cave-in. She peered around

Mike, dying to see the result of his explosion. The cave-in area was a solid, jumbled mass of boulders and smaller rocks.

A hollow ache opened within her.

With her eyes, Hope followed the left side of the tunnel upward to where it became an indistinguishable mass of rocks. The passage was blocked all the way to the top. Just like before.

No, no, no!

Hope clenched her jaw, trying to keep her breathing calm as she moved her light across the top of the tunnel where more rocks piled together.

Then she saw it.

An opening appeared in her beam on the right, near the top of the rock pile. Mike had already seen it and rose to investigate. Hope approached on his left side but stayed a distance away, giving him room to maneuver.

He finned to a gap about two feet in diameter and looked in, moving his head to throw his beam around. In their lights, particles drifted through the water. Then Mike turned toward her and nodded, excitement flashing in his eyes. Like Alex, he averted his head slightly as he stared at her, avoiding shining his light directly in her face.

A pile of rocks led from the opening down to the floor of the tunnel, some small and some larger. Using only one hand at a time, Mike carefully palmed rocks, then scooped them below him. The stones rolled with a clatter down to the floor, enlarging the opening. Once he'd made a good start, he moved over and beckoned for Hope to help.

Within minutes, they had enlarged the opening to over three feet in diameter. Rock dust and particles floated in the Hope's beam.

She stared at the cavity with a mixture of foreboding and excitement.

Chapter Thirty-Four

THE CONSTRICTING PASSAGE was called a squeeze. Large enough to get through, but not without removing their tanks and pushing them ahead. But there was something else. Something that brought desperate hope surging through her. Water gently pushed against her face, brushing her hair back.

A current.

Meaning water flowed toward them for a considerable distance. An opening likely lay on the squeeze's far side.

Mike held a hand out for her to wait, and she nodded. Unbuckling his BCD, he pushed the scuba kit into the squeeze and shimmied into the tight passage after it. He continued until only his fins hung outside, and stayed there for several minutes, his fins motionless.

Hope became concerned.

Is something wrong, or is he just studying the passage?

As soon as she completed the thought, Mike scooted backward out of the squeeze. He pulled his tank out of the stricture and gestured with his head toward the tunnel they had just traveled. As he swam back toward the entrance, he put his kit back on, but left it unbuckled.

Why are we going back? Is it too narrow to get through?

Confused, Hope followed. Mike stopped at the tree-root section and gave her a thumbs up. Comprehension dawning, she nodded enthusiastically.

He wants to talk!

They surfaced. The ceiling of the tiny chamber was less than a foot above their heads, causing them to tip their heads sideways as they removed their regulators.

"That squeeze continues a way, but it doesn't get any narrower that I could see," Mike said. "I couldn't see all the way through. I set my charges to create a passage in that area, so this is a good sign. Though I was hoping for a bigger opening. It's worth following, but you'll have to take your gear off and push it ahead. Have you ever done that?" He stared at her, dead serious.

Hope nodded, aware of what an unnerving maneuver it was. "Lots of times. There was a squeeze in the other cave passage. Alex taught me how to do it."

"Ok. Let's keep going."

"On the other side of the cave-in, the tunnel goes through some gentle S-curves for another ten or twenty yards," Hope said. "At least I hope that section is still there. Then it empties into the cavern where Alex and the kids are."

"Sounds good. Listen—if I tap my right fin on the floor five times, that means I can't go any further. You'll have to back up first, then I'll follow. We won't be able to communicate in there. We either go forward or backward. There are no other choices. Again—are you ok with this? We're at go or no go."

She pushed down her fluttery nerves. "I am. We're a go."

Mike continued to stare at her. "Are you sure, Hope? I can't help you if you get hung up or panic."

"I know. I understand the risks." She paused, her nerves settling as deeper emotion coursed within her. "Mike, *Alex* is in there. I can do this."

He nodded firmly. "All right. Let's go."

She gave him a smile, though it felt shaky. "Besides, I'll tell you the same thing I said to Alex regarding squeezes. You're a lot bigger than me. If you can make it through, so can I."

He returned her smile, and his was more confident. "That's very true. Let's dive."

This squeeze was far more unsettling than the one Hope had traversed in the big cave. It was narrower, but she also occasionally scraped against a rock and felt it *move*. Every so often, a groaning creak sounded from the rocks around them. She kept a mantra running through her head, calming her.

Mike wouldn't do this if he didn't think we could make it.

At one point, he stopped for several minutes. He shoved and pummeled his tank forward, constricted by something. The water became cloudy with silt and rocky particulate. Then his arm angle changed as he dug at something near his left shoulder. Finally, a large rock appeared at his left hip. He pushed at it with his hand, moving it behind him.

Then he scuttled forward again.

Hope paused by the rock and pushed it behind her also, pressing it into a cavity to get it out of the way. Well, somewhat out of the way. The constriction Mike had just negotiated was very narrow from top to bottom. She had to shove her tank forward and turn her head sideways to get under a lip that hung down into the squeeze. The bare rock scraped over her left shoulder, and she repeated a new mantra.

If Mike made it through, I can too. If Mike made it through, I can too.

He waited motionless just ahead, and held up his left hand, forming an ok signal. Hope returned it and they continued through the constricting and claustrophobic squeeze. Hope pushed her tank forward, relying on brute strength to fight for every inch of progress.

I forgot how much this sucks.

They continued for another ten feet. The floor of the squeeze changed from solid rock to multiple smaller stones crammed together, the stricture becoming slightly taller. Hope craned her head around Mike's shoulder. There was a narrow black opening ahead, and she nearly groaned in relief.

The other side!

She looked closer. Three huge slabs of rock formed the top and sides of the section they now traveled through. At the far end was an opening several feet wide, but it was too narrow from top to bottom.

No, no! We didn't come this far to back up now!

Mike stopped before the irregular opening, studying it patiently while Hope nearly smashed a fist into the floor. Then she thought better of that idea, instead using deep breathing to control her frustration. He brushed a hand over all three slabs at the exit, then knocked on them, testing for weaknesses. Next, he turned his beam to the floor of piled, jumbled rocks. One at a time, Mike picked them up and tossed them out of the opening in front of him.

Hope waited behind him while he worked slowly and methodically. Frustration and impatience grew within her. They were so close now! She could practically see Alex ahead.

Then she realized what he was doing.

Mike removed each rock individually, pausing to make sure the slabs above them stayed in place.

Nausea flooded her mouth with saliva—the realization she was underneath a highly unstable rock formation formed mere minutes ago. Underwater. In an area which had suffered a major earthquake recently.

Her heart rate went through the roof, her skin prickling all over her body. Hope closed her eyes.

Easy, easy. I've been through this before. Alex needs me right now. He needs me to hold it together.

Nothing matters but him. I owe him an apology, and I'm damn well going to give it to him. Focus on that. Focus on that.

Calmed, she opened her eyes to see Mike pushing his kit through the opening he had just enlarged. Hope followed, looping her right arm through the shoulder straps of her BCD to keep it from sinking as she emerged from the squeeze. Mike already had his tank back on and BCD buckled. A gentle stream of bubbles drifted up from his regulator. The tunnel was wider here, allowing Mike to help Hope with her kit.

They swam on. The passage now seemed massive after what they had just negotiated. She moved up to Mike's waist, anticipation growing as they went around a bend to the right.

We're almost there!

Hope finned faster, moving to Mike's shoulder. She bounced her headlamp around, but the passage looked the same as it had on her two previous trips. As she moved ahead, Mike held out an arm and pulled her back even with him, shaking his head.

God, you're just like Alex!

Then she almost laughed. Of course he was. Alex trained him.

She relaxed—slightly—and they swam around the soft curves. The unexplored passage with Alex's orange line blocking it off appeared undamaged. Mike ignored it, staying in the main tunnel. Hope dropped back when they reached the rocky lip jutting into the tunnel from the side. Mike went first, his right shoulder scraping against rock. Hope got through without touching.

A tumult of emotions roiled through her, building steadily. Elation that she would soon be with Alex again, and guilt and regret about the incident in the lobby. She might be overreacting about that last parting, but her swelling emotions made her snappish words feel like a terrible transgression.

After one more turn, the cavern opening appeared before them.

Hope's heart hammered once again. This time, she didn't try to slow it. Tears built in her eyes. She and Mike swam into the cavern as memories flooded through her brain. The agony of communicating through the seam. Alex looking more ill every time she saw him. And finally, the memory tortured her one last time—that the last time they'd had had the opportunity to touch, Hope had pushed him away.

The bright orange line rose toward the stony shore, and Hope surged ahead, finning as hard as she could. Mike didn't stop her this time. Breaking through the surface, she stood and clambered to the stone shelf that rose from the shore.

Alex, Jasmine, and Zach weren't in sight, but that didn't concern her. The plateau above was where they had been staying. She unbuckled her BCD and shrugged it off, the clang reverberating around the cave as her tank hit the rock. Sprinting up the slope, Hope called out, "Alex! I'm here. We're here!"

She reached the flat plateau and there they were. Hardly noticing Zach and Jasmine, Hope headed straight for Alex. He was *right there*, tall and broad in all the right places. Also obviously tired and hurting. She stumbled a few steps as her foot slipped on the wet stone, puzzling her.

Why is the ground wet up here?

But that didn't matter, and she righted herself. Tears burst from her eyes and a sob tore from her throat. Alex broke into a huge smile and held his arms out. Wanting nothing more than to launch herself at him and wrap her legs around his waist, Hope remembered his injury and looked closer. He stood on only one leg, though he wasn't using Zach for help. The two men stood six feet apart. But Alex's right leg was bent at the knee, the lower portion held behind him.

At the last second, Hope skidded to a stop, gently falling against his chest. Alex wrapped her in his solid embrace, clutching her tightly to him. Hope continued to sob, but she didn't care. All that mattered was that they were together again. She took a deep breath, just wanting to *smell* him, and inhaled a deep breath of tired sweat and struggle.

Alex cupped her face in his hands and pressed his lips to hers. A sweet, tender kiss. A kiss that reminded her of everything important in life.

But Hope was still sobbing and returned her face to his chest, wrapping her arms tightly around him. "Oh, Alex! I'm so sorry. Please forgive me."

Chapter Thirty-Five

WHEN ALEX HEARD Hope's shout that she'd arrived, he pushed up to stand on his left foot, waving Zach off.

He wanted to be on his own power for this reunion.

Anticipation shoved his pain into the background. Hope appeared at the top of the slope. His heart nearly stopped when she slipped on the wet stone, but she recovered quickly.

The wave hadn't looked very impressive when it rolled across the cavern. But Alex knew the destructive force of water first-hand, and he'd made sure they were on high ground. Fortunately, with the stone floor sloping up from the shore, the wave had lost momentum halfway across the plateau before sliding back. It never reached them.

Hope charged across the rocky ground toward him. The moment he'd been waiting for was finally here. The one that had sustained him during the long, pain-filled nights—holding Hope in his arms again. Alex broke into a face-splitting grin and held his arms wide. She was smiling and sobbing at the same time as she ran, their eyes locked together. He lifted his injured leg behind him, holding it off the ground.

Hope raced over the ground, and Alex couldn't help

worrying about her pace. If she thrust herself into his arms as she liked to do, they were going to have a problem. He couldn't support her standing on one leg like a battered flamingo. But Hope hit the brakes, softly falling against his chest. He wrapped his arms tightly around her and ignored her dripping wetsuit. He rested his cheek on the top of her head. Other than her sobs, both of them were quiet.

Oh, my brave, beautiful woman.

Alex couldn't talk over the lump in his throat. The cave and the others around them faded into the background. Even the pain in his leg diminished. Hope was the best analgesic in the world.

He inhaled deeply. Her hair was wet, but hints of her coconut shampoo remained. She smelled like home. He cupped her face and brushed a soft kiss over her lips, keeping his mouth tightly shut.

God, I hope my breath isn't too awful.

Hope didn't seem to mind, kissing him back warmly. Then she broke away and burrowed her head into his chest, her arms like a vise around him. "Oh, Alex! I'm so sorry. Please forgive me."

The smile plummeted off his face, confusion setting in.

Did I just hear her right? "What?"

She pulled back and blinked her wet eyes. "At the lobby, before the earthquake. I practically shoved you out the door and told you to leave me alone. I'm so sorry!" She broke into sobs again.

Alex bit his lip, worried laughter might upset her more, but couldn't hold it in. "Hope, what are you talking about? I pressured *you.* Baby, have you been worried I was mad at you?"

"No." She started wailing again, completely contradicting herself.

"Then why are you crying?"

"Because we're finally in each other's arms again and it's made me an emotional wreck!"

He laughed again and kissed her forehead, understanding completely how stress can magnify emotions. "Feels pretty good to be together, doesn't it?"

"God, yes! Now please tell me you forgive me."

Alex clasped her face again, staring into her wet, hazel eyes as he rubbed her cheeks with his thumbs. "I forgive you for acting like a normal human being. Is that better?"

She snuffled. "Yes. Much."

"Good. Can we get out of this cavern, then?"

She nodded and stepped back, wiping her eyes. Mike was talking to Zach and Jasmine and met Alex's gaze. He walked over and held out his hand. Alex, carefully balancing on one leg, took it and pulled him into a hug. "I can't even tell you how happy I am to see you. Thank you for coming so fast."

Mike grinned and slapped his back. "You're welcome. The beer's on you."

Turning on his headlamp as he squatted down, Mike peered at Alex's leg. Alex straightened it, holding his toes softly to the ground. As if making up for the reprieve when Hope had arrived, the pain had come roaring back. Hope came over too. She gasped at the damage, both hands flying to cover her mouth.

Mike blew a low whistle. "Monroe, that looks a little painful."

Hope turned her horrified eyes to Alex. He held them, doing his best to look reassuring. "Turns out it's a little more than a sprained ankle."

"How much more?" she whispered, letting her hands fall to her sides.

"It's broken."

Mike stood again, both brows halfway up his forehead. "I've

seen broken legs. I've had one. That thing looks like you got in an argument with a steamroller. And lost."

"I kind of did."

"You said this happened during the quake." Hope's face was pale and drawn. "What happened?"

"I'll tell you all about it. Later. Can we get out of here now?"

"Of course," Hope said, giving him a somewhat shaky smile. Then she moved to give Zach and Jasmine a quick hug.

Alex stared across the cavern. "We are very ready to leave this place."

Mike was taking a breath to speak when Hope's face strengthened. Wiping her cheeks completely dry, she turned to face Alex. "Ok," she said. "I've got just over 2000 psi in my tank. What is your air situation?"

Alex laughed ruefully, recalling his trip as a human pinball. "Zach and Jasmine both have full tanks. The ones I brought in with me."

Hope looked at Mike. "What about you?"

He tapped his fingers rhythmically against his thigh. "1500 psi."

"Baker!" Alex shouted, his blood pressure soaring. "You used *half* a tank? Goddammit, I thought you could dive."

Mike stared steadily at Alex. "Getting the path open took some work, boss."

Alex deflated, lacing his fingers on top of his head. "Shit, I'm sorry. I jumped down your throat when you first got here too."

A look passed between Mike and Hope, and Alex could have sworn they shared a tiny smile. Mike turned back to Alex and broke into a full grin. "I'm used to you layering on the charm like that."

Hope sighed. "Well, you can't continue with only half a tank." She stared at the two full cylinders standing nearby. Zach and Jasmine's half-empty ones lay on their sides. "Why don't you use one of the full tanks and swim out? You can get two fresh tanks and come back. Then we'll all go. And while you're outside, you can tell the authorities we're getting ready to come out."

Alex watched her, pride flooding through him at how she took charge. "I'm surprised you're not champing at the bit to do it yourself, Boss Lady."

Hope shook her head. "Mike is far more capable of diving alone inside a cave than I am. While he's gone, I can give you all a run-through of what you're facing. The tunnel has gotten quite a bit smaller."

As Alex watched his wife, Zach's words came back to him. About how Alex left the people he led free to make their own decisions and learn from their mistakes. Like Hope.

Mike nodded and switched over his BCD and regulator to a fresh tank. "I'll be back as soon as possible."

Alex turned back to him. "Can you grab a fresh air cylinder for my rebreather? Better safe than sorry. There's one in the gear room."

Mike nodded as Hope laughed ruefully. "You might need to dig a little, Mike. Jack is cleaning up, but the room isn't back to Alex's standards quite yet."

Which was another reminder that Alex needed to get out of this damn cave. Now. He should be repairing the damage, not Jack.

After Mike left, the quartet moved back to Alex's rock. He sat and placed his leg back on it, trying not to wince at every movement. The change in position made it throb anew. Hope stared at the limb, then swallowed thickly as she scooted next to him. She took his hand, brushing her fingers over the back of it. He turned his, lacing his fingers between hers, and held tight.

Hope swept her gaze around the group as she described the narrow passage Mike had blasted through the caved-in area.

When Jasmine found out about the squeeze, she jumped to her feet, breathing hard and her eyes widening more by the second. "What? Take my tank and BCD *off* and push them through? I can't do that!"

Alex wasn't too happy about it either. Not because of the maneuver, but he didn't have any delusions shimmying through a squeeze was going to hurt like hell.

Holy living hell.

Hope stood and took Jasmine's hands. "You can do this. You made it in here just fine. The tight section isn't that long. The rest of the passage is the same as when you came in here."

Zach pushed to his feet and stared at his girlfriend, his face grave. "I'll make sure you make it through this. I promise. You're in here because of me. You're goin' to get out again."

She gave him a shaky nod, the need to believe clear in her eyes.

"You won't be alone, Jasmine," Alex said. "We'll have to go through single file, but there will be people around you all the time. We're here to help each other."

That seemed to settle her, her eyes becoming less terrified. Hope darted a glance at Alex. She knew as well as he did the dangers of a diver panicking in a squeeze. If Jasmine became unable to move, everyone behind her would be trapped. But she seemed reassured and sat again.

Alex asked several technical questions about the tunnel and was pleased to hear it was essentially unchanged. Except for the caved-in section, which now sported a nice hole through it.

Thank God for Baker.

<hr>

OVER AN HOUR LATER, scraping sounds came from the landing area as Mike returned. He walked up the slope, one tank on his back, and another harnessed to his side. He held up the smaller rebreather cylinder with one hand. "Ok, guys. What do you say we go for a fun little dive?"

Alex took a deep breath, preparing for what lay ahead. Zach stood and retrieved his and Jasmine's wetsuits, handing Jasmine hers. Mike unhooked the spare tank, setting it next to the other full one. "I've got 2300 psi in my tank, so all five of us are good to go now."

Hope picked up the pieces of Alex's cut-up wetsuit. "Should we go out again to get you a wetsuit?"

Alex kept from shuddering at the thought of all that pain. "No. I don't want to take the time, and it won't be that long of a dive. I'll be fine."

Mike crossed to him, still fully geared up with his mask around his neck. He glanced at Alex's leg, then met his eyes and held them. "Can you do this?"

Alex knew what Mike was really asking. The same point that Alex and Hope had silently made earlier about trapping those in line behind. But Alex didn't care how badly it hurt. He was getting out of here.

So is everyone else.

He nodded firmly at Mike. "I'll make it."

Mike held his gaze a moment longer, then nodded before turning away. "Ok, I'll lead. Then—"

"No," Hope interrupted.

Mike turned to her, his face blank.

"I'll lead," she said.

"Hope, I'm not letting you go first here," Mike said. "Remember our rule?"

"Different situation, different rules." Hope crossed to stand in front of Mike. "If Alex needs help, you're the only one strong enough to do the job. You have to go in front of him. And no one else but me can lead."

Alex pressed his lips into a thin line, then nodded. "She's right, Mike. Hope goes first, then Mike, then me." He turned to look at Zach and Jasmine. "Jasmine, you go behind me, and Zach, you bring up the rear."

He gave Zach a long stare, and the young man nodded, understanding his unspoken message. By being behind Jasmine, Zach would be able to watch and evaluate her, assess whether she was spiraling into panic, and prevent it if possible. At least until she was inside the squeeze. Then she was on her own. Though Alex had one last back-up option if it became necessary.

Hope stood tall and confident as she moved her gaze around the circle of people. Alex watched her, his throat constricting at the pride and assurance in her eyes.

She turned to him last. "Let's get you guys out of here."

Chapter Thirty-Six

ALEX CAREFULLY SAT down at the shore, letting Mike help him to the stony ground. Scooping cool water into his hand, he poured it over his sweaty head, trying to breathe normally. The slope from the plateau to the waterline wasn't steep, but hobbling down on one leg while Mike had supported him made his injured leg howl like a banshee.

A deep, steady nausea roiled his stomach, the result of days of pain and stress. And maybe knowledge of the pain to come. Hope hunkered down at his feet and pulled his neoprene bootie on his left foot. Alex was still in the same board shorts and T-shirt he'd worn for several days, but now he'd attached his rebreather, the monitoring console strapped to his wrist. He'd already replaced the oxygen cylinder, and had ample air for the trip out. His mask hung around his neck. Hope picked up his nearby fin and attached it before studying his purple right foot. It was twice the size of his left. "You sure you want to do this with one fin instead of going completely without?"

"Positive," Alex said. "The propulsion will make this trip much easier." The mangled half-fin he'd worn on his right foot lay on the ground. Hope had gathered both when they'd journeyed to the water's edge. Now she picked it up and turned it over in her hands, stroking a finger over the ragged, torn blade. She met his eyes but remained quiet. Alex stared back, then nodded at her unspoken question. He'd tell her the whole story later.

All of it. They didn't keep secrets from each other.

Alex took a long breath, trying to settle his stomach. "I'm ready. Let's go."

Jasmine also breathed a long sigh and he smiled at her. "You got this, Jasmine. You'll do great." He desperately hoped that was true. What she was being asked to do was a lot for a new diver. Too much. But there was no alternative.

Mike stood nearby. "You want me to help you up?"

Alex shook his head. "It'll be easier if I just ease myself into the water from here."

Pressing his lips into a grim line, he eased away from the rough shore. The cool water was heavenly against his sweaty, clammy skin, but it wouldn't continue to feel that way. The water was twenty degrees lower than his body temperature— he'd be losing body heat every minute he was submerged.

Raising the mask onto his face and placing the bulky regulator in his mouth, Alex gave Hope an ok as the others gathered in a circle. She returned it, then got confirmation from the others in the group. Raising one arm, she pointed her thumb down, and they descended.

They fell into line immediately. Alex tried to watch Hope from around Mike's body in front of him, but forced himself to stop. She was qualified to lead, and it was time to let her. He had enough to worry about just managing himself. Holding his right leg stiffly, he took long sweeping strokes with his left as they crossed the water of the cavern.

They entered the tunnel, and Alex vividly remembered coming out of it, nearly out of his mind with pain as Zach helped him. They slowly moved through the sweeping S-turns, and Alex took his time easing through the one narrow finger, getting through without scraping his injured leg on anything. He barely spared a glance at the unexplored side passage, blocked off with orange line. *I think that's going to remain unexplored.* The pain had dulled to a constant, throbbing ache, but he could handle that. The nausea steadied as well.

Rocks appeared on the floor. First just a few, then they grew in number, creating a slope. Alex kicked up slightly, getting a good look at the cave-in which had almost killed him. His eyes automatically went to the base of the pile where he'd lain those hours. He touched his hand to the knife attached to his rebreather.

My leg might hurt like hell, but at least I've still got it.

Sinking back down, he drifted to Mike's right and approached the rock which had been his nemesis, pausing when he reached it. Alex placed his hand on it. It was mostly covered by rocks dislodged by the blast, but he had stared at the damn thing long enough to recognize it instantly. He patted the rock, then withdrew his hand.

Time to put this behind me.

Jasmine had paused, waiting for him to rejoin the line. He nodded to her, pleased her eyes weren't enlarged and she breathed steadily and slowly. A regular, even stream of bubbles exited her regulator.

Hope hovered near the top of the tunnel in front of a formation of three boulders. A small opening was left where they leaned against each other. She got ok signals from everyone, then unbuckled her BCD. Removing her tank, she hefted it inside the squeeze and crawled in after it like it was something she did every day.

Alex smiled, beyond proud of her.

Then Mike entered.

Alex unbuckled his rebreather and shrugged it off. He turned around and pointed at Jasmine, then gave her an emphatic ok signal. *You're ok.*

She met his eyes and nodded once.

Alex placed the canister of his rebreather inside the squeeze and pushed it forward, then inched forward on his elbows. As he suspected, it was impossible to crawl over the rocky ground without jostling his right leg. Bolt after bolt of agony shot up his leg. Sweat broke out over his forehead as he tried to breathe through the pain.

Forward, forward. Keep moving.

There wasn't any other choice.

An inch at a time, Alex continued. Soon he reached the even narrower section Hope had warned them about. His rebreather barely made it through—he had to push several times with both arms, each shove reverberating through his leg. Sweat dripped freely inside his mask, and he blinked back the stinging fluid. Turning his head sideways, he scrabbled forward through the tiny space, moaning now at the white-hot flame his leg had become. His shoulder scraped as he slid under the rock, but it was hardly noticeable compared to his leg.

He had to rest for a long moment when he emerged from the narrowing, rolling his head on his shoulders. The squeeze was still tight, but nothing like what he'd just gone through. Steeling himself, Alex dug his bare elbows into the rocky floor and pushed his kit forward, scooting after it.

Ahead of him, Mike made steady progress, stopping periodically so he stayed about five feet in front. The water cooled Alex's body rapidly, and goosebumps rippled his arms. He came upon a large rock wedged off to the right side and inched past it. It looked purposely placed to get it out of the way. *Better not knock my leg on that.*

Alex had to stop again to rest, calm his breathing, and let the pain diminish. Mike stopped as well. When he was ready to move again, Alex drew a circle with the beam of his headlamp, telling Mike he was ok. Mike pumped his closed fist in acknowledgement and moved on.

Alex heaved the canister forward, surprised when it slid a good distance. Pleased, he dug his elbows in, then launched himself, eager to make more progress.

His right leg slammed into the protruding rock.

A scream ripped from his throat, and black blotches appeared in his vision. He clenched his eyes shut, nausea roaring through his stomach. The pain was all-encompassing, forcing him to freeze in place. He swallowed his saliva, trying not to throw up. Technically, vomiting through a scuba regulator *was* possible—Alex had done it. Which was how he knew it was an absolutely foul, disgusting experience to be avoided if at all possible. And puking underwater inside a tight squeeze deep underground wasn't a good idea at any rate.

Alex breathed in deep, gasping heaves, getting control of himself again as the nausea diminished once more. Somewhat. Hot pulses of agony shot up his leg with every frantic beat of his heart.

Eventually, the pain diminished to a red, furious throbbing. When he finally opened his eyes, they stung so badly from sweat he couldn't keep them open. Cracking open the seal of his mask, Alex let fresh, clean water flood in. He closed his eyes, letting the mask fill completely before clearing it by exhaling into the nose pocket. This time, his eyes opened easily.

Much better.

He glanced at the dive computer on his wrist, confirming he still had plenty of air despite his desperate breathing. He concentrated on mastering the pain, embracing it.

Pain or not, get moving Monroe.

He smiled grimly. That wasn't the voice speaking. He didn't need it.

Pushing the rebreather forward yet again, he moved forward. Inch by inch. As he progressed, his leg reached a new equilibrium of pain. Still horrible, but less than the agony after striking the rock. The nausea was constant, but he was confident he wasn't going to vomit.

At last, he was at the squeeze opening.

Mike was already out and waited at the entrance. He grabbed Alex's rebreather when it appeared. Alex pushed out of the squeeze, finding a long slope of rocks descending below him. The tunnel on this side of the squeeze was wide enough for him, Hope, and Mike to hover near each other.

Hope swam over, clasping both his hands and watching his face carefully.

Alex did his best to smile at her, squeezing her hands and drawing strength from the feel of them in his. Keeping hold of one, he turned to wait for Jasmine.

And waited.

Hope looked at her dive computer, then at Alex, a deep line between her brows.

He nodded. *She'll make it. She's a tough young woman.*

But after several more minutes, Jasmine still hadn't appeared. The nausea was getting worse, making Alex sweat more. The cool water pulled the heat from his body, causing a fine tremor to run through him. That didn't help with the pain, which escalated again to a furious roar. When beads of sweat ran into his eyes again, Alex ripped off his mask, letting the cool water bathe his entire face.

After a long moment, he replaced and cleared it. He opened his eyes and Hope was watching him intently. He nodded and looked toward the squeeze.

Still no Jasmine.

Time to deploy his back-up plan.

Alex pointed to Mike and the narrow opening. Then he tapped his two index fingers together lengthwise, the signal for buddy.

Mike nodded, understanding immediately.

Maybe Jasmine just needed help with her tank. In the other cave passage where they'd found the treasure, Alex had grabbed Hope's tank inside that squeeze on several occasions, helping her move it.

Mike removed his tank and climbed into the narrowing. But this time, he maneuvered the tank between his legs instead of in front of him. The motion would make the regulator hose tight and unsteady in Mike's mouth, but he could handle that.

Hope squeezed Alex's arm.

When he looked, she urged him to continue up the tunnel, signaling him to buddy up with her.

He whipped his head back and forth. *I'm not leaving them!*

Hope's wide eyes were frightened and imploring. Her asking him to leave indicated how worried she was about him. She was concerned about Jasmine and Zach, but Alex was her priority. He knew that. But it didn't matter.

He softened his eyes and tightened his hold on her hand. This time, he shook his head more slowly and deliberately.

But no less emphatically.

Hope nodded and shifted her eyes back to the squeeze. She knew him well.

Then Mike's fins appeared, followed by the rest of his legs with the silver tank between. He pushed himself out, gently pulling a tank before him. Alex smiled, relief relaxing his shoulders somewhat. He was utterly exhausted, and dark spots danced in front of his eyes, but Jasmine's appearance at the end of the tunnel was an enormous relief.

She made eye contact with Alex immediately. He gave her

an ok with both hands, incredibly proud of her. Jasmine smiled back, her lips widening behind her regulator.

Alex and Hope moved down the passage a bit to give the rest of the group more room. As Alex turned, Mike raised both brows at him. Shaking his head, Alex gestured that he and Mike were trading places. Here the tunnel was wide enough to swim side by side, and he didn't want to let go of Hope's hand. He needed her now more than ever, as dizziness buzzed inside his head and motes floated in front of his eyes.

Zach appeared at the squeeze entrance and flashed an ok signal.

Everyone had made it through the most difficult part.

Hope tugged on Alex's arm, and they continued toward the grotto, still holding hands as the others fell in line behind them. He smiled at her, but it was forced. He felt awful—nauseous, weak, dizzy, and the spots in front of his eyes weren't going away.

Almost there, almost there. Make sure they get out. Stay awake, dammit!

As they neared the exit, the passage narrowed again, and he let go of Hope's hand so she could go first. She finned with a beautifully performed frog kick, her buoyancy perfect. He tried to appreciate her skill, but it was hard to concentrate. She appeared to have four legs, all moving in synchrony.

Then they emerged from the tunnel, and were surrounded by clear, blue water. He squinted as his eyes adjusted to daylight again, dim as it was.

It's getting dark already?

Alex wanted to feel exalted. This was what he had been dreaming of for days. But the black splotches in his vision were getting bigger, the pain harder to push back. Nausea and dizziness both threatened to eclipse him, and his body could have weighed a thousand pounds. He turned around and Hope moved her hand to grip his arm. Mike came out and joined his other side. Alex blinked hard, forcing himself to stay alert as he waited. Then Jasmine appeared, with Zach just behind. As the divemaster joined Jasmine's side, both sets of eyes nearly glowed with excitement.

Everyone had made it out. They were safe.

At last, Alex could relax. Tension eased from his body in a soothing ripple, though the lightheadedness increased. The group resumed their swim across the grotto, and buzzing was now constant in Alex's ears. A rock slope appeared. and they angled up and toward the sandy beach. When they reached waist deep water, Hope took one of his arms and Mike the other, and they stood. Alex placed his left foot on the ground, surfacing on his wobbly, uninjured leg.

He gaped at the scene in the grotto.

Loud cheering erupted in a long wave from a packed crowd standing behind yellow caution tape. Several news cameras pointed their way, people with microphones in front. An ambulance was backed up in front of the beach. In the growing darkness, spotlights mounted on towers illuminated the grotto.

The noise was deafening, especially after the near silence he had existed in for the past several days. He hadn't expected this at all. Hope had said nothing about it.

Alex blinked several times, confused.

The entire scene was spinning, tilting back and forth.

At first, he thought it was another earthquake, but no one else was reacting. People would appear with crystal-clear focus, then fade again. Heather and Robert stood cheering. Patti and her husband Gary were next to them. Others stood behind, but Alex couldn't recognize them, unable to get his eyes to work properly.

Mike quickly unbuckled Alex's rebreather, letting it fall into the water before gripping Alex's arm tightly. "Hang in there, man. I've got you." His voice was muffled, like cotton was plugging Alex's ears. He should be concerned about the rebreather just lying there, but couldn't make himself care.

Hope spun to stand before him, gripping his arms as she shouted, "Stay with me, Alex!"

Stay where?

Mike threw Alex's arm over his shoulder and wrapped his own around Alex's waist, then manhandled him toward the ambulance. Alex tried to help, to hop on one leg, but the limb wasn't responding well. His gaze wandered back to the crowd, and in a moment of clear vision, he stared at a familiar-looking, applauding couple. But he couldn't place them, maybe because they were spinning. The woman looked pregnant.

Sara held Magen in her arms, while Jack and Will stood next to her. All were cheering. He really should respond, so he raised a hand to wave. But his arm hardly moved from Mike's shoulder.

Hope grabbed his free elbow, gripping tightly as she supported his weight and helped Mike.

Alex looked forward, mesmerized by the spinning, red flashing lights on the ambulance.

They're so bright! Why are there so many?

The paramedic rushed toward him with a stretcher, alarm widening his eyes.

Alex tried to tell the man he was fine, that he didn't need any help. But his tongue wouldn't work.

Then everything went black.

Chapter Thirty-Seven

HOPE WAS CONCENTRATING SO hard on getting Alex to the ambulance, she hardly noticed the applauding crowd. When Zach and Jasmine had safely exited the tunnel, Hope was gripping Alex's arm and had *felt* the tension drain out of him. But the unfocused, glazed look in his eyes told her he was fading fast, and Mike recognized it too.

As they helped Alex across the sand, a paramedic took over for Hope. Alex's eyes closed and he crumpled. The paramedic and Mike helped Alex fall onto the stretcher between the open rear doors of the ambulance. Hope said a tiny prayer for small favors.

At least no one got him passing out on camera. Alex would hate *that.*

People cheered as Zach and Jasmine stepped onto the beach, both tossing a worried frown toward the ambulance. Hope made eye contact with Zach and nodded before giving him an ok signal. She turned back as a second paramedic appeared from inside the ambulance, a fortyish woman, her brown hair in a slick bun.

Alex was completely unconscious, his head turned slightly

to one side. The first paramedic stared at his leg as he placed two fingers on Alex's wrist. "His pulse is rapid but strong. Let's get him to the hospital."

The female paramedic's nametag read Evelyn. She helped strap Alex in and the two pushed the stretcher into the back of the ambulance. Evelyn turned to Hope. "You're family?"

Hope nodded. "His wife."

"Ok. You can ride up front with me. Chris will work on Alex in the back."

"You know my husband's name?"

Evelyn shot her a brief smile. "I think everyone does now, if they didn't before."

Hope turned to Mike, who stared fixedly at Alex in the back of the ambulance. "Can you give the onlookers and press a statement, then come to the hospital? You can drive my Jeep. The keys are in the small cave over there."

He broke away from Alex to look at her, nodding firmly. "You got it. I'll be right behind you." He walked over to the yellow tape with bold, confident steps and put his hands on his hips.

Hope climbed in the passenger seat of the ambulance, still wearing her wetsuit. As she swung in, Mike began his briefing. "My name is Mike Baker and I assisted in the rescue. I was a US Navy SEAL who worked with Alex. As you saw, everyone made it out of the cave—"

Hope shut the door as Evelyn started the ambulance, then slowly drove down the path. The extended sides of the back brushed against the tree branches and bushes on both sides. Hope gave a weak laugh. "We didn't build this path with ambulances in mind."

"It's wide enough. That's all that matters."

When Evelyn reached the highway, she turned left and hit the siren, picking up speed rapidly. Hope craned around in her seat to watch Chris, the other paramedic, work on Alex. A large bag of saline hung from a metal pole, infusing into a line he'd started on the inside of Alex's elbow.

Chris removed a stethoscope from his ears and unwrapped a blood pressure cuff. He glanced at Hope. "His vitals are stable. Does he have any injuries besides the leg?"

She shook her head, unable to speak. Her eyes darted back to her pale husband.

"Good. I think he passed out from the pain."

Hope could hardly fathom that. Alex had the highest pain tolerance of anyone she'd ever met, refusing anything stronger than ibuprofen even when he'd been shot.

As Evelyn zipped through Frederiksted, Chris grabbed the receiver of a nearby radio. "We need a surgical team and ED staff standing by. Get an OR room prepped. I've got a complex tib-fib fracture coming. Who's the orthopedic surgeon covering?"

He paused, then breathed a sigh. "Good." Chris listened for a moment, flicking his eyes to Hope. "Yeah, it's one of the people from the cave. The SEAL guy."

With lights and sirens blazing, they quickly arrived at the hospital in Christiansted. Hope stayed by Alex's side as they wheeled him into a curtained bay of the emergency department. A nurse in blue scrubs held a hand out to her. "You'll have to stay in the waiting room."

Half a dozen people worked around Alex after they transferred him from the paramedic's stretcher. Hope backed away, staring at his handsome face, calm in unconsciousness.

Someone ripped the curtain closed in front of her and she shuddered.

An older nurse with kind eyes placed a hand gently on Hope's upper arm. She smiled comfortingly. "Let me get you some scrubs to wear. Then I'll show you to the waiting room."

Blinking, Hope stared at her still-zipped black wetsuit and neoprene booties. She wore nothing but a one-piece swimsuit underneath. The nurse gave her a pair of light blue scrubs and Hope changed in the bathroom, going commando underneath. She didn't have any shoes, though, so she kept the booties on, wet or not.

The nurse led Hope down several hallways and pushed through double doors into a room Hope was already familiar with from her previous visit after the shooting. She took a seat on a hard plastic chair near the double doors.

Ten minutes later, Mike entered through two glass doors on the opposite side of the room. He had changed, now wearing a dry T-shirt and shorts with sports sandals on his feet. Spotting Hope, he crossed to sit next to her. "Heard anything?"

"No. He's being examined by emergency staff. But I think they're going to take him to surgery. I heard the paramedic talking about it." Looking for a distraction, she turned to Mike. "Did your briefing go ok?"

"Fine. I couldn't very well hide the fact that Alex was taken away in the ambulance, but I was vague about his condition. They had plenty of questions for Zach and Jasmine. Their parents were pretty happy to see them."

Hope smiled, remembering how worried they had been. The two couples hadn't left the resort at all.

"Once they started talking to the kids, I ducked out and came here."

Just then, a middle-aged man in green scrubs and a surgical cap pushed through the doors, looking around the room. "Mrs. Monroe?"

Hope stood, and the man beckoned her into a private consultation room. She waved Mike to come along.

"I'm Dr. Rawlings, the orthopedic surgeon. I'm taking Alex to the OR now. His leg is in pretty bad shape. The X-Ray showed both lower leg bones are broken, the larger of the two in several places."

Hope forced herself to ask the question. "Are you going to have to amputate it?"

Dr. Rawlings smiled. "No, not unless there are complications I don't know about. But this is going to be an extended procedure, so be prepared for a wait. A volunteer will take you to the surgical waiting room. I'll come get you as soon as I'm done."

Soon they were in an expansive, blue-painted room. Multiple rows of chairs lined across it. Hope chose a chair in the corner, next to a potted Ficus tree that looked like it had mange. The waiting room was empty except for her and Mike, and Hope looked at the wall clock. It was past 9 p.m.

A young woman slid behind the information desk and woke her computer. She called them forward. "It's after hours, but you're welcome to stay here. If you want to have a seat, I need to fill out Alex's admission information." She gestured to a plastic chair in front of the desk. "If you leave or get something to eat, just give me your cell number so I can call if I get any updates. The café on the first floor closes at midnight."

Hope reached a hand to her forehead. "I don't even have my phone. Or my wallet. I came straight from the cave."

"Tell me where they are and I'll go get them," Mike said.

She did, and asked Mike to stop by the resort lobby so he could update anyone still working. Then he was out the door again, headed without complaint or comment back where he'd just come from.

Hope returned to her chair by the ugly Ficus, a bone-deep weariness settling over her. Along with a hard, hot ball of worry growing steadily in her gut—fear that Alex's leg couldn't be repaired, or that something worse would happen in the OR.

An hour later, Mike returned with her purse and two white

containers. He passed the purse to her, then grinned as he held up the cardboard boxes. "Patti was still in the lobby and insisted on me bringing something to eat."

Hope opened her box and her stomach rumbled loudly. Gerold had filled the boxes with a sub sandwich, chips, and a banana. Mike handed her a water. She hadn't eaten anything since Mike had been on his initial exploration, which seemed like eons ago. Both of them tucked in, demolishing their dinners.

The hours passed endlessly. Mike rose to talk quietly to Emma from the other side of the room. Hope checked her phone. Dozens of messages were lined up, but the only one she answered was Sara. Her sister had been at the grotto with Jack, Magen, and Will, but Hope hadn't even seen them. She texted saying Alex was in surgery and she'd inform Sara when she knew something.

The last thing Hope wanted was a crowd of people around her, even supportive people she loved. She and Mike shared the bond of having gone through the experience. He had every right to be there. Next, she texted Alex's sister Kate, giving her the latest.

Hope tried to keep her mind off their passage through the tunnel but couldn't. She couldn't shake the tight fear that had accompanied her throughout the journey. Of not being able to communicate with Alex. Twice, Mike had stopped behind her so he could stay near him. But it had been agony for Hope, not knowing what was happening.

Until Alex finally made it out of the squeeze, ashen and sweating, his eyes hazy with pain. And of course, he'd never leave Zach and Jasmine in that tunnel without knowing they were safe. He'd pushed back the pain until everyone made it out ok, then collapsed. Hope blinked back tears and picked up a magazine to distract herself.

It was nearly 2 a.m. when Dr. Rawlings returned, looking

much more tired than he had earlier. But he gave Hope a smile and her rock-hard shoulders relaxed, the tension draining from them. "Alex is on his way up to the floor now. The surgery was successful, and I'm pretty sure I got all the broken bits back together again."

"Will he have full use of his leg?" Hope asked.

Dr. Rawlings nodded. "He'll need physical therapy, and recovery will take a while. I can't guarantee anything, but yes, he should regain full use."

The woman behind the desk gave Hope Alex's room number, and soon she and Mike were walking down a deserted hallway and past a nurse's station with several people sitting behind computer terminals. Hope reached Alex's room and pushed the door all the way open to reveal a dimly lit private room.

He lay in the bed, still asleep. She crossed to his bedside, brushing her hand over his hair. His color was much better, but he didn't respond to her touch. A heavy growth of brown and gray scruff covered his jaw. She moved to the foot of the bed and lifted the blanket. His right lower leg was covered in gauze and a beige, wrapped bandage. His toes peeked out. They were reddish purple, but all there.

A nurse entered the room. His black hair was slicked back, and his brown eyes were warm as he smiled at Hope. "Hi, I'm Rodrigo. He's still coming out of the anesthetic but should wake up before too long. Sounds like you guys had quite a day."

"We have, especially Alex." Hope brushed the back of her hand down Alex's scruffy cheek. Trying to relax now that he was safe, but unable to get the image of him passing out from her mind. She blinked back tears.

A pneumatic sound hissed, and Rodrigo glanced at a steadily beeping screen. "His blood pressure is good and so is his pulse. I'll check on him after a while. If he wakes up and needs anything, just hit your call button."

After he whisked out of the room, Mike pulled up a padded chair on one side of Alex, while Hope did the same on his other side. They sat down to wait.

She studied Alex's relaxed face, no longer pinched and tight. Her own ball of dread was slightly diminished, but still holding on inside her stomach. A fine tremor ran through her hands, and she pressed them against her thighs.

Wake up, love. I need to hear your voice.

Chapter Thirty-Eight

THE BEEPING WAS slow and steady. At first, Alex tried to ignore it. He was warm and comfortable, which was important, even if he couldn't remember why. The beeping distracted him. It was familiar—he should know what it was.

Then it came to him. It was a hospital monitor.

He should know. He'd been in a hospital for months after Syria, though the last time he'd heard this sound had been when Hope had been hospitalized.

He slowly fluttered his eyes open to a dim room.

Across from him, a sink and length of counter lay between upper and lower cabinets. Soft under-cabinet lighting provided illumination. Alex rolled his head to the left. Mike sat in a chair with his legs stretched out and crossed at the ankles. He scrolled on his phone, the screen's glow lighting his face.

Alex twitched the side of his mouth. "I really need to stop waking up in hospitals to your ugly face."

Startled, Mike dropped the phone in his lap before giving Alex a broad grin. "You're in luck. There's a much prettier face on your other side."

There was a rustle as Alex rolled his head the other way.

Hope leaned forward in a matching chair, a window behind her. The blinds were open, and it was dark outside. Her hands were pressed between her knees, and she wore scrubs for some reason. Tears welled in her eyes and a single one beaded down the right side of her face. Her eyes held a mixture of relief, shock, and fear. She looked like she was holding herself together out of sheer will.

Her expression concerned him enough that he darted his eyes to the foot of the bed. But his eyes were met with the two reassuring lumps of his feet. He still had his right leg.

Turning back, Alex cleared his dry, scratchy throat. "Hey, you."

Hope unfolded herself and stepped to the side of his bed. "Hi." She brushed her hand over the side of his head, and he closed his eyes briefly at the comforting touch. "How are you feeling?"

"Really good." He laughed weakly, realizing he wasn't just reassuring her. It was true. "My leg is completely numb, which is paradise."

Smiling, Hope leaned over and brushed her lips over his. A soft, sweet kiss that sent happiness drifting through him.

When she pulled back, he raised a brow. "Be careful with that. I haven't brushed my teeth in days."

That made her laugh like he had hoped. "Take it easy. One step at a time."

On Alex's other side, Mike stood. "Since you're awake and even coherent for once, I'll take this as my cue to leave. Hope is letting me crash in a guest bungalow, and the bed is sounding pretty good right now. I'll take a taxi."

"Of course," Hope said, moving to her purse and withdrawing a room key. She crossed and handed it to him before drawing him into an embrace. "Thank you, Mike. If you hadn't been here, I don't even want to think about what would have happened."

"You're welcome." Mike pulled back and shot a grin at Alex. "I'll tell you what would have happened. Alex would have directed the explosion, which would have been a disaster. The guy doesn't know a blasting cap from his own ass."

Alex broke into soft laughter. "Get out of here, Baker. You've earned some rack time." Then he sobered. "Thank you. For everything."

Mike crossed to him, and they shook hands. "You're welcome. Just trying to repay what you did for me. I'll be back later."

After he left, Hope took Alex's hand and stroked it. "Both your lower leg bones were broken, the tibia in several places. But the surgeon said you'd have full use of your leg."

Relief washed through him. "Thank God for that." Then he cocked his head as he took in her appearance. "Why are you wearing scrubs?"

She pointed across the room to a large plastic bag. "My wetsuit is in there. In the emergency department, they were kind enough to give me a pair of scrubs to change into. It feels strange—my swimsuit was wet, so I took it off. I'm not wearing anything underneath this."

"Hubba hubba." He grinned, a pleasant dizziness making him sleepy again.

But his comment made her smile. "Don't even think about it."

"Can't help it." He rubbed his eyes and laughed. "Besides, I'm sure I've got some pretty strong drugs in my system. I'm feeling a little loopy."

Hope pressed the call button on his bed and soon a young man with slicked back hair entered. "Hey! You're awake."

Alex reassured Rodrigo he was doing well. The nurse

flipped back the covers from the foot of the bed, giving Alex his first glimpse of the repaired leg. It was wrapped in a bandage with gauze underneath, and his toes peeked out from the edge.

All five toes.

Rodrigo wrapped his hand around Alex's toes, but he couldn't feel a thing. "My leg and foot are completely numb."

The nurse nodded and replaced the blanket over his feet. "That's normal. They gave you a nerve block which will last a day or so. Your toes are nice and warm. Though they're pretty colorful."

"How long am I going to have to stay here?"

"I can't say yet. Dr. Rawlings will be in sometime today to talk to you. But he's ordered frequent checks and blood work, so I imagine you'll be here a couple of days."

Alex sighed, already itching to get home. Hospitals weren't his happy place, though he was very grateful to be where he was.

After Rodrigo left, Alex looked out the dark window. "What time is it?"

Hope glanced at the dive computer on her wrist. "Just before five. You were in surgery for almost five hours."

"Everything is hazy in my mind once we reached the grotto pool." Alex's eyelids felt like anchors were dragging them down. He tried to stay awake, wanting to keep talking with Hope, but his body had other plans.

THE SURGEON CAME by just after noon, a middle-aged man who looked like he kept in shape. Alex was wide awake, and the groggy drugs had worn off. Dr. Rawlings immediately gave Alex a physical exam. "You're doing well. Vital signs are strong and you're not showing any signs of infection, which is a concern after being in a cave for several days then submerging that leg in water."

"My skin looked mostly unbroken."

Dr. Rawlings nodded. "Mostly, which is a blessing. You really smashed that leg up though. I didn't even try for a minimally invasive approach. So be warned—you're going to have an impressive scar running up that leg. I needed to relieve the pressure building up in there. I imagine you must have been in a lot of pain."

"It hasn't been the most pleasant couple of days."

Hope frowned at him as the doctor moved to a white digital wall monitor across from the bed. He turned it on and flipped through medical imagery until he found side-by-side images of Alex's leg.

Alex swallowed hard, not needing to be told which was the *before* picture.

"There were three breaks in the tibia. I picked out the shards and placed several screws and plates. The fibula also needed some screws, but it was a pretty clean break. You've got a broken metatarsal in your foot, but that should heal fine on its own."

"Hope told me you expect I'll get full use of my leg back?"

Dr Rawlings smiled as he drew an imaginary circle with one finger around Alex's ankle on the *after* X-Ray. "Yes. Your ankle joint is completely undamaged. If that had been smashed, you'd be in a very different situation."

Thank God for small mercies. "So does this mean I can get out of here today?"

Hope's frown deepened. "You just got here."

Dr. Rawlings shook his head. "I'm going to keep you a couple more days. I want to keep an eye on that leg and make sure there's no latent infection brewing. We'll need to re-wrap the limb as the swelling decreases."

Alex nodded, not happy, but not expecting otherwise, either.

"I've ordered pain medication if you need it. The nerve block should last the rest of the day, but then you're going to feel some pain."

Alex laughed. "It can't possibly be more than what I felt in the cave."

Dr. Rawlings shrugged. "Everyone's different. Some people have minimal post-op pain, but for others it's significant."

"I've got a fairly high pain tolerance."

Hope's mouth tightened at that.

The surgeon eyed him steadily. "I'm sure you do. While I was checking you over for injuries, I couldn't help noticing the scars on your hip. Looks like you had quite a few surgeries."

More than a few. "Yeah. In Germany and at Walter Reed."

"They did an excellent job. I imaged your hip to be thorough, and it looks solid."

"One less thing to worry about, then. Thanks, doc."

After the surgeon left, Hope faced him squarely, parking both hands on her hips. "You need to stay in the hospital for a few days, ok? So don't get all cantankerous about it."

He couldn't resist a smile. "When am I ever cantankerous?" Then he softened his expression, looking at the bags under her eyes. "When was the last time you slept?"

"The night before last. But I'm doing fine—I can stay here."

Alex pointed a finger at her. "I have a very vivid memory of someone lying in a hospital bed and ordering me to go home and rest. And make sure Cruz was fed." He knew that would get to her.

Hope pressed her lips together primly. "I already took care of him. He's outside and Patti and Clark have been feeding him."

"You're always taking care of everyone. Now you need to take care of yourself. Go home and rest."

"I'm not tired." Her mouth opened in a gigantic yawn, and her hand flew up to cover it. "Shit."

"Yeah. Not tired at all. Besides, I have an ulterior motive. When you come back, you can bring me some real food." His day-shift nurse had brought a bowl of broth and lime Jell-O. Alex had downed the broth, but refused the Jell-O. After being in the hospital in Germany, he couldn't touch the stuff.

Hope smiled at him. "Fine. I'll go lay down for a while. What do you want Gerold to make you?"

Alex closed his eyes, already blissful. "Steak, grilled shrimp, and French fries. No—a double order of French fries, with cheesecake for dessert. And a chocolate milkshake."

Hope's smile widened. "You've thought all about this, haven't you?"

"I had to think about something in that cave." He took her hand and brought it to his lips. "Besides you."

She stroked her hand down his arm. "I thought about you a lot too."

"You got me through that. When I needed strength, you gave it to me. I'm so proud of you, Hope. You managed that rescue like a true pro."

"Thank you. I was trained by the best." She bent over and kissed his forehead. He took a deep inhale. She smelled of home. "I'll let you know when I'm on my way back. And I expect the full story of what happened during the earthquake."

He nodded, dreading that conversation. "I know. I'll tell you."

Alex watched her leave the room, shutting the door softly behind her, and immediately felt her absence. He ran a hand over his layer of beard growth, needing a distraction. "Time to clean up a little."

Earlier, a physical therapist had stopped by, dropping off a pair of crutches and giving Alex permission to move as long as he felt strong enough. They would start walks in the hall later that day. The crutches were next to the bed, and he slowly, carefully, swung his legs over. After the agony of his broken leg, he was astonished at how painless the motion was. Taking a crutch in each hand, he pulled himself to stand on his left foot. Dizziness rose, but it settled quickly, leaving him clear-headed.

Alex moved across the room to the bathroom. Walking on crutches came back to him instantly, especially since his broken leg was on the same side as his hip wound. He smiled grimly. *Guess if I have to deal with another leg injury, it's better to have one bad leg instead of two.*

After opening the door, Alex entered the small bathroom. A toiletry kit lay on the vanity, complete with toothbrush and toothpaste, as well as a razor. He lifted his eyes to the mirror and was met with a solid growth of hair on his jaw. After thoroughly brushing his teeth, he lathered up his jaw and lifted the razor. Then he paused, staring at his reflection.

I haven't had facial hair since I arrived in St. Croix. Time for a change.

Alex slid the razor down his cheek and over his neck, but left a goatee. After toweling dry, he inspected his reflection and the liberal amount of gray hair on his chin. He would turn forty-four in March and couldn't deny he was aging.

"But I just learned it sure beats the alternative."

He poked through his sun-bleached hair but couldn't find more than a few grays at his temples. Nodding once at his reflection, Alex returned to the bed to find a football game on TV.

Chapter Thirty-Nine

ALEX RECEIVED his next guest in the early evening. He'd been expecting Hope, but Mike walked through his door. Alex muted the television, which was broadcasting extended local news about the earthquake. The cave rescue was the other major news item, much to his displeasure. But the reporters weren't blowing the rescue out of proportion, simply stating that Zach and Jasmine returned home with their parents while Alex needed surgery for a broken leg suffered during the earthquake. Like other news flashes, now that everyone was safe, it would blow over quickly. At least he hoped so.

Mike strolled to the counter next to the sink, which was packed with flower arrangements. One dwarfed the others in size. "That's a change from this morning."

"They've been delivering them all afternoon."

"Who are they from?"

"Not sure. I haven't looked. I'm sure Hope will want to."

Mike sat in the same chair he'd used earlier and smiled at Alex. "You missed a spot shaving."

Alex laughed. "Yeah, I decided to do something different. I was expecting Hope. Did you get some rest?"

"I did. Slept like a rock for several hours. I ran into Hope when I was eating. She'll be along before too long. She was putting together some sort of feast for you."

Alex's stomach rumbled. His appetite had grown all day, and he was more than ready to eat.

"I'm glad I saw her," Mike continued. "It gave me a chance to say goodbye."

Alex's brows flew up. "You're leaving? I've been watching the news. They said flights are still packed."

"They added a flight that takes off in a couple of hours, so I jumped on it before all the seats were gone." He studied his hands, twirling his thumbs.

"You ok, Mike?"

He snapped his head up and leaned back in his chair, straightening one leg casually. "Yeah. I got a call a couple of hours ago. About that job I've been telling you about. They offered me the position, with a lot more money than I was expecting."

"They realized how lucky they'd be to get you. Congratulations."

Mike shifted his eyes to the large window overlooking the green mountains. "I turned them down."

Mike had always been ambitious, so his response was puzzling. "Really? What changed your mind?"

He hesitated for a moment. "Watching Hope. She was totally focused on the rescue, but it was clear she was terrified for you. It made me think of how I'd feel if it had been Emma trapped in there." Mike rifled both hands through his short brown hair. "I don't need a new job and more money. I need a strong marriage."

Alex smiled. "I highly recommend it. This news should make Emma happy."

"I'm sure it will. And it's the right thing to do." Mike stared at Alex's bandaged leg before meeting his gaze. "Sounds like you're going to be ok."

"Yeah. The doctor said it will take several months, but I'll get there."

"I'm sure you will. This rehab should be easier than the last time."

Alex repressed a shudder. "Thank God."

Mike stood. "I'm on my way to the airport now. I just wanted to drop by and tell you the news about the job."

"I'm glad you did. And I'm glad you found a flight out." Then Alex grinned. "I won't have to put up with your awful jokes anymore. Finally have you out of my hair."

Mike smiled back. "I like Emma's hair better anyway. Long, blonde, and silky."

"Emma has better hair than me. I admit it."

"She smells better, too."

Alex rubbed his palms over his eyes. "After the past few days, I have no doubt of that." Dropping his hands in his lap, he eyed Mike evenly. "Take care of yourself."

"Always. Gotta stay in top shape so I can bail your ass out."

"I like to give you something to do now and then. So you feel better about all the times I snatched your ugly face out of the fire."

Smiling, Mike leaned over Alex's bed. They embraced, slapping each other's backs.

"Thanks, Mike. If not for you, I'm not sure we would have gotten out of there."

"You're welcome. I'll see you around." He turned and headed across the room.

As he reached for the door handle, Alex called out. "Mike."

He turned, arching a brow.

"If you ever need anything, I'll be there."

A slow smile raised Mike's lips. "I know that. We all do. We're part of the same team, remember?"

HOPE HURRIED down the hospital corridor, carrying Alex's dinner in a canvas shopping bag hanging off one arm. Earlier, after leaving the hospital, she'd climbed under the covers of their bed, positive she wouldn't be able to sleep.

She woke up four hours later.

After showering and changing, she'd rushed to the restaurant and ran into Mike. She made time to say goodbye, and she didn't need to play up the gratitude she felt toward him.

Now Hope pushed open the door to Alex's room and was met by a wave of tropical floral scent. The counter was crammed with flower arrangements, including one enormous explosion of flowers that took up most of the real estate.

Alex was alone, lying in bed. Smiling, she crossed the room. "Sorry it took me so long. I brought your dinner."

He pressed the button to lift the head of his bed as Hope slid his tray table over his lap. She whisked a finger over his jawline, enjoying the change in texture. "I've never seen you with more than a little stubble. Decided to keep some of it?"

"For now. As long as you like it."

"Let's find out."

Cupping the back of Alex's head, Hope leaned in and pressed her lips to his. The hairs of his goatee tickled her lips, but his mouth was soft and yielding. His kiss was a vivid reminder of what she'd been missing for the last four days. Pent-up emotion started to rise, but she pushed it down, determined to stay positive and grateful instead. Alex raised his arm and hooked his elbow over the back of her neck, drawing her closer to lengthen the kiss.

Eventually, she broke away to brush her finger down the straight bridge of his nose. "Mmm. Facial hair approved. Did you get all cleaned up?"

"No, I didn't want to get too carried away. Just brushed my teeth and shaved. I got plenty clean coming out of that cavern."

Opening the containers Gerold had packed, Alex tucked into his feast, making appropriate groaning noises. While he ate, Hope sat in a chair and watched a game show. When that was over, she crossed to the flower arrangements, pulling out cards. Several resorts had sent bouquets, as had Cindy. Finally, Hope couldn't deprive herself any longer and opened the card of the gigantic one. She barked a laugh when she read it. "This one's from The President."

Alex swallowed the last bite of cheesecake before drawing his brows together. "Of the scuba agency?"

"No, Alex. Of the *United States*. He thanks you for your service and is thrilled the rescue had such a positive outcome."

"Is it handwritten?"

"No. Typed."

Alex lost interest, stacking the empty boxes neatly on the tray table. "Uh-huh. Minions."

Hope held up the card. "It's a very nice gesture."

"He never thanked me for my service after I was nearly killed in combat."

"He wasn't in office then."

"Fine. Be all logical." He took a long drink of his milkshake, his cheeks drawing in as he sucked through the straw. "You look beautiful, by the way."

"Thank you." She fanned out the skirt of the sundress she wore, her hair up in a clip. "At least I'm wearing underwear again."

"That's highly disappointing."

Hope laughed as she crossed the room to plant a kiss on top of his head. "I've missed you so much."

Alex leaned his head against her breast, kissing the top of her cleavage. His humor was gone. "I missed you too. I can't describe how much. But thinking about you helped me in so many ways."

"You did the same for me." She enfolded her arms around his head, gently pressing him against her chest. "Will you tell me what happened?"

Hope wasn't at all sure she *wanted* to know, but she needed to. She needed to understand what he'd been through.

Alex shifted his head slightly and kissed her skin. "Yes. Have a seat."

"Great. I need to sit for this, huh?" Her poor attempt at humor fell flat this time.

The conflict within him was clear in the etched lines of his face. He wanted to tell her what she had asked for. But he also wanted to protect her from unpleasantness. And she was under no delusions his experience had been unpleasant, to put it mildly.

The *before* X-Ray flashed in her mind, and a shiver trickled down her back.

Alex began, speaking slowly at first, and the story took a long time to tell. He ended with the wave sweeping upon the rocky shore that thankfully stopped short of where the trio stood. Several times, Hope had to wipe her sweaty hands on her skirt. There was no doubt in her mind he told her everything. She understood at last why he had been in so much pain, though the knowledge made her nauseous. When he finished, they stared at each other for a long moment.

Hope was slightly dizzy. "You were about to cut your own leg off?"

"Not quite. But mostly because I couldn't think up a way to

make a tourniquet. Bleeding to death in that black passage wasn't how I wanted to go. At any rate, I didn't need to because Zach got me out. Thanks to you."

She rose and moved to him, grasping his face between her palms. Needing to touch him, though she remained dry-eyed and determined to stay strong. "How could you ever think you weren't a good leader? Mike didn't even let me explain what had happened. As soon as he knew you were in trouble, he hung up on me so he could book his flight. Alex, you're everything. To so many people—not just me."

He rested his hand on top of hers. "It was a dark, weak moment. Zach helped me overcome it. So did you."

They kissed again, another soft meeting of lips, of drawing strength and comfort from each other. Hope was afraid to push him to open up more, especially after finding out she could have lost him forever. They were in a delicate dance with each other, reconnecting while both were fragile emotionally. She could sense the currents of emotion running through him—the same as those filling her. They could continue the conversation later. Each was acutely aware of the other and their shared bond, so nearly broken because of that cavern.

Nearly.

But now stronger than ever.

Chapter Forty

ALEX ROLLED down the window of Hope's Jeep as she turned off the highway onto the resort access road, enjoying the breeze on his face. Dr. Rawlings had kept him in the hospital for four days. But that morning he'd finally discharged Alex, convinced he didn't have an infection and his leg was healing steadily. Alex had done his best to be a good patient, pleasant and polite to staff, and found it a much easier task than his previous rehabilitation stay after his combat wound. Because he had something to go home to. A profession he enjoyed. A purpose. A *wife*.

Over the past few days, Hope had made a series of trips to bring home his numerous flower bouquets and gifts. The back of her Jeep was full of the last of them, their floral scent drifting through the car. When they reached the sand parking lot, Alex turned to her. "Will you stop at the lobby? I want to say hello."

"Of course." Hope shut the engine off in front of the lobby steps.

Several guest bungalows were visible, making Alex smile. "I'm sorry I never got a chance to talk to Megan and Derek."

Hope had explained they were the couple he had spotted just prior to passing out at the grotto, and that Derek had provided the water purification tablets. The couple had left two days ago.

"So were they," Hope said. "I think they got a little more than they bargained for on their return trip! But they assured me they would come back for a third time someday."

"I'd like to get Derek's email and thank him personally for the safe drinking water. That made a big difference, especially for me."

"I'm sure we have his email on file."

In the distance, a construction worker operated a table saw near a bungalow. The sound filled the air. "How many bungalows need work?"

Hope rested her hand on the steering wheel, pointing with her index finger. "That one and Ixora fared the worst. All needed some repairs, but we've had a lot of cancellations, so work is progressing quickly. All the bungalows should be good as new in a couple of weeks."

As she exited the car, Alex collected his crutches from the back seat. Carefully crutching up the stairs, he entered the lobby through the double open doors with Hope just behind.

Martine stood alone behind the front desk. She screamed when she saw him, bolting from behind the desk to run toward him with both arms open wide. "You're home!"

Patti was hot on her heels, though a bit more sedate.

Alex returned the front desk clerk's hug with a grin. "I'm home. I just wanted to stop by and say thank you for all you did while we were in that cave."

Martine's caramel-colored face beamed. "That was somethin' else! We had people callin' from all over the world. But it's settled down now."

Alex swept his gaze over the expansive room. Other than cracked drywall, it looked largely the same. Well, except for the flower arrangements placed on every horizontal surface. The two seating areas were still on either side of the room, the desk and office on the far side. A table with baked goods and infused water sat near the front.

Alex grinned at the dolphin sculpture in the middle of the room. "The statue made it through ok?"

"Yes," Hope answered. "It toppled over during the quake, but landed on one of the couches, so it was protected."

He shared a private look with her. The sculpture had cost a small fortune, but was a private symbol for both of them. He was glad to see it undamaged.

Then he noticed something else.

The wall of staff photos was highly diminished. And one very prominent photo was missing. "Where's our wedding picture?"

Hope's eyes clouded. "It fell and broke. That was one of the first things I saw after the quake." She held his gaze, and he reached out to tuck a lock of hair behind her ear. Now he understood why she'd been such a guilty wreck over ordering him out of the lobby. He softly planted a kiss on top of her head.

"Oh, don't you two worry about that!" Patti said, alternating a pointing finger at each of them. "I've already called the frame shop in Frederiksted, and Vera is makin' another one. Said she'd have it ready by next week."

The framed copies of Hope's and his articles were in their usual places, but Alex would be glad to see the wedding photo back where it belonged.

The front-desk phone rang, sending Martine hurrying to answer it. Patti headed back to the office after a final hug from Alex.

Hope turned to him. "I don't want the flowers in the Jeep to wilt. We should head to the house."

"Can you take them? I want to head down to the pier to talk

to Zach and Jasmine." The couple had been by for a short visit while he was in the hospital, but it had been somewhat awkward and formal. Both of them felt guilty. Alex wanted to rectify that.

Hope nodded. "Don't be too long, ok? I can come get you in the golf cart if you want." Then she snorted, shaking her head. "As if you'd let me. I imagine you'd crawl back on your hands and knees rather than accept a ride."

"It's not that far. I'll go slow." He kissed the tip of her nose. "And thank you for not coddling me."

As he made his way out of the lobby, Alex smiled as the sun warmed his face. It had been seven days since he'd experienced that. Hope had him pegged. There was no way he'd accept a ride in a golf cart. And in truth, he wanted to walk along the shore, crutches and all, on the way back. To feel the ocean splash over his sandal.

Hobbling his way up the long flight of stairs took more effort than he wanted to admit, but Alex opened the door and entered the cool dive/gift shop. He took a deep breath of neoprene, always a favorite scent of his. The room showed little signs of damage, though Hope had told him it had been in a shambles after the quake.

As he entered, the bell above the door rang, and Jasmine looked up from a display. Breaking into a smile that rivaled Martine's, she trotted over. After exchanging hugs, Alex got to the reason he'd wanted to see her. "How are you holding up? You doing ok?"

She leaned back against the check-out counter and nodded. "The first couple days were pretty weird. I felt elated, guilty, and proud all at the same time. It didn't seem right that Zach and I both went straight home that night while you were in the hospital."

"I'm glad it happened that way. I'm really proud of you,

Jasmine. Getting through that squeeze was badass on a whole new level."

Her smile held a lot of pride, but it faded as she stared at him. "Thanks. I got through that because you were in front of me, and Zach was just behind. I watched you the whole time, starin' at your damn ugly leg."

They both laughed at that.

Then Jasmine became somber again. "I could tell how much pain you were in by how you moved. And when you knocked your leg on that rock, I was afraid you'd faint. You kept poundin' your hand on the wall."

Alex straightened. "Really? I don't even remember doing that."

Her expression turned rueful. "I imagine you had other things on your mind right then."

Like trying not to puke or pass out. "It wasn't a fun moment."

"But you kept goin'. And I knew if you could, then so could I. My tank got hung up. I'm still not sure on what. I tried and tried to get it unhooked, and was gettin' pretty worked up and scared. That's when Mike came back. He grabbed my tank and all I had to do was army-crawl after it."

"You were fantastic, Jasmine. I can't imagine anyone doing better." He eyed her evenly. "If you ever need to talk about any of it, I'm here, ok?"

She shuddered. "Thanks. But that cavern and tunnel are the last things I want to think about. I'm doin' all right."

"Just know the offer is there. Are you and Zach getting along ok?"

"Better now. We've talked quite a bit. My folks weren't too happy with him, but I went into that cave of my own free will. He came over and formally apologized to them for puttin' me in danger like that. He's more careful now. More... aware."

Alex was happy to hear that. They were a good couple, and after spending three straight days with them, he wanted to see them stay together.

When Alex returned to the dock below, he opened the door to the gear room and confirmed his rebreather hung neatly in its spot. Jack told him he'd grabbed it out of the water as soon as the ambulance took off. But it was a big relief to see it there—it was by far his most expensive piece of equipment. Since Alex was out of commission, Jack had come back to work early, taking over interim management duties. *Surface Interval* was currently out on the afternoon dive, the end of the pier empty.

When he exited back onto the dock, Zach was under the palapa, crossing from the ladder and dripping wet. The divemaster tossed his fins on a wooden bench. Alex made his way to the palapa and sat on the bench next to the fins. The two men exchanged greetings. "Good dive?"

"Yeah," Zach said, his face tight and guarded. "I dove the coral nursery. Several PVC trees got knocked over in the quake and will have to be repaired, but the structure itself is fine."

"Thanks. I don't think anyone has been down there yet."

"The nursery hasn't been a priority lately."

Alex nodded his head at the extra tank Zach wore. "I see you remembered your pony bottle."

Zach unbuckled his BCD, letting his tank slip to the wooden deck, and sat next to Alex, meeting his gaze squarely. "Can't imagine I'll ever forget. Like I said, I learned my lesson, Alex." His eyes filled with tears, and he moved his head to stare out at the ocean.

"How are you doing, Zach?" Alex asked quietly.

Talking to both Zach and Jasmine had been a top priority. Post-traumatic stress took several forms, and Alex was no stranger to it himself. He didn't want either of them feeling that what they were experiencing was unusual or made them weak.

"So-so. I feel so guilty. I could have gotten both you and Jasmine killed. Or myself."

"Zach, everyone has done stupid things. I've got more than my fair share of experience on that front. Most of the time, you're lucky and everything works out fine. Once in a while, it doesn't. Don't beat yourself up with what-ifs. I did that for years." Alex leaned forward, staring Zach square in the eye. "Take it from me—stewing in your misery doesn't help. I could have been a few seconds later and been buried by that cave-in. Hope could have been with me and killed. None of that matters."

Zach watched him, listening closely.

"Only two things matter. That we held together as a team, and that we all made it out of there."

"Thanks."

Alex paused for a moment. "And one other thing matters."

"What's that?"

"That I give thanks to *you*."

Zach sat back, shaking his head over and over. "No way. You should never have needed to come after us. The whole thing was my—"

Alex stopped him by grasping his upper arm. "Stop. You're doing it again. Don't let that loop get started. Zach, if you hadn't come back for me, I'm pretty sure I'd be dead right now. The air in my rebreather wouldn't have lasted forever and I couldn't lift that stone by myself. You saved my life. Plain and simple. Thank you for that." He'd never mentioned the dilemma with the knife. Only Hope knew about that.

Zach swallowed thickly. "You're welcome."

"Don't keep this bottled up inside, or let it eat you alive. If you need to talk, I'm here. I don't care if it's 2 a.m., call me."

"Thanks, Alex." Zach regarded his tank. "In a weird way, I think this experience will make me a better divemaster."

"I know it will. You're already a great divemaster." Alex was glad the experience hadn't changed Zach's mind about his career choice. The young man would face some hurdles overcoming this ordeal. But when he did, Zach would be a better man for it. "When are you back on the schedule leading dives?"

"Tomorrow... I'm lookin' forward to it. A little nervous too."

"I don't think you'll need to worry about any tunnels," Alex said with a laugh.

"I just feel like there's a spotlight on me. Or like I'm wearin' a sign sayin' *It's my fault*."

"I know exactly what you mean. That's what I felt like after Syria. Zach, the only way to get past it is through it." He paused. "Have you talked to the media?"

"A little. I said Jasmine and I were in there explorin' and you came to make sure we were ok and got trapped."

Alex nodded. "That's pretty much what happened. You don't need to say anything more."

"The whole situation proved what you said about us bein' too inexperienced to be in there. Feels like I'm shrinkin' from the truth."

"You're not. And what happened isn't anyone's damn business anyway. The court of public opinion can be brutally judgmental. Don't torture yourself unnecessarily. You're getting in the water and leading a group tomorrow. Shrinking from the truth is the last thing you're doing."

Zach's face was less troubled as he rose to rinse out his gear. Alex left him to it, crutching his way up the pier. Before the earthquake, Zach had been full of life and bluster. Alex didn't want that spark to flicker out.

He ambled along the shoreline, keeping his injured leg dry while letting the sea wash over his foot in its comforting, endless rhythm. A profound sense of peace and gratitude overcame him. Like Zach, Alex wasn't finished processing what had happened.

He still had moments of doubting himself, but the house in the distance contained everything he would need to overcome this.

Hope.

The afternoon was beautiful, with a light breeze and bouncy clouds. As Alex neared the house, a streak of yellow bounded off the porch and barreled toward him. Cruz barked nonstop, skidding to a halt in front of Alex. His tail wagged so hard his hindquarters shimmied.

Laughing, Alex transferred his crutch to the other hand so he could pet Cruz's head. "I get the feeling you missed me, guy."

"A lot of people missed you."

Alex looked up as Hope descended the stairs and came toward him. She wore a yellow sundress that brought out the gold in her eyes, and her hair was blowing softly around her shoulders. She took his breath away.

As she slid both arms around his waist, Alex wrapped her up tightly, holding her against him as he rested his cheek against her head. Closing his eyes, he was enveloped by the ocean and his wife's arms.

Eventually, Hope raised her head, standing on her toes to brush her lips over his, a soft, loving kiss that went straight to his heart. "Welcome home, sailor."

Chapter Forty-One

HOPE OPENED the slider and let Alex enter the house first, rubbing her hand over his broad back. Cruz ducked past and headed for his water bowl. Stopping just inside the slider, Alex swept his gaze around the open area, his perceptive eyes taking in everything. He halted at the sight of two wrapped loaves of bread sitting on the counter.

"Special delivery. I baked banana bread for you this morning."

"I smelled it as soon as I walked in." He gave Hope the smile that always made her heart knock against her ribs. "You're spoiling me, Boss Lady. Cupcakes yesterday, and now this."

"You deserve a little pampering."

Flower arrangements were placed everywhere, even on the floor after she'd run out of space. The ones she'd brought home that day sat in a row near the front door. Hope had done her best to clean up the house, but the damage was still apparent.

Alex crutched over to a line of floor tiles which were buckled and broken, tapping one with the tip of his crutch. His smile faded.

"Now we have an excuse to remodel," Hope said, trying to make light of it.

Alex didn't smile back. "I'm sorry you had to deal with this all alone. I should have been here."

"You had a pretty good excuse for being absent. And I wasn't alone. Sara did a lot of the work in the great room. Tommy and Will picked up the fridge. I had plenty of help."

His gaze moved to their dented, but functioning, refrigerator. Still frowning, Alex crutched into their bedroom, then into the bath and large closet they shared. Hope followed.

"Looks pretty good in here," he said, glancing around the closet.

"There wasn't too much damage in here. But your Navy box slid off and opened up. I put everything back, and I don't think anything was harmed." She thought of her project and smiled, not ready to show it off yet.

Alex's face was still troubled, and Hope grew concerned. "How are you feeling? Do you need a pain pill?"

She'd filled his oxycodone prescription despite his reluctance to use it, and set the amber bottle on his nightstand. He'd taken pain medication in the hospital to help him sleep, and she wanted to ease his way home. This time would be a delicate balance for them, as it had been after he'd been shot. Alex's natural tendency to be in charge and fully capable conflicted with the fact that he couldn't be. And Hope wanted to support him without tipping into coddling and henpecking.

Like before, they'd get through it. Together.

As she closed the distance between them, he shot her a smile. "No, I don't need any meds now. My leg feels so much better, I can hardly explain it. It hurts, yes. But the pain is so different. The leg feels *right* now, if that makes sense."

Hope slid her arm up his chest and patted it. "It does.

Would you like to hang out in the great room? Maybe watch a game?"

"No. What I'd really like to do is take my shoe off and sit on the porch with my wife and a beer—another reason to skip the pain meds. I want to have you by my side and just watch the ocean for a while."

"That sounds heavenly. And *normal*."

Alex passed through the slider while she went to the refrigerator. Her phone on the counter chimed with a text from Patti asking Hope to send a picture they'd discussed earlier for the project. Hope had to scroll through her camera roll before she found it, a picture of her and Sara from years ago, when Hope was in college. They had their arms draped over each other's shoulders and wore bright expressions, their heads tilted toward each other. Hope smiled. It was one of the few happy pictures from that time.

After texting the photo to Patti, she continued scrolling down her camera roll. Her thumb froze at the picture from her Facebook memory, the one of her with two friends. She brought the photo up, looking at that poor, shattered version of herself. Now Hope only felt compassion for her.

Well, not quite. There was something else.

Something Hope only realized because of what she'd just been through. Her heart was finally emptied of fear and rage toward Caleb. For the useless life he'd squandered. Now she only felt pity. That time in the past was truly over—inconsequential. And now he was truly out of her life. Forever.

She glanced out the window at the back of Alex's head as he looked across the beach. Her experience with Caleb had led directly to where she stood right now. Which was exactly where she was meant to be. Closing her eyes, a great sense of peace and calm overcame her.

"I forgive you, Caleb. Goodbye."

Hope deleted the photo.

Turning, she pulled two beers out of the fridge, eager to join her husband.

LATER THAT EVENING, Hope helped Alex, wearing only boxers, into bed. He'd taken an oxycodone, which let her know he was in more pain than he wanted to admit. Settling on his back, he tossed his portion of the covers toward the foot of the bed. His leg was still wrapped, but the rolled gauze underneath had been replaced by gauze pads. His incision was six inches long, though less red and angry than it had been.

Hope wore a light-blue silk nightgown as she slipped under the covers. She slid across to Alex, settling her head against the hard muscles of his chest. He encircled both arms around her, slowly stroking one hand up and down the silk covering her back.

"The night I spent in the hospital after my surgery," Hope said. "I remember you said you couldn't sleep in here alone. Neither could I. I went out and slept on the couch."

He brushed a hand over her hair. "We're together again now."

"Thank God." She pressed her lips against his warm skin.

Alex placed a knuckle under her chin, tilting her head up. He kissed her, not the sweet, hesitant kisses they'd been sharing. He met her lips fully, opening his mouth and probing with his tongue.

A jolt of arousal went through her, followed quickly by concern. She pulled back. "You can't possibly..." Hope glanced down at his boxers and smiled, the evidence obvious. "I guess you can."

"I want to make love with my wife."

"And I want to make love with my husband. But Alex, you just got out of the hospital today."

As soon as the words left her mouth, she knew they were a mistake.

Alex hissed a breath out, raking a hand through his hair. "So what? I've been lying in that bed for days, and on a rocky floor for days before that. I'm tired of being weak and useless. I need to do something. Something that matters. And I am very capable of this. Right now."

Hope slipped her panties off and stretched out next to him, making sure not to touch his right leg. "I know that. You're the most capable man I've ever met. You've never been weak or useless. And you matter. To everyone."

He tightened his mouth into a gash and shook his head.

She understood this man to his soul. The cave-in was bringing echoes of how he'd felt after Syria. Even though he'd said his dark moment in the cave was fleeting, she knew better. Alex was a man who wore the weight of the world on his broad shoulders.

"Everyone here at the resort banded together and got things repaired after the quake," he continued. "Without me. You managed all those problems. Without me. I was useless in that cave—"

Hope silenced him by placing her index finger against his lips. "What do you need?" Though Alex spoke those words more often to her, they were equally important when he needed them.

"I need to *matter*."

Hope raised onto an elbow, stroking his face with her other hand. "Did you see that crowd when we got out of the cave?"

"Yeah. They were there for the show."

"Maybe some of them. But most of the resort staff was there. Alex, they were thrilled to see Zach and Jasmine come out of that cave. Both were safe and sound—thanks to you. But make no mistake, that crowd was there because they were terrified for *you*. How can you even think you don't matter? That you can't lead people?"

He stared at her intently as she stroked his face.

"When I called Mike, the only question he asked was if you needed the entire Team. Then he hung up to book the first flight down here. That is the kind of loyalty you inspire. I've talked to both Zach and Jasmine. Both credit you and your support with getting them through that ordeal."

Hope stared deep into his eyes. "I'd like to think I'm the beating heart of Half Moon Bay. But Alex—you're its *soul*. Never question that. Ever."

His eyes became glassy, emotion building.

She took his hand and placed it over his thudding heart, holding it in place with her own. "You feel that? That is strength. That is what matters. You are what matters." She smiled softly at him. "I'll ask you again. What do you *need*, Alex?"

"You. Only you, Hope."

She bent down and brushed her lips over his. She was still getting used to the sensation of his goatee tickling her lips, and kept the pressure light, trying to be sensitive. Instead, Alex folded his arm around the back of her neck, drawing her tighter. He opened his mouth to kiss her deeply, a rough groan wrenching from his throat.

That was all she needed.

Hope rolled on top of him, digging her fingers into his shoulders, and taking her cues from him. Just as he did for her when they had made love in his office. He didn't want gentle, sweet sex. He wanted to feel powerful and passionate. Normal.

She sat up, ripping the nightgown off. Alex followed her into a sitting position, his abs rippling as he contracted them. He drew her breast into his mouth, sending hot waves directly to her core.

"How has it been only a week since we've been together?" she asked, gasping. "You turn me on so much."

He bit her gently in response, and she pushed her hips against him. Grinding and swaying.

Growling, Alex cupped her face with both hands, kissing her with hot, frantic passion. "I need you now, baby."

Reaching down, she withdrew his shaft from his boxers. She lowered herself slowly, easing herself open. Alex closed his eyes, wrapping both arms around her as he fell onto his back, pulling her down over him.

When he was seated deep within her, Hope slowly began moving. "Is this what you want?" Then she lifted and slammed down, wrenching a long, low moan from him. "Or more of that?"

"Both. Either. Anything."

She gave a titter of laughter, and Alex smiled, his eyes still closed.

"Well, then. Leave everything to me, love." She took his hand and brought it between her legs. He moved his fingers in slow, exquisite circles as she continued lifting in slow, deliberate movements, periodically punctuated by a fast, hard thrust that made Alex cry out louder each time.

Tipping her head back, she breathed his name in a long exhale. A slow pulsing radiated from her core, and the pleasure she gave him only increased her own.

Hope ran her hands over his chest, spreading her fingers over the hard muscles. His skin was smooth and still tan, even after a week indoors. Gripping his shoulders, she slid both hands down to clench his biceps. She dug her nails in. He shuddered, then gasped as she bent over and swiped her tongue into his ear, whispering against it, "You're so hard and strong. All over. So sexy."

He found her mouth again. "Oh, my Hope."

"You're all power and strength. You're everything, Alex."

He moved his fingers faster, bringing her ever closer to climax, and the sounds of their breathing filled the still room. She pressed her lips to his, plunging her tongue into his mouth as she met him in one final, powerful thrust that took them both over the edge.

Alex wrapped both arms around her, holding her against him. Hope settled against his chest, listening to his heart gradually return to its normal, steady rhythm.

"You always know exactly what to do. What to say," he whispered.

"The same way you do. Because we know each other—down to our souls."

He brushed his fingers down her back in a long stroke, lulling her. Within seconds, his movements slowed, finally stopping as his breath deepened. As carefully as possible, Hope lifted and moved off him. She pulled up the covers and lovingly drew them over him. Settling at his side, she closed her eyes, listening to the cadence of his deep, regular breaths next to her.

The universe had been righted.

HOPE WOKE JUST after 5 a.m. and Alex was already out of bed. He wasn't in the great room either, but a smile rose on her face at her coffee mug sitting ready next to the coffee machine. Fresh-brewed cup in hand, she exited onto the porch. Alex stood just behind the railing, dressed in a long-sleeved T-shirt and shorts. His crutches rested on the rail next to him.

Sliding an arm around his waist, she joined his side. "How did you sleep?"

"Better than I have in a week. Now I'm out here watching a new day wake up."

It was still dark, but there was a soft, pale glow on the horizon where the moon had recently set. Stars twinkled overhead. "Looks like it's going to be a beautiful one."

"It will be. Just like every other day I get to spend with you."

Hope turned to face him. His crystal blue eyes were a darker shade when reflected in the house's lights. "The house is still here," she said. "The resort is still here, and most importantly, all our people are still here. And we're together again."

"It takes more than a little earthquake and being trapped by a cave-in to keep us apart."

"You forgot the high-risk explosives and emergency surgery."

He shrugged one shoulder. "Immaterial. We're meant to be together."

She nodded and placed a hand over his heart. "That's what happens when *you* promise forever. When *I* promise forever."

Alex leaned his forehead against hers. "And that's how it always will be."

Epilogue

FEBRUARY...

A SINGLE BEAD of sweat appeared on Cindy's ebony forehead. As it slid down the side of her face, Alex intensified his effort, pushing hard with his right foot against her resisting hand. He went to physical therapy several times a week, his strength improving with each visit. Cindy was a physical-therapy assistant, and able to help with maneuvers such as this. Multiple dots of sweat rose on her forehead. She adjusted the position of her hand, a fine tremor appearing in her arm.

Alex sat on a padded vinyl table, and his heart hammered as he pushed his foot against her hand as hard as he could. *The pain is making me stronger. Don't give up.*

Finally, Cindy let go with a laugh. "Ok. Uncle!" She picked up a nearby hand towel and wiped her brow. "Jeez! How long could you have kept on with that?"

Grinning, he leaned back, resting his hands on the vinyl surface. "A second longer than you."

She laughed. "Well, you're makin' great progress. But don't go too far—be careful about overdoin' it."

"I am. I have my own personal drill sergeant at home monitoring my every move."

Cindy tossed her towel in the laundry bin. "Yeah, Hope told me when we had lunch yesterday. When do you get the boot off for good?"

"I see Dr. Rawlings next week. Hopefully I'll get the green light then."

"Well, your recovery is goin' great. See you on Friday."

Cindy exited the small room as Alex leaned forward to run a hand over his lower right leg. The scar was still bright red but had healed cleanly. It would fade with time, but he'd always carry his own reminder of the earthquake. Swinging off the table, he stood and placed his right foot into a gray, molded walking boot. Buckling it shut, he clomped out of the office and got into his Land Cruiser, only to remove the boot again so he could drive. Maneuvering his foot was still slightly painful. When he woke in the mornings, his leg was stiff and unyielding, but he focused on the noticeable progress.

After being discharged from the hospital, one of Alex's first tasks had been calling an underwater construction company to repair the gate into the tunnel. Now it was locked safely shut. Half Moon Grotto was closed for the foreseeable future.

As he drove, he passed the building housing the *St. Croix Chronicle*. Shortly after being discharged, Alex had relented and given an exclusive interview to John Strickland, figuring he was better off with the devil he knew. Reporters had still been nosing around, and he didn't want Zach and Jasmine being bothered. So Alex told the story of the earthquake and rescue to put the issue to bed once and for all—glossing over exactly why the kids had been in the cavern, and Jasmine's lack of dive experience.

As much as Alex disliked Strickland for outing his past when he'd barely been able to face it, he had to admit the reporter wrote a good article about the cavern ordeal and rescue. *The Chronicle* created a separate multi-page feature in the Sunday paper, using several photographs Robert had supplied of the area.

Now, six weeks later, the world had moved on. The resort was back to normal and fully booked most days.

Alex talked regularly with Mike, who had adjusted his work schedule. He and Emma had date nights once a week and their marriage was better than ever. He even hinted they might start a family.

After parking next to Hope's Jeep in the garage, Alex thumped along the beach to the pier, then up to the dive shop. Getting rid of the crutches had been a major victory. The boot was hot and made his leg sweaty as hell, but it was a big improvement.

With a wave to Jasmine, he passed into his office and sat behind his desk. He wasn't ready to dive yet, but he would be soon. Starting the next day, Tommy was taking a week's vacation, and Alex couldn't wait to fill in, driving *Surface Interval*. Anything to be out on the water. A glance at his watch confirmed he still had a few minutes before the afternoon trip came back. Today, he needed to be there when the boat arrived.

His office phone rang. Leonard from the scuba agency. They exchanged pleasantries.

"We're having a regional convention next month in Miami," Leonard said. "If you're up to traveling, we'd love to have you there."

"I got your email about it, but I have to pass this year. I'm recovering well, but not sure I'm up to participating in a convention."

"I understand. You've had plenty to deal with. I loved the article you wrote about the rescue and how instructors could incorporate what you learned into their teaching."

Alex smiled. Since he couldn't dive, he'd thrown himself into his role as PDII regional representative, holding a special meeting in Christiansted a couple of weeks prior to discuss the cave rescue and lessons learned. He'd talked to a packed room, and not a single person had been late. After his discussion with Zach, and Hope's supportive but firm insistence, he'd put the idea of resigning behind him. More importantly, he had the confidence to lead again.

After hanging up, it was almost time for *Surface Interval*'s return from the afternoon trip, so Alex descended to the pier. Sitting on a wooden bench under the palapa, he watched a school of blue-striped grunts mill around the pier, smiling at the peaceful scene around him. Further away, bubbles rose to the surface from the students Jack was teaching. Zach and Will had repaired the damage to the coral nursery and a new crop of corals were growing, one day to be transplanted to the living reef.

Alex had several reasons for wanting to meet the boat, not the least of which was Hope's unveiling of the mysterious staff project she'd been working on since before the quake. She'd called an all-staff meeting in the dive shop for that afternoon.

Stretching out his booted leg, Alex settled in to wait.

HOPE EXITED the sandy channel and turned around to check her group. She put on a neutral, bland face when Lucas appeared, a broad trail of sand rising behind him. He'd been her project all day. A new diver, he was visiting the resort with his friend, who was highly experienced. The man exited the channel right behind Lucas, brows lowered and glaring at him.

Quickly, Hope swam to the new diver and lifted his fins, pointing at the froth of sand following the man. His eyes became round as he understood.

Yeah, Lucas. People don't like it when you destroy the view they traveled a long way to see.

Hope smiled and tapped her head with a finger so he would remember. They were back under the boat, and it was time for their safety stop. Hope gave her group of six the signal and they ascended. She had been leading dives regularly for a month and was now an experienced, confident divemaster. She couldn't help a small laugh that escaped.

Guess I should be after leading the way out of the cavern!

April led the other group. She was just getting on the boat when Hope surfaced and ushered her divers aboard.

Within ten minutes, Tommy was driving the boat back to the resort. Hope and April busied themselves breaking down the scuba kits. After finishing, Hope ambled over to her. "I'm going to miss these girl power days."

"Me too," April said with a big smile. "I'm going to miss St. Croix, but it's time for a new beginning."

After the quake and all the upheaval it had caused, April delayed her departure to help them. Now that they were back on their feet, she was ready to leave the island. The previous night, the women had celebrated a special GNO at Marimba—a going away party for April. Everyone had come. Even Sara, who left Magen with Jack for some father-daughter bonding time.

"Maybe Alex and I will visit you sometime at Calypso Key," Hope said. "We really enjoyed our time there."

"I'm sure they'd welcome you. Especially since both of you can lead dives now!"

They both broke into laughter. On their honeymoon, Alex

had ended up leading dives there when the resident divemaster became sick and couldn't work.

As the boat neared the pier, Hope shaded her eyes with her hand, squinting at a person sitting under the palapa. She quickly recognized Alex. After tying up, the guests left the boat, and only Hope, Tommy, and April remained when Alex boarded.

"I'm officially prohibiting you from doing grunt work on your last day," Alex said to April with a warm smile. "If you want to take off, Hope, Tommy, and I will clean up."

April's eyes swept over the trio. "I'm going to miss you guys."

"We'll miss you too," Tommy said. "Come on in here." He held out his arms, and April folded against him. He wrapped her up and lifted her off her feet, making them all laugh.

She moved to Hope, and the two women hugged warmly. "Take care, April."

Last, she moved hesitantly to Alex, and they embraced. Their hug was somewhat stiff, and Hope found herself wondering if April would finally find her happy ending in Florida.

I hope so. She deserves it.

"You'll be missed, April," Alex said. "By all of us. Good luck." He stepped back and joined Hope's side. His body naturally melded into hers as he put an arm over her shoulders.

A single tear spilled down April's face, and she bit her bottom lip as she waved goodbye to them. Then she turned and walked up the pier for the final time.

As Hope watched April stroll away from Half Moon Bay, she got even mistier. Alex tightened his hold around her shoulders, and she leaned into his comforting presence. She wiped her cheeks. "I hope she finds what she's looking for. So many changes."

Her text tone went off.

She pulled her phone out of her pocket, her face becoming animated. "It's Patti. They're almost ready. Just waiting on Gerold and Pauline to finish lunch service. Let's head up to the dive shop."

"You're finally goin' to show us your grand project, huh?' Tommy asked with a grin.

"It's not really grand, but I'm happy with it. Let's go."

Hope wasn't sure who would show up at her meeting since it was mid-afternoon. So she almost stumbled when she opened the door to find nearly the whole staff there. Jack and Sara stood nearby, Magen in Sara's arms. Hope took her, bouncing her niece against her shoulder. Nearly two months old, Magen was starting to hold her head up and regarded the room curiously. She still had the thick mop of dark-brown hair and was a quiet, easygoing baby.

Obviously takes after her father, not her mother.

Hope smiled, then spied Robert and Heather in the back of the crowd. "Look, Alex! Let's go talk to them since we're waiting for Gerold and Pauline." She turned to Sara, who was back at work at Aqua two afternoons per week. "Don't worry—I'll bring your daughter back."

"If you don't, I know where you live. Just remember that!"

Hope and Alex made their way through the assembled crowd, Hope bouncing Magen up and down in her arms. Heather's copper hair hung in a flat sheet down her back, and she wore a sharply tailored suit. Aqua and Ember were both fully operational again and doing well. Robert stood at her side, dressed in a fitted, dark-red polo shirt embroidered with *Robert Davis Photography* on the left breast.

Hope stopped in front of Heather. "All right. We have a few minutes, so show me the hardware!"

Heather and Robert both broke into brilliant smiles as she

held out her left hand. Hope grasped her fingers, leaning over the engagement ring. "Wow! That's beautiful." The solitaire diamond looked at least one carat and was set in a modern rectangular cut. Hope arched a brow at Robert. "She said yes, so you must have come through with a decent proposal?"

He laughed. "I had to rethink my plan a little, but it worked out." At Hope's puzzled expression, he continued. "I was originally goin' to ask her durin' a private visit to the grotto."

Hope brought a hand to her mouth. "Oh, I'm sorry! We might open it again someday, but we're keeping it closed for the foreseeable future."

Robert placed a hand on her shoulder. "Don't worry about it. I wouldn't blame you if you never wanted to go near the place again. I had Gerold help me with Plan B. He baked the ring into a big slice of cake, and I took Heather to dinner. I was scared to death she'd take a huge bite and choke on the ring, but she found it as soon as she cut into the cake with her fork."

Alex laughed and shook Robert's hand. "Congratulations, and nicely done." Then he kissed Heather's cheek.

"Now we're flyin' off to Palo Alto so I can sign my life away," Robert said, but his dazzling smile ensured he wasn't upset.

"I promise!" Heather said in a tone that said they'd been over this territory multiple times. "The prenup will be as painless as possible. My dad loves you and feels horrible making you do it. But the lawyers insist." She turned to Hope and Alex. "We're heading to Carmel for a romantic weekend right after. It's the least I can do."

Robert nudged her. "If you're still feelin' guilty when we get there, I can probably think of ways you can make it up to me." He grinned at her, and a smile rose on her face in return. Simultaneously, they melted together in a kiss.

Hope laughed. "You two are going to be just fine."

Gerold and Pauline walked in the door, distracting Hope.

He spotted her. "Ok, we're here! Are we all gettin' fired?"

A round of laughter rang around the room, but some of it was nervous, bringing a pang to Hope's heart as she left Robert and Heather. She handed Magen back to Sara before taking Alex's hand.

They moved to the other side of the room, standing next to a large-screen TV. "Of course not!" Hope said. "Just the opposite. I've been working on a project. It's pretty minor compared to Ember and Aqua, but I wanted to show it to you guys before guests." She gazed around the room.

Standing next to Gerold, Patti gave Hope a slow wink. She was the only one who was in on the secret. Not even Alex knew.

"I've been trying to come up with a team-building exercise for a while now," Hope continued. "Half Moon Bay Resort has expanded so much in the last couple of years, and I didn't want to lose the sensation that we are all family here. Then the earthquake happened and the cave-in, and I got more of a team-building project than I could have ever asked for—or wanted." She stopped to swallow, taking a shaky breath. Alex placed his hand on her upper back, rubbing softly.

"Those three days in December were really hard for me. This project gave me solace—it gave me *hope*. It helped me remember that every one of you is part of our family, and it's what makes this resort so special. Our guests comment on this subject more than anything else—that coming here feels like being with family. Family you *like* being with!" she added with a laugh, then picked up a remote control.

The television on the wall next to her came to life with the resort logo. "We've had a slideshow of resort photos on all the TVs around the resort for quite some time. Photos that Robert took, I might add."

A round of cheering went around the room as Robert waved sheepishly.

"I asked him to get me some pictures he'd taken of staff and added others myself. This is the project I wanted to show you. And after this, I want all our guests to see it too. The Half Moon Bay family."

She pressed play and took Alex's hand again. The slideshow was a mixture of beautiful images of the resort and active pictures of staff. One of Clark and Heather mixing drinks, another of Patti, Martine, and Corrine at the front desk. A round of applause went up at the picture of Alex, Gerold, and Hope standing on top of the podium after they won a local triathlon. More applause rose at Clark's gigantic smile as he held up the trophy for winning the St. Croix mixology contest. This was followed by a stunning sunset Robert had captured, the sun dropping into the ocean behind the palapa.

Next were several pictures of the dive staff, including an updated group photo of all the new faces. Jack and Will appeared on screen, arms over each other's shoulders as they posed underwater, and brought a round of laughter from the crowd.

Hope leaned against Alex's side, eager for the next two. On the television, Young Alex appeared in his dress blues, around twenty years of age. A newly minted SEAL, pride glinted in his eyes as he stared confidently at the camera.

"Oh, Hope," Alex said. "No one wants to see that."

But he was nearly drowned out by the chorus of *awwwws* going around the room, and she just laughed at him. The next photo was the one she loved. Also of Alex, but older, and in this one he wore dress whites with a peaked cap, standing against a vivid sunset with his hands in his pockets. They had just been married.

In both photos, the look in his eyes was identical. Pride at having accomplished something deeply meaningful. It brought tears to her eyes again, but happy ones this time. She looked up at Alex, and he bent to brush a kiss over her lips.

She moved in front of him, and he wrapped both arms around her waist, pulling her back tightly against him. She placed her hands over his, enjoying the reactions of the people around her.

Patti had insisted on including a picture of Hope in her wedding dress, which was the next photo. A long, happy sigh went across the room. The setting was the same as Alex's—a vivid sunset beach photo.

The slideshow moved on to other staff, Gerold and Pauline both cooking. Charlotte, their head-server-turned-Ember employee, working at the gallery and smiling as she held a hand up to one of Sara's watercolors. The next one was of Sara and Jack together. Robert had taken this also, on their private beach, and their faces were radiant.

Next was a picture of Robert and Heather at the Ember opening, both in formal attire and stunning together. Then, one of Hope and Sara together—the photo taken when Hope had been in college.

The last photo was of her and Alex. Not the wedding photo, which once again prominently graced the lobby. This one had been taken by a photographer for a magazine Hope had been featured in and was one of her favorites. She and Alex stood on the pier in the golden glow of late afternoon. They wore matching staff shirts—the leaders of Half Moon Bay Resort—and she stood close to him, resting her hand against his chest. Both smiled at the camera, their happiness broadcast in their wide smiles.

Finally, this last image of the slideshow faded, and one final message flashed against a black background.

Half Moon Bay Resort... Welcome home.

THANK you for being by my side until the bittersweet end! I won't say I'll never return to Half Moon Bay, but at this point, it's time to move in a new direction. But if you're not quite ready to say goodbye, keep reading for one more chance to peek into Half Moon Bay's future!

April is a side character who has intrigued me since the second book of this series. She's an interesting woman—moral, conscientious, and positive, yet absolutely hopeless where men are concerned. Especially regarding Alex.

Is there anything sadder than unrequited love?

I've always felt that Half Moon Bay Resort represented second chances—at love and life. April was the only character who didn't find happiness there.

Could that mean she's destined to find it elsewhere?

Find out when April moves to Calypso Key in the Florida Keys! She is one of the main characters in the first book of my Calypso Key series, *Visions of You*. April quickly runs into her new resort's eldest son, returned home to save his ailing family legacy. Gabriel Markham, a grumpy single dad, doesn't believe in love after his wife left.

Then he meets April...

VISIONS OF YOU: A Small Town Single Dad Romance
CALYPSO KEY SERIES

**I'm a single dad, not the prodigal son.
And that gorgeous, sunny blonde? She's just an
employee.**

GABE:

When Dad needs help running our family resort at Calypso
Key, I can't say no. So I bring my daughter home to raise where I
grew up. Except the resort is worse off than I expected. Still, I
understand business. Women... not so much. And after my
divorce, I don't believe in love.

Then I meet new divemaster April Desmond.

She was hired before I came back. I have one job—to cut costs
everywhere I can. I try to deny the attraction. After all, I might
have to fire her. But that sheet of golden hair. Those sky-blue
eyes.

The sparks become an inferno. We're opposites in many ways. April is the sunshine to my grumpiness. But we agree on one thing—neither of us wants a serious relationship. We make a promise to keep things casual, and it works great.

Until one of us breaks our pact...

Dive into the Florida Keys with *Visions of You*. This swoony, steamy grumpy-sunshine romance will keep you riveted to the final page.

Click below to grab your copy:

VISIONS OF YOU: A Small Town Single Dad Romance

IF YOU'D LIKE one final glimpse of Half Moon Bay, I invite you to sign up for my Beach Read Update. As a thank you, I'll send you **a bonus scene featuring all our favorite characters** two years after the events in *Crowning Hope*. It's told from Hope's point of view.

My Beach Read Update subscribers hear about all my free content, plus exclusive offers and sales. I'd love to have you along!

Sign up to download this exclusive bonus today.
(erinbrockus.com/crown)

Plus, you'll stay up to date with cover reveals, sneak peeks, and exclusive content about my books!

If you're already on my list, I've got you covered! At the bottom of each newsletter is a link to all my free content for subscribers. Just find your last email from me to read this bonus, as well as any others you might have missed. Or you can simply sign up again—you'll have your bonus in a flash.

KEEP READING for my Author's Note, as well as a preview of *Visions of You*, the first book of the Calypso Key series...

Author's Note

It's funny how sometimes the act of writing can mirror the act of reading—that unrelenting sense of *I must find out what happens next*! There were times during the drafting of this book when I got up in the middle of the night because I couldn't just leave my characters hanging!

I loosely plot my novels, but usually each chapter is only summarized by a sentence or two. So, in a real sense, the act of putting the words on the page makes everything become *real*. Especially when characters do unexpected things.

Readers have asked me what happened to Barnaby Morgan, and I wanted him to have a happy ending. Which is difficult when the character died over three hundred years ago! But I'm pleased with the plot line I gave him.

Hope's resolution with Caleb was more problematic. I never felt that Hope truly dealt with this very pivotal part of her life. I wanted her to have a final conclusion, but I was very reluctant to have her horrible ex-boyfriend show up at Half Moon Bay.

An author must remain true to her characters, and Caleb showing up in person could only have one outcome where Alex was concerned. Alex would defend Hope at any and all costs, and I don't think he would care much what happened to Caleb.

And I really didn't want to go down that road—too dark for me! Hopefully, I came up with a conclusion that gave emotional closure to Hope and readers (and Alex).

Originally, when I first had the idea of Zach and Jasmine being in a cavern, I planned on Hope rushing to save them and getting trapped, with Alex going after the trio. Then I reconsidered... What if *Alex* was the one who needed rescuing this time? I think it made for a much better story, and gave Hope what she needed to come into her own as an expert diver and leader.

There are strong echoes of *Finding Hope*, Book 1, in *Crowning Hope*, which I think is appropriate for the series-ending volume, ie. Alex is involved in a survival situation and Hope has to manage the emergency. But this situation is much different and really shows the progression of the two characters (especially Hope).

I've absolutely loved writing about all these characters, especially Hope and Alex. But the great thing about books is you can fall in love with characters you know and love, then experience that heady rush all over again with new ones.

See you soon on the new adventure...

Erin Brockus
September, 2023

Excerpt from VISIONS OF YOU

April

I glanced in the rearview mirror, trying to memorize the wonder now falling behind me. Seven Mile Bridge spanned the distance between Marathon and Big Pine Key, soaring over the expanse of aquamarine water beneath. Nothing but seven solid miles of ocean and the occasional small island lay on either side of fabled Highway One.

Amazing.

Though I was sad to leave the famous bridge behind, the end of the fabled structure couldn't squelch my excitement. I spared one last glance at the scene around me—a rare experience worth the hype.

My driver's window was down, and my elbow rested on the ledge as I enjoyed the warm breeze drifting in. I was still getting used to my two-year-old Honda CR-V. I'd sold my old car before leaving St. Croix—it was easier to just buy a new one than mess with the hassle of shipping it.

A flutter rippled through me as I exited the highway and turned south.

Toward my new home.

Maia had called a few days previously and told me to take my time traveling down the Keys, and to enjoy the sites and the diving. I'd stayed in Key Largo for two days to dive some of the famous wrecks there, finding them plenty advanced for anyone's taste. I'd been buddied up with a man who wasn't quite up to the challenging conditions, and I'd spent as much time watching out for him as enjoying the enormous shipwrecks. But that was all in a day's work for me and didn't detract from the experience.

I passed a large flashing sign alerting drivers to watch out for Key deer and slowed down. I craned my neck around eagerly but didn't see any of the tiny Lower Keys inhabitants. A smile rose on my face as I turned onto a road named Calypso Causeway, then crossed over a bridge to Dove Key. The smile wasn't just due to my new surroundings. It was also the realization that for the first time in a very long while, I was happy.

I had a whole new life to start.

I'd left everything behind in St. Croix, including my emotional baggage and bruised heart. I'd always looked on the bright side, and around a year ago realized that facet of me was being inexorably worn down. A new job as a divemaster at Calypso Key Resort was exactly what I needed.

Along with a self-induced sabbatical from men. I'd proven I was lousy at picking them, so romance was officially off the table for me.

And that was tremendously freeing.

Dove Key was a decently sized island and town, though it only had two main streets, intersecting at the single traffic light. As I passed a ramshackle tavern called Salty's, a long metal building stretched in the distance along a bluff to my left. A sign alongside the road pointed toward it, proclaiming the long structure the Conch Republic Brewpub.

But exploring could wait. I continued on Calypso Causeway and the buildings thinned out, a fringe of scrubby brush and mangroves replacing them eventually. I traveled over a short bridge connecting the island to its smaller, southern neighbor, Calypso Key. The paved road rose in a gentle climb, and I could barely glimpse a sizeable multi-story house, screened by trees and brush, along a sheer bluff to my left. I reached the crest of the hill and the remainder of the island spread out before me to the south. I continued slowly rolling down the asphalt road.

Most of the western half was undeveloped, a large expanse of marsh and mangrove wetlands. Along the eastern side of the key, a road branched off toward the house and several other nearby buildings. After passing a grassy meadow decorated by several flame trees, a long two-story building appeared on my left. Two large sliding doors were open, and I spied machinery inside as I drove by.

The road ended in two parking lots, a sand one facing east and a larger, neatly paved one on my right. Directly ahead lay an airy, one-story white building. Maia had sent a text with preliminary instructions, so I pulled into the sandlot and parked next to several other employee vehicles. Maia Markham and I had recently reconnected after meeting six years ago. When she'd offered me a position at her family's resort, the opportunity was too good to pass up. The position became even more enticing after she arranged living quarters for me too.

Excitement quickened my pulse as I turned off the engine and studied a protected canal with several buildings behind it. A red flag with a diagonal white stripe running through it flew from the top of the largest building. The entire area was neat and clean, which pleased me since I was staring at my new domain.

The dive operation.

Grabbing my phone out of my purse, I sent Maia a text, letting her know I'd arrived.

Then I studied the resort around me. A lawn of neat green grass lay behind the parking lot, surrounding the long structure housing the machinery. A sand path led from the buildings on the bluff and passed near the long building. More flame trees threw shade over the area and farther to the south, I spotted a row of palm trees.

The white building where the road ended was of considerable size. I assumed it was the lobby and other resort facilities. My text tone pinged, and I grabbed my phone.

Maia: Welcome! I'll meet you in the lobby in a couple minutes.

After texting back a thumbs-up, I took a deep breath and exited the car.

Let's get this show going.

I crossed the parking lot and climbed a short flight of steps onto a covered porch. Twin doors painted a soft blue were propped open, and I entered a bright, breezy room cooled by ceiling fans. A long wooden counter lay directly across from me. It was staffed by a woman currently helping guests, and several blue couches and armchairs were spaced around the room. Soft music played from hidden speakers, and the lobby exuded a cozy, old-school tropical vibe. Several framed pictures drew my eye, and I crossed a weathered but clean wooden floor, the boards squeaking under my sandals.

Three color prints were prominently displayed, and I immediately recognized Maia, who smiled at the camera, her brunette hair pulled into a ponytail. *Maia Markham-Taylor, Lead Divemaster* read a small placard beneath. I smiled at her new name—she had been married less than two months. Next to Maia, a man with somewhat lighter hair and a full, bushy beard smiled at me. Evan Markham was the general manager. A third, larger picture was centered above both of an older man. He had Maia's eyes and darker hair with a liberal amount of gray, but he carried an obvious resemblance to both siblings. The placard read Warren Markham, Owner.

The sound of footsteps trotting up the stairs reached me. "April! You're here!"

I spun around, my blond braid swishing to one side, and broke into a grin as Maia ran toward me. I held out my arms and we hugged. She was taller and nearly knocked me back.

"Sorry it took me so long, but I'm here at last."

Maia pulled back and patted my arms. "Don't worry about it. You couldn't have predicted an earthquake. Was everything okay when you left?"

My departure from St. Croix had been delayed several weeks due to damage caused by an earthquake. My former employer had been injured in the quake and I couldn't very well take off and leave them—him—in a lurch when he'd been unable to work.

Employer. That's a good one. But men are in the past. Especially ones in love with someone else.

I smiled at Maia. "Yes. The island is more or less recovered, and Alex is back to work. Half Moon Bay Resort needed some repairs, but they're back on their feet now. And I'm extremely excited to be here."

Maia's expression sharpened, but she didn't press the point. She knew about the torch I'd carried for Alex Monroe for an embarrassing number of years, a romance that had only been on my side. And once he'd met the woman who was now his wife, I'd done my best to bury my feelings and find someone else.

Which had been another disaster.

I turned my mind back to the woman in front of me. "Congratulations! On both the baby and the wedding."

She grinned. "Thanks. It hasn't been dull lately. Today's a

little hectic—I'm helping my brother Gabe, and your apartment is being cleaned. We'll put you up in a guest cottage tonight, then you can move in tomorrow. Enjoy the experience. Beachfront views aren't part of the deal, I'm afraid."

"I can't believe you're letting me use an apartment! Thanks for hiring me, Maia." Even if mice infested my apartment, I wasn't about to complain, no matter how cramped or old it was.

We walked toward the parking lot so I could collect my suitcases. "I'm glad you're here," Maia said. "It'll be nice to have another woman around. I'm surrounded by men. There's way too much testosterone around here."

I assumed she meant her husband and family, and figured I'd get to know them all in time. I lugged my two suitcases out of the back of my SUV and Maia stared at them, both brows halfway up her forehead. "You only brought two bags?"

"My dive gear is in a duffel in the back seat, but I figured I'd leave it there for now."

"Yeah, take today off and just relax. You want to tag along on a dive tomorrow and get the lay of the land?"

"That sounds perfect."

She grabbed one of my suitcases and rolled it down a concrete path and around the lobby. We passed a casual open-air restaurant and pool area. Reggae beats thumped from a nearby bar. Maia pointed with her head at the airy restaurant, where several groups were eating lunch. "This is Dorado, our casual restaurant. Staff eat in the kitchen. Our fine dining restaurant, Orchid, is on the western side of the island and gets the great sunsets."

Everything was spotlessly clean and casually tropical, though not particularly modern or luxurious. We skirted a free-form resort pool and neared the palm trees I'd glimpsed earlier. A row of ten cinderblock cottages, all painted light blue, were spaced between the palms and sat on a white sand beach.

The Caribbean Sea washed gently on the shore and a soft breeze blew a lock of hair that had escaped my braid across my face. I tucked it behind my ear as Maia led me toward a cottage.

"This is beautiful!" I said, giving myself whiplash as I took in the area. "I had no idea you had such a big beach."

"We're very lucky. Beaches are rare in the Keys, let alone one this big. It stretches all along the southern part of the island. There are ten beach cottages, all one-bedroom units. You're in number eight."

She lifted my suitcase up a short flight of stairs onto a screened, covered porch and I followed. Producing a key from her pocket, Maia unlocked the front door, and we entered an open, very stuffy room. She picked up a remote from the coffee table and pointed it at a modular air conditioning unit on the wall. It whirred to life after she pushed a button. "It'll cool down quickly in here. Don't worry."

She left my suitcase next to a king-sized bed covered with a pale blue comforter. A blue sofa and love seat lay across the room.

Maia turned to me. "The bathroom is in the back, and feel free to use anything you want from the minibar. I need to get back to my brother, so I'll leave you to relax this afternoon. There's a hammock on the porch, and I imagine you're ready to swing in the breeze a little."

We both laughed and I nodded. "I'll keep the unpacking to a minimum since I'll be moving tomorrow."

"I'll stop by later, okay? I'm sorry I'm not more available— we've had a little family drama this morning."

My smile fell, wondering about the comments regarding her brother. Was she referring to the one whose picture I saw? I knew she had more than one brother. "Nothing serious, I hope?"

Maia waved at me casually. "Not really, and nothing I'm

going to bore you with when you've just arrived." She crossed the room and halted at the front door. "All of us are glad to have you, April. Welcome to Calypso Key!"

After a final hug, she exited and left me alone. I glanced around the room. Like the restaurant I'd glimpsed, it was clean and comfortable, though more on the modest side than luxurious. Though it was undoubtedly posher than what I'd be moving into tomorrow.

I smiled. "My *free* apartment. I'm damn lucky and I know it. I can't wait until tomorrow."

Digging a paperback out of my purse, I stepped onto the shady porch and climbed into the hammock. Settling in, I read as a warm tropical breeze gently blew me back and forth.

~

The next morning, I took a meandering journey to the dive shop, wanting to explore during the calm of my first morning at Calypso Key Resort. As I wandered up the cement path after eating breakfast at Dorado restaurant, a sand trail veered off toward the canal. I followed it, figuring if it wasn't brick or cement, it was for employees. The path turned to brick as it led between the back of the dive shop and another building directly across.

A stunning butterfly bush with a profusion of lavender and dark-purple blooms stood at the corner of the dive shop. I'd never seen one that flowered in two colors, and it was obviously lovingly tended. Colorful butterflies danced in the morning air, and as I passed by, a sense of peace filled me. I continued along the brick path, laid in a herringbone pattern. On my left, I passed an open door. A rack of hanging wetsuits lay on the far side of a crowded room, and I could hear sounds emanating from inside.

But I wasn't quite ready to meet my coworkers yet. A shady grove lay in front of me, drawing me toward it. Several sizeable white boats were tied up in the canal, and I studied the nearest. Empty white plastic tank holders lining the two side benches proclaimed this the resort's dive boat, and I was impressed by what I saw. I noted the name and smiled. *Shark Bait* was a solid forty feet long with a canvas canopy stretching over the front half. A ladder led up to a small, elevated bridge. Another boat lay behind it, Calypso Key's fishing charter.

My feet carried me toward the open end of the canal, and the adjacent grove of gumbo limbo trees lay ahead. Panning my gaze around the empty picnic tables, I could imagine the area full of waiting guests, eager for the day's adventures. But in the silent early morning, no one was there yet.

A covered patio lay to my right, and I eased forward to the rail. The morning sun was already warm, and I gathered my hair, circling it into a low bun.

Anticipation built within me, raising a smile on my lips.

Then the back of my neck tingled, and a shiver ran over my shoulders—a strong feeling I wasn't alone. Glancing to my right, I saw something out of the corner of my eye.

I nearly gasped as a man was revealed. He casually leaned against the dive shop wall behind me, one leg bent at the knee.

"Oh!" I said, my stomach flopping over. "I didn't see you there."

The stranger was very tall, I'd guess six-foot-three. He had dark hair, cut short, and his intense brown eyes gave absolutely nothing away. A trimmed scruff covered his jaw, but he didn't look sloppy.

In fact, he damn-near stopped my heart, and not just because he'd startled me.

He was dressed strangely for a diver in a button-down shirt and jeans. When he lowered his leg to stand on both feet, his work boot made a solid thump on the brick floor. Remaining silent as he eyed me intently, the man was over-the-top handsome.

A slow ripple moved from my neck farther down my body. Taking a firm imaginary grip, I got a hold of myself.

Sabbatical from men, remember?

And I sure wasn't interested in a guest, despite the gorgeous pair of bedroom eyes staring at me. However, I was still an employee. Though not leading dives today, I should be helpful.

I smiled at the stranger. "Hi, I'm April."

"I know who you are." He didn't smile back as his eyes held mine. His voice was deep yet smooth, like fine whisky.

I swallowed reflexively.

Again, I was surprised. How had word gotten around that I was here? Hopefully, he wasn't a creepy guest, though he wasn't friendly either.

Guess I'll find out.

"Can I help you get checked in at the dive shop?" I lifted my right arm to point toward the pathway.

His lips moved in what was almost—but not quite—a smirk. "I'm not a diver."

Then, without another word, he pushed away from the wall and strolled off the patio toward the guest cottages.

My mouth dropped open as I stood there watching him.

God, what an asshole!

Flustered heat spread over my face as I watched him walk away in jeans that looked like he was born wearing them. Wide, muscular shoulders tapered to trim hips.

I took a deep breath and muttered, "Why were you near the dive shop if you're not a diver? And why do I care, anyway?"

No one but a small yellow bird replied. It landed on the deck railing and chirped at me.

At least you're friendly.

Surly guests weren't the best part of my job, but at least they were temporary. They all left eventually.

Hopefully, Hot Grumpy Guy was on his way out.

I'm pretty sure you can guess that Hot Grumpy Guy isn't going anywhere...

Click below to get your copy:

Visions of You.
CALYPSO KEY SERIES

About the Author

Dive into steamy small-town romance, where passion meets paradise!

Erin Brockus writes steamy small town romances that transport readers to exotic, tropical destinations, and provide a perfect beachy getaway from everyday life. Her mature, relatable characters are impossible not to root for, and she weaves breezy romantic adventure into her stories, emphasizing scuba diving and the ocean.

Drawing on her twin passions for diving and travel, Erin infuses her characters and narratives with a sense of excitement and passion. Her idea of the perfect day involves sipping a cocktail on the beach after exploring the ocean depths.

Erin lives in Washington wine country with her husband, who is also a scuba instructor. She is currently hard at work on her next island adventure. When she's not writing, you might find her out for a run or cycling through the countryside on the next quest for adventure.